She gasped in pleasurable confusion, and broke away from his kiss, though not from him. "Geoffrey, I—"

"Serena," he coaxed, his voice rough with desire. "My sweet *jēsamina.*"

She smiled at how he'd turned the jasmine flower into a Hindi endearment, as he kissed her again, wooing her to relax. She felt her nipple tighten shamelessly against his palm, sensation and heat rippling through her body to gather low in her belly.

This was longing, this was desire and reckless passion. She'd known the words, of course, but only now did she understand their meaning. She remembered how the other women had teased her when she'd been a girl, promising that a lover's kiss should be masterful and full of glory; then she'd thought it was nonsense, but now she knew that glory was only the beginning.

"This is why I could not let you go," he whispered hoarsely. "*This,* Serena."

"It's why I came to you," she said breathlessly, rubbing her cheek against the slight bristle of his jaw. "I didn't know, and yet I did."

BY ISABELLA BRADFORD

When You Wish Upon a Duke
When the Duchess Said Yes
When the Duke Found Love
A Wicked Pursuit
A Sinful Deception

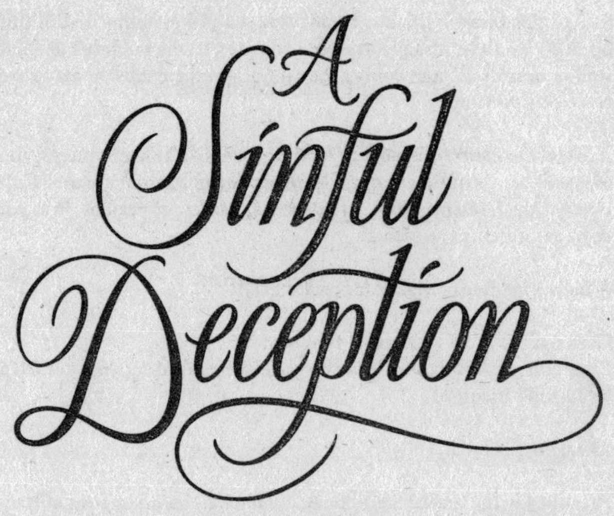

A Breconridge Brothers novel

Isabella Bradford

BALLANTINE BOOKS • NEW YORK

Sale of this book without a front cover may be unauthorized. If this book is coverless, it may have been reported to the publisher as "unsold or destroyed" and neither the author nor the publisher may have received payment for it.

A Sinful Deception is a work of fiction. Names, characters, places, and incidents are the products of the author's imagination or are used fictitiously. Any resemblance to actual events, locales, or persons, living or dead, is entirely coincidental.

A Ballantine Books Mass Market Original

Published in the United States by Ballantine Books, an imprint of Random House, a division of Random House LLC, a Penguin Random House Company, New York.

BALLANTINE and the HOUSE colophon are registered trademarks of Random House LLC.

This book contains an excerpt from the forthcoming book *A Reckless Desire* by Isabella Bradford. This excerpt has been set for this edition only and may not reflect the final content of the forthcoming edition.

ISBN 978-0-345-54814-6
eBook ISBN 978-0-345-54815-3

Cover design: Lynn Andreozzi
Cover illustration: Gregg Gulbronson

Printed in the United States of America

www.ballantinebooks.com

9 8 7 6 5 4 3 2 1

Ballantine mass market edition: March 2015

Acknowledgments

Writing may seem to be a solitary endeavor, but there are plenty of friends and colleagues behind the scenes. Many thanks to all those who so generously shared their knowledge, inspiration, support, and often their sense of humor to help me once again reach the last page: Kimberly Alexander, Melissa Blank, Loretta Chase, Abby Cox, Mary Doering, Beth Dunn, Jay Howlett, Neal Hurst, Mark Hutter, Michael McCarty, Diya Rajput, Annelise Robey, Mollie Smith, Junessa Viloria, Janea Whitacre, and Sarah Woodyard.

CHAPTER
1

London
April 1771

He knew in an instant that she was different from every other woman in the ballroom.

Lord Geoffrey Fitzroy watched the lady as she paused in the arched doorway, a figure of perfect, self-contained calm beyond all the others, with their swirling spangled silks and too-bright laughter. She didn't fidget or preen, the way women usually did while they were waiting to be announced to the company. She simply *stood,* and made standing look more elegantly fascinating than Geoffrey had ever dreamed possible.

"Who is that divine lady?" he asked his brother Harry, the Earl of Hargreave, who was beside him at the far end of the ballroom with the other gentlemen who'd rather drink than dance.

"Which lady?" Harry asked as he reached for a fresh glass of wine from the tray of a passing footman. "The room is filled with ladies."

"The one in blue," Geoffrey said, amazed that his brother needed more description. To him there was clearly only one lady among the scores in attendance who could be called divine, a term he had not used carelessly. Even at this distance, she was exceptionally beautiful, but not conventionally so, with pale skin and gleaming dark hair that she wore without powder. "There, in the doorway."

"That's Miss Serena Carew." Harry turned toward Geoffrey, one brow raised with bemusement. "I cannot believe you don't know her. Or rather, *of* her. No gentleman truly *knows* the distant Miss Serena Carew. None of us poor sots are worthy of her acquaintance."

Geoffrey emptied his glass, setting it on a nearby sideboard. "Then that's only because she has yet to know me," he said confidently, smoothing his sleeves to spruce up his already-immaculate evening coat. "A lack I intend to remedy at once."

"I thought you kept clear of unmarried ladies," Harry said. "I recall you being quite firm on the subject of remaining a bachelor as long as was humanly possible."

Geoffrey shrugged, his gaze still intent on the lady. "I'm not intending matrimony, Harry. I'm fully aware of how far I can go before her family begins demanding the banns be called. *Exactly* how far."

"A moment, Geoffrey." Harry took him by the arm to hold him back. "Take care with this one. You should know the lady's story before you begin the chase. She's old Allwyn's granddaughter, and he guards her like a hawk with a favorite chick. That's his sister, Lady Morley, with her now."

"What of it?" Geoffrey smiled, nonchalant. It didn't matter to him that she was the granddaughter of the Marquis of Allwyn, not when he himself was the son of the Duke of Breconridge. "That's hardly enough to put me off."

"There's more," Harry said. "Her father was employed by the East India Company, and she was born and spent her childhood in India."

"Truly?" Geoffrey studied her with fresh interest. "Where? In Calcutta, with all the other English?"

"At first, yes," Harry said, tapping his ebony cane lightly on the floor. "But the father had a falling out with the Company after his wife died. Resigned his commission outright. Turned Turk, as they say, and went off to make his fortune trading muskets and gunpowder for jewels and living like a pagan in the hills, complete with a harem of Hindi mistresses. I don't know all the details—I doubt Allwyn himself does—but you'll see soon enough how it has marked Miss Carew."

Geoffrey's curiosity grew as he continued to watch Miss Carew and her aunt. They had been announced to the company and were slowly making their way through the room, the older woman smiling and nodding and greeting friends. Miss Carew simply followed. It was as if she'd removed herself to another place entirely, a place she preferred far more to the gaiety and music of this ballroom. Geoffrey was not only attracted, he was intrigued. What could be more fascinating than a beauty with a mysterious past?

Not, of course, that he'd confess any of this to his brother.

"I cannot believe you'd call a lovely creature like that 'marked,'" he said instead. "Surely you exaggerate, Harry."

But Harry shook his head. "Judge the lady for yourself, and decide if I exaggerate. You'll see soon enough that she is not at ease in company—*any* company."

Geoffrey grinned. "Fifty guineas says that she'll dance with me."

"Fifty?" Harry said, chuckling. "I'll say a hundred, the surest wager I've ever made. I've never once seen that particular lady dance with anyone."

"One hundred it is, then," Geoffrey said, patting

Harry on the shoulder. "Watch me proceed, brother, and be astonished. I'll be collecting those guineas before the late supper."

Geoffrey plunged into the crowd, determined to win both the wager and the lady. Based on experience, he'd every reason to be confidant, too. He was tall and handsome, with an easy, infallible charm that women of every age and rank found nearly impossible to ignore or resist. He'd begun beguiling his nursery maids in the cradle even before he could speak, and since then the results had been the same with every other female he encountered.

It was simply a fact: he liked women, and they liked him, very much. Why should Miss Carew be any different? In his estimation, Serena Carew was the most interesting and beautiful young lady in the room. It only made sense that she should be dancing with him.

There was, of course, the faint possibility that she would reject him outright, the way his brother had predicted. Some ladies did insist on the nicety of a proper introduction, even in a crush like this, but he'd risk it for the chance to speak to her first, without the aunt or anyone else interfering. Besides, he never tired of the intoxicating challenge of pursuit, the first step toward flirtation, passion, even seduction. Anything was possible.

She was turned away from him now, her back to him as he drew closer. Her shining dark hair set her apart from all the powdered heads around her, with the pale nape of her neck an elegant, vulnerable curve above the blue silk of her gown. She wore drop earrings and a necklace of diamonds and sapphires so large that on any other woman her age, the stones would surely have been paste. Yet on Serena Carew, Geoffrey knew they were genuine; nothing about her would be so blatantly false.

"Miss Carew," he said when he was at last close enough that she'd hear him.

She did, and turned to face him in a single fluid movement. From a distance he'd seen she was a beauty, but he wasn't prepared for the impact of that beauty with only a few feet between them. Her skin was golden ivory, her mouth full and red, her nose regal, and her brows perfectly arched, but it was her eyes that stunned him: almond-shaped and the color of clearest amber, deep-set and shadowed with mystery, and perhaps melancholy as well. Geoffrey wasn't sure. Blast, he wasn't sure of anything when he stared into eyes like that.

But to his chagrin, he clearly had not affected her the same way. There wasn't a flicker of warmth in those golden eyes, nor encouragement, either.

"I do not know you, sir," she said, a simple declaration.

He smiled his most winning smile, determined to thaw her chill, and not just because he knew his brother was watching.

"Lord Geoffrey Fitzroy," he said with as much of a bow and flourish as he could manage in the crowd around them. "Your servant in every way, Miss Carew."

She did not smile in return, nor did she so much as dip her head in acknowledgment of his higher rank. Instead she regarded him impassively, her expression not changing even a fraction.

"Indeed, sir," she said. "If you are in truth the nobleman you profess to be, then you cannot be my servant. It is impossible for you to be both."

"But I am," he said, smiling still. With a different inflection, her words might have been banter, teasing and intimate, but she was making it clear enough that they weren't meant to be anything but discouraging. Damnation, could she have somehow learned of the wager he'd just made with his brother? What other reason could there be for her to be behaving so coldly toward him?

"My name and title are mine through birth," he said,

"but you, Miss Carew, are the sole reason for my devoted servitude, and I—"

"Lord Geoffrey, good evening!" exclaimed Lady Morley, joining them. "Why, Serena, my dear, I see you have already met one of the most notable gentlemen in the room."

Lady Morley beamed at Geoffrey, her dark eyes sharp beneath her oversized, frizzled wig. Clearly she'd overheard, and clearly, too, she was determined to repair matters as best she could.

"Such a splendid gathering, Lord Geoffrey," she continued. "I trust you are enjoying yourself?"

"I am, Lady Morley," he said. He didn't usually consider chaperones allies, but in this case, he'd take any help that was offered. "Especially now that I am in the company of two such lovely ladies."

Lady Morley chuckled happily and fluttered her fan. It was the response that Geoffrey had hoped to win from Miss Carew, who continued to regard him with the same degree of dispassionate interest that she'd display toward a lower order of insect.

"Lord Geoffrey is the son of His Grace the Duke of Breconridge, Serena," Lady Morley said, a not-very-subtle explanation for the younger woman, "and he is the younger brother of the Earl of Hargreave. His charm, of course, is all his own."

Geoffrey smiled, charmingly. He'd heard this kind of explanation from mothers and aunts and older sisters so many times that he could interpret its true meaning perfectly: *This handsome fellow may be a mere second son, Serena, but he's one with his own fortune and therefore well worth your attention, and while the older brother may be married, his wife has only given him a daughter, so there's still a chance for you to become a duchess.*

Geoffrey hoped that Miss Carew interpreted the message this way, too. "I see the musicians are returning to their chairs," he said, bowing toward her, "and the next set of dances will be beginning shortly. Will you honor me with the pleasure of a dance, Miss Carew?"

"Of course she would," Lady Morley swiftly answered for her. "Serena, dance with Lord Geoffrey."

"No!" protested Miss Carew with haste, and almost alarm. "That is, you know I do not dance, Aunt, and I—"

"Nonsense," Lady Morley said briskly, the merest hint of admonition in the word. "You dance like an angel, my dear. I insist. Go, take your place with Lord Geoffrey among the other couples whilst room remains on the floor."

Still Miss Carew hesitated, her unexpected reluctance an unflattering challenge to Geoffrey. Perhaps she truly did dance like a goose. A beautiful face was no guarantee she'd be light on her toes. But for the sake of that beautiful face, as well as for the wager—he could practically feel his brother's gaze in the middle of his back—he was determined to persevere.

"One dance, that is all," he said softly, coaxing, and holding his hand out to her. "I ask for nothing beyond that."

"Very well." With a sigh she looked down, avoiding his gaze, and carefully placed her hand in his palm. "One dance and no more."

"One dance, then," he repeated. He closed his fingers around hers to lead her toward the floor. Her hand was cool and soft, as reserved as the rest of her, which did not surprise him.

"I must apologize for my aunt, Lord Geoffrey," she said. "She can be unconscionably forward where I am concerned. Pray do not feel any obligation to dance with me."

"There is no obligation, Miss Carew," he said firmly,

and just as firmly pulled her along until they stood facing each other, waiting for the other dancers to take their places in line. "When we are better acquainted, you will realize that I seldom, if ever, do anything I don't wish to do. I'm stubborn that way. I wished to dance with you, and now I am, and I only hope that you will come to find the experience enjoyable as well."

Before she could answer, the gentleman at the head of the line loudly announced the dance's name: *Lady Randolph's Frolic*. At once the musicians began to play, and Geoffrey had no choice but to bow and begin leading Miss Carew through the steps. The dance was a rollicking country reel that was complicated to follow, and offered no opportunity for further conversation. All that Geoffrey could do was smile, and admire Miss Carew as she danced.

It was impossible not to. She was dressed in much the same fashion as the other ladies, and it was clear that beneath her blue silk gown, her slender figure wore the whalebone-stiffened stays and hoops that were required for every proper English lady.

But she didn't dance like an English lady. Not at all. Oh, she followed every step with a precision that would make her dancing-master proud, her back straight and her head held high. Yet there was a sinuous grace to her movements that could never be learned in any London drawing room, nor would it be entirely proper there, either. Her amber eyes lost their sadness and sparkled, and her lips parted and gradually began to smile with pleasure. The slight dip and sway to her hips, the arch to her wrists and arms, the way she unconsciously framed the rising swell of her breasts with every gesture—all of it was innately seductive, and the fact that she seemed entirely innocent of the effect she was creating only made it all the more enticing.

Geoffrey couldn't look away, and neither could any of the other men around them. He couldn't recall a dance that was over and done so swiftly, nor another that he'd wished would never end.

"Mercy," she said breathlessly, pulling free of Geoffrey's hand to draw her fan from her pocket. She spread the blades with a single sweep and began to fan her still-flushed cheeks. Belatedly she remembered to curtsey, her fan still in her hand.

"I thank you, Lord Geoffrey," she said as she rose. "If you please, I should like to return to my aunt now."

He'd won his wager with his brother. He'd had his dance with Miss Carew. He'd made every other man in the room envious. He'd no reason not to do what she asked, and lead her back to her aunt's side. But instead he stood before her, oddly off-balance and incapable of doing what he should or what was expected.

"If you please, Lord Geoffrey," she said again, uneasily this time. She was already composing herself, withdrawing back into being that proper English lady.

And he did not want to let her go.

"Another dance," he said, reaching for her hand.

She pulled away, shaking her head. "I agreed to only the one dance, Lord Geoffrey."

"You can't deny that you enjoyed yourself," he said. "You do indeed dance like an angel."

She shook her head again and closed her fan. "If you'll excuse me, Lord Geoffrey."

"Then come walk with me in the garden," he said with all the charm he possessed. "The moon is full and the stars are bright."

She blushed, gathering her skirts with one hand. "Forgive me, but I must return to my aunt directly."

"*Kāyara,*" he said, smiling still as he called her a coward in Hindi. He hadn't planned to say that; it simply came out.

But it worked. She stopped abruptly, frozen in place. "What did you say, Lord Geoffrey?"

His smile widened. "*Mairh āpakō ēka kāyara bulāyā.*" *I called you a coward.*

She raised her chin, striving to be aloof. "I am an English lady, Lord Geoffrey. You should not address me in Hindi."

"Yet you understood me, Miss Carew," he said easily. "And you *are* being something of a coward."

She blushed again and frowned. "Come with me, Lord Geoffrey," she said, turning away with a rustle of silk. "We must speak, alone, where no one else will hear."

She didn't look back to see if he followed, assuming he would. He did, of course. Hadn't he been the one who'd suggested they step outside in the first place?

He followed her from the ballroom, through the tall, arched door, and onto the stone terrace above the garden. There were a few lanterns here to light the steps down to the paths below, but most of the terrace was cast in welcoming darkness beneath the trees. Several couples lingered in the deeper shadows to take advantage of the privacy, the women's silk gowns faintly luminous and their little sighs of pleasure clear.

Steadfastly Miss Carew walked past them, not looking as she led Geoffrey to the farthest end of the terrace. At last she turned and faced him, her arms folded over her chest with discouraging determination. Moonlight spilled over her face and throat like a caress and emphasized the dusky cleft between her breasts. Clearly she'd no idea of how delectable she looked, her eyes golden and her skin velvety pale. Geoffrey certainly did, and with the memory of her sensuous dancing still fresh in his mind, it was requiring all his willpower not to take her immediately into his arms.

"Now, Lord Geoffrey," she said, her voice both low

and fierce. "Tell me why you addressed me in that—that ridiculous manner."

"It was hardly ridiculous, Miss Carew." He wasn't accustomed to wasting perfectly good moonlight in mere conversation, but if that was what it would take to win her, then he'd oblige. "You were in fact being quite cowardly."

She sighed impatiently. "I didn't mean *what* you said. It was *how* you said it, in—in a foreign language. Why did you speak so?"

"To amuse you," he said easily, shifting closer to her. "I knew you were from India, and I thought you would find it entertaining."

"What could you know of India, Lord Geoffrey?" she demanded, much more warmly than he'd expected.

"Not nearly as much as I wish to," he said. Even when she was trying to be stern, her voice enchanted him, husky and mellifluous with a hint of an exotic accent. "When I visited India, I found it the most fascinating and beautiful place on earth."

She nodded, quick little jerks of her chin. "So that is it. You are but one more younger son turned nabob."

"Like your father?" he asked, unable to resist.

"No," she said firmly. "My father was a gentleman of honor, and he sailed as an officer in the East India Company. He was never a rapacious English nabob, rushing across the sea to grasp at opportunity and make his fortune however he could."

"But I didn't go to make my fortune, either, Miss Carew," Geoffrey said. "I went for pleasure."

She raised her brows in disbelief. "I'm not a fool, Lord Geoffrey. No English gentleman goes to India for pleasure."

"I assure you I did," he said. "When I was done with school, my father wished me to travel across the Continent to complete my education in Paris and Rome. I refused, and insisted on India instead. I've always been fascinated by the East, you see."

With her mouth set, she searched his face, clearly deciding whether to accept his answer or not. She should; it was the truth, every word.

"Do you truly speak Hindi," she said quickly, shifting to that language once again, *"or did you recite those few words by rote like a trained parrot?"*

He laughed, as much at her bravado as at the words themselves, and answered her back in Hindi as proof. *"I speak it well enough to know how gravely you have insulted me."*

She drew in her breath sharply, surprised by his response.

"Then we shall consider it even between us," she said in English. "My father was the bravest European in the Company's Territories—as brave as any lion!—and he would not have taken kindly to hearing his daughter called a coward."

"Then please forgive me, Miss Carew," he said, bowing. "You've already proven your bravery by joining me here. I'll admit I made a sorry jest, but I intended it without malice."

"It no longer matters, Lord Geoffrey." She dropped her arms to her sides, as if the brief exchange had knocked the fight from her. "You startled me, that was all. It was the first time I'd heard Hindi spoken in years."

He lowered his voice, liking the idea of a confidential secret language they could share. *"Mairh khuśī sē, yaha āpa kē sātha bāta karēngē."*

I'd happily speak it with you.

"No, Lord Geoffrey," she said in English, the words turning brittle and sharp. "I am an English lady, and I intend to speak like one. I must be more careful."

"Careful, Miss Carew?" he asked, puzzled. "Careful of what? Surely not of me?"

But she only shook her head, raising her small chin with fresh resolve. "If you were so enamored of India, why did you leave? You are a gentleman of rank and wealth. You may do as you please with your life. Why are you not there still?"

"Because I was called back on account of my older brother," he said. "I had no choice."

"No choice, Lord Geoffrey?" she asked curiously. "Your brother holds such sway over you?"

"Not in the way you imply," he said. He did not like telling this story, for it brought back a time of dread and uneasiness; he had never felt so helpless as he had on that long, bleak voyage back to England. "I received a letter—a letter many months old—that informed me that my brother had suffered a grievous accident, and was not expected to live. Even though I feared I would most certainly be too late, I sailed for home at once."

"Oh, no," she said softly, resting her hand on his sleeve. "Such a loss! I am so sorry, Lord Geoffrey."

"You needn't be." He smiled crookedly, liking her touch on his arm. "Harry survived, the devil, and recovered to greet me on my return, and with a new wife at his side as well. So while all my cynical acquaintances were ready to congratulate me on taking my brother's place, the story had a far happier ending, and a good thing it was."

"How barbarously cruel of them!" Her eyes widened with indignation. "How could you ever truly replace your brother?"

"Only as my father's heir," he said quickly, wanting to reassure her. "That's all that's required of second sons, you know, to be another male in constant readiness. I could never replace Harry in any other way, nor would I wish to become Duke of Breconridge at such a price."

He knew he'd said too much. He couldn't help it. He always did when he spoke of Harry's accident, and though he'd come to realize it was only his way of dealing with such a near-tragedy, it still made him feel a bit foolish.

"I didn't intend to rattle on like that, Miss Carew," he said, "but if you had a brother or sister, then you would understand."

"But I do understand." The melancholy that he'd first glimpsed in her eyes was now in her voice as well. "Such a loss would have been intolerable for you to bear. Indeed, how fortunate for you both that the story had a happier ending."

Of course she'd understand loss. She was an orphan, the only survivor of her family in India. Instinctively he slipped his hand over hers, linking their fingers together.

"Again I find I must apologize to you," he said gently. "I'd no intention of raising old sorrows."

She glanced down at their joined hands, and slowly curled her fingers into his.

"Why should you be so kind to me?" she asked wistfully. "I've done nothing that would make me deserve that from you."

"But you did," he insisted. "I spoke without thought, and I was wrong."

She looked up, her smile small and bittersweet. "And I say you are being kind to me, and generous as well. You are not what I expected, Lord Geoffrey, not at all."

"Nor are you, Miss Carew." He used their linked hands to pull her close, gambling that she wouldn't reject him. "The gossips do you great injustice."

"I'd rather not imagine what they say of me." She came to him effortlessly, as if she belonged in his arms.

"But I must be careful in all things, you see, and especially cautious in whom I trust."

"I'm eminently trustworthy," he said, though as soon as he'd spoken he realized how hollow his words must sound, given that he'd just slipped his arm around her waist.

She knew it, too. But while her smile turned wry, she didn't pull away. "You did not come here into the moonlight to make empty declarations like that one, Lord Geoffrey. I would rather guess that your intention was to seduce me."

"Ahh," he said gruffly, chagrined. Of course that had been exactly what he'd intended, more or less, but he hadn't expected her to acknowledge it quite so bluntly, and especially not after such a somber conversation. "You are very direct, Miss Carew."

"It's the truth, isn't it?" Her sapphire earrings bobbed against her cheeks as she rested her open palm lightly on his chest. "That is the reason all gentlemen—no, all *men*—pursue women. It is no great secret. I may be a lady, Lord Geoffrey, but I am not a fool."

"I never thought you were, sweet," he said softly, grazing the back of his fingers over her cheek. If she was going to be so deuced frank, then he saw no reason not to show her that he, too, knew what was supposed to happen in the moonlight. "You strike me as being remarkably clever."

"Oh, I am, Lord Geoffrey," she said. "You've no notion of how clever I can be."

"Then you must educate me," he murmured, no longer really paying much attention to what she was saying. She fit neatly against him, her waist delectably small. He liked how she was gazing up at him, how her amber eyes were filled with warmth, and he liked her scent, an exotic mix of sandalwood and roses. "I'd enjoy that."

"So would I." She hesitated for a long moment before continuing, tracing her fingers absently over the silk embroidered scrolls along the front of his coat. "Have you heard of *kismet,* Lord Geoffrey? It is a Persian word, not Hindi, but it was much used in India. Do you know its meaning?"

His Persian was practically nonexistent, but that was one word he knew, just as he knew the trouble it could bring him.

"One moment now, Miss Carew," he said, his well-practiced bachelor instincts instantly turning wary. "I don't believe in love at first sight, no matter the language."

"Love?" she repeated, astonished. "I said nothing of *love*, Lord Geoffrey. I spoke of kismet. Of fate, or destiny, or fortune. Of how our lives are pre-ordained, and we are helpless to make them otherwise. I spoke nothing of love."

He frowned and drew back from her a fraction. "But what other destiny is there for a beautiful lady than love?"

"Not for me," she said softly, sadly. "Never for me."

He was accustomed to arch beauties who pretended to scorn the men around them as unworthy of their love, but never a lady who described herself in this way. The sorrowful conviction in her voice made no sense, even as it touched him.

"Don't say such grim things, Miss Carew," he said, striving to cheer her as once again he drew her into his arms. "You simply haven't found the proper man, that is all."

She shook her head, watching her hand settle over the front of his coat, over his heart.

"When first I took notice of you," she said, her voice barely above a whisper, "I believed you were no better than any of the other foolish young gentlemen my aunt has presented to me. Yet as soon as you spoke, I sensed you were not like the others. How, or why, or in what fashion, I cannot yet tell, but you are. You were sent to me for a purpose. That was what I meant by kismet. And though I wish with all my heart that it were not so, I feel the pull of kismet, and of you."

Kismet. He realized with dismay that there was absolutely no way that he could kiss her now. She was still as beautiful, still eminently desirable, but she'd changed everything with her belief in fate, in destiny, in kismet.

Because in some devilish way he couldn't begin to understand, he believed it, too.

"I must go," she said, suddenly slipping free of his embrace with the same sinuous grace that she'd shown while dancing. "This is wrong. I can't be alone with you any longer."

He reached out, determined to capture her, but her blue silk gown was already disappearing into the shadows.

"A moment, Miss Carew," he called, following swiftly after her. "Don't go just yet. What of fate? What of kismet?"

She paused, her head bent, before finally glancing back at him over one pale shoulder. "Each day I ride in Hyde Park at half-past two."

Then she fled, nearly running, her slippered feet silent on the stone.

Geoffrey stopped, staring after her as he raked his fingers back through his hair. She could run as fast as she pleased, but she couldn't escape, not from him, and not from herself, either. He'd played this game before. He knew how it would end. No matter how deuced mysterious she tried to be, he'd solve her puzzle in the end. He nodded, reassuring himself. Of course he'd win. He always did where ladies were concerned.

Yet even as he sauntered back into the brightly lit ballroom and the scores of other ladies, he did not put Serena Carew from his thoughts, or that single word she'd whispered to him.

Kismet.

CHAPTER 2

As soon as Serena had fallen asleep, the old nightmare began again and would not let go, no matter how much she struggled to waken.

She was thirteen again, in her bedchamber at Sundara Manōra, the large house with pink marble columns that her father had built long before she'd been born, away in the hills and three days' ride from Hyderabad. She was still called Savitri, the daughter of the sun god, a name that both flattered and amused Father; the only time she heard her English name, Rachel, was when Father was being stern.

It was June and the rains began early, flooding the lake on their estate and turning the paths in their gardens to constant ponds. The summer heat arrived early, too, the fiery sun appearing from behind the rain-clouds only long enough to make the standing water steam and send shimmering waves of heat over the tops of the rose trees.

To no one's surprise, the fevers that always came with the rainy season had begun earlier as well. In the *zenana*, or women's quarters, there were already handmaids, slaves, and eunuchs who were too ill to perform their duties, and Father worried about how many of the others about the estate would fall sick as well.

Then her half sister, Asha, became ill and was confined to her room, and two days after that, the fever claimed Savitri herself. Two handmaids had fanned her with palm leaves, while her *ayah,* her nursemaid since she'd been a baby, had washed her hands and feet in cooling rose-water and given her a special drink to help her sleep, sitting on the floor beside her bed and singing softly until Savitri had slept, falling into the deep fever-sleep.

Two days passed, and nights to match. When Savitri finally woke, she was alone, and sicker than before. Her body was on fire, and her head ached so badly she could scarce open her eyes. She called, her voice a rough croak, yet no one came to her. The *zenana* was far too quiet. Where had they all gone? Why had they left her behind? She dragged herself from the bed, her legs swaying beneath her, and slowly made her way from her room and into the hall, leaning against the walls for support.

On the floor in the hall lay one of the handmaids, the pitcher she'd been carrying smashed beside her. Savitri didn't have to look closer to know that the woman was dead, and had been for some time.

Her panic rising, Savitri staggered toward the servants' quarters, wrongly silent for this time of day. The door was open, with more corpses curled on their pallets on the floor. Around them were scattered clothes and baskets and other signs of great haste, proof that those who could flee had done so.

With a little cry of despair, Savitri went to the door to the courtyard, a door she had never opened for herself. She must find Father. He would save her, and he would know where the others had all gone. Weak as she was, it took all her strength to unlatch the heavy door and push it open.

To her horror, the front gate to their estate yawned open, the porter and guards who so loyally defended them gone. Only one remained: he lay across the center path, his turban askew and his bald, shaven head gleaming in the sun, and his drawn sword still in his hand. Standing over his body were three hyenas, their muzzles stained red with the man's blood as they raised their heads to stare boldly at Savitri, challenging.

Whimpering with fear, she shoved the door shut against the beasts, and forced her shaking legs to carry her to her sister's bedchamber. Asha was two years older; together they could decide what to do.

But as soon as she saw Asha, lying on her bed in a tangle of sheets, Savitri knew her sister would have no answers for her. Her skin was yellow and gleamed with sweat, her cheeks hollowed and her lips cracked.

"Asha!" she cried, throwing herself onto the bed beside her sister. "You must not die, too. You cannot!"

Asha's eyes fluttered open, and she managed a faint, ghastly smile. "Savitri," she whispered. "You came."

Savitri was crying, her tears falling as she smoothed her sister's tangled dark hair back from her face.

"Lie with me," Asha said. "We must be together."

Savitri curled beside her sister, her head heavy on the shared pillow. They would die together, side by side, as they always had lived. She knew that now. With trembling fingers, she pulled off the oversized locket she always wore, a miniature of her mother framed in diamonds. She pressed the locket in her palm, and linked her fingers with her sister's over it.

"Mama will watch over us, as she always has, Asha," she whispered, exhausted with fever and despair. "She'll keep us safe."

Unable to keep her eyes open any longer, she felt herself falling, falling into the darkness.

"This one lives still," the Englishman said. "Barely."

Through a fever-haze, Savitri saw three men standing over her: two in the red uniform that matched the old one that Father kept in his trunk, another dressed in black, and all with scarves tied over their noses and mouths. Their faces above the white cloths seemed shockingly pale to her, with faded blue eyes and yellow hair. Englishmen, she thought, more Englishmen than she'd ever seen together in her life.

The black-clad man bent over her, chafing her hands and forcing her eyelid upward to peer at her eye. "We must do our best to save her for poor Carew's sake," he said. "She's his daughter, of course. He always boasted of her beauty."

"Brave little lady," one of the others said. "She can't stay here, that's for certain. Here, miss, we'll be as gentle as we can."

Strong arms gathered her up, lifting her from the bed and her sister's lifeless body. The necklace with her mother's picture slipped from her fingers and dropped into the tangled sheets. She struggled weakly, wanting to tell them to bring Asha, to spare her from the hyenas, but her mouth was too dry and the words too far away.

"Take her to the wagon, Abbot," said the man in black. "I'll do what I can for her, but it will be a miracle if she survives to see Calcutta. The sooner this entire place is burned to the ground, the better. This fever's like a plague, and fire's the only way to purify it. I've never seen so many struck dead so fast."

Now she could smell the smoke and hear the pop and crack of flames. Through the window she saw more soldiers with lit brands, setting fire to their great house. She tried to twist back for Asha, but the man's arms were so much stronger as he carried her from the room and away from her sister.

"Be easy, miss, be easy," he said. "You'll be safe among your own people now, good Christian Englishmen."

But she wasn't. Her final glimpse of her home was red flames leaping through the roof, consuming all she'd known and everything she loved.

"Serena."

She woke abruptly. Aunt Morley was holding her by the shoulders, her face full of concern. Her lady's maid, Martha, stood holding the candlestick, and there were two rumpled-looking footmen, clearly roused from their own beds, standing near the door.

She took a deep breath, pulling free of her aunt as she struggled to orient herself. Her cheeks were wet with tears, and she was shaking with emotion after the horror of what she'd just witnessed.

But she hadn't, not really. It was only a dream, a nightmare. She must remember that. Nothing could hurt her now. She wasn't in Sundara Manōra any longer, and hadn't been for seven years. She was safe in London, in her grandfather's elegant town house in St. James's Square. Everything was familiar, exactly as it should be, from the framed prints of the seven virtues on the wall over the mantelpiece to her mahogany dressing table to her armchair near the window, covered in pink damask to match the curtains. There were no ravening hyenas, or corpses in the hall, or soldiers with flaming brands.

She was awake, and she was *safe*.

"My dear child," said her aunt gently. "It was the old nightmare again, wasn't it?"

Wearily Serena nodded. She took a huge, shuddering gulp of air, and wiped her tears away with the sleeve of her night rail.

"Poor lamb," Aunt Morley murmured, her voice low and soothing as she smoothed Serena's hair back from her tearstained face. Widowed twice and her own children long grown, she had welcomed the chance to look after Serena. "I know how terrible they are for you."

"It's done now," Serena said, her voice so hoarse that she realized she must have been crying out in her sleep. Her plaited hair was tangled, and her bedsheets were twisted and rumpled. It was always the same after she'd struggled to free herself from the dream, and the force of it left her shaken and anxious, her heart racing with terror. Determined to calm herself, she reached for the crystal glass of water on the table beside her bed, and Martha hurried forward to hand it to her.

"It's been at least a year since you've had one of those nightmares," Aunt Morley said. "I'd dared to hope you'd outgrown night terrors like that. I don't know what could have brought it on tonight, especially after having such an agreeable time at the ball, dancing with his lordship and all."

But Serena knew. Her conversation with Lord Geoffrey Fitzroy had reminded her of India, of her childhood, of far too many things that would be better forgotten than remembered.

"Now that I'm awake, Aunt, I shall be fine," she said. This was real, she reminded herself again, and the dream had been only a dream. "Forgive me for disturbing you."

Her aunt smiled, her eyes still filled with concern. "It was nothing to me, child," she said. "Though I do believe you gave Martha quite a fright."

Martha nodded vigorously, unable to keep quiet. "Oh, miss, it was terrible to hear! You was weeping and crying out and thrashing about like there was very demons attacking you, and—"

"That's enough, Martha," Aunt Morley said firmly. "Serena, I believe I still have some of that decoction that the doctor left last time to help you sleep."

"None of that," Serena said swiftly, then sighed. Her aunt meant well, but the laudanum the doctors prescribed only made the nightmares impossible to avoid, playing them over and over in a heavy sleep that she couldn't escape. "The best thing for me now is simply to stay awake. I'll read. I promise I'll be well enough in the morning."

Her aunt released a small, wounded *harrumph* of disapproval, tucking her hands into the sleeves of her dressing gown. "I do not believe that is wise, Serena."

"Of course it's wise, Aunt," she said, striving to be patient, "because it's the only remedy that works."

When Serena had first arrived in London, her health had indeed been fragile, and not entirely from the lingering effects of the fever that had nearly killed her, either. The troop of doctors that had hovered around her that first year had never figured out the reason, but she had. While the long, difficult voyage from Calcutta coupled with the perpetual damp and cold of the English climate had taken their toll, most punishing of all had been the grief and guilt that she had survived when her father and sister hadn't.

But that had been seven years ago. The sorrow would never completely disappear, yet she'd found it did soften with time. Her health had recovered, and she'd grown from the pale and sickly girl arriving from India into an English lady who was admired wherever she went. Only Grandpapa and Aunt Morley seemed unable to accept the transformation, and continued to regard her as delicate.

"I will be fine, Aunt," she said again. "You'll see in the morning."

Unconvinced, her aunt touched her palm to Serena's cheek, ever-vigilant for signs of fever, and glanced at the little porcelain clock on the chimneypiece.

"It's nearly four, and not much longer until daybreak," she said. "I suppose no lasting damage will be done to your constitution."

"It won't," Serena agreed. At least now she understood why she felt so exhausted: likely the nightmare had been playing itself over and over in her dreams for hours before her aunt had awakened her. She reached for one of the wool paisley shawls that she always kept nearby and wrapped it around her shoulders, and then purposefully took a novel from the table. "I'll distract my thoughts by reading."

"Very well, my dear," said Aunt Morley with obvious reluctance. "As you wish. I shall leave you to the solace of your book. But because I do not wish you to tire yourself unduly after so little sleep, I shall cancel your engagements tomorrow, so that you may rest."

"No!" Serena exclaimed, thinking of how she'd told Lord Geoffrey that she'd be riding in Hyde Park. "That is, you may postpone my gown-fitting with Mrs. Delamore in the morning, but I wish very much to go riding as I always do. The fresh air will do me good."

"Then we shall take the carriage," Aunt Morley said, leaning forward to kiss Serena's forehead. "You'll have your fresh air, without the exertion of sitting in a saddle. Good night, niece, or what is left of it."

Serena watched her leave, followed by the two footmen. No matter what her aunt said, she would not be sitting in the carriage with her this afternoon, but riding her mare instead, and she'd wear her bright blue habit with the silver lacing, so that Lord Geoffrey would be sure to see her.

"Is there anything else you'll be wanting, miss?" asked Martha hesitantly. "The kitchen fires will already be lit for breakfast."

"Only tea," Serena said, and with a curtsey, Martha, too, retreated, closing the door quietly after her.

Alone, Serena sank back against the pillows and pulled the soft woolen shawl more closely over her shoulders. She should have asked Martha to put fresh coals on the fire before she'd left. The embers in her hearth, banked when she'd gone to bed, were barely glowing. Although the faint light of first dawn was beginning to show through her windows, her bedchamber was holding on to the chill of the night. She was almost never sufficiently warm in London, even if everyone else was remarking on the balminess of this spring.

But she hadn't been cold last night when she'd stood

beneath the stars with Lord Geoffrey. She smiled, remembering. It was the first time she'd ever left a ball with a gentleman like that. To be sure, there had been any number over the last two years who'd wished her to join them in such an intimate conversation, and she'd refused them all. Of course she understood exactly why these gentlemen had hovered around her with such determination. Grandpapa assured her that because of Father's gift for trading, she was worth £10,000 a year, an astonishing fortune, and she'd quickly learned that there were a great many more poor bachelors than wealthy unmarried ladies in London society. They reminded her of mosquitoes, buzzing about her with annoying persistence everywhere she went, and she brushed them all away like mosquitoes, too.

But absolutely nothing about Lord Geoffrey reminded her of mosquitoes. He was tall and lean and his shoulders were broad, and he'd worn his elaborately embroidered evening suit with a disarming nonchalance. He had black hair and brilliant blue eyes, with little lines that fanned out at the corners when he'd teased her. And when he'd smiled at her—ah, when he'd smiled she'd felt as if the very sun had burst out from behind the clouds.

He'd dazzled Serena when she'd first confronted him, his handsomeness overwhelming her so thoroughly that she'd turned wooden and awkward. Then he'd begun to speak of India, and her first impressions had been swept aside by rising panic. Could he possibly have discovered her secret? Was he toying with her, amusing himself before he shamed her in front of all the others at the ball?

She'd hidden her fear behind her most practiced mask, acting aloof and distant. She'd tried to avoid dancing with him, yet her aunt had insisted until it could not be helped. Even then she'd feigned such disinterest that any ordinary gentleman would simply have bowed and retreated.

Yet it had not stopped Lord Geoffrey. Far from it. He had pursued her, not with flowery, false compliments, but with Hindi and a genuine—or at least it had seemed genuine—interest in her. He said nothing of her secret, nothing she couldn't deflect with ease. Gradually she'd let her initial fears slip away, and let her guard down as well. He'd held her in his arms, but he hadn't tried to kiss her, though she was quite certain he'd wished to. She'd almost wished it herself.

Almost, almost. Her smile turned wistful, remembering the warmth and desire in his eyes when he'd gazed down at her, and how safe she'd felt in the circle of his arms. She'd tested him with the Hindi, and in turn he'd teased her until she'd blushed. She'd felt so comfortable with him that she'd foolishly begun babbling on about kismet, and how it must have been fated that they meet—a confidence that was in itself dangerous to make.

Oh, she'd been so foolish, betraying herself to him like that! Speaking of India, their conversation in Hindi, even the way she'd danced were all little clues to her past, and she'd freely revealed them. It was entirely her own fault, her own weakness, because she couldn't deny that she'd liked him. She'd met so many gentlemen since she'd come into Society last year, but not one of them had tempted her as he had.

Yet nothing could ever come of it. If their conversation had been enough to inspire her nightmares, then that same nightmare in turn should have been a potent reminder of why she must never again let herself be beguiled by a man like Lord Geoffrey. The fact that he'd traveled to India and knew her homeland only made him all the more dangerous. Even she knew that love required more than desire: it required trust, and she could never risk trusting anyone, not even a man she'd accept as a husband. How could she, with the secret she kept buried deep within her?

Perhaps, in time, she might marry a lesser man, a man who would be so grateful for her fortune that he wouldn't ask questions that she couldn't answer. But to entangle herself with the son of the Duke of Breconridge, blessed with all his power, wealth, and royal blood, could only lead to disaster.

With a groan of frustration she hurled the unread book across the room, where it thumped against the wall. She'd no doubt that Lord Geoffrey would come to Hyde Park to meet her today; the hunger in his expression when they'd parted last night had assured her of that. He would come, and she would greet him, and her aunt, sitting in the carriage at a discreet distance, would be overjoyed and already planning their wedding.

But Serena intended to tell him that this first meeting between them would also be the last. She'd invent some sort of foolishness, the kind of polite excuse that ladies were always concocting, and he would be forced to accept it, as a gentleman must.

She could never tell him, or anyone else, the truth: that she was an imposter. She was Father's daughter, true, but her mother had been a dancing-girl from a brothel near the fort at Golconda that he had bought and brought back to Sundara Manōra. He always said it was her beauty that had caught his eye, but her spirit that had captured his heart. Her mother had been beautiful indeed, with a heart-shaped face, dark golden brown skin, and enormous dark eyes beneath arching black brows.

She and Father had never married; being his mistress, his *bibi,* had been enough for her. To Father it hadn't mattered, nor to anyone else in his little self-created kingdom of Sundara Manōra. Marriage had proven to be a great disappointment to him, a dutifully British union filled with bitterness and misunderstanding that had ended only with his wife's death in childbirth. It was no wonder that marriage had had no place in the happiness he'd found with her mother. Serena's mother had come from Lucknow, while Asha's had been born in Scotland. Beyond that Serena was simply one of Lord Thomas Carew's two daughters, girls whose mothers had died too soon, and he loved the two of them exactly the same.

But in England, it would matter very much. Serena was illegitimate and she was half-Indian, and worst of all, she was not the daughter who had died. She was entitled to none of the kindness that had been shown to her, none of the love that Grandpapa and Aunt Morley had given, none of the regard showered on her by Society, none of the jewels or silk gowns or the rich furnishings in this room. Even the name she was called wasn't her own, but her dead sister's. She was only Savitri, the *nautch* girl's bastard, and if the benevolent English ladies who'd nursed her in the hospital in Calcutta had realized the mistake they had made, they would have instantly cast her off into the streets and the oblivion of poverty that should have been her lot.

The authorities here in London would not be any more understanding. She would not be forgiven for the error of the kind people in Calcutta; she would instead be punished for not telling the truth. She knew the courts were not merciful. Grandpapa had a fierce devotion to English law, and with relish he would often read aloud from the papers of cases that pleased him in their awful justice. In mute terror, she would listen, and recognize the crimes she shared—fraud, theft, criminal deception, and false impersonation—and imagine the sentence that could be read over her own bowed head if she was ever discovered for what she was.

That was the truth, and she carried the inescapable burden of it within her always, day and night, through waking and through dreams and nightmares, too. As the years had slipped by, she'd realized that the danger of being discovered had lessened. She tried to tell herself that the possibility was slight, especially since the English ladies in Calcutta had told her that the doctor who'd rescued her had also sickened from the same fever and died, as had the soldiers with him. They'd sacrificed their lives to save hers. Any records of her birth would have burned with their house, and the truest source—her father—had perished as well.

Yet no matter how she strived to believe she was safe, her conscience refused to accept it. Somewhere there could still be someone who knew the truth, or some damning paper or record that could reveal who she truly was. Her greatest fear, however, was that she would somehow unwittingly betray herself. That was her fate, her punishment, and in it there was no place at all for moonlight and English lords with charming smiles.

And so she must be strong, and see no more of Lord Geoffrey. She must be as brave as her father had been, and as resilient as her mother, and pray for the courage to withstand whatever other twists and turns her life's path might take.

She buried her face in her hands in too-familiar despair, and thought again of how much better and more fair everything would have been had she died from the fever instead of her sister.

CHAPTER 3

The afternoon was warm and bright with sunshine, and Hyde Park was crowded. To Geoffrey it seemed that all of fashionable London must have decided to take a turn around the park, and a good deal of unfashionable London with it. The ways were packed with carriages of ladies displaying overwrought new bonnets, middle-aged gentlemen pretending to be country squires, and officers in red coats on prancing, high-strung mounts. Every kind of street-hawker selling oranges and gingerbread and primroses was boldly darting between the horses and carriages in search of customers, and mixed in among them beneath the trees were fiddlers with their hats on the grass before them and showmen with their puppets and trained squirrels.

It was all just one massive, cacophonous distraction to Geoffrey, whose single concern was finding Serena Carew. How in blazes he was supposed to accomplish this was a challenge he hadn't expected. He never came to the park at this hour, and he was irritated and frustrated by how slow his progress was now, forced to ride at the trudging pace of a stately snail.

He'd been picturing Miss Carew as a daring rider, one of those rare ladies who feared nothing as she raced over the open lawns, and looked quite fetching whilst doing it.

In fact from the moment she'd slipped back into the ballroom and from his sight, he hadn't been able to stop imagining her doing a great many things, most of which had been wickedly entertaining to him, if not very respectful of Miss Carew's heretofore impeccable reputation.

But now he not only despaired of witnessing any daring or entertainment this afternoon, he despaired of seeing the lady herself. As he came to the end of Rotten Row yet again, nodding at one more of his father's friends, he heard the half-hour chime of a nearby church bell, and his despair deepened to pure misery. She'd said she rode in the park at two-thirty, and now it was half-past three. He was generally good-natured about women and time, understanding that they required more of that commodity than men to prepare themselves to face the world.

But an hour was his limit for waiting, and Miss Carew had now exceeded that. Far worse, however, was the nagging suspicion that she wasn't delayed by vanity or accident, but had instead simply chosen not to join him, and regarded their appointment of so little significance that she hadn't bothered to send word that she'd changed her mind. All that feverish talk of kismet and fate from her in the moonlight might have evaporated with the common sense of dawn. For that matter, he could well have been doing a bit of imagining himself, remembering more of an attraction between them than had actually existed.

It would serve him right, he thought with gloomy resignation, lusting after a genteel, romantic virgin like that. He was much better off with actresses and bored married women who wouldn't turn skittish and not keep assignations. As intriguing as Miss Carew had been, he wasn't going to let her play him for a fool, and with a muttered oath of frustration he turned his horse toward home.

And there, of course, she was.

She was riding toward him on a neat black mare, riding with exactly the same grace that he'd imagined. She sat tall yet easy, with her back making a long, sinuous curve over the sidesaddle. Her habit was nearly the same brilliant blue as her gown had been last night, with silver lace that glittered in the sun, and on her head was a stylish black silk hat inspired by a jockey's cap, and crowned by a curling black plume. Tied diagonally over her breast was a patterned, scarlet sash knotted at the shoulder, with gold silk fringes that danced and rippled against her hip in the breeze.

In short she looked quite, quite perfect, and instantly made him forget all the bustling crowds and racket and his impatience as well. He lifted his hat and rode forward to join her.

"Good day, Miss Carew," he said, smiling warmly as he guided his horse to fall into step beside hers. "A beautiful afternoon is made all the better because you are now in it."

The compliment didn't make her smile, and seemingly neither did his presence. But then she'd been like this when they'd first met last night as well; he must remember that, and do his best to thaw her.

"Good day to you, Lord Geoffrey," she said, her voice solemn. "I must beg your forgiveness for being so much later than I had originally said."

"I took no notice," he lied, beaming. It was always a good thing to have a lady indebted to him, even over something as foolish as this. "All that matters is that you are here now."

"It was due to my aunt, you see," she continued, as if he hadn't spoken at all. "She wished me to sit in the carriage, while I preferred to ride. Our, ah, conversation took longer than I anticipated."

Pointedly she glanced over her shoulder, and he followed her gaze. A pair of burly grooms in her grandfather's pale gray livery were riding directly behind her, and behind them was an open carriage with Lady Morley, sitting in the center of the seat in an extravagantly beribboned hat and a parasol on her shoulder.

How in blazes had he forgotten? Miss Carew was a young, unmarried lady, and young, unmarried ladies were never permitted to go anywhere unattended, from fear that men like him would swoop down and snatch away their virtue.

Which, given how beguiling Miss Carew appeared today, was a very genuine possibility. Or at least it had been, until he'd realized she was being guarded as closely as the crown jewels in the Tower. The odds against him having her to himself alone again as he had last night were slim, very slim. He would simply have to be more inventive. Kisses and caresses were the easiest path toward seduction, yet from experience he'd found the right words could be effective as well. More challenging, yes, but this lady was well worth the extra effort.

"I must go to Lady Morley and pay my respects," he said gallantly, knowing how important it was to keep in her aunt's good graces. "The older ladies merit that, you know."

"No," Miss Carew said swiftly, reaching out to place her small gloved hand on his arm to hold him back. "That is not necessary. She will already be pleased beyond measure to have you join us. Besides, I wish to speak to you. At once, if I may."

Happily he complied, and reined his horse back beside hers. "I am glad of it, Miss Carew, because I have things I wish to say to you as well."

Her eyes widened beneath the curving black brim of her hat. "You do, Lord Geoffrey?"

"I do," he said. "You needn't look so wary, either. I promise you I'll say nothing that merits that kind of look from you."

"Hah." She ducked her chin for a moment, visibly composing herself before she raised her gaze once again to meet his. She'd done this last night, too, shifting her emotions as easily as other women took off their gloves, and he found it intriguing. Now her unusual amber-colored eyes only showed curiosity. "I can only begin to guess what you'd say to me."

"Then I suppose I must tell you at once," he said easily, "and end your suffering."

She gave a disdainful little flick to her hand. "I assure you, Lord Geoffrey, that you flatter yourself very much if you believe that I would suffer on your account."

He laughed. "So whilst I am determined to spare you, you in turn refuse to be in sufficient peril to be rescued. A fine conundrum, that."

"Only because you have made it so," she said. "It's no wonder that you turned to Hindi last night, Lord Geoffrey, since you appear so incapable of plain-speaking in your own tongue."

He laughed again, delighting in her banter. Not once did she smile, let alone laugh, but her expressive eyes were filled with teasing amusement, made all the more beguiling by her outward solemnity. Last night he'd assumed that she wore paint and powder and rouge on her face, the way all women did, but now in the sunlight he realized the sooty darkness of her lashes and the ivory of her skin were truly hers, and owed nothing to artifice.

"I thought I was never to breathe a word of that language to you again," he said. "I recall being quite strictly forbidden."

"And so you were," she said promptly, adding a quick nod for emphasis, enough to send the plume on her hat fluttering over her head. "I commend you for being so obliging."

"I will always oblige you in everything, Miss Carew," he said, lowering his voice just enough to make his words more confidential. "Whatever you wish, and it shall be yours."

"In everything, Lord Geoffrey?" she asked, without even a hint of coyness. "That's a very bold promise for you to make, considering how little you know of me."

"In everything," he repeated, and at that moment, with her watching him with a slanting, sidelong glance, he meant it. "Try me. Test me. Ask a favor of me, and see how swiftly I will agree."

"Oh, I could not," she said, and if she weren't the famously cold Miss Carew, he'd swear she was flirting with him. "It would not be right."

"Of course it would be." He'd been expecting her to make the usual requests that ladies did, a nosegay from a flower-seller or some such, but clearly she'd something more in mind, something that wasn't entirely proper, and he couldn't wait to learn what it might be. "Ask me your favor. Anything your heart might wish."

"To ask what I wish most—ah, Lord Geoffrey, what I long for is a champion," she said fiercely, her words tumbling out in a rush. "A champion, yes, and not one of these pitiful modern English gentlemen, either. Instead I'd summon the ancient warriors of Greece and of Rome and of Persia for my choosing, men who were honorable and fearless in their loyalties."

He smiled, intrigued. He remembered this intensity of hers from last night; it had been much of what had drawn him back in the hope of seeing her again today. Passion in a woman was a fine thing, no matter what inspired it.

"You have so little use for us poor Englishmen?" he asked. "We are of so little worth in your estimation?"

Her gaze swept over him in a swift, efficient appraisal. "Not you, Lord Geoffrey," she said. "I did not mean *all* Englishmen."

He laughed, wondering if she realized how brazen her accounting of his physical attributes would be considered by her aunt. Or perhaps not; he did recall Lady Morley also conducting a brisk accounting of him last night. "How relieved I am to learn that I suffice, and that my humble self will meet your measure."

"You know you do, Lord Geoffrey," she said with charming indignation, "and no lady would say otherwise. But a good many of your fellows are sad creatures indeed, macaronis and dandies and other idle jacks lolling in their coffeehouses and clubs. They are pitiful, Lord Geoffrey, quite, quite pitiful, and I'll have none of them."

It was clear she was taking this conversation quite seriously, while he—well, what he was doing was enjoying the fire in those golden eyes as she declaimed against the sad Englishmen, and how rosy her cheeks had become.

"For a husband?" he asked.

"For a champion, Lord Geoffrey," she said, and her cheeks flushed a fraction more deeply. "I explained to you last night that I have no intention of marrying."

He remembered, but he still didn't believe it.

"Not even if some ancient Greek or Persian warrior were to come thundering around Hyde Park Corner with his sword drawn, intent on plunder and carrying you off as his wife?" he asked. "You wouldn't take him?"

"No, Lord Geoffrey, I would not." She raised her chin a fraction higher. "But if such a man also displayed bravery and loyalty and intelligence, then I'd consider him as my champion."

"A champion." He wondered if, in her mind, this was the same thing as a lover. Obviously, he rather hoped it was. "So those are the sole requirements for being your champion? Bravery, loyalty, and intelligence?"

"I would not encourage the plundering," she said. "That is not acceptable in London. But you were wise to suggest the swords. Father always said you could judge the innate worth of a man by the strength of his sword-arm."

He raised his brows at that. "In India possessing a good sword-arm means one can lop off an enemy's head with a single blow."

She nodded. "I believe that was what Father meant, too. It would be a most useful talent for a champion. The hills where we lived were home to many bandits and outlaws, and all the men at Sundara Manōra were skilled swordsmen. Father wouldn't have had it otherwise."

"I fear, Miss Carew, that you may have to adjust your requirements, this being London." He'd never engaged in a more unusual flirtation, nor one that was more exciting. If they weren't on horseback, they'd be tearing at each other's clothes by now. "But I do know of a possible candidate for your champion. Will you consider him?"

She smiled, with the exact degree of assurance to show that she knew what he was really asking.

"Oh, Lord Geoffrey, I wouldn't dare do that," she said. "It wouldn't be proper."

"*Proper?*" he repeated, incredulous. "You won't dare tell me because of propriety?"

She didn't reply, letting her smile be her only answer.

But as far as he was concerned, it was too late for that. It was the dancing all over again. She could swear up and down that she was a proper English lady, but she wasn't. Not in the least. No matter how carefully she'd been educated and groomed and refined the way her bloodlines demanded, part of her had clearly resisted becoming one more proper but excruciatingly dull young lady.

He understood forced propriety, for his own family

and tutors had attempted to instill much the same with him, with an equal degree of success. Rebellion was always bubbling within him, and a natural contrariness to authority and expectations. No wonder he was so drawn to her. Propriety simply wasn't in her soul any more than it was in his, and he liked her all the more for it.

She gave another defiant, determined toss to her head, her gaze never leaving his. Surely this must be a challenge; he could think of no other way to interpret it.

He'd no intention of disappointing her, either.

As if avoiding another rider, he nudged his horse a fraction closer to hers so that his knee above the top of his boot brushed lightly against the skirts of her habit.

Her skirts, and her thigh beneath. His instincts were infallible that way. Even if his knee hadn't bumped against her, he would have known by the way her eyes widened and her lips parted with a startled little gasp.

Yet she made no attempt to draw back, or to show any kind of maidenly fluster or indignation. Instead she looked directly at him, her chin slightly ducked so that her gaze was shadowed by her lashes. Even so there was no mistaking the longing he saw in her eyes, so keen that now he was the one startled.

"You should dare in everything you do, Miss Carew," he said, coaxing. "Daring is much like courage, and both trump propriety in my book."

Her eyes flashed with determination. "You cannot know how much I've already dared in my life, Lord Geoffrey."

"Then dare again," he said. "Dare to tell me what I must do to prove myself your champion."

"My champion." She caught her breath. "Do not tempt me like that, Lord Geoffrey, I beg you."

"What about kismet, Miss Carew?" he said, his voice rough with urgency. "That fate that's brought us together? You believed in kismet last night, and I believe it still."

Abruptly she looked away, lowering her eyes and bowing her head, her mouth twisting with obvious distress.

"Forgive me, Miss Carew," he said with concern. "I did not intend to—"

"It is nothing," she said, even as her fingers knotted the reins in her hands. With a shuddering sigh, she raised her face and turned toward him again.

The transformation stunned him. The fire, the spirit, the passion that he'd seen in her before had vanished, snuffed out as surely as a candle's flame. Instead she'd again become the distant beauty from the ballroom, and she'd done it as swiftly as if she'd put on a mask. How many times had she done this before, buried her true self away like this?

"It's you who must forgive me, Lord Geoffrey," she said, her voice reduced to a refined murmur. "I fear again that I've said too much."

"Not yet, Miss Carew, don't retreat from me," he said, determined not to let her disappear like this. "You don't have to be this way for my sake."

"But I do," she said, with the same regret he'd heard when she'd left him last night. "I forget myself, you see, and I shouldn't."

"I'll remember for you," he said. "I won't forget."

"You won't, will you?" Her smile was bittersweet, its brightness gone. "You said you wished to speak to me, Lord Geoffrey. Have you finished?"

"I've only begun, Miss Carew," he said, frustration making him direct. "When you left me at the ball, my thoughts were so full of you that I couldn't sleep, and I'll wager fifty guineas that it will be the same tonight. I counted the hours until I would see you again, and

I cursed the possibility that you would not come. You are unlike any other lady I have ever met, and yet at the same time I feel as if I've always known you, and if that is not kismet, then I don't know what is."

He'd spoken with far more honesty than he usually did, but he didn't regret it, not with her.

She flushed and looked away, staring out at the bright new green of the budding trees and the first spring flowers and the curving silver strip of the Serpentine glittering in the late afternoon sun. One wispy tendril of her hair had slipped free of her hairpins and hat, and he watched how the breeze made it bounce lightly against the side of her throat.

"My father always tried to see the splendor in each day," she said softly, still not looking his way. "He said it was the surest way to contentment. In India, it was easy, for there's splendor to be found in every bright flower and bird, but when I came to England, everything seemed shrouded in gray and misery. Yet today, I see nothing but splendor, Lord Geoffrey, because you are here to see it with me."

"Kismet," he said without thinking. After vowing she wouldn't speak of India, she'd done it twice today, and he understood what a sign of trust and confidence this must be for her. And then like a great, thoughtless lunk, he'd said the one word that had made her pull back from him. It *did* feel like kismet, or fate, or whatever in blazes it was that was simmering between them; she just didn't want it said aloud, and he could understand that, too. Now he held his breath, hoping he hadn't upset her again.

But her thoughts, it seemed, were somewhere else entirely.

"We're at the Gate again," she said as if she hadn't heard him at all. "I must bid you farewell here, Lord Geoffrey."

"Farewell?" he repeated, not happy. "Now?"

"Yes," she said succinctly. "My aunt's limit is three turns of the drive, which we have done. If I pretend I haven't noticed, she'll soon send one of the footmen forward to remind me."

She turned her horse back to join her aunt's carriage, and he swiftly followed. He'd been thinking of the usual next step for a late afternoon ride like this one: a light refreshment that would lead to an invitation to a leisurely, seductive dinner and a romantic night in her bed. He'd conveniently forgotten the fact that Miss Carew was not one of his ordinary lady-loves, but a chaperoned, genteel virgin, and that the rest of the day and night that he'd envisioned were completely out of the question.

"Then permit me to accompany you home," he said, hoping for a few more minutes of her company. "You live in St. James's Square, don't you?"

"My grandfather's house is there, yes," she said. "But if you were to appear there with us, I do not believe his welcome would be very warm."

She didn't have to explain further. His brother Harry had warned him how the elderly marquis guarded his granddaughter's virtue like a hawk, and it didn't take much effort by Geoffrey to imagine how he'd be received if he came trailing along after the ladies. There'd be no surer way for her to be locked completely from him, and that he did not want.

"I must see you again," he said, keeping his voice low so the footmen would not overhear. "When?"

"I shouldn't," she said with a small shrug. "There's nothing to be gained for either of us."

"There is," he said, "and you know it as well as I."

She glanced at him swiftly, her expression carefully unchanged. "I will be here in the park again tomorrow."

"Good day to you, Lord Geoffrey," Lady Morley said, smiling brightly from the carriage. Before her marriage, she, too, had been a Carew, but Geoffrey could see little family resemblance in her plump, overpowdered face. She was swathed in a fur-edged pelisse and hood and a great many ruffles, and only now did Geoffrey notice the small black dog curled on the seat beside her. "I'd no idea we'd be favored with your company today."

"A fortuitous accident, Lady Morley," he said easily. "Although given this fine spring afternoon, it would appear that most of London had the same notion."

"You have certainly improved my niece's afternoon," Lady Morley said. There was sufficient shrewdness in her smile to prove that she realized the truth behind their meeting, but also that she wouldn't contradict him. "Serena, my dear, have you asked Lord Geoffrey to join us for tea?"

Serena. The name suited her precisely, and he made the subtle shift in his head to think of her in that way instead of the formal "Miss Carew."

She blushed. "He has other obligations, Aunt."

"Is that true, Lord Geoffrey?" Lady Morley said. "I cannot believe that you have any obligation more pressing than taking a dish of tea with a beautiful young lady."

"Aunt Morley, please," Serena said, her discomfort clear. "Do not press."

"My dear, it is not 'pressing' when spoken by someone of my vast age," Lady Morley said, smiling not at Serena, but at Geoffrey. "Another time, then, Lord Geoffrey. I shall be delighted to receive you whenever you may call."

"I shall be honored, Lady Morley," Geoffrey said, bowing his head. As much as he hated parting with Serena, it was high time he left before her aunt began seeing him even more clearly as a prime matrimonial prospect for her niece. Tomorrow would be another day, and perhaps a better chance to meet with Serena alone. "Good day to you both. Lady Morley, Miss Carew. I shall count the minutes until tomorrow."

Serena watched him ride away, trying as hard as she could to keep her face impassive so as to betray nothing to Aunt Morley. Her gaze lingered on his tall figure on the chestnut, his blue riding coat with the buff facings perfectly tailored for his broad shoulders and buckskin breeches snugly fitting his thighs above his boots. Other women turned to stare when he passed by, and she could not blame them. She was finding it impossible to look away herself, and he'd been with her for the last hour.

"Stop gawking at the gentleman, Serena," her aunt said. "It's very common."

"Yes, Aunt," she said, quickly looking away as if it were her own idea. She gathered her reins and smoothed her gloves over her hands, avoiding meeting her aunt's gaze. "Shall we ride home?"

"We shall," her aunt said. "But I would like you to join me here in the carriage so that we may speak more privately. I believe you and I have some matters that need discussion. Here, let John hold your horse and help you down."

Reluctantly Serena did as she was bid, letting the footman help her from the saddle and then up into the carriage to sit beside her aunt. Aunt Morley could call what was coming a "discussion," but Serena already knew it was going to be more of a sermon, with very little discussing to it.

"Well, now," Aunt Morley began. "Pray enlighten me, Serena. If I am to believe the proof of my eyes, Lord Geoffrey did not meet us here by accident, but by appointment, just as there is an arrangement for him to return here and repeat the exercise tomorrow. Is that the truth?"

Serena smoothed the fringed end of her sash across her lap, deliberately combing and arranging the silken fringes as neatly as she could with her fingers as she decided what to say next.

"Last night at the ball he mentioned that he rode in the park each day," she finally began. "I told him that I did the same. That is as much of an appointment that there was between us."

Aunt Morley sighed. "I suppose I must accept that, no matter that it has the taint of a half truth to it."

"Aunt Morley, please, Lord Geoffrey and I didn't—"

"No more, Serena, no more," the older woman said with resignation, holding her palm up. "Let us leave that to the past, and anticipate the future. It's not that I am displeased by Lord Geoffrey's attentions. Far from it. He is the most imminently suitable gentleman that has yet to present himself to you as a suitor."

This was exactly what Serena had expected her aunt to say, but that didn't make it any more bearable. "He has done nothing of the sort, Aunt."

"Oh?" Her aunt's mouth formed a perfect oval of doubt and disappointment. "Then how exactly does he wish you to consider him, if not as a suitor for your hand?"

Serena didn't answer. She'd nearly blurted out that he was her champion, a blunder that her aunt would never have understood. She still didn't know why she'd used that particular word with Geoffrey—she'd already begun thinking of him by his Christian name alone, without his title—earlier, for she wouldn't have been able to explain it to him, either.

But for him to be her champion—ah, it made perfect sense to her. In the *zenana* at Sundara Manōra the language had been quite frank regarding men and women and how they pleasured one another, and there had even been books with bawdy pictures passed around in case mere words failed. No one had tried to keep any of this from Savitri or her sister, and even Father had openly chosen concubines from among the servant-girls, young women who would eagerly spend the night in his bed in return for special privileges and trinkets. It followed naturally that Savitri and Asha, too, had been teased about their own future husbands and wedding nights.

The teasing been good-natured, but as two of the few virgins in the house, she and Asha had shied away from the coarser comments. Alone together, they'd invented much more romantic tales of the unknown men in their future, full of gallantry and true love. They'd called these men their "champions," taking the word from a bedraggled book about knights and chivalry that Savitri had found in Father's library. In their fantasies, their champions were always handsome men of courage with noble hearts and high-minded devotion, and they never expected any of the terrifyingly robust lovemaking that was all around them.

But then today with Geoffrey, she'd unwittingly mentioned the champions aloud, the first time she'd done so with anyone since Asha had died. Geoffrey had seized upon the word and not let it go, turning it into something else entirely—something exciting and romantic and a little dangerous, and more than enough to make her forget her resolution to not see him again.

"Well, Serena?" her aunt said eagerly, not hiding her impatience. "What was Lord Geoffrey saying to you in all that time you were riding side by side? If you mean that he has raised false hopes or behaved in any other dishonorable way, why, then—"

"No, Aunt, not at all," Serena said. "He was most civil to me."

He had flirted with her, and she had flirted back. She'd never done that before, and it had been . . . pleasurable.

And civil. That *was* the truth.

"I am glad to hear of it." Her aunt sank back against the carriage's leather squabs, drawing her spaniel, Fanfan, across her lap. Lightly she stroked the dog's feathery ears, thinking. "You've done well for yourself to attract such a gentleman, Serena. Lord Geoffrey has a great deal to recommend himself."

"Please don't begin," Serena said with dismay. "Please, Aunt."

"Hush, and listen to me," her aunt said, unperturbed. "He is young and handsome and charming, which pleases you. He is a second son, true, but he is wealthy in his own right, having been left diverse properties and interests in several profitable ventures by an unmarried uncle on his mother's side. He will not be looking at you and seeing only golden guineas, all of which pleases me."

Serena winced, uncomfortable with her aunt's obvious relish over such mercenary details of Lord Geoffrey's private affairs. "How do you come to know that of him?"

"I have my informants," Aunt Morley said. "I know financial matters seem tawdry to you, my dear, but for your future security, it is wise to have them known and settled now, before any attachments are made. He has had the usual *petite amours*, but nothing of any consequence. There is also a fair chance that he may inherit the dukedom from his brother, whose wife has yet to produce a son. No, the only unfortunate aspect to Lord Geoffrey lies in his family history, and it will be a sizable objection to your grandfather."

"But Lord Geoffrey's father is a *duke*!" Serena exclaimed. "How could Grandpapa object to that?"

"Because he is the Duke of Breconridge, my dear." Aunt Morley lowered her voice, as if whispering about a scandal would somehow lessen its wickedness. "Which means to your grandfather, he is not quite a proper duke. Our family's title and lands were honorably won centuries ago beside the Plantagenets on the battlefield, but the Fitzroys owe their fortune to a certain immoral Frenchwoman and her bastards by the king, not a hundred years past. Oh, I know Lord Geoffrey's father is as close as can be to His Majesty and cuts a fine figure at court, but the whole family still has the blood of that dreadful woman in their veins, and your grandfather will not be easily won over. You know how proud he is of our family's heritage."

"I do know," Serena said faintly. How could she not? From the first night she'd spent in the grand house in St. James's Square, she'd realized that Grandpapa had no notion of the life his younger son—her father—had led in India, let alone the truth about herself.

"I shall simply have to convince him of Lord Geoffrey's other merits," Aunt Morley continued, nodding graciously at a friend in a passing carriage. "He shall fuss and rage in the beginning, but when he calms himself he shall see what a splendid suitor Lord Geoffrey is for you, then—"

"Please don't say a word to Grandpapa," Serena said, twisting on the seat to face her aunt. "Lord Fitzroy is not my suitor, not now or ever. He is simply an acquaintance."

"But perhaps with time, your acquaintance will grow, and he will become—"

"It will not happen, Aunt, because I do not wish to marry," Serena said swiftly. "Father left me the means to be independent, and I shall be far more content as a spinster than having to answer to a husband. I have told you and Grandpapa this before, and I intend to keep my word."

Aunt Morley's expression darkened beneath the ruffled brim of her cap as she clucked her tongue with disapproval.

"Such nonsense, Serena," she said. "As if repeating it will make it any less foolish! Of course you shall marry. All the money in the world will be a cold comfort to you without the love and companionship of a husband and children."

The words rang true to Serena as they always did. How could she not want love and companionship? In the seven years since she'd lost everything and been brought to England, her heart had ached for exactly that. But to keep her secret safe, she had to keep herself apart from others, and not risk the danger of revealing too much. She knew she'd no alternative, yet meeting a man like Geoffrey had only sharpened the too-familiar longing for that elusive, imagined love and a respite from her loneliness. How could she not crave the love and friendship that would come with marriage?

"Yes, you have no counter to that, do you?" Aunt Morley continued. "Independence at your age may seem like a fine dream, but it will sour quickly, and then where shall you be?"

Serena raised her chin, determined to stand firm. "I will be content, Aunt Morley."

"What you will be is alone and pitied," her aunt declared, "and neither your grandfather nor I wish to see you reduced to such a sorry state. It is completely unnatural and unwomanly, especially after all that your poor father did to ensure you had a suitable settlement. You are a Carew, my dear. You will have your choice of gentlemen, an opportunity very few young women are granted. Why you insist on this stubborn, misguided course of spinsterhood is beyond me."

Serena stared down at her hands in her lap, struggling to keep back her tears. She'd had nearly this same conversation with her aunt more times than she could count, and before this she'd always been strong and sure of herself. But now, because of Geoffrey, she felt the strength that had always held her steady ebbing away and her resolution grow weak and shaken.

Today as they'd ridden side by side, he'd reminded her once more of kismet, and again she wondered if this—if he—was truly her fate. What if he was meant to be her champion, not just in flirtatious jest, but in reality? What if he was in fact the one man in the world for her to love?

And what if they did marry? She would have his love, his trust, his loyalty, and she would become part of his family. But would all that be enough to face the truth of her past?

What would the proud, powerful Duke of Breconridge say if he was to learn that his son had married the illegitimate daughter of a Golconda brothel-dancer? And what would Geoffrey himself say if, in time, she presented him with the ultimate proof of her heritage and her deception: a child with dark hair and dark skin and nothing English in his features?

She had already dared so much. Now she must decide if she could dare much more for the sake of love.

Her aunt sighed so loudly beside her that Fanfan growled softly in sympathy. They were nearly home now. The carriage had just turned the corner into St. James's Square.

"I intend to say nothing to your grandfather of your encounter with Lord Geoffrey today, Serena," she said, more gently, "nor will I tell him of your plans to see him again tomorrow in the park. Day by day, my dear, day by day. Perhaps then Lord Geoffrey will be able to succeed where I have failed, and make you see sense. All I ask at present is that you put aside your stubbornness, and listen to the gentleman, not just with your ears, but with your heart. Is that too much to ask?"

Slowly Serena shook her head. Riding in the park with Geoffrey, listening to him say glorious things meant only for her ears, did not mean she was going to marry him. She was only sharing his company for less than an hour, day by day, with her aunt and hundreds of people in the park as her chaperone. Surely, in the grand plan of her life, there could be no lasting harm in that.

Especially not if it was fated to be.

CHAPTER 4

Over the next four days, Geoffrey met Serena in the park, and rode beside her as he'd done the first afternoon. Each time she was followed by Lady Morley's carriage and the two mounted grooms, making for a small procession of propriety. As much as he wished otherwise, he and Serena never left the sight of the others, nor did they dismount to stroll into any of the more shady and private areas of the park. All they did was ride slowly, side by side, and talk. Their physical contact was limited to the occasional, electrifying brush of his hand against hers or his leg to her skirts with the pretense of accident, and the night he'd held her in his arms at the ball had come to seem a distant dream. He'd never before shown such patience or restraint with a woman, and it was at once both maddening and captivating.

He had no choice, of course, considering her position, but to his surprise he also found the time in her company to be completely fascinating. He never knew what she'd say, for she was as changeable as the weather, one moment being distant and lost in her own thoughts, and the next her gaze fairly smoldering as their eyes met. She called him her champion, at first in teasing flirtation, and then more seriously, and though she didn't seem to expect him to do anything to earn the title, he still took it seriously because she did.

But the more time he spent in her company, the more muddled his own goals became. When he'd first seen Serena at the ball, he'd intended a full seduction, and perhaps making her his mistress. After he'd learned from Harry that she was much more innocent than she seemed, an unmarried lady who could not be seduced without the gravest consequences, he had reconsidered his intentions and aimed only at a kiss, just enough to prove to his brother that she wasn't as chilly as she appeared.

Now, however, that didn't seem sufficient. As a rule, he didn't generally listen to what ladies said, yet Serena's talk of champions and kismet and splendor had drawn him in. He was certain she wasn't intentionally trying to ensnare him, but it was happening just the same.

It was the damnedest thing. Each day she seemed to grow more beautiful and desirable, and he could not believe the speed with which every rendezvous—always the same three turns of the way as proscribed by Lady Morley—would end. When they parted, he could think of nothing and no one else, and no matter how he tried to distract himself with his friends and his usual diversions at the playhouse, clubs, or gaming houses, she remained in the center of his thoughts.

But on the fifth afternoon, the fair spring weather gave way to an equally typical spring downpour. No one would ride in the park today. Geoffrey stood at the window and glumly stared out at the rain that pelted the glass. Weather like this always left him restless, and made his house feel especially empty as well.

He considered summoning his carriage to call upon Serena, and then thought better of it. To appear at her door like that would be answering her aunt's constant invitation, an invitation that always felt more like a summons. Worse yet, he'd be officially considered A Suitor. He liked being her champion well enough, but a suitor—no. He wasn't that, and he'd no intention of being so just yet, either, not for any lady.

And so as much as Geoffrey longed to see her, he settled on the safer course. He sent a footman to the flower-seller and had him deliver a bouquet of conservatory roses to Serena. He enclosed his card, and nothing more: no endearments that could be misinterpreted by Lady Morley.

Then, still feeling at loose ends, he left for White's, and the convivial, if not as alluring, society of cards and wine.

"*Non, non, non,* Mademoiselle Carew!" exclaimed Monsieur Passard with exasperation, his pale blue satin coat the only bright spot in the music room on this dreary afternoon. "Heed me, if you please, and mind the time of the tune."

Hands at her waist, Serena sighed with dismay and glanced out at the rain pelting against the glass. With the weather making a ride in the park impossible, Aunt Morley had asked the dancing-master to remain for an extra lesson today. It was, thought Serena, hardly a fair trade.

The lesson was not going well. Usually Serena earned Monsieur's approval, but today her thoughts were filled not with dancing, but with Geoffrey. She had tried to tell herself that a day apart would mean nothing, that what they'd been sharing while they rode together was only the kind of polite conversation that engaged any lady and gentleman. That was all it should be between them; no, that was all it *must* be, the mildest of flirtation that would lead to nothing more.

But as hard as she tried to be coolly objective, she wasn't. Her disappointment at the rain had been so sharp that she'd shocked herself, and no amount of reasoning in her head had helped.

Now she kept glancing at the window in the empty hope that the weather would improve, and imagining how Geoffrey himself was passing the afternoon. She was too distracted to pay close attention to the complicated steps Monsieur demanded, and over and over she began a beat too late to match the cue of the fiddler sitting patiently in one corner. It was just as well Aunt Morley had been called away by a question in the servants' hall, and wasn't there to see her blunders.

"*Non, non, non,* Mademoiselle Carew," Monsieur said again, his exasperation now bordering on despair. "First you forget the steps and the figures, and now your *posture.* Without proper deportment everything is clumsy and meaningless. I beg you not to wilt, mademoiselle, yet still you forget!"

Serena nodded and again drew her shoulders back, striving to make her shoulder blades touch the way every lady desired. For the past three years, poor Monsieur had labored to correct her posture, imploring her to keep her upper body straight and unyielding so as to better display the curving arc of her arms. This, he argued, was the posture of a genteel lady, and he was particularly vigilant against *se déhancher,* which her embarrassed aunt had defined as wiggling. Aunt Morley blamed this on the fact that she'd begun proper dancing lessons so late in her life, but Serena knew the real reason was exactly the opposite.

She couldn't remember a time when she hadn't danced. Dancing was something that every Indian woman did, for holidays and celebrations and to entertain guests and family, and simply for the joy of it. She had learned from the older women, and had been praised for her grace and fluidity and the emotion she brought to her movements. Father had loved to watch her dance, and had wept openly because she'd so much resembled her mother.

In Serena's opinion, London dancing was hardly dancing at all, but a stiff, joyless exercise that reduced ladies to awkward cranes, their bodies so encased in stays and hoops that all their grace was snuffed away. She had tried her best to learn what Monsieur taught, wanting desperately to appear English and not give herself away, but she still felt so self-conscious that she rarely danced at balls and routs and assemblies, no matter how many times she was asked.

Yet she had danced with Geoffrey. She'd danced the steps exactly as Monsieur had taught her and had held her back straight, the same as every other English lady in the room. She knew she'd succeeded, because she'd seen the admiration and pleasure in Geoffrey's eyes as he'd watched her, which in turn had given her pleasure, too. If she'd been able to do it then, she could do it now, and she faced Monsieur with fresh resolution.

"*Répetér,* mademoiselle," Monsieur said, briskly clapping his hands twice. "We shall begin again. *Une, deux, trois, et quatre,* and step."

As the fiddler began again, she could hear raised voices in the distance, most likely in the front hall. She tried to ignore them and concentrate on the music, but one voice was growing louder, coming closer through the house, and because it belonged to her grandfather, it was impossible to ignore.

"Serena!" he roared. "Where in blazes are you, girl?"

"Here, Grandpapa," she called, nodding to Monsieur in apology for the interrupted lesson. "I'm in the music room."

The footman barely had time to open the door before her grandfather came charging into the room first. Although the Marquis of Allwyn was nearly seventy, there was nothing frail about him, and when he was as angry as he was now, he was a formidable figure indeed: his broad chest puffed with outrage, his face ruddy, and his old-fashioned, full-bottomed wig flying around his shoulders and scattering hair powder like snow over the front of his dark green coat.

"What is it, Grandpapa?" Serena asked, clasping her hands together at her waist. When she'd first come to London, she'd been terrified of him, but since then she'd learned two things: that he loved her deeply because of her father, and that the best way to deflate his blustery rages was with reasoned calm. "What has upset you so?"

"*This* has upset me," he said, thrusting a sizable bouquet of white roses into her face. "Do you know anything of *this*?"

"No, Grandpapa, not at all." He was brandishing the bouquet like a beribboned weapon, shaking it so fiercely that white petals and green leaves were beginning to fall to the carpet. It was a shame to see such a pretty thing destroyed; even in its battered state, the bouquet was lovely, and the out-of-season roses must have been quite costly. "How did you come by it?"

"It didn't come *by* me at all," he fumed. "It was brought to my door, and carried into my house by my own servants like the false horse that destroyed Troy!"

"It will take far more than a nosegay to destroy this house, Grandpapa," she said, wondering why the flowers hadn't first gone to Aunt Morley, as such deliveries usually did. "Surely there must have been a card from whomever sent them."

"Oh, there was a card," he said, "just as there was a rascally jackanapes of a footman delivering it. He tried to skulk away back to his rogue of a master, but I spied him just the same. A good thing I was passing through the hall when he came. I'd recognize that livery anywhere."

He pulled the card from his cuff, holding it at arm's length to read.

"'Lord Geoffrey Fitzroy,'" he read. "Lord Impudent Scoundrel is more the truth. How dare he address you, Serena? How dare he send his wicked offerings to an innocent lady like you?"

She gasped and felt her cheeks grow hot, unable to help herself. She couldn't believe that Geoffrey had sent flowers to her, here, and that somehow her grandfather had intercepted them.

It wasn't just that this was the first time a bouquet of flowers had arrived for her from a gentleman. What mattered most was that the gentleman was Geoffrey. She'd told him enough about how protective her grandfather was of her that he should have known better than to make so blatant a romantic gesture, but still, in a way, she was overjoyed that he had. A bouquet of white roses was exactly what a champion should send. What more proof did she need that he, too, regretted today's rain?

Wistfully she looked at Geoffrey's flowers, wishing she could rescue them. Misinterpreting her reaction, her grandfather's eyes gleamed with fresh indignation.

"Don't distress yourself, Serena," he said gruffly. "My poor gentle girl! I see how it grieves you to be insulted by that rogue's attentions."

"Grandpapa, please," she began, striving to calm him. Clearly Aunt Morley had kept her word and said nothing to Grandpapa. Serena was grateful for that, but her secrecy had created other problems, and she wished now that her aunt were here, too, to help soothe her grandfather. "I'm not distressed. Truly, it's of no consequence."

But he wasn't yet ready to be appeased.

"No, no, I'll be failing in my duty to you if I didn't end this now, Serena," he said. "I'll make sure Fitzroy doesn't trouble you again. I won't have him sniffing about you. My God! A *Fitzroy*!"

The name alone seemed to inflame him all over again. Shaking his head, he hurled the bouquet contemptuously to the floor.

"No!" wailed Serena, and without thinking she dropped to her knees to retrieve Geoffrey's roses, gathering the now-broken stems into her arms.

"Enough of that, Serena," Grandpapa said crossly. "You needn't be gathering up the rubbish. Leave it for the servants."

"Whatever is happening here?" Aunt Morley stood in the doorway, looking from Grandpapa to Serena and back again. "Serena, what *are* you doing on the floor with those flowers?"

Grandpapa glared at his sister, aware of the disapproval that she wasn't trying to contain. "It's perfectly obvious what she's doing, Deborah," he said. "She's picking up the damned flowers that I threw there. If that infernal rascal Fitzroy hadn't presumed to send them to this house and to her, then I wouldn't have been provoked to throw them."

"Lord Geoffrey sent you flowers, Serena?" Aunt Morley asked, her humor instantly improving. "How generous of him."

The marquis swung around to face her. "Do you know of this, Deborah? You are supposed to be watching over the girl. How in blazes did Fitzroy get to her?"

"In the most proper way possible, Allwyn," Aunt Morley said. "They danced together at the ball last week, and they have addressed each other whilst riding in the park."

"There's not one thing that's proper about Fitzroy," Grandpapa snapped, "and I won't have him intriguing with Serena. He must keep from her, or answer to me, and the sooner he knows my feelings, the better, too."

He reached down and snatched the battered flowers from Serena's lap, and stalked from the room.

"We must stop him, Aunt," Serena said urgently, scrambling to her feet. "He can't call on Lord Geoffrey."

"If he does, he will only say things we shall all regret," Aunt Morley said grimly, and the two of them hurried down the passage after the marquis.

He was standing by the front door, thrusting his fists into the sleeves of the greatcoat that his manservant was holding for him. Another footman held the offending flowers, gingerly. Her grandfather's hat was already on his head and the carriage was waiting at the bottom of the steps, but what terrified Serena was the sight of his sword buckled around his waist. She knew that Grandpapa was of the school of older gentlemen who did not feel entirely dressed without his sword slapping at his thigh, and that it was a formality as much as anything. Yet still she feared for the combination of Grandpapa's bellicose temper with Grandpapa's sword, and what he might rashly do if he confronted Geoffrey.

"Don't make a fool of yourself over nothing, Allwyn," Aunt Morley said tartly. "You are far too old to go traipsing about all over town in the rain after a young lord who dared smile at your granddaughter."

"Don't you scold me, Deborah," he said, glowering. "It wouldn't be necessary if you'd heeded your own responsibilities toward the girl."

"My duty is to see that Serena is happily wed to a suitable gentleman," Aunt Morley said. "How that is to be accomplished without her being permitted to converse with young men is an utter mystery to me."

"It's not the conversation, Deborah, it's the suitability," her grandfather said. "The Fitzroys are the spawn of a wastrel king and a French whore. None of them are fit company for Serena, nor would I ever wish such filth to be introduced into our family lines."

"Please, Grandpapa, there's no need for any of this,"

Serena pleaded. "Lord Geoffrey has made no designs upon me, none at all."

Grandfather shook his head, his expression stern.

"Say what you wish, Serena," he said, "but I saw your face when you learned who sent those flowers, and I saw the truth in it, too. Fitzroy has beguiled your affections. No, don't deny it. He is not worthy of a lady from this family, and he must be made to understand that."

She already understood that she'd never be permitted to see Geoffrey again. Yet as much as that grieved her, she still feared for him, too.

"Don't hurt him, Grandpapa," she pleaded. "For my sake, I beg you."

Her grandfather's mouth only tightened with fresh determination. "It's a matter of honor, Serena. I'll serve the rogue as he deserves."

"Honor!" she cried with dismay. It was one thing to make jests with Geoffrey about being her champion, but she'd no desire to have the two men she cared for most slashing away at each other because of her. As a girl, she'd witnessed the grievous wounds caused by swords and male tempers, and there was nothing romantic about it. "You do not mean to challenge him to a duel, do you? Not over me?"

"A duel? With a Fitzroy?" He grimaced. "Show some sense. A rascal like him merits a thrashing, not a duel."

Then he seized the bedraggled flowers from the footman and plunged out into the rain to the waiting carriage.

"Oh, Serena, I am sorry," Aunt Morley said, coming to stand behind her. "We must hope he will not say too many things that cannot be undone."

But Serena knew it was already too late for that.

She'd told herself that Geoffrey was only a passing diversion, with no lasting consequence in her life, and that it was better that way. There could be no shared future between them, and she'd tried to pretend that she could be like other London ladies with their careless flirtations. She'd tried, and she'd failed, and now it was done.

The bitter irony, of course, was that her grandfather believed she was too fine a lady for Geoffrey, when the reality was that she was not nearly fine enough. Her secret had given her wealth and security and a life that most would envy, but in return she must live that life without love or intimacy or real trust, and she was just beginning to realize how steep a price that would be.

A single bruised rosebud, snapped from its stem, lay on the polished marble floor. Before one of the footmen could sweep it away, she picked it up and tucked it into her pocket as a keepsake.

For what else, truly, did she have left?

Geoffrey sat in a leather-covered armchair not far from the fire, a glass of Madeira on the table beside him. This was his favorite time of day, when the clocks had chimed for early evening and the curtains had been drawn against the twilight and the rain with it. He was making a show of reading the newspaper he held open before him, but in reality he was so thoroughly enveloped in the comfort and quiet of the club that he was having a difficult time staying awake. He hadn't slept well all this week on account of thinking too much of Serena, and on this rainy evening it was finally catching up with him. His father was meeting him here to dine; he could close his eyes for a few moments before then, and none of the other members of the club would be so ill-mannered as to notice.

He let his thoughts drift back to their favorite topic. He imagined Serena receiving the roses, her happy little cry of pleasure. She'd hold them to her nose and breathe deeply of their fragrance, and then she'd ask a servant to bring her a vase to keep them fresh. Some ladies simply plunked bouquets into the water, but he was sure Serena would untie the ribbons and rearrange the flowers into something new to suit her own tastes.

It was so easy for him to picture her with the flowers, humming to herself as she leaned over the porcelain vase with her breasts plump and high above the front of her bodice. She was turning this simple task into a dance, twisting and swaying with the roses in her hands with the sensuous grace he remembered from the ball. She smiled, and leaned toward him, her lips parted in invitation, and—

"There's the rascal, damn him!"

Geoffrey woke with a jolt, abruptly pulled away from his dream. It wasn't usual for anyone to raise his voice inside the club, especially not in this room, and he looked toward the doorway to see who the loudmouthed culprit might be.

He didn't have far to look, for the culprit himself was standing in the arched doorway to the room: a sturdy older gentleman in an oversized wig and rain-splattered greatcoat, his face flushed and his eyes glowing with fury, and a battered bouquet of white roses in his hand, the white satin ribbons trailing around his wrist. The sight was so incongruous that Geoffrey wondered if he still was dreaming . . . until the man came charging like a bull directly to his chair, with the flowers raised over his head.

"Here you are, you damnable rogue!" he roared, and Geoffrey scarcely had time to roll clear before the man whipped the flowers against the back of the now-empty chair. "Are you a coward, too, Fitzroy, that you try to run from me?"

"I don't even know who in blazes you are, sir," said

Geoffrey, striving to stay calm in deference to the man's age, "let alone what your quarrel with me may be."

"You should know me, Fitzroy," the man said furiously, "considering you've tried to rob me of my only granddaughter!"

Of course: the man must be Serena's grandfather, the Marquis of Allwyn. He felt an instant wave of automatic guilt, and just as instantly put it aside. For once in regard to a lady, he was completely innocent.

"You're mistaken, Lord Allwyn," he said, wishing they'd met under different circumstances. "I've only regarded Miss Carew with the most complete respect."

"The devil with your respect!" the marquis bellowed. "I won't have you so much as speak my granddaughter's name!"

He raised the flowers again to lash at Geoffrey, but this time Geoffrey reached out and seized the bouquet from the marquis. It was, he realized, the same bouquet about which he'd been fantasizing so pleasantly, now sadly battered and bedraggled, and he wondered if Serena had even had the chance to see it before her grandfather had appropriated it to use as a cudgel.

"I'll tell you again, Lord Allwyn: I've done nothing to dishonor Miss Carew," he said, slowly and firmly. As was to be expected, they'd drawn a small crowd of other members, and he wished to make his innocence clear before so many witnesses. "Nothing. Ask her, or ask Lady Morley. They'll tell you the same."

Allwyn's face flushed a deeper red. "You impudent cur!" he sputtered. "How dare you pretend you're innocent?"

He reached for his sword, struggling to shove aside the skirts of his greatcoat. The bystanders exclaimed and drew back. Belatedly the club's porter and two stout footmen came hurrying into the room and seized him by the arms to restrain him. The marquis fought against them, swearing loudly at Geoffrey, who heartily wished he were anywhere else.

And then, as they always did, matters grew worse. His father, His Grace the Duke of Breconridge, appeared. Even if he were not a duke, Father had a way of commanding all the attention in the room the moment he entered, and he did it with such easy, elegant confidence that it seemed like the most natural thing in the world. Of all the other gentlemen in the room, he was the only one who seemed to have arrived at the club without a single drop of rain falling upon his impeccably tailored, silk-covered shoulders, and the only one who appeared completely unsurprised by the sight of the Marquis of Allwyn whipping his second son with a bouquet of white roses.

If only Father had arrived ten minutes later; Geoffrey would have resolved everything with Allwyn himself by then. Now, with Father involved, it was bound to become much more complicated.

"Good day, Geoffrey," Father said evenly. "Allwyn, good day to you as well. I hope I have not interrupted a private discussion?"

"Discussion, my foot!" Allwyn exclaimed hotly, still struggling to free himself. "Do you know what your blaggard of a son has done to my granddaughter?"

Father's brows rose, but that was all. Geoffrey didn't know if the raised brows were for the display of Allwyn's temper, or the allegation he was making toward Geoffrey, or how Allwyn had pointedly made no deference to Father's higher rank.

"No, Allwyn, I fear I do not," Father said mildly. "But I do believe you intend to remedy my ignorance at once."

"Oh, you can be certain of that," Allwyn said. "What this wastrel son—"

"Allwyn, please," said Father, adding a pleasant smile

to his mildness. Geoffrey wasn't fooled; he'd seen enough of that pleasant smile over his lifetime to know that Father now was angry himself, very angry, but far too well-bred to let it show to the world at large. "There is no need to abuse my son's name."

Wonderful, thought Geoffrey. How was it Father always knew the exact way to make him feel like a schoolboy on the carpet again? He was twenty-five years old. He did not need his father settling his disputes for him, and he most certainly did not want him meddling in his affair with Serena.

"Lord Allwyn," Geoffrey began. "If you would only—"

"It's called plain-speaking, Breconridge." The marquis snorted derisively, ignoring Geoffrey. "I didn't *abuse* your son. I was only speaking the truth of his damnable behavior."

"Lord Allwyn," Geoffrey interrupted. "Father. Why don't we continue this in a more quiet place?"

To his relief, Father nodded, and Allwyn, too, agreed. The porter showed them to a small room, likely designed for exactly this kind of uncomfortable conversation between gentlemen. At least they were removed from the public audience; no doubt the tale of him being confronted with roses by the Marquis of Allwyn in the middle of White's had already taken wings through Society without adding any more salacious details.

The porter brought them more wine and had barely closed the door before Allwyn began again.

"What I want, Breconridge, is for this young rake to stop debauching my granddaughter," he demanded. "That's fair, isn't it?"

Deliberately Father sipped his wine, watching Geoffrey. "Is this true?" he asked finally. "Have you debauched the young lady?"

"I most certainly have not," Geoffrey answered tersely. "I've already told Lord Allwyn that. I've done absolutely nothing to compromise Miss Carew's honor, let alone debauch her."

"Lies," Allwyn said, striking his fist onto the small table between them. "You've danced with my Serena at a ball. You've ridden with her in the park and filled her head with pretty lies and fancies. And you've sent her that damned posy. Don't tell me you haven't compromised her."

Geoffrey sighed with exasperation. "That's hardly a debauch," he said. "Believe me, if I'd intended to debauch her, then there would be no question of it now."

"Geoffrey," Father said curtly. "Do not boast of things you have not done."

"I am not boasting, Father, I am simply—"

"You enjoy the lady's company?" Father asked: a foolish and obvious question in Geoffrey's opinion.

"Of course I enjoy her company," he answered, fondly imagining Serena, and wondering how she could have come from the same family as her boorish grandfather. "I wouldn't keep it if I didn't. Miss Carew is a charming, beautiful lady."

The marquis sputtered. "Don't you say anything about her, you cur, not a word!"

"A moment's patience, Allwyn," Father said, holding up his hand for silence. "Geoffrey, can you envision continuing to enjoy Miss Carew's company for one more evening?"

"I can indeed," Geoffrey said, "which is why I had the roses—"

"Geoffrey, I should appreciate patience from you as well," Father said, the warning in his voice unmistakable. "All I wish is to preserve the lady's unblemished reputation. Allwyn, would you agree to permitting your granddaughter to be my wife's guest one evening, at our house?"

Down came Allwyn's fist again. "I will not!" he declared. "I do not wish her to be anywhere near your son or the rest of your family."

"Indeed," murmured Father, his expression quizzical. "I find that astonishing. Most people welcome an invitation to Breconridge House."

"My granddaughter will not be among them," Allwyn said curtly. "She's a Carew, through and through, and I want better for her than any of your baseborn lot, Breconridge."

Geoffrey rose, unable to contain himself in the face of such an insult, but Father placed a restraining hand on his arm.

"Then let me explain it another way, Allwyn," Father said, his voice deceptively even. "My son has done nothing to dishonor your granddaughter. You, however, have now made her name common on the lips of every gentleman in this club by your rash actions, and what will be said of her will be far, far worse than the innocent truth. But if she was to attend some gathering as my wife's guest, the scandalmongers would see our approval in their conversation, and remove the odious taint of impropriety."

The marquis scowled, his bushy brows working as he considered the duke's logic. Geoffrey would grant Father that much: there was no one better at wringing unquestionable truth from a situation, especially if it served his own purpose.

"One gathering, then," Allwyn said grudgingly. "She'll accept one invitation. But that is all, mind you, and my sister must be included to watch over her."

"Oh, of course," Father said, smiling again. "You would be welcome, too, if you could bring yourself to enter my house."

"Nothing would induce me to do that, Breconridge." He rose abruptly. "One invitation, and then your son leaves her alone."

"One invitation," Father said, and Geoffrey wondered why Allwyn didn't seem to notice that Father hadn't actually agreed to anything. Even better was the fact that Geoffrey hadn't had to swear to give up Serena, which, despite her grandfather's wishes, he'd no intention of doing.

"The duchess will write to Miss Carew," Father continued. "She may count upon it."

"But nothing from your son, mind?" Allwyn said. "Not a single blasted word. This isn't a match."

Father rose and bowed. "No, it's not," he agreed. "Not at all. I expect my son to marry at least the daughter of a duke. Good evening, Allwyn."

The marquis muttered a few dark oaths by way of farewell, and left.

"What a wretched old gentleman," Geoffrey said, glad to have this little scene past. "I wonder how he forced his way past the porter."

"Forcing wasn't required," Father said. "The man's a member, and has been forever. He's an unpleasant bully, true, but I suspect he acted only from devotion to his granddaughter."

"Likely so," Geoffrey said, eager to move on to a more enjoyable part of the evening. "Shall we dine?"

"Not quite yet," Father said, gently closing the open door. "I wish a few words with you first. I took your side, because you are my son. But I suspect that there is more truth to Allwyn's story than you admitted."

Geoffrey sighed, and squared his hands on the back of the chair before him, reminded again of being that long-ago schoolboy.

"It was exactly as I explained, Father," he said. "I danced with Miss Carew at the ball last week. For four days this week, I have met her and her aunt in the park. Today I had flowers brought to her to show I regretted the rain. That is all."

Father folded his arms over his chest and lowered his chin, never a good sign.

"What of the wager with your brother at that same ball?" he asked. "A wager that I understand you won, given that you spent a good half hour out-of-doors in the moonlight with Miss Carew. And before you ask, no, Harry didn't tell me. I heard it from another, which means you are most fortunate that Allwyn didn't hear it as well."

Geoffrey drew in his breath. "At least there is still some honor among thieves and brothers."

"Geoffrey, please," Father said, looking pained. "You know I do not care how you amuse yourself around the town. You're young. It's to be expected. But when you begin to make idle wagers about seducing noble-born virgins, then I must object."

"It may have begun like that, Father, but the lady—the lady changed that," Geoffrey said, striving to make clear what he didn't entirely understand himself. How could he explain being her champion, and flirtations in Hindi, and kismet? "Miss Carew is unlike any other lady."

Father frowned. "Do you fancy yourself in love with her?"

"*No,*" Geoffrey said quickly, because he wasn't. Not at all. "No, I am not in love with her. But I won't deny that there is an attraction, an affection, perhaps even a friendship, between us. She is different."

"Miss Carew *is* different," Father agreed, the planes of his face sharp and stern in the candlelight. "From what I understand, she has suffered unimaginable loss, and endured tragedies that should never befall a lady. She is the treasured granddaughter of that old gentleman, and all he has left of a favorite son. To toy with her affections would not only be dishonorable, but unconscionably cruel."

Geoffrey didn't answer. It wasn't that Father had said

anything that he hadn't considered himself. When he'd first spotted Serena at the ball, lovely yet almost disdainfully aloof, the wager with Harry had seemed like fair sport, a challenge and a chance to take a haughty beauty down a peg or two. But he realized now that by the time she'd left him standing alone in the moonlight, his attitude toward her had subtly changed.

Yes, he still desired her—she'd only grown more bewitching to him with each passing day, and he thought endlessly of how he'd like to bed her—but he'd become equally fascinated by who she *was*. He wanted to learn everything about her, from her mysterious childhood to what made her laugh. The fact that she spoke so little of herself only made her more intriguing to him. Every graceful gesture, every glance from her held meaning, and he'd become almost desperate to discover more.

When she'd first spoken of him being her champion, he'd thought it some manner of flirtatious jest, but the more time he'd spent in her company, the more he'd realized she'd been perfectly serious—and that he couldn't imagine a role he'd more willingly accept. From that first night, he'd seen that being a chilly beauty was a defensive disguise she assumed to keep the rest of the world at bay. Behind it, she was achingly vulnerable. Fragile. She *needed* a champion to defend her. Dishonoring her in any fashion, as Father was now describing, was utterly unthinkable.

"You're damned quiet, Geoffrey," Father said sharply, breaking into his reverie. "This is not the time for more of your habitual stubbornness."

Geoffrey drew in his breath, taken off guard. "My intention was not to disappoint you, Father."

"Then God only knows what you were intending." For the first time in this conversation, Father let a note of unmitigated disgust creep into his words—a note that Geoffrey recognized all too well. "There has always been a selfishness about you, Geoffrey, a certain determination to put your own desires above everything and everyone else, and this sorry business with Miss Carew is only the latest example."

" 'The latest example,' " Geoffrey repeated, permitting himself a bit of his own disgust in return; this was a very old song from his father, and one he heartily wished never to hear again. He had never believed himself to be a selfish individual, but then he could never see his actions from the lofty view of being the Duke of Breconridge, either. "I suppose I am next to hear the usual catalog of every misstep I have made from the cradle onward."

"If you had chosen to learn from your missteps," Father rumbled, "then the catalog would not be quite so vast. All I ask is that you behave honorably, with a mind toward your duty to this family."

"Oh, honor and duty, the eternal twin verities." Geoffrey knew he was pushing his father toward losing his temper—a virtually impossible challenge, true—but his own temper was so close to bubbling over that he could not help himself. "And once again, I have failed twice over, and can never dare to approach Harry's perfection."

Father shook his head, his dark brows drawing ominously together. "I said nothing of your brother."

"You needn't have, not again," Geoffrey said. "I've heard it often enough before."

"If you have, it is because Harry does not forget the responsibilities of his place and his title."

"While mine, of course, will always be so much less exalted, being as I am the mere second son." Geoffrey glanced down at his cuff, brushing away an infinitesimal speck of lint. "Though as you may recall, I did return home at once as soon as I received word of Harry's fall.

Not that I shall ever receive praise from you for journeying halfway around the world in haste to do so."

"If you had not insisted on removing yourself to that distant, heathen place, then your journey would not have been so arduous," Father said, each word clipped and edged. "You did so by your own choice. As for duty: that is never to be rewarded or acknowledged, Geoffrey, not that you have ever appeared to possess an understanding of that particular nicety."

What Geoffrey understood was that he'd come back home not because of duty, but because he loved his brother. That alone had driven him across the sea on his desperate voyage and had sustained him through long days of hope and sorrow at sea that he'd no wish to repeat. His joy at finding his brother alive should have been reward enough, had it not been tainted by Father's incessant lectures on duty.

"Until Lady Augusta gives your brother a son, you are his heir, and mine as well," Father continued, intoning as if being his heir was the most glorious role possible. "I expect you to comport yourself as a future Duke of Breconridge should."

No one believed Geoffrey when he swore he'd no interest in becoming the next Duke of Breconridge, particularly if the title came at the price of his brother's life. He'd never wanted to be a duke, nor did he want any part of the awful honor and duty that came with the title. Once he'd been reassured that Harry was healthy, he'd wished with all his heart that he'd remained in India, where no one gave a damn about duty or dukedoms.

And yet, if he had stayed in Calcutta, he wouldn't have met Serena, just as if her family had survived, she would not have come to London. Whenever she spoke to him of kismet, he'd always thought of how they'd danced together that first night, but really, if he thought harder, he realized that coincidences and accidents on a much grander scale had brought them together, and would not now pull them apart.

"You do understand what I am saying, don't you?" Father said, once again misinterpreting his silence.

Rain drummed against the windows, as if to drive home every one of his father's words.

Slowly Geoffrey nodded, thinking how in truth it was Father who did not understand about him, or Miss Carew.

"I understand," he said softly, his own anger curiously spent. "I understand."

Father was watching him closely. "You will behave honorably toward the lady? There will be no more unpleasant scenes with old Allwyn?"

Geoffrey straightened, and tapped his hand on the carved back of the chair. "You have my word that there will not."

He would behave honorably, and he would not upset Lord Allwyn. He'd given his word. But he would see Serena again, and what happened when he did—ahh, he'd make no promises about that.

Who would dare tamper with kismet?

CHAPTER 5

"At last we're nearly before His Grace's house," Aunt Morley said, pressing close to the window's glass to peer beyond the carriage's lanterns and into the darkness. "What a crush! I've never seen so many carriages attempting to squeeze their way before a private residence. Though to be sure, the London home of the Duke of Breconridge is no ordinary private residence."

Restlessly Serena smoothed her gloved fingers over the white fox fur that trimmed her black evening cloak. "It's very generous of the duchess to invite us here tonight after Grandpapa behaved so badly at White's last week."

Aunt Morley sighed dramatically. "I have told you before, Serena, and I shall tell you again. Your grandfather and His Grace came to an understanding, and decided that the very best way to smooth away their disagreement before the world was for you to be included as Her Grace's guest at the rout this evening. That way no one will perceive any ill will between the duke and your grandfather, nor contrive any mischievous slander involving you and Lord Geoffrey."

"There will be no mischievous slander, Aunt, because Grandpapa absolutely forbids me to speak to Lord Geoffrey tonight," Serena said, striving to keep the unhappiness from her voice. "No one shall observe us so much as glance at each other."

"He didn't forbid you conversation with Lord Geoffrey or any other gentlemen, Serena," Aunt Morley said patiently. "He asked you to be circumspect."

But Serena shook her head, unable to see whatever fine shade of difference her aunt perceived. Grandpapa had made his wishes perfectly clear.

She slipped her hand into the pocket beneath her gown, searching for the little pressed rosebud that was all she had left of the infamous bouquet Geoffrey had sent to her. She'd stitched together two pieces of silk ribbon to make a little bag to keep the rosebud safe, a secret keepsake. To see Geoffrey tonight but only at a distance, to watch him across the crowd laughing and talking with other ladies would be an unbearable torment. She'd wondered if Grandpapa had intended it to be her punishment, for certainly there could be few things more painful to her.

Even as her grandfather had railed against Geoffrey and his family, she had taken care to act as if none of it had mattered. She had not complained, nor begged for him to relent. Instead she'd simply nodded, and agreed to follow his orders. All of this had happened because she'd betrayed too much of her true feelings, and she was determined not to do it again.

And yet, deep down, it was her feelings that she trusted most. This should be the last time she saw Geoffrey. Instead she believed he would find a way to be with her again, and again after that. He was her champion, and her grandfather's warning would only make him more loyal to her.

Lightly her fingers played over the fragile rosebud, her thoughts racing as fast as her heart. If she truly were an English lady, bred to be practical and logical and obedient, then none of this would make any sense. Because instead she believed in kismet, she must trust her illogical heart, and Geoffrey with it.

"There will be many gentlemen in attendance this evening," Aunt Morley continued, excitement making her offer more than her usual amount of advice. "You would do well to look about you, Serena, and make yourself agreeable. There are plenty of other fish in every sea, even if one fat trout wriggles free from the hook."

"Yes, Aunt Morley," Serena murmured, preferring not to think of Geoffrey as a trout—or herself as the baited hook, either. "I shall be agreeable."

"I can only pray that you will," Aunt Morley said, clearly not believing that prayer would be sufficient. "Ah, our turn at last. Mind your skirts when you climb down, Serena. No lady offers a tawdry display of leg to the gaping footmen and link-boys."

As soon as the door had opened and a pair of footmen had helped her aunt climb down, Serena made her own exit in a graceful *shush* of silk. Beneath the flickering flames of the lanterns, she walked up the marble steps of the duke's grand house with her head high and a half smile on her face, determined not to let the rest of the guests guess how fast her heart was racing.

Following her aunt, she acknowledged the greetings of others as they entered the duke's house, but never paused for longer conversation, not even in the antechamber set aside for ladies' cloaks. She knew she was being discussed, pointed out, the subject of excited whispers behind fans. How could she not be, after how Grandpapa had behaved? Of course she couldn't stop their talk, but she could ignore it, and not give any of them a chance to be curious and ask how it felt to be the center of such an interesting scandal. Being distant came easily to her from habitual practice, a way of keeping secrets by keeping apart, and tonight she simply moved a little faster.

Besides, the only opinion that mattered to her tonight was Geoffrey's. She'd dressed so he wouldn't miss her.

Her gown was a brilliant golden silk *robe à la Française*, the unstitched pleats drifting from the back of her shoulders like angels' wings, and her jewels were the magnificent suite of sapphires and diamonds that Father had sent back to London long ago. She hadn't powdered her hair, preferring to leave it in contrast with her pale skin, and had scattered more diamonds among the dark waves. She wore gold silk shoes with buckles studded with brilliants and emerald-green embroidered stockings, and carried an oversized fan of black Italian lace. She was, in short, dressed to perfection and the very height of fashion, and as she stood beside her aunt, ready to be presented to the Duke and Duchess of Breconridge, she should have been as confident as any lady in the house that night.

Instead her heart was racing and her palms were damp and her stomach was twisting so much from nervousness that she feared she'd lose her afternoon tea right here while she waited. These were Geoffrey's parents. They would be as protective of him as Grandpapa was of her. What if they could sense her falseness, her deception? What if they could *tell*?

"Your Grace, may I present my grand-niece, Miss Serena Carew," Aunt Morley was saying. "Serena, Her Grace the Duchess of Breconridge."

At once Serena sank into her curtsey, her head bowed. Grandpapa might have no regard for the Fitzroys, but she was well aware of their rank and prestige at the Court. Geoffrey spoke in an offhanded manner of this cousin and that cousin—all dukes—and how often his parents were at the palace for special gatherings with the king and queen, and all of it far grander than anything the Carews could muster. This was the first time that she and her aunt had been invited to Breconridge House, and even though she knew the circumstances were not ideal, she still felt honored to be included.

"Please, Miss Carew, rise up, rise up," the duchess said. "I long to see the pretty face that's driven poor Geoffrey into such fits of distraction."

Serena turned her face upward, and then slowly rose the way Monsieur Passard had taught her, like a flower turning toward the sun. Not that she was thinking overmuch of her own first impression: she was too dazzled by the duchess for that. Her Grace was beautiful in the pink-and-white porcelain way that was so undeniably English, her gown a costly ice-blue brocade enriched with a small fortune in lace and pearls.

"Now I understand why most of the males in London have fallen beneath your spell, Miss Carew," the duchess said, waving her fan languidly before her. "No wonder Geoffrey feels he must defend you with such vigor."

"Thank you, Your Grace," Serena said, the safest answer. She couldn't help blushing with confusion; she could understand Geoffrey defending her, for that was what a champion was supposed to do, but falling into "fits of distraction" was something else altogether. "You are too kind."

"Oh, I am not being kind, my dear, but truthful." She turned away briefly, drawing a tall, elegant gentleman by his arm to her side. "Brecon, this is Geoffrey's Miss Carew, come to us at last."

Serena opened her mouth to tell the duchess that she didn't belong to Geoffrey, wasn't *his* Miss Carew, before she realized that the tall gentleman was Geoffrey's father, the Duke of Breconridge. At once she sank hastily into another curtsey, and when she rose again, the Duke of Breconridge was studying her closely—too closely for comfort, or true welcome, either.

Though the duke must be over fifty, he was still strikingly handsome, tall and lean, much like his sons. He was dressed in a dark purple velvet suit in the French style, lavish with silk embroidery and brilliants, yet on him it wasn't foppish. Beneath the extravagant elegance she sensed a powerful man accustomed to having his way, and doing whatever was necessary to get it. She understood now why Geoffrey spoke of often being at odds with his father, for she felt herself instantly wary and on guard as well. Clearly the duke was not a man to be offended without consequences.

"You cannot know how pleased I am to make your acquaintance, Miss Carew," he said now, his voice deep and rich. "Geoffrey told me you were a great beauty, but for once he is guilty of understatement, rather than exaggeration."

"You're very kind, Your Grace," Serena murmured, and smiled as she was expected to do, wincing inwardly as she realized she'd repeated herself. She wished Geoffrey were here beside her to help lessen this awkwardness.

Her aunt must have been aware of it, too. "My grandniece and I are most honored by your invitation, Your Grace," she said, smiling too brightly. "Such brilliant company!"

"You are ornaments to our evening's entertainment, Lady Morley," the duke said with an excess of gallantry (or so it seemed to Serena), his smile making her aunt turn starry-eyed before he turned back to Serena. "Especially Miss Carew. This is, you see, the first time we have ever met the very eye of one of my son's little romantic storms."

He chuckled, as if this were meant as a jest, but Serena found no humor in his condescension.

"Forgive me, Your Grace," she said, unable to keep silent, "but I would not deem my friendship with Lord Geoffrey a 'romantic storm.'"

"Would you not, now?" the duke asked, bemused. "Having witnessed the veritable typhoon of emotions that erupted between your grandfather and my son, I can think of no better description. A typhoon, a hurricane, a raging gale at sea. Any of those would suffice."

"Perhaps such descriptions would do for the conversation between my grandfather and Lord Geoffrey, Your Grace," Serena said, more warmly than was perhaps wise. "I was not a witness, and thus I cannot offer an opinion."

"Yet undoubtedly you will, Miss Carew," the duke said drily. "I feel certain of that."

"Then you are mistaken, Your Grace," Serena said defensively, "for I won't. But I can assure you that what exists between Lord Geoffrey and me is neither romantic nor stormy, but merely the shared regard between two acquaintances."

"A shared regard, Miss Carew? That is all?" the duke repeated, openly skeptical. "I'd have thought otherwise, given what I have seen of my son. But then, you ladies often do possess a harder heart than we men choose to credit."

"Oh, hush, Brecon," the duchess scolded, tapping him on the shoulder with her fan. "That is rubbish, and you know it. Miss Carew, pray forgive my husband. He watches over his sons like an old biddy-hen, and believes that every female in London is determined to wound them and play them false."

"You exaggerate, Celia," the duke said mildly, his gaze not leaving Serena, nor losing any of its intensity, either. "But there's no doubt Miss Carew possesses the spirit to make any conquest she pleases. Since I've already come near to blows with her grandfather, I am not inclined to do the same with her as well. Ladies, your servant, and pray enjoy yourselves in my house."

Serena nodded, and with her aunt moved along into the first drawing room, leaving the duke and duchess to greet the guests arriving after them. Aunt Morley seized Serena's arm the instant they were out of hearing.

"Whatever possessed you, Serena?" she demanded in a sharp whisper. "At most affairs, I can scarcely compel you to speak two words to our hosts, and yet here tonight, you insist on *challenging* His Grace over some imagined slight! The duchess is one of the most important ladies in Society, and I can't begin to imagine what she must be thinking of you now."

"His Grace was wrong, Aunt," Serena protested. "I shouldn't have corrected him, but he shouldn't have made a jest of my friendship with Lord Geoffrey."

"A friendship that is as good as done now," Aunt Morley said grimly. "You'll be fortunate if he so much as comes near you this evening after you've quarreled with his father like that. First your grandfather, and now you. No wonder the Fitzroys have no use for the Carews."

For once Serena feared her aunt might be right, and she sighed miserably. What *had* possessed her? "I suppose we must enjoy ourselves tonight, as His Grace bid us. We'll likely never be invited back."

"Then do not squander the time you have here tonight," Aunt Morley said, already scanning the crowd for possible acquaintances. "You are being widely admired. There are a number of gentlemen here whom I never see in company elsewhere."

"It doesn't signify, Aunt," Serena said, her gaze sweeping the crowded room before them. She was scarcely aware of the carved and gilded paneling, or the enormous looking glasses, or the chandeliers ablaze with candles, or even the duke's magnificent collection of paintings. All she wanted to see was Geoffrey. "I could have raved and torn my hair like a madwoman, and it would have made no difference. Recall that by agreement the duchess invited us here for this single night, and no more. Grandpapa wouldn't allow it otherwise."

"Yes, yes, Serena," Aunt Morley said impatiently, "but if you can but manage to capture the interest of another gentleman here tonight, then I'm certain your grandfather would permit—"

"Not again, Aunt, please," Serena said wearily. "I do not wish to interest any gentlemen, for I do not intend to marry any of them."

Aunt Morley puffed out her cheeks in indignation. "You have been interested enough in Lord Geoffrey."

"As a friend, Aunt Morley, only as a friend," Serena insisted. "And now it seems even that is done, so you and everyone else may cease your worry."

She had truly expected to see him here, no matter what their families had arranged. Although the hall and the three rooms that they'd passed through were filled with guests, drinking and conversing and flirting, she would have spotted Geoffrey at once, if only on account of his height, and she struggled to contain her disappointment.

"You are the one who worries too much, Serena, not I," Aunt Morley said with a sigh. "There's Lady Ralston waving to us from the whist table in the next room. Come, a few hands will cheer you."

But Serena hung back, in no mood for the exuberant gossip of her aunt's friend.

"You may go ahead," she said. "I mean to survey the supper table first."

Her aunt nodded with approval. "Remember to be agreeable, Serena. There's always a cluster of hungry gentlemen about the meats."

In truth Serena had no interest in either supper or the gentlemen about the meats, but both served to give her a few moments alone before she must follow her aunt to the gaming room. She stood before one of the tall windows, staring out into the dark back court. Perhaps this was the true kismet, that her acquaintance with Geoffrey last for a matter of days instead of a lifetime. There was nothing now that could be done to change it, nothing that she could have done before.

The bright candles and the company reflected in the glass before her like a distant blurred painting come to life, making her feel even more apart from the gaiety. Suddenly chill, she drew the black lace scarf over her shoulders; she never was warm enough in England, one more way that she didn't belong.

As she absently watched the reflection, she became aware of a figure entering the room behind her, purposefully making his way through the crowd. He came closer until it was clear he was approaching her, and to her joy she realized it was Geoffrey. Eagerly she turned around to greet him, her smile warm with welcome and relief as she curtseyed quickly and offered him her hand.

She'd thought she'd never forget anything about him—his easy smile, his well-muscled figure and unexpected grace, his blue eyes and unruly dark hair and the sharp, clean line of his jaw—but there was no way she could ever truly remember the intoxicating masculine perfection that all those random parts, however pleasing, could create when combined. As was to be expected, he was richly dressed in a suit of deep plum-colored silk, exactly tailored to show off his broad shoulders, with the coat and waistcoat cut away in the newest fashion to shamelessly display the close fit of his breeches. It was *devastating*.

"Good evening, Lord Geoffrey," she said, her voice husky with pleasure. "I feared you weren't here, and now—now you are."

But instead of the happy reunion she'd expected, his expression was impassive and slightly bored as he bowed over her hand.

"We are being watched," he said softly, so only she could hear him as he leaned forward. "Act as if my company were the most tedious thing in the world."

She didn't have to look to know he was right. She could sense it all around them. She was always being watched: not only by her aunt and grandfather, but by people who believed her to be a beautiful, exotic curiosity, deserving of the same stares and bold attention as animals in a menagerie.

At once she banished her happy smile, and composed her features into her usual guarded indifference. Inside, however, she was bubbling with excitement and pleasure that he'd sought her out, and how the ruse he was asking her to share was making them conspirators.

"Thank you for warning me," she said, scarcely above a whisper. "It's wise to be careful."

"With you, always," he said. To those who were watching, his expression, his posture, could not have been more dispassionate. But when he looked up at her over her hand, his eyes were full of fire and daring and a little bit of mischief, exactly as she remembered. "How lovely you are tonight."

She blushed, unable to control her response. "I chose this gown so you would see me first among all the other ladies here."

"It's not your clothes that are beautiful," he said. "It's you. Your face, your form, your soul. I would have found you if you'd worn nothing but your shift."

Her blush deepened, immediately imagining herself standing before him wearing so scandalously little. From the way his gaze was drifting lower over her body, she suspected he was imagining it as well.

"You shouldn't say such things if you wish me to appear bored," she said. "You shouldn't be saying them to me at all."

He tipped his head in acknowledgment. "Very well," he said. "Then instead I shall say how much I've missed you."

She had to remind herself to breathe. "I've missed you, too," she whispered. "Oh, so much."

"It has been . . . torment." He'd held her hand too long for the ennui they were pretending, but she could feel his reluctance as he let go, a match for her own need. "Especially for a champion."

She smiled at how he'd remembered. She couldn't help it, even as she finally slipped her hand free.

"I need to be with you alone, Serena," he said, a statement that was almost an order, not a request. "Count off five minutes' time, then meet me in the library."

She very nearly gasped aloud. She didn't know which was more startling: that he'd used her given name so intimately, or that he proposed such an audacious assignation. And yet what was truly scandalous was that she wasn't as shocked as she should be. To hear him call her by name seemed the most natural thing in the world, and to be with him alone was all that she desired.

"Five minutes, Serena," he said, his voice low and urgent. "I pray you won't disappoint either of us."

She was only half-aware of another gentleman joining them until Geoffrey smiled at him, placing his hand on the newcomer's shoulder.

"Here you are at last, Millbury," Geoffrey said heartily, his manner shifting to one full of bravado. "And here's the lady I promised to present to you. Miss Carew, this is one of my oldest friends, Edmund Castle, Earl of Millbury. He has been gazing at you like a lovesick mooncalf all evening."

"I'm honored, Miss Carew," Lord Millbury said, bobbing quickly over her hand. His face was good-natured if not handsome, round-cheeked and ruddy beneath an exuberant wig. "Your servant."

"Good evening, Lord Millbury." Bewildered, Serena smiled and curtseyed, and looked to Geoffrey for an explanation that did not come. "You are, ah, an old friend of Lord Geoffrey's?"

"The oldest, Miss Carew," the earl said cheerfully. "At least a thousand years. Perhaps more."

"There now, I knew you two would have much in common," Geoffrey said in the same too-hearty voice. "Now I shall leave you together, as you doubtless wish, and return to the gaming."

Without another glance, he left them, plunging back into the crowded room.

"You needn't look so devastated, Miss Carew," the earl said. "You've only to bear my lesser company for five minutes, and then off you go to the library."

"You are party to this, my lord?" Serena asked with surprise.

He grinned, puckish and gallant at the same time. "As Fitzroy explained, we are the oldest of old friends, more than willing to perform certain, ah, services to the betterment of the other's circumstances. Now you and I will converse for the next four-and-a-half minutes, and then I shall point you in the proper direction of the library, and you'll be done with me. It's all for the show, isn't it?"

Serena wasn't sure she could agree. It was one thing for Geoffrey to suggest they meet elsewhere in the house, but another entirely for him to have involved his friend. What had first seemed pure impulse now smacked of all that she'd been warned against regarding gentlemen, and though she'd never become involved in an intrigue before, this had the distinct taint of being one.

Sensing her hesitation, Lord Millbury sighed dramatically. "All he desires, Miss Carew—at least at present—is to say a few words to you in private. Besides, how could anything untoward occur in a library, surrounded by the gathered wisdom of the ages as witness?"

The chance to speak alone with Geoffrey was a heady temptation. When she'd gone onto the garden walk with him on that first night they'd met she'd no idea how rare such conversations would become. Geoffrey might have a few words for her, but she had just as many that she'd like to say to him. Where could be the harm or scandal in that?

"It's almost time, Miss Carew," Lord Millbury said. "Pray do not feel obligated to attend our friend—he would not wish that—but I am certain he will be gravely disappointed if you decline his invitation. It's your decision entirely."

It *was* her decision. She'd gone through every day they'd been apart thinking of ideas and experiences she longed to share with him, things she knew would make him smile or think or simply agree with her. The truth was that she hadn't realized how much she'd miss his company until it had been taken from her. She hadn't expected it to be that way, but it was, and in the end, that was what decided for her now.

"If it pleases you, Miss Carew," Lord Millbury said, "I can show you to the library."

"Thank you, my lord, but no." He was only trying to be helpful, as any gentleman would, but this was her decision, not his, and like everything else in her life, she'd be more at ease doing this alone. "If you'll excuse me, I should rejoin my aunt."

His nodded, understanding. "I would have you know that if ever you tire of Fitzroy and his shenanigans, I would be honored to step into the fray. All you need do is give me a sign that you are . . . intrigued."

Serena blushed furiously, surprised by the attention that she did not want. "I don't believe that is what Lord Geoffrey expects from a gentleman he considers his friend."

Millbury chuckled. "Oh, I assure you, Miss Carew, he has done far, far worse to me," he said wryly. "All's fair in love and war, yes?"

She wouldn't answer that. "Good evening, Lord Millbury."

"As you wish, Miss Carew," he said, his eyes twinkling as he bowed and stepped away. "Pray enjoy the remainder of your evening with your aunt."

She curtseyed, and turned from him, melting in with the other guests as if hunting for her aunt. In truth the last person she wished to see now was Aunt Morley, and as soon as she could she slipped back into the hall. She stopped a footman and asked directions to the library, and then hurried off down the hall and in the direction he'd pointed in the grand house.

It occurred to her that the library wasn't simply any library, but the library belonging to the duke, a realization that added an extra layer of trepidation. She could only trust that Geoffrey was sufficiently aware of his father's habits to know that he wouldn't retreat to his library with a houseful of guests. In fact she was trusting Geoffrey a great deal in everything, yet still she hurried up the stairs toward the library, and him.

To her relief, with all servants pressed into service with the rout, there was no footman standing ready at the door to open it for her, and no one to witness what she now would do. With her heart racing, she turned the knob herself and slipped inside.

There was a fire in the grate, but no candles lit, and she blinked to accustom her eyes to the relative darkness. She'd a rapid impression of the walls lined with book-filled shelves, of leather-covered armchairs and a soft Chinese rug underfoot, and then she saw nothing else because Geoffrey was standing before her.

"You came," he said simply, one side of his handsome face burnished by the golden light of the flames and the other hidden in shadow. The half-light seemed to lessen the refinement of his evening clothes, and instead emphasized his height and the size of his leanly muscular frame. He'd put aside the air of disinterest that he'd affected earlier, and while he did not seem to share her giddy happiness—what gentleman would?—he did look intensely satisfied to see her there, as if he'd already won a battle she hadn't realized was being waged. "I wasn't certain you would, you know."

"How could I not?" she asked, breathless with excitement and a bit of trepidation, too. He seemed somehow larger and more intoxicatingly male now, or maybe it was only that she was so focused on him that she could see nothing else in comparison. "I came by myself, too."

He raised a single brow with surprise. "Millbury didn't bring you?"

She shook her head, and swallowed. This was the first time in her life that she'd been alone in a room with a gentleman who wasn't her father or grandfather, and she'd been trained to think only of the danger of such a situation. It might indeed be dangerous; Geoffrey was a man, after all, and men of every class did pose a certain risk to a lady's reputation as well as to her person, no matter if it was Britain or India.

But none of the warnings had mentioned the frisson of the forbidden, or how that undercurrent simmered between them, as if the three feet of emptiness between them didn't exist.

"If I am sufficiently brave—or mad—to come here," she said, "then I am likewise brave or mad enough to come here on my own."

He chuckled, a sound she'd missed. "If you are brave or mad, then I must be as well."

"Most likely." She smiled, glad that they'd fallen into their familiar pattern of banter. "But I did not require an escort."

"Poor Millbury!" he said wryly. "I didn't intend him to be an escort so much as an alibi in the event your aunt saw me with you. There is no more stolidly proper fellow than Millbury, and he was glad to oblige me where a beautiful lady was concerned."

She tipped her head to one side, watching him. "His lordship seemed thoroughly familiar with the role."

"Not as familiar as you might think," he said. "This particular ruse is new to me as well."

"A ruse?" she repeated, wishing he hadn't used that word. Her entire life was a ruse, though of course he couldn't know that, and she didn't want to be reminded of how perilous any kind of true intimacy could be.

"A ruse, a gambit, a deception, a deceit," he continued, amusing himself with a litany of duplicity. "All arranged by your loyal champion. May I offer you a glass of canary?"

"I must go," she said, backing away. "Forgive me, but I've been away from the others too long."

"Hush, hush, no, you haven't," he said softly, reaching to take one of her hands. "I've missed you too much to give you up so soon."

"I must go," she said again, but not pulling her hand away as she warred with herself. "My aunt—"

"Your aunt will be well enough without you," he said, coaxing. "You're cold, Serena. Come stand by the fire with me first and warm yourself."

She stilled, and looked up at him. "That's the second time you've used my given name this night."

He smiled, charming enough to warm her better than the fire. "I'd hoped it would make you use mine in turn. Go on: it's not difficult."

"Geoffrey," she said, for it was in fact easy for her to do. "Geoffrey, please."

"Please me, and stay." Gently he drew her farther into the room to stand before the fire. "I don't want you to be cold."

"How do you know I'm cold?" she blurted out: a foolish question, considering her fingers were likely icicles in his hand. She stood facing him, closer than they had been before. One side of her was warmed by the fire, while the other, which faced the door, was still chilled, and as she gazed up at him, she thought of how apt that was. The door was her path back to the others, to a cold life alone, while here with him by the fire was warmth and happiness.

He smiled down at her, his gaze so intense that she could almost feel it on her skin. He was the fire, and she was the foolish moth, determined to immolate herself in the bright, irresistible flame that was Geoffrey. To stay here in this room much longer could destroy her good name, and yet like that moth, she was unable to keep from dancing ever-closer to the fire, no matter the peril.

"I knew you were cold because everyone is cold in England once they've lived in India," he said easily, saying nothing of her cold fingers as he circled his arm around her waist, above her hoops. "You're a sweet jasmine flower, roughly dropped into harsh old London."

"No one here knows of jasmines," she said wistfully. His arm felt natural around her waist, secure and steady. "They grew everywhere in our gardens at Sundara Manōra."

She liked having him before her, an excuse to study the handsome perfection of his face. With his arm at her waist, she dared to rest her hands lightly on his shoulders, and that, too, felt right. Beneath the silk of his coat she felt the powerful muscles of his chest and shoulders, and realized her hands were no longer cold. None of her was.

"Did you wear the jasmine flowers in your hair?" he asked, the words rumbling low in his chest.

"Oh, yes," she said softly, letting herself drift back into the memories she usually kept bound tight inside her. "All the girls and women did. We'd pick the blossoms early in the day, when the petals were still tightly shut, and keep them in a special dark cabinet through the heat of the day. Then, in the evening, we would pin them into our braids, and the petals would slowly open as the stars came into the sky. When the moon was high, the fragrance would be at its sweetest."

He pulled her nearer, closing the gap between them. "I wish I could tuck one into your hair now."

He lightly touched her temple, running his fingers over her hair as if pretending to put a flower in place.

She laughed softly, imagining her hair once again crowned with white jasmine, instead of the hard glitter of diamonds.

"The scent was *magical,*" she said. "I can remember it exactly, although it's been years ago now. Oh, Geoffrey, this is exactly—exactly!—why I have missed you so!"

"It's why I've missed you, too, Serena," he said, his eyes hooded and his voice bewitchingly low. "Will you be my own jasmine flower now, ready to blossom in the night?"

He leaned closer, his mouth slanting above hers. There was no doubt in her mind that he was going to kiss her, and no doubt, either, that she would let him, and in that instant she realized how fast everything was changing between them.

She had liked calling him her champion, for the title had come swathed in her long-ago girlish innocence, a chaste and idealized champion. But Geoffrey wasn't an ideal in a book: he was very real flesh and blood and bone, and what was even more surprising was that she was, too. She wasn't granting him a kiss. She *wanted* him to kiss her, and as he bent over her, she eagerly turned her face up to his, her lips puckered into what she thought a kiss should be.

She wasn't prepared for the reality of his mouth pressing boldly over hers, sliding skillfully over her lips until they parted with a startled little gasp that was lost between them. She'd no notion of how his tongue against hers could be so intimate, or so arousing. She hadn't expected him to tangle his fingers in the back of her hair and hold her head captive as he kissed her, making it impossible for her to turn away even if she'd wished to, and she'd never thought that arm around her waist would pull her body close to his until her breasts were pressed to his chest and his thigh was hard against hers through the silk skirts of her petticoat.

Tentatively she began to answer his kiss, widening her lips to let him come deeper into her mouth and pressing back even as she prayed she was doing it right, and he rewarded her with a groan that told her she'd done it exactly right. She felt his kiss not just on her lips, but dancing through her entire body like the flames in the fire before them.

His hands slid along her sides, along the hard bones of her stays around her waist. One roamed higher still, tracing the low, curving neckline of her gown, and his fingers lightly grazed her breast, plumped high by her stays. She shivered, startled by how small a touch could have such an effect on her senses. In a single deft motion, his long fingers slipped inside her bodice to caress her breast.

She gasped in pleasurable confusion, and broke away from his kiss, though not from him. "Geoffrey, I—"

"Serena," he coaxed, his voice rough with desire. "My sweet *jēsamina*."

She smiled at how he'd turned the jasmine flower into a Hindi endearment, as he kissed her again, wooing her to relax. She felt her nipple tighten shamelessly against his palm, sensation and heat rippling through her body to gather low in her belly.

This was longing, this was desire and reckless passion. She'd known the words, of course, but only now did she understand their meaning. She remembered how the women had teased her when she'd been a girl, promising that a lover's kiss should be masterful and full of glory; then she'd thought it was nonsense, but now she knew that glory was only the beginning.

"This is why I could not let you go," he whispered hoarsely. "*This,* Serena."

"It's why I came to you," she said breathlessly, rubbing her cheek against the slight bristle of his jaw. "I didn't know, and yet I did."

He turned her face up to kiss again, and as she parted her lips in welcome, the ormolu clock on the mantel chimed the hour. Distracted, she lost count of the chimes, and glanced over her shoulder to see the time: eleven o'clock.

"Eleven!" she cried with dismay, pulling away from him and tugging her neckline back over her breast. "Oh, Geoffrey, I'd no notion it was so late! I must go back directly, I must—"

He reached for her, drawing her to him once again. "Stay with me, Serena," he said, his voice rough with urgency. "It's where you belong."

"I can't," she said, her palms spread against his chest. She was breathing hard, and so was he, and beneath her hand she could feel how swiftly his heart was beating. "I've been away far too long. If my aunt discovers I'm not at the rout with the others, she'll become distraught, and everyone will *know.*"

His eyes were dark, full of desire. "When can I see you next?"

She bowed her head, unable to meet his gaze. "We should not do this, Geoffrey," she said, unable to keep the longing from her voice. "We cannot. What future could there be for us? I've told you before that I have no intention of marrying."

"Nor do I," he said, lightly stroking her cheek with his thumb. "But there are other ways to share our future than marriage."

Swiftly she raised her gaze. It was clear enough what he was proposing. Long ago she'd resigned herself to a life without the love that a husband would give. She'd never let herself consider this kind of illicit, ruinous love as an alternative, the kind that she'd been taught no respectable Englishwoman should ever accept. In India, such liaisons had been common enough—her own parents had not been married—but not here, and especially not for a lady.

She shook her head. "That's madness. It is not possible, Geoffrey."

"Anything is possible," he said. "Anything can be arranged for those who dare."

The intensity in his expression reminded her of his father, a determination that would not be denied. Yet while she'd found it intimidating in the duke, with Geoffrey it was wildly exciting.

She saw it in his eyes. He would do whatever was necessary to be with her. Nothing would keep him away. Anything, truly, was possible.

She took a deep breath, her heart pounding in her chest. "I've no wish to wound those who care most for me."

"Yet you would leave me." He tipped his head to one side, watching her closely. "I cannot put you from my thoughts, Serena. Awake or asleep, you're there."

"You *are* mad," she whispered. "Geoffrey, we scarcely know each other. Why should I believe you? Why should I believe anything you say?"

"Because if it is meant to happen, it will," he said, his expression surprisingly vulnerable. "Kismet."

Kismet.

She gasped. "You shouldn't say that."

"Why not, when you said it to me first," he countered. "In the moonlight you told me you believed it. Do you still?"

She felt like a fledgling seabird, poised on the edge of a nest built into the wall of a yawning precipice. Far below her were sharp rocks and crashing waves. If she let uncertainty claim her, then surely she would plummet downward to her own destruction. But if she raised her face upward toward the sun and the stars and dared spread her wings to fly, then she would find soaring freedom, joy, elation beyond her imagination.

The rocks, and ruin. The stars, and Geoffrey.

Did she dare? Would she?

"I am always watched," she said in a breathless rush. "My aunt, my grandfather, the servants. I'm never alone."

He smiled, sensing her indecision. "You're not alone now, either, are you?"

"My days are too full. I have no freedom. No English lady does. What you want is not possible," she protested again, even as she realized the obstacles she was naming were more to convince herself than him. "Not at all."

"Then what will your day be tomorrow, Miss Carew?" he asked, feathering teasing little kisses along her jaw. "Surely you do more than sit by the fire reading sermons."

"I-I do," she said, struggling to concentrate. "I have a dancing lesson, and will dine with Grandpapa, and make calls with Aunt Morley, after which we shall return her week's books to Widdicomb's. And in the evening, there's a musicale at Lady Ralston's house, and—"

He stopped her words by kissing her again, his mouth warm and purposeful and enough to make her melt against him.

The ormolu clock chimed again, this time the quarter hour: eleven-fifteen.

She tore herself away, her lace scarf catching on his sleeve. “I must go.”

“Go,” he said. “Fate will bring us back together.”

Finally she fled, and did not look back.

CHAPTER 6

"So where exactly did you vanish to last night?" Harry asked as he plunged his fork into the shirred eggs and bacon on his plate. He was only half-dressed for the day, with a bright red silk banyan over his breeches and shirt, and slippers still on his stockinged feet. "Don't tell me you were in the drawing rooms all that time, either, because you weren't. The elders might accept such a protestation from you, but I won't. I'm assuming it was some delightful lady that kept you away from the guests."

"It was," Geoffrey admitted, sipping at his coffee. He, of course, was properly dressed, having ridden from his own house. "Though that is all I'm admitting."

Ever since his brother had married, it had become their custom when both were in town to take breakfast together at Hargreave House, here in this sunny back parlor overlooking the walled garden. This was the only hour of the day when Geoffrey knew he'd have Harry to himself, before Harry's wife, Lady Augusta, finished addressing the servants for the morning and came to join the two brothers. It wasn't that Geoffrey disliked Gus (as she was called within the family); far from it, for Gus was so cheerful and agreeable that it would be impossible not to love her as a true sister, which Geoffrey did. But the mornings without her wifely presence were the one time when he could regale his very-married older brother with tales of his bachelor exploits, of what he'd done the night before, with relish and unexpurgated detail.

At least that was how matters usually proceeded. This breakfast, however, felt different. The longer Harry poked and prodded at him for more information about his activities during their stepmother's rout last night, the less inclined Geoffrey was to reveal them.

Actually, Harry's questions had little to do with his reticence. Geoffrey had arrived at the table determined to say nothing about his rendezvous with Serena Carew, and he'd kept his resolution. He was generally very open with his older brother where women were concerned, but Serena was different. She was an unmarried noble lady, not an actress or a milliner's apprentice, and she didn't deserve to be discussed like one of his more usual conquests.

He also didn't want to talk about her because he wasn't sure what he'd say. He'd told himself that he'd gone through the trouble of meeting her alone last night because he'd missed her, and wanted to see her again, and kiss her, too, if she was agreeable. In his experience, absence did make the heart grow fonder, and the surest cure for an infatuation with a lady was to see more of her. To a lesser and perverse degree, he'd also done it because he'd been ordered not to by Lord Allwyn, and he'd been too stubborn to resist the challenge. All that was obvious enough, and perfectly suitable to share with Harry.

But as soon as Serena had walked into the library, things had stopped being obvious. She bewitched him. There was no other way he could think of it. Every graceful twist of her body, every turn of her head or glance from her golden eyes enchanted him further.

Yet it wasn't just her beauty that fascinated him. There

was an air of mystery to her that he found irresistible, something that he'd never encountered in any other English lady. Once she'd put aside the mask of aloofness that kept the rest of the world at bay, she had shared with him a rare, unexpected vulnerability. He could listen by the hour to her speak of her childhood in India, and after last night, he'd always associate jasmine flowers with her. He'd often told women that he thought of them constantly when he was apart from them, but with Serena Carew, he'd meant it.

When she'd first whispered "kismet" to him, he'd been ready to dismiss it as meaningless mumbo jumbo. Yet the longer he was with her, the more he'd come to believe that fate truly was bringing them together. Holding her and kissing her had only confirmed it. He could not forget the intoxicating taste of her mouth or the lush way she'd filled his arms, or, perhaps best of all, the starry-eyed way she'd looked at him after they'd kissed.

Kismet, indeed.

That was what he couldn't explain to his brother, or to himself, either. He wasn't even going to try.

Instead he reached for another piece of toast from the silver rack, and dropped a large dollop of marmalade in the center of it.

"Discretion, Harry, discretion," he said as he spread the marmalade neatly to the very edges of the toast. "The lady feared that her honor would be damaged, and I shall respect that."

"Of course her honor was in peril," Harry said. "She was with you."

"Exactly," Geoffrey said. "All the more reason for me not to tell more."

Harry sighed with frustration. "Just her name, then."

"*Just* her name?" Geoffrey repeated, incredulous. "Really, Harry. If you have her name, you can guess the rest."

"Then let me guess her name as well," Harry said, trying another course. "Was it the luscious Lady Pencroft? I saw her wafting about you earlier, displaying a prodigious amount of her justly famous breasts for your admiration."

"Who possesses famous breasts?" asked Gus cheerfully as she joined them in the little back parlor. "I should like very much to know who she is, in the event she is among my acquaintances."

At once Geoffrey rose along with his brother, who hurried forward to greet his wife. Gus had not been born a great beauty, but love and happiness had turned her into one, and her round, freckled face always made Geoffrey smile nearly as broadly as her husband did. She and Harry had been married for almost three years and still behaved like the freshest of sweethearts, billing and cooing and kissing with such unabashed affection that Geoffrey was forced to stare down at his coffee to hide his embarrassment. They really were shameless for a wedded couple, especially since Gus was eight months pregnant with their second child.

Cautiously he waited until he heard Gus settle into her chair with a sigh before he once again glanced up. She was looking directly at him, sitting a bit away from the table on account of the large swell of her belly beneath a spotless linen apron. She took considerable pride in the management of her servants, and in the mornings she often dressed in linen and wool, more like a housekeeper than a countess.

"I know you'll tell me the truth, Geoffrey, even if Harry won't," she said, her eyes bright with mischief. "Who is this lady with the prodigious breasts?"

"*I* wasn't being secretive, Gus," Harry said, a little wounded. "That's Geoffrey. He has made a great secret of the latest lady to capture his interest, and I am striving to guess her name. You overheard my suggestion of Lady Pencroft."

"The one with the breasts." Gus nodded, adding a dollop of cream to her tea. "That makes sense. She's rather sweet, in addition to her other more notable attributes."

"Was it Lady Pencroft, then, Geoff?" Harry asked eagerly. "Was she the one you swept away from the party for a bit of, ah, private conversation last night?"

"Oh, I can tell you that," Gus said, clearly disappointed that there wasn't a more elusive secret. "It wasn't Lady Pencroft at all. It was Miss Carew."

Surprised, Geoffrey's toast hung in midair. "What makes you say that?"

"Because it's the truth." Gus shrugged, holding her cup cradled in her fingers as she raised it to her lips. "I'd heard so much about Miss Carew that I was curious, and asked Celia to point her out to me. I watched you talk with her, then separate with more fuss than was necessary. Soon after both of you vanished, and then later returned, also separately, but within five minutes of each other. When all I could do last night was sit with my feet up on a cushion, it wasn't a difficult puzzle to solve."

"That's hardly proof of anything," Geoffrey said. It was a weak rebuttal at best and he knew it, but he'd been so sure his ruse had worked that Gus had taken him by surprise. "Many people came and went from the parlors in the course of the evening."

"That they did," Gus agreed. "But they didn't gaze at one another like a pair of billing turtledoves the way that you and Miss Carew did."

Harry, however, saw it in a less romantic light.

"You're an ass to involve yourself further with that particular lady, Geoffrey," he said flatly. "I explained the peril to you on that first night, and God knows Father has had his say in the matter, too."

"This is between the lady and me," Geoffrey said, more curtly than he'd intended. "I don't see that it's anyone else's affair than ours."

Gus nodded in sympathy. "He's right, Harry," she said. "I don't see why everyone is in such a righteous fuss about this. If Geoffrey and the lady enjoy each other's company, then where is the harm to it? She's certainly beautiful, in an exotic sort of way. I can understand why Geoffrey is so beguiled by her."

But Harry shook his head, looking stern and judgmental, and entirely too much like their father.

"You can say that because you haven't conversed with her, Gus," he said. "She's undeniably beautiful, but there's an unsettled air to her that's . . . well, disconcerting. She's distant. She keeps herself apart. I suspect it's likely due to her curious upbringing, but you can't begin to tell what she's thinking."

"Which is precisely why I find Miss Carew so intriguing," Geoffrey said. "Most ladies her age have little of use to say, but Miss Carew's conversation is quite fascinating."

Harry grumbled, unconvinced. "I do not believe it is entirely her conversation that fascinates you. It wouldn't be the first time you've been led by your—not by your head. If you're not careful, you'll find yourself standing before the parson beside the lady, with old Allwyn's blunderbuss at your back."

This was enough to end any man's appetite. Geoffrey shoved aside his plate with much of his breakfast remaining uneaten, and at once a footman removed it.

"The last thing Allwyn would wish is to see her wed into our family," he said. "He thinks we Fitzroys are disreputable upstarts, and nothing but whores and bastards."

Gus's brows rose at the strong language. "That seems rather uncharitable of him."

"That *is* the charitable version," Geoffrey said, relieved to have shifted the conversation over to the old marquis. "What he spewed in the front room at White's was much more, ah, colorful. He nearly made Father lose his temper."

"Oh, my, he must have pushed wickedly hard for that to happen," Gus said, her eyes wide. "All Celia told me was that Lord Allwyn was unhappy."

"Allwyn will be a great deal more than unhappy if you debauch his granddaughter, Geoffrey," Harry said sternly. "And the poor man's right. You can't keep toying with a lady like this. It's not honorable, and it reflects badly on our entire family."

Geoffrey sat back in his chair, folding his arms over his chest and wondering how in blazes this once-pleasant breakfast had deteriorated into a fraternal lecture on honor and duty. He'd grudgingly accept that part of his brother's meddling was founded in genuine concern; a too-public love affair with Serena Carew would not exactly bring honor and glory to the family name, or to his own. It was, however, his decision alone to make—or, rather, his and Serena's together.

"I don't wish to discuss the matter further, Harry," he said. "Speak to me of something else."

But his brother wasn't about to give up yet. "As far as I can see, you only have two choices before you," he said. "Either you must quit Miss Carew's company entirely, or make her an offer of marriage."

"Enough, Harry," Geoffrey said, his temper beginning to fray. "I told you. I do not wish to discuss the lady any further."

"You've never done that before," Gus said, marveling. "You're defending her. How very gallant of you, Geoffrey."

Harry snorted with disgust. "It's not gallantry, Gus. Ruining a lady's prospects never is."

"I am following the lady's wishes in the matter, with discretion and attention," Geoffrey said sharply. He sensed that he and Harry were dangerously close to scuffling, the way they had years ago as boys, flailing away and rolling across the floor like mongrel dogs. "As I always do."

Now Harry shoved his chair back from the table, his expression determined and ready for whatever Geoffrey might offer. "The only desire of a virtuous lady should be marriage."

At once Geoffrey rose to his feet, his hands in fists at his sides.

"I pray I am misunderstanding you in regard to Miss Carew's virtue, for I assure you there are no stains upon either her character or her honor," he said. "As for marriage, the lady has made it clear that she has no interest in that article. If I were to ask for her hand, she would unequivocally refuse."

"Hush, hush, you two!" Gus scolded sharply, clapping her hands twice to break the tension between the brothers. "Both of you should be ashamed, carrying on like this before the breakfast dishes are even cleared. Now sit down directly, and drink your coffee like gentlemen instead of snarling away like wild beasts."

With great reluctance, Geoffrey slowly retook his chair, still staring warily at his brother. No one countered Gus in her house, not dogs, servants, children, or men, and when she expected peace beneath her roof, she received it. With the large silver coffeepot in her hand, she refilled first Harry's cup and then Geoffrey's, without spilling a drop. She dropped one precise spoonful of sugar and another of cream into her husband's coffee, knowing exactly how he liked it, and added a small, coaxing smile as she handed him the steaming cup. To

Geoffrey's surprise, Harry smiled warmly in return, his animosity melting as swiftly as it had risen. Truly Gus had amazing powers.

But before Geoffrey could marvel too much, she turned toward him, and lightly rested her small hand on his arm.

"I beg you, Geoffrey, listen more to *how* Miss Carew speaks than her words alone," she said, her round, freckled face solemn, even troubled. "Because she is young, she may say she has no interest in marriage, but in her heart she might believe quite the opposite. She could even be saying what she thinks you wish to hear to please you."

Geoffrey smiled wryly. Gus being Gus, he'd expected her to say something sweetly sentimental like that. But Serena was a different kind of lady entirely, and she had indeed vowed that she'd never wed. He remembered that quite distinctly; it was the important linchpin to whatever happened next between them, and a salve to his own conscience as well. Still, he'd only to remember how she'd kissed him last night to know that she was that rare lady who put passion before propriety, and that it was clear enough they wanted the same things—or, in the case of marriage, didn't want them.

"I believe Miss Carew knows her own heart, Gus," he said with care, not wanting to hurt his sister-in-law's feelings, "especially in such an important matter."

"But that's exactly what I'm saying, Geoffrey," Gus said earnestly. "She may not know what she truly wants until it is offered to her. Love, devotion, friendship, the joy of children, and the pleasure to be found in a loving husband: what lady would ever reject such gifts?"

"Ah, here's my little darling now!" Harry exclaimed eagerly, turning in his chair toward the opening door.

A nursemaid entered, carrying Lady Emily Fitzroy, the daughter of Gus and Harry. The baby was not a usual feature of their breakfasts, and uneasily Geoffrey hoped she wouldn't be thrust into his arms. Parents were always doing that with babies, expecting him to share their besottedness over their damp and sticky progeny.

He guessed Lady Emily must be about a year old now—as a bachelor, he was a little hazy about infant ages—and to him she seemed like a small doll in her nurse's arms, a wriggling confection of wispy blond hair, round cheeks, and a great deal of white linen ruffles and ribbons. The main thing he recalled about her birth was disappointment, felt from his father through every other member of their considerable family. Only a son, destined to take Geoffrey's own place as heir to the dukedom and all its fortunes, would have truly been welcomed.

But there certainly wasn't any disappointment in his brother's eyes now.

"How's my girl this morning?" Harry asked in the kind of foolish, crooning voice that most men reserved for addressing their dogs and horses. "How's my little queen?"

The baby made a chortling gurgle and flailed her arms in Harry's direction.

Harry beamed like a simpleton. "Did you hear that, Geoff? She said 'Father,' clear as day! Who's my clever girl? Who's my little Em?"

"How did she do with the porridge this morning, Betty?" Gus asked the nurse, more practical as usual.

"Oh, Lady Emily did wonderful fine, my lady," Betty said, struggling to contain her squirming charge. "Ate every bit of it, neat as could be. But what she likes best is moving about, my lady. I vow she'll be dancing before long."

"Then put her down, Betty, so she might walk for my brother," Harry said proudly, bending down with his arms outstretched in encouragement. "Watch this now, Geoff. She's already walking like a little lady through Hyde Park. Here, Em, come to me."

Carefully the nurse set the little girl down, holding her firmly by the leading-strings on the back of her gown to keep her upright. Lady Emily scowled with determination as she put one small red shoe unsteadily down after the other.

"Come along, Emily, come along," Gus said, slipping from her chair to stand beside Harry. "Come to Mama and Father, sweetheart."

Resolutely the little girl lurched and staggered stiff-legged across the floor, her plump hands held out for balance. It was the most ungainly process that Geoffrey had ever seen, yet he realized he was holding his breath along with Gus and Harry, willing the unsteady Lady Emily across those last few feet of patterned carpet. Finally she toppled into her father's waiting hands with a squeal of delight. Harry swept her up in his arms, raising her high to make her laugh, then bringing her back down to cradle her in the crook of his arm. Gus leaned forward to kiss her daughter's forehead, not minding at all that the little girl deposited a very wet kiss in return on her cheek.

"Did you see that, Geoffrey?" Harry asked, his grin wide and full of fatherly pride. "Wasn't that something rare?"

What Geoffrey saw was rare indeed, and something he'd never expected to see: Harry standing before him in the morning sunshine with his daughter in his arms and his pregnant wife's head against his shoulder, the three of them together a perfect picture of love and contentment. Clearly his brother didn't regret for a moment his lost bachelorhood, and just as clearly he wasn't living vicariously through Geoffrey, either. Instead Harry had found utter happiness beyond Geoffrey's imagining.

Geoffrey didn't exactly envy Harry, not with all the responsibilities of a wife and child, but he did catch himself wishing he'd a measure of this love and happiness that appeared to come with a family.

Fortunately, his brother had no idea what Geoffrey was thinking.

"Have you ever seen such spirit in a mite, Geoff?" he said, giving his daughter's arm a fond little pat. "My sweet Emily won't be denied in anything, once she sets her mind to it."

"She's a marvel, no doubt," Geoffrey agreed. "Why, if your next child's a boy, consider all he'll be able to accomplish with that kind of determination."

He'd intended it as a compliment, a joyful prediction for the future, but he couldn't miss how Gus's smile faded and her cheeks flushed, and how she placed her hand over her belly as if to protect her unborn child.

"It won't matter if this one's a girl or a boy," she said, fiercely defensive. "We'll love her or him the same as we love Emily."

"Forgive me, Gus," Geoffrey said, contrite. "I never meant to imply you wouldn't."

"Gus knows that," Harry said, a bit too heartily. "Just as you know, sweetheart, that we might have a half-dozen daughters more, and I would not love any of them one whit less for not being boys."

"Of course Geoffrey would approve of that," Gus said, her voice strained. "If I bear nothing but daughters to you, then he'll be the one who'll claim the dukedom."

"I've never wanted that," Geoffrey said, aghast that she'd say such a thing. "Not ever."

"Oh, what does it matter?" Gus said, her cheeks flushed and her eyes perilously red-rimmed. "You'll make my poor daughter suffer anyway, burdened as she'll be with a notorious, selfish uncle known for—for debauching young ladies like Miss Carew without the *shred* of a conscience!"

Lady Emily sensed the tension around her and began

to whimper fretfully, wriggling against her father. That was enough for Gus, who didn't wait for either Harry or Geoffrey to reply before she plucked the little girl from his arms and into hers, holding her closely to reassure her as she backed away from the two brothers.

"Excuse me, but I must take Lady Emily back to the nursery." She studiously concentrated on her daughter to avoid meeting the gaze of either Harry or Geoffrey and hurried from the room, the nurse following close behind her.

The silence she left was painfully empty.

"Should I go after her, Harry?" Geoffrey asked after a moment, contrite and knowing he'd somehow erred badly, but mystified as to the details. "I can apologize again if that will help, or—"

"No, no, let her go." Harry sighed, and dropped back into his chair. "It's best to give her a short time alone to gather herself, and then I'll find her and make things right. She didn't believe any of that, you know. Not a word."

"Are you certain?" Geoffrey asked uneasily. He'd no experience with pregnant ladies. He genuinely liked Gus, and he'd hate to have brought any harm to her or her unborn child, even if it was unintentional. "She seems quite, ah, distressed."

"Most likely," Harry said. "But you know how Gus usually is, Geoffrey. There's not a speck of meanness to her. She's very fond of you as well. That tirade isn't like her, not at all, but this second child has made her so blasted sensitive. Every little thing upsets her now, and in the most irrational ways, too."

"Then tell her I won't upset her, either," Geoffrey said, motioning for the footman to bring him his hat. There'd been a time when he and Harry had been thick as the proverbial thieves, with never a secret between them. Geoffrey had spent his entire life bucking against Father's wishes, but Harry was different. Geoffrey would do anything for Harry. It was the reason he'd come rushing back from India when Harry had been hurt. His brother had meant that much to him.

But then Harry had married Gus, and everything changed. Harry's first loyalty was now to his wife, not to his brother, and while Geoffrey knew that this was for the best, he was forever left behind, on the outside. Yet his loyalty to his brother remained, unable to be ignored, or forgotten, or rationalized away.

"Gus's concerns are all easily remedied, of course," Geoffrey continued. "Assure her that I will not be bringing any further shame or worry to her or the rest of the family on account of Miss Carew."

"You will break with Miss Carew?" Harry asked, surprised.

"What did I just say?" Geoffrey was unable to keep a note of bitterness from creeping into his voice as he thought of Serena and remembered the wonder that had shone in her eyes after they'd kissed: pure magic. *That* was what his family wished him to abandon, what he was supposed to give up for their sake. The day as he'd planned it was already going to be complicated, and now this miserable breakfast had made it infinitely more so. "I would never wish to disgrace Gus, or you, or young Lady Emily, or even Miss Carew, by my notoriously selfish behavior."

Harry winced. "I told you, Geoff, Gus didn't mean that."

"She must have meant it to a certain degree, or else she wouldn't have bothered to say it." Geoffrey took his hat from the footman, and settled it on his head with what he hoped was offhanded nonchalance. "I'll cause no shame, no disgrace, to this family. I trust that will please everyone. Now go to your wife, Harry, and good day to you both."

* * *

Widdicomb's Circulating Library stood at Otway's Head in King Street, Covent Garden, and like every other London establishment dependent on the taste and custom of ladies, it was tidy, commodious, and so easy to locate that even the wife of the most backwater country squire, up to town for the first time, would have no difficulty finding it. The Library was like honey to a certain kind of lady-bee, one for whom the latest gothic novel was the very nectar of life, and the two floors of tightly packed bookshelves were always abuzz with the gentle hum of these ladies indulging their pleasure and discussing it with their fellows.

Or so Geoffrey had heard. Like most gentlemen, he'd never ventured into the place himself, let alone pursued a lady into those hallowed, bookish halls of ten thousand volumes waiting to be borrowed. Today would be his first time, and as he strolled absently among the market stalls across the street, he flipped open his watch to check the time. Nearly three o'clock. The carriage with Serena and Lady Morley inside could appear before Widdicomb's at any moment, and he meant to be ready.

It had been easy enough to determine their arrival. Geoffrey knew from his own aunts that older ladies tended to set their days to a precise schedule, and from what Serena had told him, he'd guessed Lady Morley would be much the same. He'd sent one of his maidservants to Widdicomb's earlier in the day to make an inquiry, and she'd learned that yes, indeed, Lady Morley was in the habit of visiting every Thursday afternoon at three, when she would meet with several other bookish ladies of her acquaintance. The trick for Geoffrey would be to catch Serena alone among the bookshelves without her aunt.

Not quite: the real trick would be determining what

he'd say to Serena when he found her. After the scene this morning at his brother's house, he'd resolved not to see her again. He considered writing to tell her so, but after the disastrous business with the flowers, he was certain her grandfather would intercept any letter he might send. He could have called on her at home, and risked more of the wrath of her grandfather in person. He could have waited until their paths crossed once again at some other ball or musicale. Or he could have done what most men would, nothing, and let her figure out for herself why he'd chosen to vanish from her life.

Geoffrey, however, had more of a conscience than most men. He couldn't bring himself to treat Serena like that; after all, none of this was her fault, and it didn't seem fair to kiss her and then disappear. No, the honorable thing was to explain how it was impossible for them to continue to see each other, and how family trumped kismet.

The conversation would not be enjoyable. He expected she'd cry, though he rather hoped she wouldn't.

He saw the carriage with the Carew arms on the door draw up before the Library. The footman hurried to unfold the carriage-step and help Lady Morley down, and after her came Serena, gliding effortlessly from the carriage to the pavement. She wore a white embroidered pelisse over a dark plum gown and white shoes with curving red heels, and as she moved, the ruffled edges of the pelisse floated around her like butterfly wings.

He frowned a little, unable to look away. Damnation, but she moved like a goddess with her head held high, lithe and effortless and full of seductive grace. Breaking off with her this afternoon might make him cry, too.

He waited until they entered the Library, then waited ten minutes more, hoping that would be sufficient for Lady Morley to find her friends and be distracted by them. Finally he crossed the street, striving to be as nonchalant as possible, and entered the Library.

"Good day, sir, good day," said an older man standing behind the front counter, a speckled quill pen tucked behind his ear. "How may we serve you, sir?"

"I am on the hunt for a book," Geoffrey said, the most obvious—and the most vague—answer possible. Not wanting to create a fuss, he had purposefully dressed plainly, as a gentleman but not a duke's son, and he'd come by hansom cab rather than his own carriage.

The man smiled warmly. "Of course, sir, of course," he said. "We have titles for every interest. History, plays, voyages and travels, chronicles of ancient wars, philosophy, and sermons."

Geoffrey glanced around the Library as if considering this wealth of variety. While there were many ladies and a few gentlemen browsing the shelves, Serena and her aunt were not among them. That was good. He'd rather find Serena alone among the shelves than risk causing a scene before the front counter, and the sooner he could begin hunting for her, the better.

"I, ah, wasn't looking for myself," he said. He wouldn't, of course; he didn't borrow books at a circulating library, but bought and had them bound, the way any gentleman would. "I'm looking for something for my, ah, my aunt."

The clerk's smile widened. "Oh, yes, sir. We have all the freshest novels and romances for ladies, as well as collections of sermons and lectures. If your aunt is a subscriber, sir, then I can consult our records, and see her favorite authors and interests so I might better advise you as to—"

"That won't be necessary," Geoffrey said quickly, with no interest of his own in an invented aunt. "I've a fair notion of her tastes."

He turned away and headed through the main room

and up the staircase to the upper floor. He was half-aware of how ladies turned to look at him as he passed by, of little sighs and smiles that this time held no interest for him. He was determined to find Serena; no, after that single glimpse of her stepping down from the carriage, he was almost *desperate* to find her.

Upstairs there were far more books than patrons, with shelves that rose nearly to the ceiling arranged in close-set rows. Before the windows overlooking the street were several chairs for the convenience of readers. Sitting there with two other ladies was Lady Morley, their conversation animated and, fortunately, their backs turned toward Geoffrey. He ducked into the first aisle of shelves, looking for Serena, and found only a woman with a small dog peeking from her oversized muff. The next row had a clerical gentleman in a flat parson's hat, advising an older lady.

She *had* to be here somewhere, Geoffrey thought with a muttered oath of frustration. He'd seen her enter, and there was no other way from the building. He moved into the third aisle, and there, at last, stood Serena.

She was turned slightly away from him, engrossed in the large, open book in her hands. Strange how he'd met her in his father's library last night, and now in another library.

She had flipped back the front edges of her pelisse over her shoulders to free her arms, and he'd now a clear view of the curves of her breasts beneath her sheer white kerchief, and the narrowness of her waist in her plum-colored silk gown. Her head was bowed over the book and her wide-brimmed hat pinned to slope forward over her face, leaving the pale nape of her neck temptingly exposed. A single wisp of dark hair had slipped free to curl like a comma to one side of her throat, and as he watched, she absently raised her gloved hand to tuck it back into place. The late afternoon sunlight through the window played over the curve of her cheek, and made the rich silks and embroidery of her clothing glow against the worn leather spines of the books.

She had never looked more beautiful, and with a little lurch somewhere in his chest, he realized that this was how he'd have to remember her.

"Miss Carew," he said softly. "*Jēsamina.*"

Startled from her reading, she caught her breath, and spun toward him, closing the book in her hands with a snap.

"Lord Geoffrey," she said, her surprise melting into a shy smile. "You said you'd find me, and you did."

"I did." He knew he shouldn't waste this time alone with her, should tell her at once what he needed to say, yet he couldn't quite do it, not yet. "What are you reading?"

She glanced down at the book and blushed, self-consciously tucking it to her side, into the folds of her silk skirts so he couldn't see it.

"It's nothing," she said. "A whim, a fancy to pass the time while I wait for my aunt, that is all."

He grinned. Most likely it was the kind of rubbish most young ladies devoured, a novel filled with ruined castles and thwarted love. "Might I see the title?"

She shook her head, lowering her chin to look up at him from beneath the curving brim of her hat, and he wondered if she'd any notion how devastating a small gesture such as that could be.

"I'd rather not," she said in a breathy whisper. "It's—it's not what you think, anyway."

"I doubt that," he said easily. "Does it feature a princely lover and a steadfast heroine, their lives snared in a web of lies and deceit?"

Her eyes widened. "Oh, no, not at all."

"Then where is the shame in showing it to me?" he coaxed, holding his hand out for the book. "Come, let me see it and judge its merit for myself."

She hesitated a moment longer before, with a deep breath, she thrust the book out for him to read the elaborate gold lettering on the cover.

"A Narrative of an Englishman's Journey through the Mughal Orient," he read aloud, surprised. "You have my apology. No idle frivolity between those covers, I'll wager."

"I know that India is my past and that there's no use in remembering it now," she said quickly, her words rushing with what he could only think was misplaced guilt. "That's what my grandfather and Aunt Morley say, and they are right. I know I'll never return and that there's nothing to be gained by regretting what is lost forever, and yet I cannot help myself when I am here. It's the pictures that draw me back, you see."

She'd kept her thumb inside the pages to mark her place, and now she held the book open for Geoffrey to see as well.

"This shows a prosperous gentleman's estate not far from Hyderabad," she said. "The author was a guest there, but it could have been Sundara Manōra, my father's house. There were more trees about our gate, and the arches over the windows were different, but otherwise it could be my home before . . . before it was gone."

He gazed down at the hand-colored plate, trying to imagine what her life had been as a child. *Sundara Manōra* would translate roughly to *Lovely Mansion,* and it must have been exactly that. The house, outbuildings, and grounds in the print were spacious and grand, clearly the estate of a wealthy man who wanted to live like a prince—which, of course, her father must have done. The son of an English marquis who dealt in precious stones, weapons, and favors would have expected nothing less.

Yet Geoffrey noted how she'd put everything decisively in the past tense. He knew that she'd been the only survivor of an illness that had claimed the rest of her family and that she'd been brought to England soon afterward. That much was common knowledge in London society, although she'd never spoken of it to him.

What else had happened to her to make her so reluctant to speak of it now? Why did she consider it wrong to remember that past, to so much as look at this book? His brother might not have much use for him any longer, but he'd the distinct feeling that Serena needed him for—

Steady now, steady, he warned himself. *You're not here to be drawn back into her mysteries. You're here to bid her farewell.*

"Serena," he said gently, beginning. "Miss Carew."

Still she studied the picture, too lost in the image and the memories it raised to hear him.

"I could look at this by the hour," she said longingly, running her fingers around the raised edge of the print. "Behind this tall wall, here, would have been the garden for the women. Ours was so beautiful—a slice of Heaven, Father had called it. We'd trees for shade and so many flowers and a pond with golden fish, and silk pillows strewn everywhere for us to take our ease. But what I loved best was our swing, with red cords of silk and gold thread, and tassels that fluttered in the breeze when I pushed it back and forth. The swing made me feel free, as if I were a bird flying through the air, and I'd pretend if I could swing just a little higher, I might fly over the garden walls themselves. I know it must sound foolish, but that is what I wanted."

"Not at all, Miss Carew." He was enchanted by the

image she was painting of herself, of the silken skirts of her sari fluttering around her bare legs and slippered feet as she pushed higher and higher in the red swing. "Not at all."

She smiled sadly. "Seven years have passed since I left, and no matter how hard I try to keep it all in my head, little things are slipping away. That's why I like this picture, you see. It helps me to remember. I never tire of it."

"Then why don't you borrow the book and take it home with you?" he asked, unable not to. "I doubt it's in much demand."

"I told you," she said, closing the book and shoving it back onto the shelf. "There's nothing to be gained from thinking of the past."

"But the pictures give you pleasure, Serena," he said. "Isn't that enough?"

"Perhaps," she said wistfully, yet in a polite way that still made it clear she didn't think it was enough at all. She kept her hand on the book's spine, not quite breaking free of the image inside. "Perhaps."

"I wish I could have seen your father's house for myself," he said. "It must have been quite beautiful."

She looked at him sharply, her eyes bright in the slanting sunlight. "Why do you say that?"

"Because it's true," he said. "The estates in the hills near Hyderabad have a rare beauty unlike anything to be seen here in England. To have seen it with you as my guide would have made my journey incomparably better."

She gave a quick shake to her head. "It's impossible for you to know," she said, incredulous. "I've never told anyone. Yet you understand, exactly as you have over and over again. You understand this, and you understand me."

"I'm afraid I don't understand now," he said, smiling.

"What miraculous knowledge do I unwittingly possess?"

The group of ladies that included her aunt laughed loudly over some remark or another on the other side of the shelf, and Serena stepped closer, so close that her skirts brushed against Geoffrey's legs like a whispering caress.

"We haven't much time alone," she said, her voice rushed and taut with urgency. "I dreamed of you last night, Geoffrey. That's what I meant, and it's why I was so certain you would keep your word and find me."

"Ah," he said, disconcerted yet intrigued by the intimacy she was implying. To invade a woman's dreams was only one step away from sharing her bed. He had to end this now, *now*, yet he couldn't, not while she looked at him like this. "Most likely that's because you saw me earlier in the evening."

"No." She lifted her chin with unquestioning certainty. "I see many people here in England every day, and none of them appears in my dreams. You are the first."

He drew in his breath, trying to remember his brother and Gus and their little daughter, and ignore how full and tempting Serena's lips were with her chin raised toward him.

Trying, and failing miserably.

"Miss Carew," he began again. "We must, ah, talk."

"We *are* talking," she said, her words coming more swiftly. "I was telling you of my dream, how you were in it and so was I. We were together in the west garden at Sundara Manōra, near the silver pond and beneath the old banyans, and I'd a jasmine flower pinned in my hair, just as you'd wished it."

"I would like that," he said, unable to resist the lure of her dream as she painted it. "We were in India together, then?"

She nodded eagerly. "Last night when I left you, I was agitated beyond measure, and my thoughts were so jumbled that I couldn't tell what to do next. But my dream made everything clear. You were right. We are meant to be together, no matter what anyone else may say or do or think or—or—"

She broke off suddenly, and to his surprise she arched up against his chest and kissed him. Her inexperience showed in her awkwardness, but that same innocence was like a spark to his own desires, and at once all his well-intended restraint shattered. The moment her lips touched his, he began kissing her back, kissing her hard. He slid his tongue into her mouth to taste her and to mark her as his own. She moaned softly, widening her lips for more of him, and he curled his arm around her waist to pull her close. Her hands fluttered over his chest before they instinctively settled on his shoulders, trusting him.

She shouldn't, not now. He shoved his hands inside her pelisse to find her waist and urged her backward until she bumped against the wall of bookcases. Her hat fell forward, and impatiently he swept it from her head, letting it fall to the floor. One carefully curled lock of her hair came unpinned with it, falling over her shoulder, yet still he did not stop kissing her. She made him forget Harry and Gus entirely, made him forget what he'd promised them, made him forget everything except her own bewitching, intoxicating self.

He trapped her against the books and wooden shelves and pressed his body to hers so she'd be sure to understand his desire as he deepened the kiss, ravishing her mouth as in return she instinctively moved against him. That was what drove him, knowing that she wanted this as much as he did, and he could not get enough of her. Surrounded as they were by others in the Library, he realized they could be discovered at any moment, yet that only gave an extra urgency to how he kissed her, demanding and hot and full of the need they shared.

She whimpered with pleasure, an enticing sound that vibrated between them, but too loud for this place. Reluctantly he dragged his mouth away from hers, pressing his finger across her lips to quiet her.

"Shhh," he whispered. "We don't want company."

Her face was flushed, feverish, and her eyes were heavy-lidded as they searched his face. "When can I see you again?"

"You tell me," he said.

Her hands slid up and down over his chest, unwilling to part with him. "Sunday."

"Sunday?" he repeated. He hadn't expected her to have such a ready answer. Usually he was the one who planned the details of an assignation, but the fact that she had only showed her eagerness. "Where?"

Her breath was coming so quickly that she was nearly panting, the tops of her breasts rising and falling beneath the sheer linen of her kerchief.

"My grandfather's house," she whispered, her voice husky with excitement. "He and my aunt and most of the servants will be away at church in the morning until past noon. Come to the back garden gate, and I shall let you in."

Damnation, but that was an invitation with a double meaning. "When?"

She swallowed, and ran her tongue lightly across her lower lip, a simple gesture that nearly undid him.

"Half-past nine," she said. "I'll be waiting for you at the gate."

He bent down to retrieve her fallen hat and handed it to her. He had to ask; he'd be a despicable cad if he didn't. "You are certain you wish to do this?"

She smiled, the daring in her eyes proof that she knew exactly what she doing. With her hair disheveled and her mouth swollen from his kisses, she looked more like some wild mountain bandit-queen than a noble-born virgin from St. James's Square, and he'd never found her more fascinating.

"If it is meant to happen," she said slowly, fiercely, "then it will."

He smiled in return. How, really, could he not?

"You'd toss my own words back at me, Miss Carew?"

Never breaking her gaze from his, she twisted the loose lock of hair back into place and set her hat back onto her head, deftly tying the silk ribbon that held it in place.

"Not so many words, Lord Geoffrey," she said, smoothing her clothes. "There's only one that matters."

"Kismet," he said softly.

She nodded, her smile full of longing and promise and secrets shared, even as she once again transformed herself back into a proper English lady. He'd seen her do it before, but the change still startled him.

"Until Sunday," she said, adding the most gracefully sweeping curtsey he'd ever seen. "Good day, Lord Geoffrey."

She didn't run away from him as she had last night, but walked with her back straight and her head high and the black bows on her hat fluttering gently with each step of her red-heeled shoes. She did not turn to look back at him at the end of the aisle of tall bookshelves—to do so would risk having her aunt take notice—but she did pause and hesitate, just enough to show she wished she could.

He hated to see her go, even with the promise of seeing her again Sunday. It wasn't just how much he desired her, which of course he did. But that desire ran much deeper than simply wanting her in his bed. He wanted to be in her thoughts as much as she was in his. He wanted to know her secrets, and do whatever was necessary to take away the melancholy and sadness that so clearly haunted her. She *needed* him, and if that was the definition of kismet, then he'd take it.

His family worried that he'd be responsible for the ruin of Miss Carew. That was still a possibility, even a likelihood, considering they'd be alone on Sunday. But infinitely more astonishing to Geoffrey was the realization that Miss Carew was going to ruin *him*.

And he could not wait for it to happen.

CHAPTER 7

"I'm sorry you found nothing new to read, Serena," Aunt Morley said as the footman latched the carriage door shut. "Reading is a great comfort to a lady. You must not forget that."

"I haven't, Aunt," Serena said, pulling the brim of her hat lower over her eyes. She was sure that having kissed Geoffrey must show on her face, that there must be some difference to her eyes, her expression, her lips. How could such a monumental change within her not be clear to the rest of the world as well? "I still have several books at home that I've yet to finish."

"I suppose we can return to Widdicomb's if you complete them before next week," Aunt Morley said, placated for now. "You should, you know. Reading keeps the mind nimble."

"Yes, Aunt," Serena said, her thoughts a thousand miles away from the little stack of unfinished books on the table beside her bed.

Her dream last night had shocked her. Most nights if she dreamed of India, it was the old nightmare, the terror of it never fading, but the one last night had been the sweetest dream imaginable. Everything at Sundara Manōra was exactly as it had been, the beautiful, shimmering paradise on earth that Father had built it to be. He had been in her dream, too, as handsome and dashing as she remembered, as well as her sister, Asha. They had not changed, but in the odd way of dreams, Serena herself had been her present age, yet dressed in a flowing silk sari, her bare arms covered with gold bangles and her hair plaited in a single braid that fell heavily between her shoulder blades in the old familiar way.

No one had thought this strange, nor had they been surprised to have Geoffrey as their guest. He had sat beside Father at the table, in the spot reserved for the most honored guests, and Serena had sat beside him, making sure his glass was always filled with wine and the best dishes were presented to him first. The sun had been warm and the air fragrant with the flowers in the garden. Everyone had talked and laughed with the freedom she remembered from her childhood, and none of the stiff manners and false politeness that she'd been forced to learn since she'd come to London. Geoffrey had been accepted as part of their family, which had made Serena extraordinarily happy. He belonged at Sundara Manōra; he belonged with *her*. When he leaned forward to kiss her at the table, she'd smiled, and leaned toward him.

And then she'd awakened, alone in her chilly bedchamber with a gray London dawn just beginning to show beyond the curtains. There had been tears on her cheeks, but this time they'd been from joy, not fear. With a muffled cry of disappointment, she'd tried to steal back into the dream by closing her eyes, tried to will herself back into its spell, even as the dream had already slipped irrevocably beyond her reach.

"Permit yourself a short rest before you have Martha dress you for dinner, Serena," Aunt Morley was saying, concern in her voice. "You've seemed out of sorts to me all day. Perhaps we should send our regrets to Lady Ralston for this evening. You're not feverish, are you?"

She reached forward to lay her hand on Serena's brow.

"I'm perfectly well, Aunt," Serena protested, drawing

back, "and there's no reason we can't go out this evening."

Aunt Morley sighed. "Very well," she said reluctantly. "I only pray you'll tell me if you truly are unwell."

"I promise I will," Serena said, giving her aunt's hand a fond, if guilty, squeeze. She'd never doubted that Aunt Morley cared very much for her. She hated knowing that her aunt would be wounded to the quick if she ever learned—which she must never, ever do—what Serena had just done with Geoffrey.

One more secret, she thought, one more deception layered on all the others she carried inside her. . . .

Her aunt smiled in return, fortunately unaware of Serena's thoughts.

"I pray you'll feel sufficiently well to attend Lady Ralston tonight," she said. "There should be a good-sized company there. Perhaps you'll even see that charming Lord Millbury again."

Serena blushed. Her aunt was supposed to have seen her talking to Lord Millbury last night only as a diversion from Geoffrey, but the plan had worked a bit too well. Her aunt had become captivated by the possibility of the earl as Serena's new suitor, and nothing Serena said to dissuade her had had the slightest effect.

"Lord Millbury is a very nice gentleman, Aunt," she said yet again, "but I do not believe he has any further interest in me, or I in him."

Aunt Morley smiled. "I understand entirely if you wish to keep your interest to yourself, Serena," she said coyly. "But know that his lordship would make a pretty match for you, and one that would please your grandfather. The Earls of Millbury are of quite ancient lineage, you know. Entirely different from those Fitzroys."

"The Earls of Millbury are of no more consequence to me than the Dukes of Breconridge," Serena said as firmly as she could. "I wish you would understand, Aunt Morley."

But her aunt chose to hear only part of what she'd said. "I am glad to hear you say that, Serena. Your grandfather can be overbearing at times, but he was entirely right to object to Lord Geoffrey. As charming as that young gentleman is, I heard something today that paints him in much less gallant light. Were you aware that last night he went off from the rout for nearly an hour with some unsavory lady or another?"

"Oh, Aunt," Serena said uneasily, knowing well enough who that "unsavory lady" might be. "You are always cautioning me against repeating empty tattle, and now you are doing the same."

"It wasn't empty tattle," Aunt Morley said soundly. "It was noted by several of the guests, plain as the day. The only question was the identity of the lady with which he was dallying. Some said it was Lady Pencroft, while others were certain it was that dreadful Mrs. Tate. Either way you are better without him, Serena. You made a fortuitous escape."

"I'm sure," Serena murmured, hoping that a lack of interest would make her aunt move to another topic.

It didn't. "No, we do not need the likes of Lord Geoffrey in our family," she continued. "I don't like to speak ill of the deceased, but your poor father was something of a rake in his youth as well, and too often ruled by illicit animal passions. Pursuing actresses and low strumpets, carousing about the town, wasting his money on buying them wine and cheap baubles—it was all a source of great unhappiness for everyone, particularly your grandfather."

Serena went very still. Aunt Morley had never spoken so freely about her father, or faulted him in any way.

"I did not intend to shock you, Serena," her aunt continued, noticing Serena's silence. "I only meant to show how a young gentleman's folly can cause grief and suffering to his family. Fortunately your father was able to put his immoral behavior behind him in the East Indies, and become a sober Christian gentleman. His hard work transformed him into a responsible husband and father, and a son your grandfather could be proud of. To be sure, he was disappointed when he learned your father had resigned his commission, but to become a diplomatic liaison for one of those foreign courts instead was quite the honor. I can only hope that for the sake of His Grace, Lord Geoffrey will one day become as respectable and accomplished as your poor father."

Serena didn't answer, her heart racing. This was more about her father's life than her aunt had ever shared with her, and most of it was wrong. What had he written back to his family in England? Was deception a part of his life as well?

He had never been a sober Christian gentleman, not the way it was defined here in England. He had not worked hard, not that she had seen: he had been endlessly charming, but he'd also been cunning and resourceful. His much-vaunted physical courage included daring to the point of recklessness. He had never been a diplomat, yet he had made himself a favorite with the princes of their region because he had been willing to sell them the European weapons that they craved, guns and muskets that other Englishmen would not. Most of all he had been lucky; he'd said that himself. She thought of Father and the beautiful, lissome concubines that slipped in and out of his bed, of the troupes of *nautch* girls he'd hire for entertainment, of how her own mother would have been one of the "low strumpets" that so disgusted her aunt.

Perhaps in her heart Serena was one herself.

She thought again of how brazenly she'd kissed Geoffrey last night, and today as well. She'd practically leaped into his embrace, and when he'd caressed her breast as he'd kissed her, she'd given herself freely to desire. And she liked it, at least with Geoffrey. She liked it very much, so much that the memory alone was enough to make her breath quicken.

Illicit animal passions. That's what Aunt Morley was calling it, and making it sound like the heights (or depths) of tawdry wickedness. Serena had heard variations of this before, of course. Any well-bred young English lady would.

Yet on the other side of the world, where she'd been born, there'd been no sin to pleasure, and no disgrace to it, either. It hadn't been illicit at all at Sundara Manōra. She'd learned that from the other women around her, as well as from her father's example. Pleasure had always been considered a part of love, a rare joy to be embraced and shared.

But where did she belong now? Should she obey the strict morality of Aunt Morley, or let herself develop this newfound taste for pleasure, a taste that she must have inherited from her parents?

Troubled, Serena did not go directly to her rooms when she and Aunt Morley returned home, but instead headed to the upstairs back parlor. There, in a place of prominence over the fireplace, hung the house's only portrait of her father. Serena had never cared for the painting, and had avoided it as much as was possible, not wanting the image to cloud her memories of her father.

The portrait had been painted shortly before he had left to take his commission with the East India Company, when he was nineteen, and about the same age when he'd been the rakehell about town that Aunt Morley had described. He was expected to return to London after he'd put in a respectable amount of time with the Company. Instead he had resigned his commission, turned his back on the British community at Calcutta, and retreated into Hyderabad to make his fortune his own way.

Serena curtseyed to the portrait, then stared up at it, trying to find any real resemblance between this handsome, haughty young man and her ever-fainter memory of her father. In the painting, he was close to her own age, tall and lean and dressed in the Company's uniform: polished black boots, cream-colored breeches and waistcoat, a close-fitting red coat bright with gold braid and gleaming gold buttons, and his sword slung low around his hips. His hair was tightly curled on the sides with a clubbed queue, and in one hand he held the reins to the horse that stood beside him. He was the very picture of an imperious young officer, English to the tips of the fawn-colored gloves he grasped in his hand.

The father she'd known had not looked like this at all. True, he'd been older by then, and his young man's lean frame had broadened considerably, but he had also abandoned English fashions and customs. Instead he habitually wore a long, narrow moustache and covered his hair with a turban, and in place of a stiff English coat he preferred a flowing, pleated *jama* over loose striped trousers, with embroidered silk slippers on his feet and jeweled necklaces around his neck. He'd looked much more like a Hindi Mughal than an English gentleman, which was exactly how he'd wished it.

The way she remembered Father best were the times when he sat in his favorite rosewood chair and she'd perch on his knee. His clothes were scented with the fragrance of the tobacco in his hookah, and he'd laugh uproariously over silly things, like trying to teach a parakeet to talk. When she'd been taken to Calcutta, she'd overheard her father described by the English officers as ruthless, brash, and unscrupulous, a man too much at ease with native ways to be trusted. What she remembered, however, were Father's great love for her and her sister, his boundless good humor, and how much he had laughed.

And that, really, was the greatest difference between the young Lord Thomas Carew in the portrait and the father she'd loved. Lord Thomas looked guarded and arrogant, even angry, while Father had been happy. He'd claimed he lived his life without regrets, and Serena believed it, for she had been happy at Sundara Manōra, too. Father had kept more than his share of secrets in his life, but she realized now that she might have discovered the most important one. He had dared to turn his back on everything that he had been and everything that was expected of him, and had instead found happiness five thousand miles away from where he'd been born.

She could hear the servants in the passage, going from room to room to draw the curtains for the evening. She'd have to leave this parlor soon if she didn't want to be caught in here, and she gazed up at the portrait one last time, striving to consider the painted face with fresh eyes. She was often told she looked much like Father, but she'd never seen it herself in the mirror.

Perhaps her real inheritance from him was not in the shape of her nose or the arch of her brows. It wasn't in the jewels and gold he'd sent back to England, or even in the taste for pleasure she'd discovered with Geoffrey. No, the most important thing Father had left her was the willingness to risk everything for happiness.

He'd given her permission.

"*Should I* send for the physician, my dear?" Aunt Morley stood by Serena's bed, her hands folded at her waist and her brow drawn with concern. She was already dressed for church, a large plumed hat on her head and her prayer book in her hand. "Perhaps it would be the wisest course if you are in such pain."

"Thank you, no, Aunt, it's not so serious as that," Serena said as wanly as she could. "When I waken with a headache like this, the only cure is to lie abed and let it pass. You know I've had them before."

"What I know is that I hate to see you suffer like this," Aunt Morley said. "But if you are certain you do not feel well enough to dress and join your grandfather and me for services, then it can't be helped."

"I'll be better by supper," Serena said, pressing her palm to her forehead. "I always am."

"Yes, but this morning you are not," her aunt said, tucking her prayer book into her pocket. "Your grandfather can get along well enough without me. I'll stay home today, here with you. There's nothing worse than suffering alone."

"No!" exclaimed Serena, remembering just in time that she was supposed to be ill, and making her voice again feeble and weak. "That is, I shall be perfectly fine by myself. I know you wish to go with Grandfather. Today's sermon is being given by Dr. Bracegirdle, isn't it? Visiting from Winchester? He's a special favorite of yours."

"He is," admitted her aunt. "Dr. Bracegirdle can take the most common of scripture verses and find an entirely new and salient meaning in it. And his voice! Gracious, if the man hadn't a calling, he could have been an actor in Drury Lane with that voice."

"Then you must go hear him," Serena insisted. "I would not want you to miss his sermon and be disappointed on my account. I'll be perfectly fine here. Most likely all I shall do is sleep."

It was clear that her aunt was hesitating. "I suppose I could ask Martha to sit with you."

"She needn't do that," Serena said, reminding herself

again to keep the excitement from her voice and sound ill—but not too ill. Ah, she didn't have the patience for intrigue like this! "She can occupy herself with other tasks in the servants' hall. So long as she's within hearing of the bell, then that will be sufficient."

While Sundays were usually the day that servants were given to tend to their own affairs and amusements, Serena suspected that Martha would not mind staying in the near-empty house, as long as Parker, the second footman, was also at home. Her lady's maid had confessed a special fondness for Parker, and while romances between servants were forbidden in the house, Serena had kept their secret—never dreaming that it might in time be a useful twin to her own.

Aunt Morley sighed, her prayer book once again in her hand. "There's nothing I could do for you that Martha couldn't as well," she said slowly. "And it's only for a few hours. We'll be back in time for dinner."

"Yes, Aunt." Serena closed her eyes and rested her palm across her forehead. "Forgive me, I'm already feeling drowsy."

"That's for the best," her aunt said, patting Serena on the arm. "You rest, and I'll speak to Martha. Most likely your grandfather and I will be back when you wake."

But as Serena lay in her bed, it wasn't the return of her aunt and grandfather that concerned her most. It was their departure; or rather, their lack of one. Although the house was large, it was still possible for her to hear Grandpapa storming about in the front hall, unhappy with something or another about the carriage or the horses. His raging continued while the problem was corrected, for what seemed like an eternity to Serena, and with growing frustration she reached for her little enameled watch from the table beside the bed.

When she'd told Geoffrey to meet her at half-past nine, she'd thought she'd have plenty of time after her grandfather and aunt had left to dress herself, but it was already that, and she groaned with despair.

How long would Geoffrey wait at the gate for her? How long would he stand there before he'd think she'd changed her mind, and leave?

She slipped from the bed and went to peek through the curtains to the street before the front of the house. Finally her grandfather was climbing into the carriage, and the footmen were closing the door and climbing on the post behind. She watched the carriage draw away and roll slowly down the street before she rushed to the window on the other side of the room. She craned her neck and pressed against the glass, trying to see if Geoffrey was there, but the angle wasn't right, and she couldn't open the window to lean out.

The clock on her mantelpiece chimed the quarter hour: 9:45. She didn't dare take the time to dress herself; instead, she swiftly tied a yellow silk sultana over her night rail and thrust her bare feet into slippers. She paused before her looking glass long enough to pull the plaits from her hair and twist it into a loose knot, then quickly secure it in place with three hairpins. Martha would have fits if she knew her lady was going to receive anyone, let alone a gentleman, like this, in a dressing gown without stays, paint, or jewels, but she was already so late that it couldn't be helped.

She opened her bedchamber door a crack to make sure no servants were in the hall. She hurried down the stairs and through the back hall, her slippered feet making no sound, and into the little back parlor that overlooked the garden.

Ordinarily she took breakfast here each morning with Grandfather and Aunt Morley. The table had already been cleared, the cloth drawn, the chairs set back along the wall, and the cushioned bench where her aunt liked to read tucked neatly beneath one of the windows. No one would likely return to this room for the rest of the day, but Serena had an important reason for coming here. All the keys to the house were kept by the butler, but because her aunt often liked to carry her tea into the garden, an extra set to both the garden door and the gardener's gate were kept in a small box on the mantelpiece. These Serena now took from the box, and let herself outside.

The morning was clear and bright, with dew sparkling on every leaf, and she couldn't help but feel her spirits soar with excitement and anticipation. The light silk of her sultana fluttered and slipped around her bare legs, and it was, she realized, the first time since she'd been in England that she'd been out-of-doors without stays, her body as uninhibited as when she'd been a girl. Perhaps not having time to dress properly had been kismet, too, and her exhilaration rose. She only hoped that Geoffrey would approve, and not be scandalized by her informality. She smiled; no, being male, he wouldn't be, she was sure.

She followed the path along the garden wall, the one that ran along the outer perimeter of the flower beds, where the boxwood bushes would hide her from the windows in the servants' hall. The last thing she needed now was to have Martha or any of the others glimpse her flitting by when she was supposed to be sick in her bed. At last she reached the gate at the far corner of the garden. This gate was used only by the gardener, and the door was heavy and practical, with an iron padlock instead of a lock. There was also a small grated window high in the door, and with her heart racing, she stood on her toes and peeked through.

He wasn't there.

The street and the walk beside it were empty, and disappointment swamped her. She was too late. He'd given up and left, or worse, he'd changed his mind and hadn't come at all.

"Geoffrey?" she called forlornly, not really expecting an answer. She dropped back down on her heels, feeling very much back to earth.

Suddenly Geoffrey's blue eyes filled the grate. "Jēsamina?"

She gasped with relief. "So you did come!"

"I did," he said wryly. "And unlike others I might name, I was prompt about it. Perhaps even early."

"Oh, I'm so sorry, Geoffrey," she said, arching back up on her toes to be more level with him. "My grandfather was so vastly slow leaving for church, and I couldn't come downstairs until he and my aunt were—"

"Serena," Geoffrey interrupted wryly. "Forgive me, but I feel rather like the turnkey at Newgate, waiting on the other side of a locked door from you."

"One moment, if you please." With hands shaking from anticipation, she fit the oversized key into the padlock and pulled on the heavy door. At once he shoved it the rest of the way open, slipped inside, and shut it closed again.

She smiled and blushed, excited but uncharacteristically shy at the same time. He was dressed in much the same fashion as he'd worn when they'd gone riding in the park, in a red waistcoat, a black cocked hat, a blue superfine coat that made his eyes even brighter, and pale buckskin breeches, all of it tailored to fit his broad shoulders and lean hips within a breath of decency.

There was no question of decency in the way he was smiling at her, however, or in the way he was watching even the slightest movement she made. She'd been admired ever since she'd come out into Society, but she'd never had a man study her with this thoroughness or intensity. She'd no doubt that he approved—that was clear enough—but he made her feel as if she'd mislaid some of her clothing. In her haste, she supposed she had. The light silk of the sultana hid very little, and the purple sash that she'd tied so tightly around her waist must only accentuate how soft and rounded she was without the rigid control of whalebone and buckram. Too late she realized that more of her actual form and shape was visible than he or any other gentleman had ever seen, and her blush deepened.

With all that to consider, she'd overlooked the large bouquet of white roses in his hand. Sweeping his hat from his head, he made a courtly bow to her, one leg before him, and held the flowers out to her.

"For you," he said, looking up at her as he bowed. "I trust you'll find more pleasure in these roses than in the last ones I sent."

"Because of my grandfather," she said quickly, wincing inwardly at how unnecessary that was. She raised the bouquet to her face, and breathed deeply of the flowers' fragrance. She thought of telling him how she'd preserved the single battered rosebud from the first bouquet, tucked away for safekeeping upstairs in her bedchamber, but decided such an act sounded too sentimental and girlish.

"Because of your grandfather, yes," he said, rising. The morning sun was making him cast a long shadow over the path and over her. "But you deserve roses every day, if they please you. You deserve everything you wish for."

"You don't know what I wish," she said over the roses. "You can't."

His blue eyes were hooded against the sun, focusing their intensity entirely on her. When he looked at her like that, her blood raced through her veins and her entire body warmed, and her heart was beating so loudly that she was certain he could tell exactly what she wished for.

Perhaps he heard it. He smiled slowly, just enough to

reveal the rakishly lopsided dimple he had in only his left cheek.

"I can guess," he said. "Should I?"

She smiled, too, and shook her head. "You shouldn't," she said. "It wouldn't be wise."

"Unwise because I might well guess the truth?" he asked, chuckling as his gaze wandered freely up and down her person with obvious approval.

"Exactly," she said succinctly, and dipped her chin for emphasis. Ahh, he was so wickedly handsome and male that it almost hurt to look at him.

"Then I'll answer your riddle with another of my own," he said, his voice rumbling seductively low as if sharing a secret. "I would guess, my sweet Jēsamina, that your wish at this moment is exactly the same as mine."

Lightly he touched his fingertips to her lips. She held her breath as he traced the bow, and then pressed his forefinger to the plump cushion of her lower lip. Instinctively she kissed it, pressing back, and he smiled.

"The same as mine, then," he said softly, slanting his face as he leaned forward to kiss her.

But instead of offering her lips to him, she raised her hand between them and pressed her own fingers across his mouth to stop him.

"Not here," she whispered, even though there was no one to overhear. "Not when there's a chance we'll be seen. Come into the house instead."

His brows rose, questioning. "You're certain?"

"My aunt and grandfather have gone to church," she said confidently, "and nearly all of the servants are out as well, exactly as I thought they would be. That's why I asked you to arrive now."

"Clever lass," he said with approval, cupping her cheek with his hand. She turned her face to brush her lips over his palm before she pulled free.

"Let me lock the gate." She tucked the flowers beneath

her arm as she pulled the key from her pocket and turned back to the door. "It will only take a moment."

"Are you trying to make me your prisoner?" he asked, unhappy at being interrupted and not quite teasing.

"Oh, no," she said, bending to turn the key in the padlock. "It's more about keeping out thieves than keeping you in."

When she turned around again, it was clear that he hadn't been listening, but rather studying her backside as she'd bent over the lock.

"That is the most captivating attire I have ever seen on a lady," he said, his gaze still lingering well below her face. "Why can't you dress like that all the time?"

She laughed, more from nervousness than humor, and linked her fingers into his to lead him toward the house. "Because I'd be condemned to Bedlam as a madwoman for roaming about town in my dressing gown."

"Not by me," he said, hanging back to let her go before him. "My God, I could watch you walk all day."

"Me?" she said self-consciously. She thought of how often Monsieur Passard had chided her for her walk, calling it vulgar. It must be even worse now with her wearing the flat-soled slippers in place of proper heeled shoes. How could he ever admire her like this?

But he did, his eyes glowing. "Look at you," he said, marveling. "Your walk is like a dance. You're like a goddess."

She blushed again, this time with pleasure. She slipped free of his hand and spun lightly on her toes before she made a curtsey of acknowledgment. "I'm the Terpsichore of the garden, if you please."

He didn't smile. "No, you're much more like Kamadeva, the Hindu goddess of passion."

"*Kamadeva?*" she repeated wryly, skipping out of his reach and making her skirt flutter away from her bare ankles. "That could be a compliment, I suppose, except that Kamadeva is a god, not a goddess, and that he has green skin. But then, that's a common mistake for an Englishman to make, believing every name that ends in an *a* belongs to a female."

His eyes gleamed. "Just as Terpsichore was a muse, not a goddess," he said. "A common mistake for an English lady who, apparently, knows no Greek."

She raised her chin, delighting in the challenge. "The English lady knows no Greek, for she has no Greeks among her acquaintance with which to converse."

"A sorry excuse," he said, lunging to grab her.

She laughed, barely escaping, the flowers in one hand. She ducked beneath a tree's branch and danced backward, just far enough to keep from his reach. Being hunted like this was a flirtatious game, full of risk, and the thrill of not knowing exactly when he'd capture her—which, inevitably, he would, just as she wanted—made her heart race.

"An English lady requires no excuses, nor apologies," she said, breathless with excitement. "And an English gentleman never expects either one, not from a lady."

"Oh, an English gentleman has certain expectations," he said, following her slowly. "Every English lady knows that."

Before she realized it, he swiftly reached out and caught the end of her sultana's sash. He pulled the length of purple silk taut to pull the looped bow at her waist apart, then snapped it free. Freed of the sash, the dressing gown at once unfurled like the petals of a silk flower, leaving her with only her night shift covering her.

She gasped at his audacity but did not move, frozen in place as he studied her with frank appraisal. The shift's white linen was a very fine Holland, so fine as to be almost translucent, and from the look in his eyes she knew it was revealing more of her than it hid. Her breasts, her waist, her hips, and the dark patch of hair at the top of her thighs—he must be seeing everything that was usually masked by the armor of her clothing, *everything*, illuminated by the bright sunlight.

Yet far more shocking was how her body was responding to his scrutiny. Her breath quickened and her nipples tightened with arousal and there was a warmth curling low in her belly, the way it had when he'd kissed her. Despite Aunt Morley's training, she wasn't ashamed, and she made no move to pull her sultana closed and cover herself. She didn't want to hide, and she didn't want him to look away. None of it was how a proper English lady should feel, and she didn't care. All that mattered to her now was Geoffrey, and the urgency of the desire flickering like a flame between them.

"Jēsamina," he said, his voice rough and seductive and with the slightest edge of desperation. He didn't just look as if he was hungry for her; from the expression on his face, he wanted to *devour* her. "My Jēsamina."

She smiled, the only answer she could give, and brushed aside a stray wisp of hair that was tossing about her temple in the breeze. She wasn't being purposefully silent or mysterious; she was simply too overwhelmed for words.

He took a single step toward her and stopped, as if barely controlling himself. "Do you know what you do to me, Serena? Can you see it for yourself?"

"I could be blind and still know it," she said in a rush, "for you've done the same to me."

He smiled, turning his head slightly to one side, and held his hand out to her, beckoning. "Then we should be together, yes?"

"It's fate," she breathed. "Kismet."

"Passion," he said firmly. "Passion."

Her smile widened, for she understood that, too. Aunt Morley never mentioned passion, but at Sundara Manōra, the women had spoken of it incessantly as an important and undeniable part of life. She'd listened, but had never understood the power, the magic that passion represented, until now with Geoffrey.

The sudden clatter of a dropped pot and a servant's oath came from the kitchen across the garden, enough to break the moment and make Serena gasp. It was also a reminder that they'd likely already lingered here in the garden too long.

"We can't stay here," she whispered urgently. "Come, this way."

She slipped her hand into his and at once his much larger fingers swallowed hers in his grasp. She led him along the narrow outer path next to the wall, and yet the closer they came to the house, the more she felt as if he were the one leading her, and not the other way around. To her relief, the few servants remaining at home had kept indoors, and she and Geoffrey entered the house the same way that she'd left it. She pulled her hand free and turned away to latch the door after them.

"This is where we take our breakfast each morning," she said, and winced inwardly. She sounded so hopelessly *English*. She was babbling from nervous excitement, filling space with empty words. "Everything's been cleared away for the day, you see, so no one will return here again until tomorrow, and then—"

"Serena," he said softly. "Jēsamina. Hush."

She blushed and turned back to him. He seemed so much larger here in the small room, the slanting sun through the windowpanes crisscrossing over his broad shoulders. His eyes never left her, and his gaze alone made her feel almost feverish with longing. He dropped his hat onto the table and ran his fingers back through his dark hair. He shrugged his coat from his shoulders and tossed it on the back of a nearby chair, and her blush deepened. True, he still wore considerably more clothing than she did, but to see him there in his shirt-sleeves, his body defined by his close-fitting waistcoat, seemed shockingly, deliciously intimate.

Then he smiled, a dark and seductive smile. Of course none of this would be any mystery to him; she was the one who'd no notion of what should happen next.

Yet still she couldn't stop her babble. "I can send for tea, if you wish."

"No," he said, coming to stand before her. "All I want, my own sweet, is you."

He cradled her jaw with his palm, turning her face up toward him, and kissed her. Her lips welcomed him, for it felt as if she'd been waiting forever for this moment, and for him. His fingers slid back to the nape of her neck, tangling in her hair to hold her steady as he kissed her.

The possession of that kiss stunned her. His mouth was hot and demanding with a ferocity that he hadn't shown when they'd kissed before. It was as if he was claiming her in this way, marking her as his, and she longed to do the same to him in return. Shamelessly she leaned into him and circled her arms around his waist, her fingers running over the broad muscles beneath his silk waistcoat. Besides, she needed the support, for this kiss was making her head spin and her body grow warm, almost feverish, and restlessly she shifted against him.

His fingers tangled in her hair, and impatiently he yanked away the few hairpins she'd used. Her hair fell heavily down her back to her waist, and at once he brushed his cheek against it, clearly reveling in the silky dark curtain. He kissed her forehead, her nose, her cheeks.

"*Tōtā mērē, mērī jāna,*" he murmured, the beautiful Hindi endearments shimmering against her skin. "*Tuma pūrnatā haiṁ.*"

My lovebird, my darling, you are perfection. . . .

She searched his handsome face, trying not to think of how very far from perfection she was.

"Oh, Geoffrey, you do not know," she whispered. "You can never know, except how much I need you."

With a low growl by way of reply, he kissed her again, and thrust a hand inside her open sultana to find her. With only the thin linen between them, she was aware of the heat of his palm as he explored the narrowness of her waist and the swell of her hips. His hand settled and spread over her bottom, caressing the softness, and then pulled her snug against his hips and the thick, hard length of his shaft, filling the front of his breeches.

Virgin though she was, she understood. She remembered the explicit prints that had been passed about the women's quarters, and she remembered the equally explicit raillery that had accompanied them, leaving no mysteries.

But this wasn't a painted picture or a lewd jest. This was Geoffrey, and she hadn't lied: she *did* need him, more than he would likely ever know. This wasn't a surrender, or a seduction, or even an acquiescence, but a gift of pleasure that they would offer to each other. Since the afternoon in the Library when she'd invited him here, she'd anticipated this moment—this moment that was happening far too fast.

He was kissing her and she was kissing him, but somehow he had also managed to guide her to the cushioned bench near the window. She was half-lying on the bench, her head on her aunt's striped silk cushions, and he was lying with her, or rather, beside her—no, halfway on top of her.

She'd lost her slippers and her feet were bare, and the silk of her sultana had slipped down her arm to uncover her shoulder. His hand slid blindly along her leg, from her shin to over her knee, pushing aside her night shift, and she shivered with excitement as he found the inside of her bare thigh. She clung to him tightly, afraid of letting go, and still they kissed, bound by the ever-increasing fever of passion. The passion consumed them, and in the haze of growing pleasure, neither of them heard the footsteps in the hall, or the voices with them, or even the little scrape of the door's latch as it turned.

She had taken such care to lock every gate and door, except the one that mattered most. The door swung open, and over Geoffrey's shoulder she saw the single sight she hadn't wanted to see: the horrified faces of Grandpapa, Aunt Morley, and the Reverend Dr. Bracegirdle.

And for the first time she truly understood what it meant to be ruined.

CHAPTER 8

"*You were trapped*, Geoffrey," his father said with succinct disgust. "The snare was set, and you marched right into it, or at least marched as well as you could with your breeches around your knees."

"Father, please," Geoffrey said wearily. The day that had begun with such excitement and promise had deteriorated into a farcical disaster, and now, inevitably, it must end like this, in the company of his father. Of course he *had* been caught, captured along with Serena in a thoroughly compromising situation, and only the presence of that pompous clergyman had stopped her grandfather from running him through with his sword. But the last thing he needed now was a paternal lecture, or the disappointment that would come with it.

"You needn't tell me you'd told me so, Father," he continued. "I freely acknowledge that."

"Well, that is something," Father said. "Perhaps there's a small measure of contrition in you after all."

They were standing in the red drawing room before the fire in Father's house, both too agitated to sit. With the sequins and silk embroidery on his coat glinting by the firelight, Father was already dressed for their Sunday midday dinner, a meal that usually included Harry and Gus, and their younger brother, Rivers, if he was in town, plus assorted cousins and their spouses. Geoffrey supposed it was a blessing that they hadn't arrived yet, to add more witnesses to his disgrace: a small blessing, very small, but at this point, he'd take whatever came his way.

"I'm well aware of the situation, Father," he said, "and of what I have done, so there's no need—"

"What *you* have done?" Father exclaimed. "The strumpet deserves at least half the blame."

Geoffrey struggled to keep his temper in check. Losing it now would accomplish nothing—but damnation, it would be impossible if Father insisted on provoking him.

He took a deep breath, then another, before he spoke as calmly as he could. "Pray recall, Father, that Miss Carew is a lady, not a strumpet."

"Very well, then. She is a lady who has behaved like a strumpet." Father glared at him, the flames from the hearth reflected in his eyes. "Regardless, I hope she pleased you well enough, since you will be wedded to her for the remainder of your lives."

There it was, spelled out as plain as was possible and more than enough to send a chill down his spine. *Marriage*. He hadn't wanted to marry anyone, not yet, and neither did she, but after this morning, he had no other honorable choice. As Father had said, they both were trapped, and the grim certainty of their situation was settling on Geoffrey with a wave of bitterness and regret.

"You must ask for her hand as soon as is possible," Father continued, unaware of Geoffrey's thoughts. "Not today, of course. I doubt Allwyn would permit you within a mile of his house. But write to him this evening, asking permission to call upon him. Let him determine the time, and by God, be prompt, whatever he says."

"May I assume I have your approval?" Geoffrey asked, unable to keep the unhappiness from his voice.

"You do," Father said curtly. "The honor of our family demands that, doesn't it?"

"Most likely old Allwyn will say the same."

"You'd best hope he does," Father said. "I'm not convinced he won't put his own pride before the lady's reputation, and refuse your suit outright."

Geoffrey frowned. He hadn't considered that, but given the marquis's wrath this morning, it was a distinct possibility. "He'd be a fool if he did that."

Shrewdly Father raised his brows and feigned surprise. "And here I thought you'd no wish to marry."

Damnation, Geoffrey thought, he'd blundered into that one. "I am attempting to behave honorably, and put Miss Carew first."

"You should have remembered that pretty notion before you left home this morning." Father said, tapping his fingers on the edge of the mantel while he thought. "Still and all, I'll grant you that this is far from the worst match you could have made, whatever the circumstances. I do not care for the lady's boor of a grandfather, but her family is respectable, and she'll bring you a decent fortune. There's no denying she's a beauty, too. His Majesty will be pleased to see you settled, and I'm sure the gossips will declare it to be a good pairing for you both."

Geoffrey gave a derisive little snort. "Their opinion has always been my first consideration."

"Often it must be, where a lady's virtue is concerned," Father said. "Truly, what is a good name, except the fortuitous report of a hundred other tattling folk?"

He sighed deeply, the first small sign that he might share a part of Geoffrey's misery. "Would you join me in a brandy?"

Geoffrey nodded, and watched his father cross the room, pour the brandy himself, and return with the two crystal glasses. He handed one to Geoffrey, and raised his own glass, the liquor golden.

"To Miss Carew," he said. "May she bring you joy and contentment as your wife."

"To Miss Carew," Geoffrey echoed, but without his father's enthusiasm.

It was impossible for him to forget his last memory of Serena from this morning: her face pale and streaked with tears, her dark hair wild and tangled, and her yellow dressing gown billowing around her as her aunt and a maidservant had half-dragged her from the room.

He'd done that to her. She'd invited him there, but he was the one who should have known better, who should have considered her innocence, who shouldn't have let himself be blinded by raging lust. Even now he recalled the taste of her lips, the lush softness of her body beneath his, the honey-sweet fragrance of her blossoming desire; if he wasn't careful, he'd be hard again from the memory alone.

But desire was only part of her attraction. He was fascinated by the air of wary vulnerability that surrounded her, and the mystery she wore like her sapphires. She'd come to trust him, a trust he treasured all the more because he realized how rarely it was given.

And then this morning he'd betrayed that trust, and taken nearly every advantage she'd offered. It didn't matter that she'd invited him to take the liberties he had; she was the innocent and a lady at that, and he should have been the one to know better. He could try to make it up to her by asking for her hand, but he wasn't sure that would be enough.

And the longer he stood here with his father, thinking of Serena, the more he came to realize that marriage might not be such an odious thing. He didn't want her to refuse, and he didn't want her grandfather to deny him, either. He wanted Serena to say yes, because he wanted her to be his wife.

True, this wasn't the most romantic of circumstances—

but then, few noble marriages in their circle were. Most were carefully arranged alliances for money and power, and marriages based on love like his parents' had been, and how Harry's and Gus's was now, were rare. He was certain that with time, he and Serena could find love, too. They were friends already, which would make for an agreeable start, and God only knew there was passion between them.

"Drink up," his father said. "The lady deserves it from you."

Chagrined at being caught so lost in thought, Geoffrey quickly raised his glass, and drank. "She deserves far more than that."

"I am glad to hear you say so." Father nodded. "You're hardly the first groom who didn't wait for the banns to try to claim his bride. Consider your brother. I've no wish to slander his delightful Augusta, but Harry did test those waters more deeply than he should have before they were betrothed. If you and Miss Carew are rewarded with as fortuitous an outcome as those two, then you'll be happy indeed."

Geoffrey didn't answer, staring into his brandy. There could not be two women who were less alike than the freckle-faced, practical Gus and his elegant, exotic Serena. By all reports, Gus had as much as saved Harry's life, and for that alone she could do no wrong in Father's eyes. If he was expecting Serena to make the same sort of cheery, capable addition to the family, then she was bound to disappoint. It didn't help that Gus was always regarded as a paragon of virtue, while Father was already judging Serena to be a strumpet.

No, the only way Serena could rival Gus in Father's eyes was to produce a son first, a little heir to his precious dukedom. The irony of that was unmistakable: before marriage, ladies were to be kept virtuously untouched, but from the wedding night onward, the sooner they could be gotten with child (and preferably a male child), the better.

"I'll have the family's jewels brought out of safekeeping tomorrow," Father was saying, "so you can choose something suitable for a betrothal ring. The Fitzroy women have acquired a veritable hoard of baubles over the years. You're sure to find a jewel for your lady."

"Thank you, no," Geoffrey said. "I already know the ring I wish for her."

Father shook his head. "You should not turn away from the family pieces, Geoffrey. From what I've observed, your Miss Carew already wears a fortune in jewels of her own. You'll have to go deep into your pockets to buy a ring to impress a lady like that. You're going to have expenses enough setting up housekeeping without—"

"I'll manage, Father," he said firmly. He didn't doubt it, either, even without considering Serena's fortune. "*We* shall manage."

Slowly Father smiled, the first time he'd done so since Geoffrey had told him what had happened earlier, and patted him on the shoulder.

"Win the lady first," he said. "That will be the real challenge. After that, the rest should come easily."

Serena had been certain that being discovered with Geoffrey had been the most humiliating moment of her life. Grandpapa's fury, Aunt Morley's unhappiness, Geoffrey swearing, and her in the middle of it, trying to explain, trying to pull her clothes back to rights, and trying not to weep with frustration and mortification as they'd pulled her away from Geoffrey. Geoffrey, dearest Geoffrey: that had been the hardest part, knowing that the price of such a magical morning might be that she would never see him again.

But that had been only the beginning.

Considering her disgrace sufficiently serious to be a family affair, Grandpapa had summoned his eldest son and heir to join him. Serena's father had felt no love for his brother, and Serena remembered how he'd said this animosity had been part of the reason he'd so happily left England behind.

Serena understood why: she found Uncle Radnor to be self-righteous and ambitious to improve his station in society, full of bullying bravado and an arrogance that easily turned to cruelty. In turn her uncle had made no secret of how little use or affection he had for her. It was a considerable relief to her that her uncle did not live with them, but in his own lodgings in Hanover Square; whenever he came to his father's house he would slyly tease and belittle her out of Grandpapa's hearing, trying to reduce her to tears for his own amusement. But it was her guilt that had always given his torment a special edge, her fear that somehow he knew her secret. As long as Grandpapa lived, she'd be safe, but she dreaded what could become of her when Uncle Radnor became the Marquis of Allwyn, and her guardian.

His appearance at the house that Sunday afternoon had only made everything worse. Her aunt had been accused of failing at her duty, and not included in the meeting between the two men. It was likely just as well for Aunt Morley. Behind closed doors, they had quarreled loudly over her; Serena had heard their raised voices all the way in her bedchamber. Uncle Radnor had been furious, and denounced her as a slattern and a whore with such vehemence that even Grandpapa, as angry as he was, had been forced to defend her. It had been enough to make Serena grateful to be shut away in her rooms and out of her uncle's path while he and her grandfather decided her fate.

Yet that decision, if it had been made, was not shared with her. For the last three days, she had been locked alone in her bedchamber, and her meals brought to her. But this morning, while her grandfather was out, her uncle had gone too far. Refusing to believe that Serena was still a virgin, he had brought a grim-faced midwife and her assistant, each wearing a white cap and apron, to Serena's rooms, and ordered them to determine the truth.

Horrified, Serena had tried to refuse, but the two women were larger and stronger, and apparently accustomed to such scenes. Together they pushed her onto her back on her bed, and though she kicked and flailed and screamed for help, they held her fast. The midwife tossed up her skirts and pushed apart her legs, and without ceremony shoved her fingers deep inside her. Serena had gasped and bucked at the invasion, but it was over quickly. The midwife nodded, wiping her fingers on her apron—something she hadn't bothered to do before she'd assaulted Serena.

"You—you are *vile*!" Serena said, her cheeks flaming with mortification over what had just been done to her. She sat upright, curling her legs beneath her, and yanked her skirts back over her legs and held them tightly at her ankles. "I shall report you to the constables for what you have done to me!"

"Then you'll have to report His Lordship, too, miss, for I only acted on his orders," the midwife said, unperturbed. She opened the door, and Lord Radnor joined them.

"Miss Carew is still a maid, my lord," she proclaimed with inflated authority. "There's no doubt of it. Her maidenhead's tight as a drum, and I'll swear to it in any court you wish."

"That won't be necessary, Mrs. Powell," he said, pressing a coin into the woman's palm. "The footman will show you out."

The women curtseyed, and as they passed through the

door, Aunt Morley appeared, with Serena's frightened maidservant behind her.

"What has happened, Serena?" she asked sternly, and then saw Lord Radnor. "Radnor, why are you in Serena's bedchamber? You have no right to be here."

"Go away, Aunt," Radnor ordered. "This is none of your affair."

"It most certainly is," she said staunchly, trying to press her way into the room. "I could hear all manner of disturbances clear from my rooms even before poor Martha came to fetch me. Serena, tell me. What manner of—"

"I told you to leave us," Radnor snarled, and rudely shoved her backward. He closed the door and latched it, ignoring Lady Morley's indignant protests on the other side, and turned back to where Serena was still sitting huddled on the bed.

"You shouldn't treat her like that," Serena said as fiercely as she could. She was almost more shocked by what he'd just done to her aunt than what he'd ordered done to her. "Villain! You wouldn't have dared do any of this if Grandpapa were home."

"You should be grateful I did not stay in here to watch those women go about their work," he said, coming to stand over her. "I would have been in my rights to do so, as a witness."

"You are *wicked*," she said, striving to use her anger and be brave, and not to cower away from him. He seemed enormous, dressed in a costly dark green suit and looming over her. He was a tall man with a powerful build, much like her father had been. In fact it was that likeness that disturbed her the most, for Uncle Radnor had Father's face as well as coloring, and even the timbre of his voice was similar. But while Father's face had always been filled with joy and love and roguish charm, her uncle's was twisted with scorn and arrogance and a darkness that frightened her, especially now.

"You'll see," she continued, her voice trembling. "Aunt Morley will summon the footmen, and they'll break that lock open."

"Why should they do that?" he asked contemptuously. "One day I will be their master, and if they challenge me now, they can be sure their places will be gone. No, we will not be disturbed, niece, and you will listen to what I have to say."

In spite of her intentions not to be afraid, she shrank away from him. Her heart was pounding, and she felt almost sick with dread.

"You have been a shame and an embarrassment to this family from the day you were carried from that East India man," he began. "If it had been up to me, you wouldn't have been allowed into this house, but sent to an institution where you would have had the decency to die far from the the rest of us. But instead my father chose to coddle you here, a parasite and a constant reminder of my brother's vile infatuation with that heathen foreign land."

She would not cry, not before him, and as resolutely as she could she raised her chin in trembling defiance.

"I am not a parasite," she said, her voice quavering more than she wanted. "My father provided for me before he died."

"Money that should have gone into the estate, not to you," he said, the bitterness in his eyes welling into open hatred. "My God, what was Thomas thinking, to squander such a sum on a wretched little harlot like you?"

"He did it because he loved me!" she cried. "Because I was his daughter, and he *loved* me!"

"Love," he repeated scornfully. "How like your father you are, Serena, weak and romantic. No doubt Fitzroy seduced you in the name of love. How many empty promises did he have to make to you before you spread your legs for him?"

She gasped, hating to hear him speak so of Geoffrey. "He never did that, never. He was far too honorable."

He drew back, sneering as if her words had a foul smell.

"To my mind, there are only two ways for you to repair the damage you have done to this family's name," he said. "You can marry Fitzroy—"

"*No!*" she exclaimed, at once imagining the perfect disaster of being married to Geoffrey, of his family's resentment, of how out of place she'd be, of how her secret could be revealed horrifically if she presented the Duke of Breconridge with a dark-skinned grandchild. But now, too, she also imagined how humiliating such a possibility would be for Geoffrey, having to acknowledge such a wife and child as his own. Her entire life might be a lie, but she didn't want to inflict that kind of dreadful deceit on him. He didn't deserve it, not at all.

"I cannot marry him," she said, despair creeping into her voice. "I can't."

"It would have been easier to coerce Fitzroy if he'd taken your virginity," Radnor continued as if she hadn't spoken. "Or better yet, if he'd gotten you with his bastard. Without that trump, and considering his disreputable family's lack of honor, it may be impossible to persuade him to take you."

"But you don't understand," she said, urgency now combined with her fear. "Lord Geoffrey does not wish to marry, me or any other lady at this time, and neither do I."

He wrapped his hand around the post of her bed, leaning slightly toward her. "It is you who does not understand, Serena. I despise the Fitzroys as much as Father does. However, I desire a place at Court. Your Lord Geoffrey's father is as thick as can be with His Majesty. It would help my suit immeasurably if you were the duke's daughter-in-law. We would all be as . . . family."

She bowed her head, her thoughts racing. Her uncle must not know her secret after all; if he did, he'd never suggest this marriage. But knowing his reason only increased her peril. If the truth of who she truly was ever came out, then he'd be blamed as well, and he'd never, ever forgive her.

"I can't marry Lord Geoffrey, Uncle Radnor," she said, her head still bowed over her knees. "I cannot."

"Then perhaps you would prefer the alternative," her uncle said sharply, a vein in his forehead below the front of his wig pulsing with displeasure. "It would be easy enough to make you simply vanish completely. I know of an esteemed physician who would be willing to accept you as a patient."

"But I am not ill," she protested. "I'm in perfect health."

"Of course you would say that," her uncle said, smiling. "Yet I'm sure that the physician would consider both your irrational behavior and the wantonness that is so unnatural for a lady of our family, and declare your wits are unsettled. He would suggest a lengthy treatment at his private asylum in Lancastershire, a place that welcomes inconvenient ladies like yourself until they regain their wits and decorum. Sadly, so few of them do."

She gasped, stunned, and stared at him in horror. How misguided she'd been to believe that she was her own mistress because her father had left her his fortune! Her dream of being Geoffrey's lover and then traveling on her own abroad had been no more than a fool's fancy. This was her reality, harsh and unrelenting. Her grandfather was an elderly man. After his death, she would become her uncle's ward, and the law declared that she'd have no rights as an unwed woman. He would have all the control, and always would.

"An asylum," she repeated, reeling. "A *madhouse*! Grandpapa would never believe you or your charlatan of a physician. He would never have me committed to such a place!"

"He would if he believed a stay there could help you, Serena," he said. "He remembers all too well when your father began to behave in outrageous ways, until at last he was lost to us forever."

"*No!*" she exclaimed, denying everything. "You are the mad one, Uncle, for only a madman would say such evil things."

He nodded, his smile chilly and without humor. "It is entirely your decision to make, my dear niece, and the consequences will be yours as well. My advice is to choose wisely."

"Radnor!" Her grandfather's voice sounded crossly from the other side of the door as he rattled the latch. "What the devil are you doing in there? Why is this door locked? I'll have no doors locked against me in my own house!"

Her uncle glanced at her one more time and opened the door.

"I'm sorry, Father," he said mildly. "I suppose it was stuck. You should tell your housekeeper to oil your locks more frequently."

"Damn the locks." Grandpapa pushed past him and into the room. "Are you well, Serena? Your aunt said Radnor was causing you some, ah, some distress."

Aunt Morley was in the hall, peering anxiously through the half-open door, with several servants behind her.

Serena sucked in her breath. If she repeated everything that her uncle had just said to her, he would simply deny it. Worse, she would appear the irrational one, and play exactly into his scheme.

"I am perfectly well, Grandpapa," she said carefully, without looking at her aunt. "I'm not distressed in the least."

Her grandfather nodded, clearly relieved. "I am glad

of it, Serena, most glad. I want you in fine spirits." He pulled a letter from his pocket, holding it up for her to see. "That rogue Fitzroy has written, asking permission to call and address me. I have put off my reply for two days, but I cannot avoid it any longer."

"Address you?" asked Serena, not understanding. "Address you how?"

"Don't be thick, Serena," he said grimly. "There's only one decent way this entire wretched adventure of yours can be resolved, and Fitzroy is showing himself more of a gentleman than I credited. He is coming to do the honorable thing, and ask for your hand in marriage. And by God, if he pleases me, I intend to give it to him."

The following afternoon, Geoffrey sat alone in Lord Allwyn's empty parlor, waiting for the marquis to join him. He had (uncharacteristically) made such a point of being prompt that he had arrived a quarter hour earlier than the time that Allwyn had written. Now he'd nothing to do but remain as calm as he could, and pray that the old man would not make this conversation any more difficult than it needed to be, so that he could once again see Serena.

He had thought of her incessantly since they'd been forced apart. It had been no surprise that she hadn't written to him, and he hadn't tried to send word to her, knowing how closely she must be being watched. He imagined her kept as a virtual prisoner, locked away in the house since Sunday, and he could only hope her aunt and grandfather were not being too harsh with her.

He, on the other hand, had gone about his life as usual, albeit cautiously, expecting that the winds of gossip had seized upon him and Serena. He'd been prepared, even eager, to defend her name and her virtue, but to his amazement, no one had said a word to him.

From his club to the playhouse to the park, he didn't hear a single whisper about what could have become the season's *scandale célèbre,* nor was there a single breathless syllable of it in any of the news-sheets. He'd been certain that the clergyman who'd accompanied Allwyn would have told at least one person what he'd witnessed—in Geoffrey's experience, clerics were among the most judgmental of tattles—but somehow this one had held his tongue. And what of the servants? They were always whispering what they'd seen to people outside the house.

He was relieved, of course, but mystified as well. Because of his father's rank and place at Court and his family's royal blood, the Fitzroys were often in the public eye. He was accustomed to the attention, to being peered at by strangers and seeing his name reduced to initials and dashes in popular journals. As a result, he couldn't understand how the son of the Duke of Breconridge and the wealthiest, unwed titled lady in London had been caught together in a compromising situation and yet somehow had completely escaped the notice of the world. There was no sense to it, but at least it might make this conversation with Serena's grandfather less of an ordeal.

Or, if he was to believe his father, it might make it easier for Allwyn to refuse his suit outright.

Geoffrey reached into the pocket of his waistcoat where he'd put the betrothal ring for safekeeping, giving the leather-covered box an extra little pat of reassurance. He hadn't wanted Serena to wear a ring that carried another woman's story, even if the woman had been his own mother. He wanted this ring to be hers alone, and one that reflected her, too.

This ring did. The center stone was a glorious oval golden-yellow topaz from Brazil by way of Portugal, and once the jeweler had shown him that, the rest had been easy to decide. The topaz had been surrounded with diamonds, which were set in silver to make the stones brighter, and the band was yellow gold, fashioned into a wreath of flowers that could very well have been jasmine. The topaz was like a concentration of the clearest sunshine, bright and intense, and its golden glow reminded him of the amber fire in Serena's eyes. No other woman in London had eyes like hers, and no other woman would wear this ring, either, and he smiled to think of slipping it on her finger.

He heard the door open behind him, and immediately he turned and bowed as Lord Allwyn entered the room. He was determined to be respectful and obliging to the old man, knowing that Serena would be his reward afterward.

As he rose, however, he saw that Allwyn wasn't alone, but flanked by a large, stern-faced, glowering gentleman: Lord Radnor, his older son and heir and Serena's uncle. Now he understood why Allwyn had given himself three days before they met: not to cool his temper, but to bring in his son from the country as reinforcement.

Damnation, if he'd known the marquis was going to play things this way, he would have brought his brothers with him.

"Good day, Fitzroy," Allwyn said, already sounding testy. "I'm glad to see you're man enough to answer for your misdeeds."

"I am honored by your invitation, Lord Allwyn," Geoffrey said, striving to sound pleasant, as if this were any other social call. "Lord Radnor. Good day to you both."

"It's hardly a good day when my brother's only daughter is debauched by a scoundrel," Lord Radnor began heatedly. "When I think upon how—"

"None of that, Radnor," Allwyn said, raising his hand. "Let us see first if Lord Geoffrey is prepared to do what an honorable gentleman must."

Geoffrey nodded. He fully intended to be an honorable gentleman; and he didn't doubt that he was the only civilized one in the room, either.

"Indeed I have, Lord Allwyn," he said, falling back into the little speech he'd rehearsed earlier. "I have the greatest admiration and regard for Miss Carew, and I dare to hope that she is not adverse to my attentions. I have in fact formed such an attachment for the lady, that I come to you now to ask for the honor of her hand in marriage."

There, he'd said it, the words he'd never thought to utter, or at least not for another ten years. If he'd expected to be congratulated on his bravery (which, fortunately, he hadn't), then he was sure to be disappointed. But if he'd likewise hoped to receive a swift affirmative to his request (which he rather had), followed by being ushered through the next set of doors to the prize that was Serena, then that was another disappointment.

Instead, the Allwyn men continued to stare at him in a menacing silence, as if he'd just made the most dastardly of declarations. While Geoffrey's inclination was to say more to fill that yawning, unpleasant silence, he didn't. He'd already said what was necessary. Anything more wouldn't be.

Finally the marquis made a gruff grunt.

"You surprise me, Fitzroy," he said grudgingly. "I would've wagered against you stepping forward like this. Not that it changes my opinion of you in the least. You aren't my first choice for my granddaughter's hand, and never will be."

Geoffrey gave a small nod of acknowledgment, not agreement. "My wife will want for nothing," he said. "My estate is—"

"Your estate is well enough," Allwyn said. "I've already had my people look into that. At least I know you're not after Serena's fortune."

"Not at all," Geoffrey said. He was likely the only gentleman she'd met in town who wasn't.

"No, I've no doubt you'll keep her well enough," Allwyn continued. "It's your honor that I doubt."

"My honor has never been in question, Lord Allwyn," Geoffrey said, sharpness creeping into his voice. He sensed that the marquis was purposefully goading him, yet he was finding it impossible not to respond. "If you can find one instance—"

"Oh, come, come, Fitzroy," the marquis said. "It's not a question of a single *instance*. Your entire family is riddled and rotten with dishonorable doings. You can't deny it. Even your father's dukedom was founded on whoring."

"Lord Allwyn," Geoffrey said curtly. He had purposefully not worn a sword to this meeting, but now he wished he had. "I cannot let you refer to the first duchess in that way."

The old marquis's eyes glinted with smugness. "You can't, eh? Could you deny that she was made a duchess without a duke, a whore's price for sharing the king's bed?"

"Lord Allwyn," he said, biting each syllable even as his fingers clutched at his side where his sword should be. "If you continue in this fashion, I shall be compelled to defend my family's honor in the only way a gentleman can."

"Your family's *honor,*" scoffed Lord Radnor disdainfully. "I should scarcely believe that merits your defense."

"To me it does," Geoffrey retorted. "Nor do I see that Miss Carew has thus far suffered from her connection to me or my family."

"That's only because no one knows of it yet," Lord Radnor said. "We've kept word of your iniquity to this house, not for the sake of my slatternly niece, but for the good of the entire family. Our people, our servants, are loyal to us. It's you who shall benefit from a connection with us. We're not like you Fitzroys, parading your dirty shifts and shirts about for all the world to—"

"Radnor, enough," the marquis said. "Serena is no slattern, and never has been. It's this fellow who led her astray, and now he must make good on his actions."

The older man's gaze hadn't left Geoffrey's face. "Would you defend your wife's honor with the same fervor? Would you run through any rascal who spoke ill of her?"

So that was the old man's game. At least Geoffrey could answer his question with perfect honesty.

"I would, Lord Allwyn," he said. "Not only because the lady would be a member of my family, but, most important, because she would be my wife."

The marquis nodded. "Serena has suffered much in her life," he said, his face losing its flintiness as he mentioned his granddaughter. "To lose both her parents in the fashion she has, and to have endured so much that a young lady shouldn't in that heathen part of the world. She's never spoken the half of it, I know, but still it breaks my heart to think of her alone in that dreadful foreign place."

The emotion in his voice touched Geoffrey, and he thought of the sorrow he himself had sometimes glimpsed in Serena's eyes.

"I would do all in my power to see that my wife never suffers," he said, and as soon as he spoke the words, he realized how much he meant them. "Above all things, I would want to make her happy."

The marquis leaned a fraction closer. "Would you swear to that?" he demanded gruffly. "On your honor, on your life, on your family's name, such as it is? Would you give up whoring and the rest of your rakish ways for the sake of your wife?"

Geoffrey didn't hesitate. "I would, Lord Allwyn," he said firmly. He wasn't at all sure exactly what was entailed by such a promise, or how he would keep it, but for Serena's sake, he would find a way. "For Miss Carew, you have my word that I will."

Allwyn nodded again. "You had better keep that pledge," he warned. "Because if I ever learn that you've hurt her, Fitzroy, or betrayed her in any way, then by God, I shall hunt you down. And if I am no longer on this earth, then my son shall act for me."

To Geoffrey's surprise, the marquis seized his hand and shook it.

"There," he said, pumping Geoffrey's hand. "As two gentlemen should. You're still not my choice for my granddaughter, but she's as headstrong as her father was before her. She has decided upon you, and I must agree. You see, I believe in making her happy as well."

He laughed, a strange sort of guffaw that his son echoed, and uneasily Geoffrey joined them.

"You do not wish to have me as your enemy," Lord Radnor said with a grimace of a smile, taking his turn to shake Geoffrey's hand. "We shall do much better as family, and as allies."

"Indeed," Geoffrey said, finding both prospects singularly unpleasant. He was determined to make everything work out as it should with Serena in the future, for he'd no wish to be confronted like this again by her male relatives. Which was, of course, the point of this entire conversation, but it was a damnably queasy way to be welcomed into the family.

"So Miss Carew will approve of my suit?" he asked, just to make certain. "She will give me the, ah, answer I seek?"

"If the answer you is seek 'yes,' then you'll have it," Allwyn said briskly. "Serena knows her duty."

Duty was not a word Geoffrey ever wished to associate with a proposal of marriage. Given the circumstances, however, it did not seem wise to object.

"Is there an agreeable time when I might call upon Miss Carew?" he asked instead, the safer course.

"Call upon her now," Allwyn said, still watching Geoffrey with all the charity of a wary old hawk. "She is in the garden, waiting for you. I daresay you already know the way, eh?"

He did, but decided that a silent bow was likely the safest course, especially with Radnor once again grim-faced. If Allwyn was the hawk, then his son was more the buzzard, ready to pounce on whatever random carrion was left behind.

"Address her as you please, Lord Geoffrey," the marquis continued. "You may prattle whatever honeyed words you choose. I know you must have a stock of them. But that is all. No more of your rakish tricks before you're wed. Mind you, we shall be watching you from the window to make certain you don't."

Geoffrey had had enough of this, and he'd no reason to linger in such company. He bowed one last time and left them, following the footman to the door that led to the garden—not through the small parlor where he'd been with Serena, but through the grander entrance in the center hall.

Instantly he felt relieved to be free of the house and its overbearing inhabitants, and he took a deep breath that he hadn't realized he'd needed. He glanced up at the sky, the clear blue framed by the surrounding houses. He was going to propose to Serena, and she was going to say yes, and become Lady Geoffrey Fitzroy. She'd be his wife, there at his side for the rest of their lives, and the mother of his children.

He felt all manner of lurching butterflies in his belly at the momentous step he was about to take, at all the responsibilities and commitments that being a married man entailed. Then he thought of Serena herself, and all the butterflies vanished. This was *right,* and he realized how very much he wanted it, and her.

He walked down into the garden, past the first row of boxwood, and there, at last, was his prize.

Serena.

CHAPTER 9

As soon as Geoffrey walked down the steps to the garden, he saw Serena, sitting on a carved bench, her aunt beside her. Lady Morley was holding an old stocking out to her black spaniel, and the small dog was growling fiercely as he tugged and worried the stretching stocking. Lady Morley was chuckling, urging her pet on, but it was clear Serena wasn't sharing her amusement.

Far from it. She was sitting with her hands folded in her lap, her back straight and not touching the bench; on her head was a wide-brimmed straw hat, tied at her nape to slant over her face. She was dressed entirely in white, which Geoffrey guessed was intended to make her appear more demure and virginal, or perhaps penitent. He didn't care for it; the white diminished her somehow, and he preferred her in the bright, more intense (if unfashionable) colors that she usually favored. It was as if his brilliant butterfly had been reduced to a pale, papery moth.

But the closer he came, the more he could see how it wasn't just her clothes. Her face was pale as well, her golden skin turned almost sallow, and her amber-colored eyes were uncharacteristically ringed with shadows making them flat and expressionless. He was accustomed to seeing a touch of sadness or melancholy in her expression, but not the abject misery he found there now. With concern he wondered what her family had done or said to her by way of a punishment to reduce her to this condition, and he wondered, too, what he could do to relieve it.

"Good day to you, Lord Geoffrey," Lady Morley said, granting him a slight nod as she rose from the bench. The little dog jumped up to the place she'd been sitting and leaped into her arms, where she turned him on his back and cradled him like a fat, furry baby. "Such a pleasant day, is it not?"

She was doing her best to make it seem as if they all were in fact back in the days when he would meet the two ladies in the park, as if nothing else had happened in the meantime. But there was sadness behind her smile as well, and a disappointment behind her determination to be cheerful.

"Good day, Lady Morley," he said. He raised his hat to her, even as he couldn't keep his gaze from sliding back to Serena. "I trust Fanfan is well?"

"Oh, yes, he's in splendid fettle, as you can see for yourself," she said, giving the dog a fond pat on his rounded belly. "But you did not come here to visit with me, or Fanfan, either. Serena, my dear, Lord Geoffrey has come to call upon you."

Slowly Serena rose from the bench to face Geoffrey, and sank into a curtsey before him like a white-petaled flower crushing to the ground.

"Good day, Lord Geoffrey," she murmured with her head bowed to avoid meeting his eye. There was misery in her voice as well, misery and unhappiness nearly beyond bearing.

"Well, then, Fanfan and I will leave you to each other," Lady Morley said. "But I shall not be far away, Lord Geoffrey, and I will ask you be most decorous in your attentions to my niece."

She smiled purposefully, and retreated toward the house, Fanfan in her arms. Geoffrey assumed she went inside; but he did not know for certain, because he couldn't look away from Serena, her head still bowed and hidden by the brim of her hat.

"*Jēsamina,*" he said softly. They were too far away from the house's open windows to be overheard, yet the knowledge that they were being watched made him lower his voice just the same. "Will you not look at me?"

Slowly she raised her chin, and her gaze with it. Now he could see how her eyes were red-rimmed from weeping. Of course she would have shed tears; the brimming unhappiness in her eyes must have spilled over at some point.

"I'm sorry," he said, an all-encompassing apology for having put her in this situation, for contributing to her suffering; even, perhaps, for first approaching her and asking her to dance for the sake of a wager. He hadn't needed the promise to her grandfather to make him wish to make her happy. He had felt that way toward her almost from the beginning. "I'm sorry for everything."

"You needn't apologize," she said swiftly. "You did nothing that merited it. No matter what Grandpapa and my—my *uncle* said to you in the house, there is no blame, no fault that can ever be attached to you."

He was taken aback by the vehemence in her words.

"They were somewhat forceful in their arguments, yes," he admitted. "But I would venture the reason is that they care very much for your welfare."

"My uncle does not care for me," she said, and for the first time he saw the familiar spark light her golden eyes. "All Uncle Radnor cares about is that I bring no shame to him, or his place in the world. My father despised him. He called his brother the worst kind of bully, and he *is*. I despise him, too."

Abruptly she turned away, again hiding her face from him. She should be resting her face against his chest instead, with his arms around her to comfort her.

"Walk with me," he urged. "Please."

She shook her head. "We shouldn't."

"Please, Serena," he said. "It will be much better than standing here like a pair of stone statues."

She sighed restlessly. "We must stay in sight, or else they'll come out and hunt you down."

"They wouldn't dare," he said, even though he didn't exactly believe it himself. Her father had been right: her uncle did have all the marks of a prime bully, and no matter how Radnor had shaken his hand, Geoffrey suspected he would like nothing more than an excuse to try to pound him to an insensible pulp. But he'd risk it for Serena, and he held his hand out to her.

"We'll walk back and forth across this path," he said, "six paces one way, six paces the other. Not even I can be accused of seducing you like that."

She stared down at his offered hand for a long moment. "We cannot touch," she said at last. "But I will walk beside you."

She folded her arms over her chest as if to remind her wayward hands to keep from his, and began to walk, taking two quick short steps before Geoffrey joined her.

"They did not believe me when I said you hadn't ruined me," she said, the words tight and bitter. "Uncle Radnor was the worst. He called me a slattern and a whore, and—and many other things. It was not pleasant."

Anger swept through Geoffrey, but for her sake he kept his voice calm. "He had no right to call you any of that."

He wasn't sure she heard him.

"It was his idea to send for a midwife to examine me," she continued. "He accepted her word over mine that I was still a virgin."

"Damnation, Serena, that is unspeakable," he said, appalled. If for no other reason, he should marry her just to remove her from her dreadful family. "That he would humiliate you like that because of his own—"

"It is done," she said, with a resolution that left no opening for further discussion. "I know why you've come today, Geoffrey, just as I know it's not what either of us want."

"Perhaps it is," he said slowly. "What of kismet?"

She glanced at him sharply. "This would not be kismet. This would be my grandfather and my uncle forcing their will upon us."

"Fate, and kismet, can take circuitous paths to the same place," he said. "You can see it as coercion, or as that different path."

She shook her head, unconvinced. "You are not obliged to follow their demands."

"But I am," he said. "By my honor as a gentleman, and by my regard for you."

"Please don't, Geoffrey," she said, looking down. He could hear the warble of more tears in her voice, equaled by the determination not to shed them. "If you ask, then I must say yes. That is what my grandfather wants."

He reached into his pocket and drew out a clean handkerchief. He'd learned long ago, from his father, to always carry a spare or two for occasions such as this one, and he offered it to her now. She looked at the snowy handkerchief marked with his monogram and sniffed, then shook her head, refusing it. From that sniff, he believed he knew better, and gently tucked the white linen square into the crook of her arm. Startled by his touch, she looked down, and after a moment she plucked the handkerchief free and used it to blot her eyes. She didn't thank him; he didn't expect it, either.

"Your grandfather seemed to believe you would welcome my, ah, attentions," he said ruefully. "After everything that has passed between us, I rather believed that was the case as well."

She shook her head again, pressing his now-damp handkerchief into a tight ball of linen in her palm. "I wished to be your lover, to belong to you in that way, as you would to me. I never wanted to be your wife."

He considered this, chagrined. He'd always thought that when the time came for him to wed, the lady he chose would be eager to marry him. He'd never imagined this unequivocal refusal.

"It is possible to be both, you know," he said, striving to turn her argument around. "For every gentleman I know who keeps a mistress, I could name another who cannot wait to return home each night to the happiness he finds with his lady-wife. I've witnessed it within my own family, with my cousins and my father and older brother. I see no reason for us to be any—"

"My father loved his concubines far more than his wife," she shot back. "That was never in question."

Surely she must be the only lady in town who would manage to introduce concubines into a marriage proposal. Still, it also explained her reluctance. If she'd witnessed how her father had neglected her mother in favor of his mistresses, then she'd every right to be wary of marriage.

"When I marry," he countered, "I don't intend to keep a mistress or a concubine. I dare to hope I'll be sufficiently content with my wife."

The look she gave him showed she did not believe him, and worse, was faintly pitying him for being naïve.

"You will not persuade me, Geoffrey," she said. "Especially not with an argument like that."

"Even for the sake of love?"

"This has nothing to do with love," she said wistfully. "How can it?"

She was right, of course. To the best of his knowledge, what existed between them wasn't love, not in the grand poetical sense—or at least it wasn't love yet. He liked

Serena; he liked her very much. He thought about her constantly when they were apart, he relished her conversation and company, he desired her more than he had any other woman, enough to have gotten himself into this mess in the first place. But he wasn't in love with her, not enough to make a comment like that. He didn't know what had made him say it, anyway, and he deserved her rebuff. But in some perverse way, the more determined she became to refuse him, the more he wanted to marry her. "Yet if I ask you, will you say yes?"

"I will, because I *must,*" she said, her unhappiness and desperation clear. "Because I have no *choice*. Oh, Geoffrey, can't you understand? You should marry some cheerful, fair-haired lady who will give you fat-cheeked sons and daughters with golden curls. *That* is who will make you content. You deserve a lady who is worthy of you, who is without complications, who is not me."

She'd painted a nearly exact portrait of the wedded life he'd previously envisioned for himself, at least when he'd bothered to envision it. But that was before he'd met her, and before he'd realized she would make a much better wife for him than all those fair-haired, uncomplicated ladies he had danced with in his life. He *had* realized that. Now all he'd have to do was convince her.

"Forgive me, but I believe I know what kind of lady suits me best," he said. "I would be bored within a week with one of those fair-haired ladies you describe. It's the one—the only one—with complications who intrigues me."

She stopped walking to look up at him, tipping her head back so that he could see all of her face beneath the hat's curving brim. She was fragile and achingly beautiful, and when she gazed at him like this with her eyes so large, he knew that honor had nothing to do with him making the right decision.

"Oh, my dear, dear Geoffrey," she said softly. "You do not understand, do you? You couldn't. You can't. And yet I so want you to!"

"But I do understand, Serena," he said, kneeling before her on the garden path. He reached into his waistcoat and pulled out the small, leather-covered box. "I understand this. Will you do me the inestimable honor of becoming my wife?"

She pressed one hand over her mouth, and made a small whimper: of dismay, of surprise, of happiness? He wasn't sure, but he decided to consider it enough of a consent, and persevered.

Gently he took her free hand and uncurled her fingers. His balled-up handkerchief dropped to the path, and he saw that she'd been gripping it so tightly in her hand that her nails had left little crescent-shaped marks on her palm. The vulnerability of those marks touched him deeply, and he couldn't help kissing them lightly, barely grazing his lips across her palm. Then he slipped the ring on her finger, gliding it down its length. It looked right there, as if it could belong on no other hand, the golden stone and diamonds winking in the sunlight.

He rose, still keeping hold of her hand. He knew they'd have only a few more moments alone before the others in the house came to join them.

"My own Serena," he said, happiness welling up within him. "My own Jēsamina."

But she did not smile as she looked down at the new ring on her finger.

"Oh, Geoffrey," she said sorrowfully. "What have we done? What have we done?"

"We've done what we both wanted," he said firmly. "To be together always, never to part. That is kismet, and so is this."

He raised her hand to his lips, and she let her gaze follow. He was looking at her with such intensity that she nearly couldn't bear it. No, it went deeper than that. The last time anyone had looked at her like this had been Father, because he had loved her.

She had always believed that a broken heart was a contrivance of poets, not reality. Yet when Geoffrey looked at her in this way, with such warmth, she felt something in her chest break open and give way, and the pain of it made fresh tears fill her eyes.

"I would take you from this house and marry you to-night if I could," he was saying. "I want you with me always, Serena. I want to keep you safe, and make you happier than you've ever been. I never want to see tears on your cheeks again, unless they're tears of joy—which I certainly hope that those are."

He found yet another handkerchief in his pocket and gently blotted the corners of her eyes with it.

"There," he said softly, intent on wiping away her tears. "I told you I would do whatever I must to make you happy, because I want you to be my lover and my lady-wife, my dear *begum*."

His dear *begum*: oh, it was that single Hindi word that undid her. In India, she would never have been re-garded as a *begum,* a genteel married lady of high rank, because of her mother. But here Geoffrey was giving her his name and his rank and his protection because he wanted to, and because he wanted *her*.

If only he knew the truth. If only she could tell him.

He was smiling crookedly, and she realized she hadn't said a word in response.

"I'll ruin you," she said, as close to that truth as she could dare to be.

His smile relaxed, with a relief that only tormented her more.

"Then we are even," he said. "By all counts, that's what I've done to you already."

She could only shake her head. But she did not pull off

the ring he'd given her: such a beautiful, beautiful ring, made a thousand times more so because he had put it on her finger.

"Say yes," he said, half-teasing and half-serious. "That one word is all I wish to hear from you now. Say yes."

He linked his fingers more closely into hers. With his thumb, he traced lazy small circles over the inside of her wrist, over her pulse, in the exact place to make her shiver. He was right when he'd said she wanted this. She'd never wanted anything more than to be his, no matter the risk, the challenges, the dangers.

She heard the garden door open behind her, and Grandpapa already beginning his bellowed congratulations. She didn't look back, but instead turned her face up toward Geoffrey.

"Yes," she whispered, for only him to hear. "*Yes.*"

The wedding date was set for the first week of June, exactly three weeks from the date that Geoffrey had proposed. Three Sundays fell into that span, just sufficient for reading the marriage banns. There was considerable speculation about town as to the haste of the wedding, but once the Duke of Breconridge publicly smiled and said he could think of no good reason for his second son to wait any longer than that to marry the beautiful Miss Carew, the whispers quieted, and the gossips instead settled down to the more serious topic of the lady's dress and jewels, who would be attending the ceremony, and where the newlyweds would reside.

While an engagement of three weeks' duration might be adequate for the Church of England, it was shockingly short to the tradespeople who were responsible for Serena's wedding clothes. Although the ceremony was going to be modest, with only the closest of family in attendance, Serena's gown would also be the same one she would wear to be presented at Court as Geoffrey's new wife. No expense was spared, for she was marrying into one of the wealthiest and most influential of noble families, and she would be expected to dress like it.

The gown was a *robe à la Française* with elegant pleats trailing from the back shoulders. The fabric was a shimmering silk cloth-of-gold over wide hoops, with swirling embellishments of costly Venetian lace and silk ribbon on the skirts. More lace trimmed the sleeve flounces, and pearls and brilliants were scattered over the entire dress to catch the light and sparkle. When she was presented at Court, she would of course wear three tall, white ostrich plumes in her hair to signify her status as a newly married lady, but for the wedding, she would have a scarf of more lace pinned like a veil to the top of her hair and falling over her shoulders.

There was, however, much more than her dress to be created and purchased in these three short weeks before the wedding. According to Aunt Morley, Serena required an entire new wardrobe to befit her soon-to-be position, and their days were filled with unending visits to mantua-makers, drapers, shoemakers, hosiers, lace-makers, and milliners. Also to be purchased was a prodigious amount of linen for the tables and beds in her new house, plus china to be ordered and silverware to be engraved with her new husband's monogram.

Geoffrey possessed a small yet elegant house in Bloomsbury Square, but while the house was undoubtedly well furnished and staffed, Aunt Morley had instantly observed many matters in these bachelor quarters that were in dire need of a feminine touch. Like every noble lady, Serena had been educated in how to manage her husband's household, but the notion of suddenly having to do so on her own in three weeks' time was daunting indeed, and she struggled to take note of all the improvements and suggestions that Aunt Morley was offering in regard to her new establishment.

To Serena's great regret, she saw nothing of Geoffrey during those three weeks. Her grandfather insisted that they be separated until their wedding, and no matter if Grandpapa believed he was keeping her from the temptation that Geoffrey represented, or that this was in itself a punishment, or perhaps he could not resist one last chance to irritate the Duke of Breconridge, the result was the same.

Still, it was just as well that Serena's last days as a spinster were so full, leaving little time for her to reflect on what exactly she'd done by accepting Geoffrey's proposal. She tried to tell herself that after so long, her secret was safe. She tried to believe that the odds were against her giving Geoffrey a child who looked more Indian than English. She tried to convince herself that the past was done, that at last she'd found the security she so desperately wanted and needed, and that she'd find only peace and happiness and another sanctuary in her future with Geoffrey, and a chance at love besides.

She tried, and failed. Her conscience knew the difference, and each night sent to her the old nightmares of the last days at Sundara Manōra, as terrifying to her now as when they'd first invaded her dreams. She woke shaking with panic and her night shift soaked with sweat, and with trembling fingers she'd light the candle beside her bed, staring at the bright flame to keep away the nightmare's darkness until the dawn.

She had never described her dreams in detail to anyone. They were too much a part of her secret, and part of her as well. What would she do if the nightmares followed her to Geoffrey's bed? Would he wake her, the way her maidservant and aunt did when she startled them with her cries, or would he wonder if she was a madwoman, the way her uncle wanted her to be? Geoffrey had promised to protect her, but even he could offer no protection from the kind of demons that plagued her at night.

And so once again she tried to calm her fears and her racing heart as she stared into the candle's dancing flame.

Happiness and peace, and a chance at love. Yet alone in the dark with her past, nothing seemed more elusive.

"*Here you* are, Serena." Her grandfather smiled broadly and rose from behind his desk as she entered the library. "Come, sit here close to me, my dear, so you can see properly."

Curious, Serena took the armchair that had been arranged for her on the near side of the desk. Her wedding was tomorrow, and she and Aunt Morley had been reviewing the last of the trunks with her new belongings when Grandpapa had summoned her here. On one side of him stood his longtime man of business, the dour Mr. Gormley, but on the other side was an equally somber man, a stranger, accompanied by a sizable man who looked to be a guard of some sort, with a brace of pistols poking out from beneath his coat.

"This is Mr. Cartwright," Grandpapa said, "and his, ah, associate Mr. Finn. Mr. Cartwright is a jeweler, Serena, and you'll understand the presence of Mr. Finn in a moment."

"Your late father was a most unusual gentleman, Miss Carew," Mr. Cartwright said, bowing toward Serena. "I understand that his primary occupation in India was the procurement and sale of fine jewels, a trade that requires both courage and political delicacy in that dangerous part of the world."

Serena nodded warily, volunteering nothing else. Father hadn't been an ordinary English father in a specific, easily definable trade. If Grandpapa and Mr. Cartwright and everyone else in London wished to believe his fortune had come from trading jewels alone, then so be it. Although she'd been too young to know the details, she was aware that Father had been involved with a number of other occupations, some of which had brought various frightening men to their house to conduct business with him. She'd suspected there had been good reason for the strong walls and armed guards that had surrounded their paradise of a home, and as she'd grown older, she came to realize there were likely things her father had done that were not entirely worthy of being a Carew, or entirely legal, either.

With trepidation she glanced at the large, handled bag sitting on the desk. She had always remained loyal to Father's memory, and kept his secrets as well as her own. But what could this Mr. Gormley have brought to her now, on this particular day?

"Don't look so distressed, Serena," Grandpapa said, even as he was clearly enjoying her confusion. "It's not as if Gormley here has brought you a nest of water snakes."

"Indeed not, my lord," Mr. Gormley said, smiling politely as he unfastened the buckles and leather straps on the bag. "I can assure you, Miss Carew, that there is nothing serpentine in this bag. Rather, I have brought you proof of your father's providential devotion for you. During the time in which he lived in India, he took care to have a number of items of great value shipped back to England, to be held in safekeeping by our agents. His express wishes were that the items should be given to you on the event of your marriage. There is a letter here for you, too, that had accompanied the first shipment."

He handed her the neatly sealed letter, the stock still fresh and white and the red wax seal imprinted with the Carew signet. But what shocked her was seeing Father's familiar handwriting for the first time since his death, as surely as if he'd reached from the grave to touch her.

With trembling fingers, she cracked the seal. The letter wasn't long; no more than a note, really, but that was like Father, who'd always been impatient with written words.

My dearest Asha,

When you read this, you will be nearly a Bride. How I wish I were there in London with You to see You in your finery! Tho perhaps 'tis best I am not, for how could I bear to give You away to another man's Care & Love? I pray he will be worthy of You, & love You & cherish You as You deserve. I will count upon your Grandmama & Grandpapa to represent me whilst I am Absent, & see You do my little family Proud.

You know I do like surprises, & here is mine for You, a few Baubles & Pretties. It is my Fond Hope that You will find them Agreeable, & wear them on Your wedding day, & remember your Father so far away who Loves You more than anyone,

My dearest Daughter,
Father

Emotion swelled inside her as she stared down at the letter, the words swimming before her tear-filled eyes. She'd had nothing of Father to remember him, no little memento to carry with her, and to have this letter now was far more precious to her than any other gift he might have sent with it.

Except that all of it, the letter and the love from Father and whatever jewels he'd sent, hadn't been meant for her. They'd been intended for her sister, Asha, the daughter of his wife.

Father had always claimed that he'd loved both of them equally, and as a child she'd never had any indication that he hadn't. Yet here was the undeniable proof that he had differentiated between them. He'd always meant for Asha—the real Serena—to return to England and marry an Englishman. Asha's mother had been a fair-haired Scottish lady with an impeccable pedigree named Miss Katherine Dalton, the lady whose portrait had hung in a place of honor in their dining room, and whose father had been a senior officer in the East India Company. Asha had been a sickly girl with none of her mother's beauty, but her pinched, milky-pale face and blue eyes would have been accepted instantly in London, where she would have done his "little family proud."

There was no mention in his letter of Savitri, her own real name, or even of Rachel, her English name. Yet she had to know for certain: she had to ask, even if it put her secret at risk.

"I thank you for bringing this letter to me, Mr. Gormley," she said. The jeweler was already lifting boxes from the bag, the kind of flat, leather-covered boxes that always contained the most precious pieces. "It means more to me than you shall ever know."

Mr. Gormley's cheeks pinked. "You are most welcome, Miss Carew. I am honored to have been the messenger of your late father's devotion."

She tried to smile. "Did he send things from India for, ah, for other members of our family?"

"Not to my knowledge, no," Mr. Gormley said, pausing with a little bow before he returned to arranging the boxes on the desk. One by one, he opened them to display the contents, setting them out to face Serena. "Only to you, his single child."

His single child. There could be no doubt—or hope—after that, could there?

She felt utterly abandoned, and more alone than she'd ever been. Mute, she looked down at the array of "baubles and pretties" that had been Father's gift to her sister. There were four bracelets, a long necklace and a short one, three rings, and several brooches and ornaments; the stones included diamonds, pearls, sapphires, emeralds, and rubies. Some of the jewels had been placed in European-style settings, while others remained in their original Indian settings, the colors of the stones set off by brilliant enamel-work in the gold.

"How much he must have loved you, Serena," Grandpapa said beside her, his voice thick with emotion as well—though likely a far different emotion than what she was feeling. "Of course I'd known of the sapphires and diamonds, since he'd sent that directly to me, but I'd no notion that he'd intended this for you as well. Might I read his letter?"

Silently Serena handed him the letter, a letter that had lost much of its magic.

But not for Grandpapa, fumbling now with his handkerchief, his eyes and nose red.

"Poor Tom," he said gruffly. "He always was generous, even as a lad. Not a day goes by that I do not miss him still. Not one day."

"Lord Thomas was generous indeed," Mr. Gormley said, standing proudly beside the arranged jewels as if they'd been his own to bestow. "His gift is a significant collection, Miss Carew, and of considerable value."

Obediently she tried to focus on the open boxes before her. Most of the jewels were new to her, things she'd never seen, but one of them was achingly familiar. Gently she lifted the nearest ornament from its plush box, turning it over in her fingers. It was a sizable piece, nearly seven inches long, with a hexagonal center of diamonds and emeralds set in gold. On one end was a long green enameled spike made for tucking it into clothing for wearing, and at the other was an oversized, curving teardrop with more emeralds and diamonds.

It was an ornament made to be worn in a courtier's turban, an elegant and costly sign of a gentleman's nobility and rank. She remembered the day that Father had acquired it. He'd shown it to her and Asha after they'd dined, explaining how the curving teardrop was called a *boteh*, a Persian word for flower. Then he'd thrust the spiked end into the front of his own turban to demonstrate how it should be worn, and had strutted around the table with his head high and his fists at his hips, pretending to be a great pretentious nobleman from the court at Hyderabad until they'd all laughed so hard they'd wept.

"That's a queer sort of thing," Grandpapa said, frowning at the jewel in her hand. "Some manner of Musselman's gewgaw, I warrant. You'll want to have the stones reset."

"We should be delighted to contrive a new setting for you, Miss Carew," said Mr. Gormley. "In the latest fashion, of course. Or if you should prefer to sell—"

"Thank you, no," Serena said quietly, the ornament still cradled in her hand. At least she had the memory of Father's love, and of how happy her childhood had been. Nothing could take that away, no matter what he'd written to her sister. "I believe I shall keep it as it is, and wear it on my gown tomorrow."

"As you wish, Miss Carew," Mr. Gormley murmured. He drew one last item from the bag, a large ledger that he opened and laid on the desk before Serena, smoothing the page for her with his palm. "If you please, Miss Carew, please sign on that line, there, that you have received the jewels from our custody. For our records, you see."

"Here, Serena, use my pen," her grandfather said, pushing his gilt inkstand across the desk as well.

There was an itemized listing and brief description of the jewels with her father's name and her own beside them, and a space left for her signature. She dipped the pen into the ink, and paused, pen over paper, suddenly reluctant to sign the name that wasn't hers.

She didn't know why she hesitated. The decision to become Serena had already been made, not just when she'd accepted Geoffrey's proposal, but long before, in Calcutta, when she had wakened and the first kind English lady had called her by her dead sister's Christian name and she hadn't corrected her.

"Have we made an error in the accounting, Miss Carew?" asked Mr. Gormley, misreading her hesitation.

"No, no," Serena said softly. "Everything appears correct."

Yet still she hesitated, thinking of her father, and her sister, too, and missing them both very much. Surely they would forgive her for what she'd done, and what she was doing. Surely they would have understood.

"Come along, lass, you cannot keep these fellows waiting all day while you dawdle," Grandpapa said, a trifle impatiently. "Consider it practice for the registry in the church tomorrow."

Tomorrow, when she would become Geoffrey's wife. She imagined him smiling at her, taking her hand, kissing her, and she smiled herself. She wasn't alone, not at all. She'd have Geoffrey, and if she doubted the love that she'd had in her childhood, she might now have another kind of love waiting before her, if only she'd dare to claim it. She'd have to put aside the past, the good memories and the bad dreams, forever, and look only to the future, and with Geoffrey, she believed she could do it. It would not be easy, but for him, she *would* do it.

She lowered the pen and wrote her name—*Serena Carew*—in the ledger, boldly, so it wouldn't be missed.

With that Mr. Gormley and the guard quickly took their leave, and Serena rose as well, intending to return to her packing. But as she did, her grandfather reached out to cover her hand with his.

"Stay a moment, Serena, if you please," he said, returning her father's letter. "I've a few things I wish to say to you, and if I do not say them now, they'll be lost in the confusion of your wedding tomorrow."

She smiled with expectation, and sat back down in her chair, tucking the letter into her pocket.

He sighed heavily, and began to shut the open jewel boxes and hook each lid closed, concentrating on that small task instead of looking at Serena.

"It's no secret that Fitzroy's not my choice for you," he began at last. "But if he makes you happy as he should, then I shall abide by it and keep my peace, and if he doesn't—"

"He *will,* Grandpapa," Serena said firmly, thinking again of Geoffrey. "I know he will."

"Ah, well, then he will, he will." He sighed again, and began to stack the boxes, taking care to square the corner together into a neat pyramid. "The weary truth is that no man would be good enough for you, Serena. I loathe the notion of giving you away, to leave this house forever."

"Oh, Grandpapa," she said gently, touched. Her grandfather had never spoken to her like this. "You know I shall be back, and soon, too. You won't be done with me."

He nodded to the stack of boxes. "Your father said nearly the same thing to me, you know. He promised he'd come back once he'd made his fortune, if only to rub Radnor's nose in it."

He chuckled at the memory before his face once again grew somber. "But he didn't, did he? He didn't. You were the fortune he sent back to me, my dear, a scrap of warmth and sunshine that I'd never expected in my dotage. You're like him in so many ways, Serena, always a reminder of what I've lost in him, and gained in you."

"You gave me shelter when I had none," Serena said, her voice breaking. "You showed me charity, and gave me a home and a family when I'd lost everything."

"You were my Tom's daughter, born of his lady-wife," he said. "What else could I have done, eh? Blood's thicker than water. It's not as if you were some whore's mongrel chit abandoned on my doorstep instead of its rightful place at the foundling hospital."

Some whore's mongrel chit: oh, that cut like the sharpest blade through the affection of this conversation. Because no matter how fond her grandfather had become of her, that was exactly what she would have been to him if he'd ever learned the truth. It would have been the same fate for her in London as it would have been in Calcutta. No more than a mongrel chit, to be sent off to the almshouse.

"Family always comes first," he continued, unaware of her thoughts. "As a wife, you'll look to your husband first for counsel, but if you're ever in need, you'll always have Radnor."

"Uncle Radnor!" she exclaimed, appalled. She'd never told her grandfather about what her uncle had said to her, or what he'd ordered done to her, either. How could she, when Radnor, his only surviving son, could do no wrong in Grandpapa's eyes?

"Yes, Radnor," Grandpapa said patiently. "I know you find him a bit, ah, forceful. Your Aunt Morley does as well. But he means well, and only wants what's best for you and the family. Even now, with all his other responsibilities, he took the time to tell me how worried he was that the trials of this wedding would be too much for you. He feared you'd make yourself ill."

"I'm perfectly well, Grandpapa," she said quickly. Her uncle had threatened to question her health and her wits if she became inconvenient, but she hadn't expected him to begin already. "The preparations have kept Aunt Morley and me very busy, but it's hardly taxing enough to make me ill."

"Oh, that's just Radnor's way," Grandpapa scoffed, making excuses. "He can't help showing concern for you as his niece. No doubt deep down, if you were honest, you feel the same regard for him. If in the way of things you see an opportunity to say a word or two in Radnor's favor with His Grace, why, I'm sure you would. You're both Carews, and Carews stand together."

She nodded, unable to think of an acceptable reply. Once she was wed to Geoffrey, she'd be safely beyond her uncle's machinations, and no matter what Grandpapa might wish, she'd absolutely no intention of ever saying a word in Uncle Radnor's favor.

Mistaking her silence for emotion, Grandpapa awkwardly patted her hand.

"Strange to think how you'll go into that church tomorrow as a Carew," he said, "and step out a Fitzroy. But that's the way of it with women, isn't it? The leopard may not change his spots, but you ladies can change who you are in the blink of an eye. Isn't that so?"

"Yes, Grandpapa, it is," she said softly, sadly, and with a hint of bitterness in her voice, too. "It is."

CHAPTER 10

Geoffrey stood near the front pew in the west chapel of St. Stephen's, trying to hide his nervousness, and not particularly succeeding. It was his wedding day, and he guessed he was entitled to some degree of nervousness, but it was still not a pleasant sensation, and he would have given a great deal to have the entire ordeal already behind him, and Serena his wife.

"I don't know where they could be," he said to his brother Harry, standing beside him. As discreetly as he could, he drew his watch from his pocket to check it once again. "It's well past time for them to be here."

"It's only five minutes past two," Harry said mildly. "That's hardly cause for concern. It's the prerogative of brides to be late."

Geoffrey shook his head. "I cannot help but fear that that uncle of hers might have meddled again."

"What, to keep her away from marrying you?" Harry asked. "The Carews were the ones who pushed for this wedding. There's no reason in the world for them to balk and turn tail now."

Geoffrey sighed, unconvinced, and shot his shirt cuffs again. No matter what Harry said, not even he could deny the proof: his father and stepmother sitting in the chapel's front pew (Harry's wife, Gus, was too close to her confinement to leave home, or else she would have been there as well), the minister in his vestments standing behind them, and not a hint of Serena or any of her family. It was just as well that they'd limited the ceremony to only the immediate family so that all his various cousins and their wives and children wouldn't be here to witness his humiliation, too.

"Then where the devil are they?" He worked his shoulders inside his stiff new wedding coat. Father had insisted on him having a new suit made for this occasion, with more gold embroidery than was his usual taste. He swore he could feel a scrap of wiry gold thread jabbing into his back, stinging him like the most annoying gnat in the world. "This is awkward, deuced awkward."

"Stop fidgeting, Geoffrey," his brother said, poking at Geoffrey's shoe with the tip of his cane for emphasis. "I'll wager you a guinea that she's here within five minutes."

"Five guineas that she won't be," Geoffrey said gloomily. Old Carew had insisted that they be kept apart until the wedding, and he hadn't had so much as a glimpse of Serena since she'd accepted his proposal. For all he knew, they'd shipped her off to some convent in Belgium, just to spite him. He glanced at Harry. "How long did Gus keep you waiting when you wed?"

"Gus?" Harry smiled smugly. Geoffrey had missed his brother's wedding, having been somewhere off the coast of Madagascar on his voyage back from India. "Gus is always prompt. No, more than prompt. She was early."

"You told me every bride is late!"

"Gus had more incentive," he said. "She was marrying me."

"The devil take you, Harry, you—"

"Their carriages are here," said Rivers, hurrying up the aisle from the front of the chapel. At twenty-four, Rivers was the youngest brother; with three weeks' notice, Father had arranged to have him brought home from Paris in time for the wedding, dragging him from the lovely arms of his current mistress, a tempestuous opera dancer.

"They've just drawn up directly to the door," Rivers continued. "They should be on the steps in a minute or two, if the crowds don't block their way."

Geoffrey's initial relief was stopped cold by this new complication. The fact that the wedding was small, a private family affair, had done nothing to end the interest of the public for anything related to the Duke of Breconridge and his family, and the scandal-sheets and other papers had been full of it these last weeks. When Geoffrey had arrived with his brother, the street outside St. Stephen's had already been thick with curious gawkers, barely kept in check by the men his father had hired for the purpose. It would only serve to confirm the marquis's worst suspicions about the Fitzroys, and for once Geoffrey couldn't deny it.

But it was Serena's reaction that worried him. She was by nature reserved in public, and the last thing she'd wish on her wedding day was the attention of a boisterous crowd. All too well he could imagine her face, wide-eyed and pale with panic, if the curious pressed too close.

"I must go to Serena," he said, but Harry caught him by the arm.

"No, you can't," Harry said, holding Geoffrey back. "The last thing she'd wish now is to have you see her wrestling with her hoops and finery as she climbs from the carriage. Let her make her entrance."

"But the crowds," Geoffrey protested. "We know how they can be—I want to save her from that."

Harry held fast. "Do you really believe Carew and Radnor and their footmen would let the riffraff come near her?"

That was entirely true, but Geoffrey wasn't in the mood

to be rational. "That is very easy for you to say, Harry, when only a fool would—"

"Turn around, and stop your babbling," Harry said quietly, releasing Geoffrey's arm. "She's here, and she's beautiful."

Quickly Geoffrey turned, and caught his breath. When he told the story later, he swore that his heart had stopped in his chest at the sight of Serena. Harry had called her beautiful, but that word didn't begin to seem adequate for how she looked.

She was standing beside her grandfather, turned slightly back toward the door as she waited for her aunt to join them. A single sunbeam slanted through one of the chapel's arched windows to bathe her in a golden light, as if to set her apart from everyone else.

Her golden gown caught every fraction of light of that sunbeam, making it dance and sparkle around her slender form even as she stood still. Her dark hair was pinned high, with lace veiling that trailed gracefully behind; the full curves of her breasts were also swathed, for decency, in more lace. He smiled to see her holding the bouquet of white roses he'd sent her; he wished they could have been jasmines, but not in London. As was the fashion for aristocratic brides, she was wearing a fortune in jewels that glittered, too, with diamonds pinned on her gown and in her hair, around her throat and wrist, and hanging from her ears.

But while most such brides would rely on borrowing pieces from around her family to make an impressive show, he was sure that what she wore was hers: not only because of her father's trade, but also because so many of the settings weren't English, but Indian, with curving swirls of gold and silver, bright with colored enamel and studded with pearls. She was like a gorgeous, gilded, glittering statue of some exotic goddess, one which—he later claimed this, too—he would have worshipped happily, even there in the middle of St. Stephen's.

Then she turned toward him, creating the heart-stopping moment. She caught his gaze, and her eyes came to life with a warmth and fire that was just for him. She raised her chin a fraction, and slowly, slowly smiled at him.

Oh, yes, his heart most certainly stopped, and his brain did, too. How could it not?

For the last three weeks his brain had been engaged in a balancing act worthy of the most accomplished rope-dancer. On the one hand was the weighty advice that his father had been giving him—almost without pause—about how a wife must be treated differently from a mistress. On the other was his memory of that last morning he'd been with Serena, when she'd behaved very much like a mistress, and a favorite one at that.

All this balancing had made him wonder if he was making the most enormous mistake of his life by marrying at all, when he still felt as if he'd so much of his life before him. He had never planned to marry this young, and Serena felt the same. Every unclever jest that he'd heard from his bachelor friends about nooses and leg-irons had only made him wonder more, and also had made the memory of Serena fade and flicker a little less brightly.

But now, with a single smile, all doubts vanished. That smile was magically shy and seductive, knowing and yet innocent, all at the same time—much as Serena was herself.

As smiles went, it had the power to make him stop thinking entirely, and only feel. And what he felt was the *rightness* of marrying her.

That, and the rightness of being able to have her in his bed beside him for the rest of his life.

"Oh, well done, Geoffrey," Rivers whispered with unabashed admiration. "You *have* improved the family stock."

Under ordinary circumstances, Geoffrey would have knocked his younger brother outright for his insolence, simply on fraternal principle. Serena wasn't another doxy; she was going to be his wife. But he was so lost in the sight of her walking toward him on her grandfather's arm that he forgot his brother and everything else.

She seemed very small beside her grandfather, small and solitary. While he had his brothers beside him, she had no sisters, and appeared to have no lady-friends to support her, as most brides would. He couldn't wait to introduce her to his brothers and the rest of his own sprawling, extended family. As a newly minted Fitzroy, she would never again be alone or lonely, and she would always be protected—and not with the boorish heavy hand that her uncle, Radnor, had shown toward her, either.

Her eyes hadn't looked away from his since their gazes had first met, nor had his from hers. When at last they were standing before each other, she blushed, and he winked, by way of jovial reassurance. Geoffrey was vaguely aware of her grandfather making a grumble of disapproval at that, but he didn't care. Serena was almost his.

He was only half-aware of the service being read around them, of his own automatic responses to the questions that the minister was asking. When he took Serena's hand in his, he smiled again at how her palm was damp and her fingers trembled with a nervousness that was at odds with her jewel-covered appearance.

He wanted to tell her to trust him, and he wanted to say whatever would put her at ease. Instead he could only continue with the simple words that were required of him, and pray that she understood.

And then, suddenly, it was done, and the minister was

telling him to kiss her. She was blushing again, turning her face expectantly up toward him. As he bent down, he fully intended the kind of chaste kiss that was required under the circumstances.

But the instant their lips met, he forgot that chaste intention. Her mouth was irresistible to him, sweet and ripe and full of heady promise, and he couldn't stop himself from kissing her more deeply. With a tiny sigh of pleasure, she parted her lips for him, and reached one hand up to rest on his shoulder. Possessively he curled his arm around her waist and pulled her closer, against his chest and into the kiss. She dropped her bouquet and slipped her other hand to the back of his neck, beneath his queue.

In front of them, the minister loudly cleared his throat. "Lord Geoffrey, Lady Geoffrey," he murmured. "Please recall that you are in Our Lord's house."

At once Serena slipped away, and sheepishly bent to retrieve her bouquet. Geoffrey reached down to help her back to her feet, and she rose with such seductive grace that he very nearly ignored the disapproving minister and kissed her again.

But while a throat-clearing minister was one thing, his father was quite another. Before Serena had even risen, Father had stepped forward to forcibly offer his congratulations, seizing Geoffrey's hand to shake it and kissing Serena's cheek. The rest of the two families followed suit in a flurry of good wishes that continued back to the marquis's house in St. James's Square, and through the endless rounds of toasts that followed at the light collation in their honor.

The only time Geoffrey released Serena's hand was when she was taken by her aunt upstairs to change clothes, and the only reason he agreed to that was because it meant that they soon would leave, and finally be alone together. It was just as well, too. He'd spent the last two hours since the wedding in a haze of simmering lust that made him oblivious to everything else that was happening around him.

It hadn't helped that Serena seemed to feel much the same, twisting her fingers around his and touching her toes against his foot beneath the curtain of her skirts. Each time she glanced up at him sideways from under her lashes and smiled shyly, he seriously considered taking her back to that same infamous breakfast parlor and finishing what they'd started—except this time he'd lock the door.

"How long can it take for her to shift from one gown to another?" he asked Harry impatiently. He held out his empty glass for a passing footman to refill. "I can assure you that I will be able to remove her gown faster than a half-dozen lady's maids."

"You nearly did that in the church," Harry said drily. "I thought Father was going to suffer an apoplexy then and there."

"Not our father, Harry," Geoffrey said, once again scowling at the staircase as if that alone could bring her down. "You know he's likely done far worse himself."

Harry chuckled. "Be grateful we live in modern times. A hundred years or so ago, and he would have lurked outside your drawn bed curtains to sing bawdy songs and make certain you took your bride's maidenhead properly."

"The hell he would have," Geoffrey muttered, wishing his older brother's attempts at bonhomie weren't quite so heavy-handed. "Where the devil is Serena, anyway? She's my wife now. She should be here with me."

"Likely that old aunt of hers is imparting last words of womanly wisdom," Harry said. "What to expect from your wedding night ravishment, that manner of rubbish. No doubt she has the poor lamb quaking in sacrificial terror."

Geoffrey emptied his glass again. He was already uneasy about their wedding night without jests like this. He had never been with a virgin, let alone a virgin wife. There were men he knew who boasted of taking maidenheads, relishing their partner's fear and suffering. He didn't want that for Serena; he wanted her to feel only pleasure.

"Serena is no poor sacrificial lamb," he said firmly. "Not in the least. And that is all I shall share of my wife's private temperament."

"You needn't tell me a word," Harry said. "I had already guessed she must be of a, ah, warm nature, or else you would not have been compelled to marry her today."

Geoffrey swung around to face his brother. "It was *my* desire to marry her, Harry," he said crossly, "and I'll not have it said by you or anyone else that I've done this against my will. And as for speculating as to the warmth of her nature—"

"Not that it will matter, dear brother, if you keep drinking." Unperturbed, Harry plucked the empty glass from Geoffrey's fingers. "She'll be ardent, and you'll be snoring."

"Don't judge me by your own meager capacities," Geoffrey growled. "I am serious, Harry. She is *my wife,* and I won't stand for anyone slandering her, including you."

"There was no slander intended, brother," Harry said mildly. "She is your wife now, but also my sister, and I'll defend her just as you would defend Gus."

"Indeed." Geoffrey looked back up the staircase once again. "Perhaps I should go upstairs to urge her onward."

Harry slung his arm over Geoffrey's shoulders, effectively (and fondly) keeping him from doing anything so rash. "Trust my word as a married man, Geoffrey: there could be no worse way to begin your wedded life. Now, come, have a slice or two of old Carew's veal pie to fortify yourself."

Upstairs, Aunt Morley was likewise urging Serena to eat.

"At least have this piece of toast with your favorite marmalade," she coaxed, holding the toast up before Serena's mouth as two lady's maids bent behind her, arranging the looped-up skirts of her *polonaise* over her petticoats. "Heaven only knows when you'll have supper."

"I'm sure that Lord Geoffrey's household has a cook," Serena said, taking the diamond drop earrings from the tray held by another maid. "He does not appear to be underfed in the least."

"That's because most gentlemen dine at their clubs," Aunt Morley said. "It will be up to you as his wife to make sure that his table at home is always agreeable, so that he'll prefer being there than off among the other gentlemen."

Not more advice, thought Serena wistfully, so eager to be back with Geoffrey that she was nearly sick with it. To hear him speak his vows with such force, confidently promising so much on her behalf, had been one of the most joyful moments of her life, and one that had left her in awe.

But when he had kissed her with passion enough to make her light-headed with desire, there before their families, she was quite certain she'd crossed into some sort of blissful, seductive Heaven on this earth. No matter the forced circumstances of their marriage: at that moment she'd truly believed they were meant to be together, and while there was no place for kismet among the marble saints of St. Stephen's, the minister's words about how no man should put their union asunder had sounded close enough for her.

Impatiently she glanced at the little clock on her mantel. She couldn't believe how long this ritual of undressing from her wedding gown, removing her jewels, and dressing again into more ordinary clothing was taking. Usually she and Martha could between them manage to make her presentable in ten minutes' time, but with her aunt to supervise, three maids instead of one to assist, and her aunt's dog, Fanfan, racing circles around her, the entire process seemed to be dragging on for the better part of an hour, and all of it time spent away from Geoffrey.

No, not just Geoffrey. Her *husband* Geoffrey.

"Come now, Serena," Aunt Morley said, brandishing the toast. "You really must eat something."

"There," she said, taking an enormous bite from the offered toast to please her. "Are you nearly done, Martha?"

"Yes, Lady Geoffrey," her maid said. "All that's left is your hat."

Serena paused, an earring dangling from her fingers, and grinned foolishly. She couldn't help it. How wonderful it was to be called by her new name, linked forever to Geoffrey!

"I'll see that the rest of your jewels are counted and packed back into their boxes," Aunt Morley was saying, fussing over all the baubles that had been removed from Serena's clothes and laid on her dressing table. "I'll have them carried to you tomorrow, along with your clothes. I'm sure his lordship's family has their own arrangements for safekeeping their jewels."

"And none of those could ever be as valuable to me as the ones that Father chose," Serena said, glancing back at the glittering display. Impulsively she picked up the turban ornament with the emeralds and diamonds, and wove it into the ribbons of her stomacher.

"For luck," she said, bending down to admire the effect in the looking glass. It was a striking way to wear an unusual jewel, and with his appreciation of Indian things, Geoffrey was sure to find it beguiling. That, and the fact that the top of the curving *boteh* was nestled between her breasts.

"Oh, Serena, you cannot mean to wear that . . . *there*," exclaimed her aunt with dismay. "It's a queer sort of brooch by any judgment, but worn like that, it's vulgar."

"Diamonds are never vulgar, Aunt Morley," Serena said, taking her hat from Martha and tying it on her head. "You've often said that yourself. And I'm certain that my husband will approve."

"Your husband." Aunt Morley sighed mightily. "I should wonder at that, Serena. I'll grant that the stones are very lovely, but the setting is peculiar. Consider the beautiful pieces Her Grace must have, jewels set with true artistry."

"Meaning set by London jewelers, not Hindi or Muslim." It was not something she would have dared say before, never wishing to remind anyone, even her aunt, of her past. But she'd often thought such things whenever her aunt or grandfather or anyone else made snide remarks or found fault with India and Indians, and now, made brave by her new status as Geoffrey's wife, she finally spoke the truth.

"I prefer settings like these, Aunt Morley," she said, lightly touching the ornament. "They're brighter, and not as solemn, and they remind me of Father. Besides, Aunt, recall that I've wed Lord Geoffrey, not Lord Hargreave. Whatever jewels Her Grace possesses will go to Lady Hargreave, not to me."

"You don't know that, Serena," Aunt Morley said, glad to seize upon another, less troubling, topic. "If poor Lady Hargreave fails to produce a son, then you may still one day be a duchess."

"That's not why I married Lord Geoffrey, Aunt," Serena said firmly, and she meant it, too. She wished a dozen sons to Lady Hargreave, because the last thing she ever wanted was to become Duchess of Breconridge. "Not at all."

"Ahh." Her aunt nodded, clasping her hands before her. "I'd rather dared hope that you'd chosen him because you loved him."

Serena flushed, taken by surprise. Love was not a subject often mentioned by Aunt Morley. To be sure, Serena had endured several intensely uncomfortable lectures from her aunt over the last three weeks about what to expect from her new husband on their wedding night—lectures that had pointedly lacked the more pertinent details that Serena had long ago learned from the women in the *zenana*—but not once had love figured into the message.

"I care for him, yes," she said slowly, carefully. "I never tire of his company, and I wish to be with him, always, and when he kisses me, it is the finest thing imaginable. But as for love—"

"I think you already do love him, Serena," Aunt Morley said gently. "You may not wish to admit it yet, either to him or yourself, but you do. And from the way Lord Geoffrey looks at you, I should venture that he loves you in return."

Serena pressed her hand to her mouth, struggling to keep back her tears. Her aunt was right. She did love Geoffrey, and she had likely loved him from that first night in the ballroom, when she had turned about and there he'd been. In her heart she'd known it, but because of her past, she had fought that knowledge, even as she'd taken greater and greater risks to be with him.

And now, of course, she'd taken the biggest risk of all, and was married to him. For love, she thought, and for love she would contrive a way to make their marriage succeed.

All for love, and for Geoffrey.

"Now, now, no tears," her aunt said briskly. "You needn't tell me. It's between the two of you to sort out, and I'm sure you will, one way or another. Especially now that your grandpapa can no longer meddle in your affairs."

Impulsively Serena threw her arms around her aunt and hugged her close. They would continue to see each other, of course, but it would never be the same. Aunt Morley had been as near to a mother as she'd had since she'd come to England. Her aunt had always been her champion, and she realized now just how much she was going to miss her.

"Thank you, Aunt," she said, her voice unsteady with emotion. "Thank you for—for everything."

"You are most welcome, Serena," Aunt Morley replied, disentangling herself from Serena's enthusiastic embrace. "Heavens, you nearly impaled me with that dreadful ornament! Mind you take care with Lord Geoffrey. It wouldn't do to inadvertently stab your husband on your wedding day. Now, if you're finally ready, it's time we returned to the others."

"I am ready," Serena said. She gathered up her bouquet, and took one last glance at the looking glass to adjust the angle of her hat. She wanted to be perfect for Geoffrey when she came down the stairs.

Her aunt swept her hands through the air, shooing her onward.

"I will offer this last scrap of wisdom, my dear," she said as Serena hurried ahead of her. "Love is all very well, but honesty must be the cornerstone of any marriage. Be honest in all things with your husband, Serena, and pray that he will be honest with you. The rest will follow."

Abruptly Serena stopped, her happiness equally halted and her optimism chilled. Complete honesty was the one thing she could never give Geoffrey, no matter how much she loved him. She couldn't do it. In most ways, yes, but in one very large matter, he must never know the truth.

"Come along, Serena, please," Aunt Morley said. "People are generally forgiving of a bride, but there are limits."

"One moment, Aunt." Serena turned and ran swiftly in the opposite direction, down the hall to the back parlor.

The seldom-used room was gray with shadows, the wooden blinds drawn to preserve the carpet and chair-coverings against fading from sunlight, but she'd no trouble making out her father's portrait over the mantel. She went and curtseyed before it, as she always did, then stood and gazed up at the handsome, painted face.

"I'm married, Father," she said, her voice barely above a whisper. "Today. I'm Lady Geoffrey Fitzroy now. I think you would approve of Geoffrey. He's much like you. If you'd had the chance, you would have enjoyed a hookah together."

She smiled sadly, imagining the two men lounging in the shade of her father's garden. They would have liked each other; she'd no doubt of it.

"I wore your favorite jewel today, Father," she said, lightly touching the emerald ornament tucked into her stomacher. "I'm wearing it still, much to Aunt Morley's consternation. I do not know if it was meant for me, or for Asha, but I know for certain it was from you, and that—that made it special to me."

She nodded for emphasis, and sighed. "I must go now, Father, and leave with Geoffrey. You sailed to Calcutta for your great adventure, and now I'll begin mine in London. It's all kismet, yes?"

She pressed her fingers to her lips and blew the kiss up toward the painting, wishing she could instead kiss his cheek as she used to do. Then she bowed her head, and with a heart that was heavier than any bride's had a right to be, she went to rejoin the others downstairs.

From the landing she could hear the voices of the two families rising up from the drawing room, more jovial than they'd been earlier. She wondered if that was from relief that she and Geoffrey had finally been married, or simply the effect of the wine that was no doubt being liberally poured and drunk. There would likely be one more round of toasts in their honor, and then the final farewells before she and Geoffrey left in his carriage.

It was strange to think that this house that had been her haven was no longer her home, stranger still to think that Geoffrey's house was now hers, and always would be. She couldn't help but remember how she'd already left one life behind her in India to find a sanctuary, and now she would do it yet again. She took a deep breath to steady the nervousness that was suddenly welling up within her. She ran her fingers along the polished mahogany rail for the final time as she turned, and began down the last flight.

Waiting alone at the bottom of the stairs was Geoffrey. His handsome face was impassive, almost stern, in a way she hadn't seen before, and if she'd hoped to see in his eyes a measure of the love she'd just realized she felt for him, she was disappointed. That dazzled look he'd had when she'd walked down the aisle in the church was gone. Now his gaze raked over her, studying her from the toes of her shoes to the brim of her hat and lingering pointedly on her breasts, where the emerald-studded ornament was tucked.

She smiled, a bit tremulously, hoping he'd smile in return.

He didn't.

Instead he held his hand up to her. "Come, Lady Geoffrey," he said, the first time he'd called her by her new married name. "I am ready to leave."

Swiftly she glided down the steps toward him, her skirts rustling. "I'll say my farewells, and then—"

"I've said them for you." He took her hand, his fingers swallowing hers. "We're leaving now."

Could he tell how uncertain she was from the chill of her hand? "But I should say good-bye—"

"They'll understand," he said brusquely. "This has already been the longest farewell in history."

A footman, who must have been summoned earlier, appeared with Geoffrey's hat and her pelisse. It was all arranged, then. That was the way of English marriages, or at least what she'd observed. She'd had no say in Geoffrey's decision, and she must accept it now unless she wished to begin their life together with quarreling. Geoffrey's expression was more daunting than his words, and disappointed, she nodded as the footman held her pelisse for her. The instant it was on her shoulders, Geoffrey began to lead her to the door held open by another footman.

But in the doorway, he stopped abruptly. A step behind him, Serena stopped, too, and gasped with delight.

Geoffrey's neat dark-green carriage with the Fitzroy arms on the door had lost all of its usual stylish sobriety. Clusters of bridal-white ribbons and flowers were tied to the corners of the roof, with streamers fluttering behind in the breeze. More ribbons and flowers decked the bridles of the horses, and even the grinning footmen and driver sported white flowers pinned to the fronts of their dark-green livery.

"Oh, Geoffrey, how wonderful!" she exclaimed, linking her fingers fondly into his. "That you would have had this done for me—for *me*!"

"I did nothing of the sort," he retorted crossly. "How the devil this fool's mischief was perpetrated upon my carriage and people is—"

"It was Gus's notion," Harry said proudly, coming up behind them. "Although she was too close to her time to be here herself, she was determined to see that you were sent off in proper hymeneal style."

Enchanted, Serena stared at the decorated carriage, while passersby in the street paused and gathered to admire it as well. It was the kindness of the gesture that touched her as much as the flowers and ribbons, that a lady she'd never met had ordered this done simply to please her. She couldn't understand why Geoffrey should be so offended by it, and she didn't want Harry to tell his wife that her thoughtfulness had not been appreciated.

"Please tell Lady Augusta how much her surprise pleased me, my lord," she said, turning back toward Harry. "Give her my thanks, and tell her I look forward to when I may thank her in person."

"You like this manner of carnival show?" Geoffrey asked, clearly dumbfounded.

"I do," she said bravely. "It's *pretty*."

"Pretty," he repeated, and shook his head. "Pretty."

"There's nothing wrong with pretty, Geoffrey," Harry said in a way that was purposefully, overly helpful. "It pleases the ladies."

Geoffrey glowered, and although Serena had no experience with brothers, she suspected these two Fitzroys were very close to exchanging blows. Silently she squeezed her fingers around Geoffrey's, wishing she knew what to say to calm him.

Because obviously her hand wasn't enough. "To the devil with prettiness," he grumbled. "I don't need you to tell me that, Harry."

"Are they leaving now?" The duchess's voice rose behind them. "Geoffrey, you're not stealing your bride away from us so soon, are you?"

"Come," Geoffrey said sharply. He pulled Serena forward through the door and down the marble front steps, so fast that she had to skip along to keep pace with his longer legs. He hustled her into the carriage and jumped in after her, barking at the driver to commence, before she'd barely time to settle herself. As the horses jumped forward, she fell back against the leather squabs with a startled little cry, her bouquet flying from her hand.

"There," said Geoffrey, looking back at the house as they clattered off. "We're away at last."

"We most certainly are," Serena said, unable to keep her indignation to herself any longer. "Faith, Geoffrey, if we weren't already wed, I'd think you were carrying me off to Gretna. Why this haste? Why this ridiculous urgency? It's madness!"

He dropped onto the other end of the seat and placed his hat on the cushion between them.

"I don't know what you mean by madness," he said, testy, his dark brows drawn together. "I was weary of waiting, so we left."

"Yes, we did do that," she said, bending to retrieve her bouquet from the floor of the carriage, "and as quickly as if a pack of bailiffs were at our heels instead of our families."

He grunted, and leaned back against the squabs with his arms folded over his chest. Alone together in the small space, he seemed more imposing somehow, more daunting. She felt the tension in him vibrating outward to fill the carriage, as taut as overwound clockwork, and she hadn't a clue why. He was staring directly ahead and not at her, almost if she weren't there beside him. She supposed that was some small blessing, but she would have much preferred that he smile in her direction, as a happy bridegroom should.

Unless he *wasn't* happy, she thought uneasily. He'd smiled at the church, but since then his mood seemed to have grown darker and darker until it had reached this present black state.

She raised her bouquet to her nose, watching him over the white flowers. She had to ask; she needed to know.

"What is wrong, Geoffrey?" she asked softly. "What has happened?"

"Nothing has happened." He grumbled with wordless frustration. "I couldn't wait to be alone with you to explain, and now that I am, the devil only knows how I am to begin."

"Explain what?" she asked warily, fearing the worst. She understood secrets all too well, and this had all the earmarks of one. Had someone in his family preached painful honesty to him, just as Aunt Morley had to her? Perhaps he kept a favorite mistress, as Father had done, or he'd some dreadful infirmity, or he'd lost all his fortune gaming?

Or perhaps it wasn't his secret at all. What if, instead, he'd somehow learned hers?

"Things will be said of us," he began, still avoiding her gaze. "No, they already *are* being said. Ordinarily I don't give a damn—that is, a fig, about gossip, but I don't want you hurt by it."

She didn't say anything, her fears twisting into a sickening knot in the pit of her stomach. He said he didn't wish for her to be hurt. Now she might never have the chance to tell him how much she loved him: what could possibly hurt more than that?

He took a deep breath, obviously steeling himself, and still not looking her way.

"No one has forced me to marry you, Serena," he said firmly. "Not your grandfather, and not your uncle, either. I want you to know that. I wasn't trapped, like some hapless rabbit in a snare. There will be fools who'll say otherwise, but it's not true. I married you today because I wished to, and I don't want you ever, not once, to think otherwise."

Her heart fluttered with relief, scarcely daring to hope.

He didn't know her secret, and he didn't have one of his own. All this manly stoicism was simply because he cared for her. For *her*.

"That is what you wished to tell me?" she asked slowly, hardly daring to believe it was so. "That you feared I'd doubt you, or your reasons for marrying me?"

He nodded. "God knows you've had reason to, given the circumstances of our wedding."

"But that has nothing to do with you, or with us," she reasoned. "To be sure, this was not how I had planned things to be, but now that it's done, I'd never wish it otherwise. How could I ever doubt you?"

"You could," he insisted. "Most ladies would."

"Well, then, most gentlemen might say the same of me," she said. "But you never would."

"I wouldn't," he said gruffly. "Because beginning today, I mean to keep every one of those vows I made to you, and if—"

But Serena had heard enough. Dropping her bouquet, she twisted across the seat, flung her arms around Geoffrey's shoulders, and kissed him.

It wasn't a wifely kiss, either, because it had a great deal more to convey than a mere dutiful kiss could manage. She remembered how he'd kissed her before and what he'd liked, and she tried to do it again, boldly slanting her mouth over his and kissing him with as much eagerness as she dared. She wanted him to understand how much she appreciated his concern for her, and how she'd never take the word of others over his. She wanted him to know that she regarded the vows she'd made earlier every bit as seriously.

But most of all, she wanted to show him that she loved him, even if she still wasn't certain of the words, and she guessed that kissing him would be the next-best way to express herself.

It didn't take long for her to realize she'd guessed correctly.

As her lips moved over his, he made a muttered, rumbling sound of surprise and pleasure. At once he curved one arm around her waist to pull her close to him, while his other hand cradled the back of her head as if to make sure she wouldn't escape. She was sitting across his lap, their faces so close she felt his breath on her cheek, swaying together with the motion of the carriage. She was struck all over again by how stunningly handsome he was, from the sharply sculpted lines of his cheekbones and jaw to the sensuous temptation of his lips, the slash of dark brows over the most beautifully blue eyes she'd ever seen on a man.

Eyes that were, at present, entirely focused on her.

"My wife," he said, managing to sound commanding and awestruck at the same time. "*Mērī patnī.* My wife."

"*Mērē pati,* my husband." Overwhelmed with emotion and suddenly shy, she struggled to smile. She ran her hands over his chest, marveling again at how he was all hard muscle and bone and strength beneath his extravagantly embroidered wedding clothes. "It sounds as fine in English as it does in Hindi, doesn't it?"

"No matter the language, it means you're mine." The edge to his voice remained from earlier, dark and a little dangerous. He tangled his fingers into her hair to draw her closer, heedless of the havoc he was doubtless causing to her elaborate wedding curls. When he sealed his lips over hers and claimed her mouth, he made her forget everything except that she was his.

He made her first little kiss seem as insubstantial as a feather by comparison. Instead he kissed her as if he'd devour her, his mouth hot and demanding. Her hat toppled backward, and she didn't care, nor did she care that he'd somehow whisked away the filmy lace kerchief that had modestly covered the top of her bodice. Deftly he scooped one of her breasts free from the low neckline, cupping it in his palm and teasing the nipple into a stiff little peak with his thumb.

"You like that, don't you?" he said, a question that seemed to her to be completely unnecessary. Sensation rippled through her with astonishing speed, and she caught her breath even as he kissed her again. He was so much more skilled at this, so much more adept at both giving and taking pleasure, that she felt light-headed from it. Effortlessly he eased her from his lap to the cushioned seat, and her eyes fluttered open just enough for her to see the blue afternoon sky over his shoulder.

She circled her hands around his back to draw him down, too, relishing his weight atop her and his hand on her breast. She adored how he kissed, demanding and possessive in a way that left her breathless with excitement. It was as if the few weeks they'd been kept apart had vanished, and they were once again lying together on the cushioned bench in the breakfast parlor.

Except they weren't. Then she'd been wearing only the insubstantial silk sultana over a shift, and now she was trapped by her own finery. With a whimper of impatience, she struggled to shift beneath Geoffrey, fighting against the boned stays and the turban ornament, hoops, and petticoats and other sundry layers of clothing that were keeping her apart from him.

"Damnation, this is wrong." Abruptly Geoffrey left her and sat upright.

"What is wrong?" Serena asked in breathless confusion, propping herself up on her elbows. "We're married now."

"That's exactly why it's wrong," he said, his expression showing exactly how difficult this was for him. "You're my wife. I can't ravish you on the seat of a carriage as if you were some tawdry Covent Garden strumpet."

She realized that she must look very much like that strumpet with her breasts exposed and her pelisse shoved aside, and heaven knows she'd been behaving like one, too. Swiftly she pulled her bodice back in place and sat upright, her cheeks flaming.

"I'm sorry," she said contritely. "It's my fault."

"You've done nothing wrong," he said sharply. "Not one thing."

He seized her hand and pressed it to the fall of his breeches. Behind it his cock was large and hard, its throbbing heat palpable through the layers of cloth. Shocked, she tried to pull her hand away, but he held it there.

"*That* is what you've done to me, Serena," he said, his voice harsh, "and I'd never wish it otherwise. But what I want now, this moment, is to throw up your skirts and spread you wide and take you hard and fast, the way I've been imagining ever since I first saw you. I want to make you cry out with pleasure, and I want to bury my cock so deep inside you that you'd never wish me to stop. Then I want to do it again in my bed, in my room, and again and again after that, in every manner and posture we can contrive, and still I'll want more. More of you, Serena."

She should have been stunned, even appalled, and she'd vague memories of how her aunt had warned her to be prepared for the marital demands that even the most well-bred of gentlemen might make upon a wife.

But she wasn't stunned or appalled. Not at all. To sit here now, tousled and aching from his kisses and caresses, with her hand pressed to his cock while he told her of what exactly he wished to do to her, was the most exciting thing she'd experienced in her life. Her lips were parted with anticipation, her entire body feverish for everything he described. He wanted *her,* and oh, how she wanted him.

"Yes," she whispered, all she could manage, all that was necessary. "*Yes.*"

Before he could respond, the carriage door swung open. Neither of them had noticed that the carriage had stopped, or that the footmen had stepped down to unfasten the door and unfold the steps. Now four liveried footmen, their wedding ribbons pinned to their chests, stood at attention on either side of the carriage's open door while the butler himself stood at the front door of Geoffrey's house, with the rest of the staff doubtless waiting just inside.

And their first glimpse of their mortified new mistress would be of her hatless and her clothing crumpled and in disarray, with her hand held firmly to the front of their master's breeches.

CHAPTER

11

"Come with me," Geoffrey said, climbing down and reaching for Serena's hand to help her from the carriage. For her sake, he regretted that they'd been taken by surprise like this. He never gave much thought to his servants—they'd seen him in plenty more embarrassing situations over the years—but she was bound to feel differently as the new mistress, and he could understand why she might be distressed.

Even now she hesitated in the carriage doorway, like a beautiful exotic bird on a perch. She'd lost her hat, her hair was half-unpinned, her silk skirts were crushed and creased. Her eyes were wide, and her cheeks and lips were still flushed from his kisses. She looked equally ravishing and ravishable, and the unified thought of his brain and his cock (not necessarily in that order) was to lead her inside and upstairs to his bedchamber as quickly as possible.

She'd retrieved her wedding bouquet, and was clutching it tightly in her hand. At some point, the bouquet must have ended up beneath them, leaving the white roses broken and crushed. Ruefully he thought of how none of the roses he'd given her ever seemed to stand much of a chance; yet forlorn as the bouquet was, it also served as a caution for him, a reminder not to let his own desire run roughshod over her. She was making a brave show, much as the roses had done, but she was also so much smaller and more delicate than he was that if he didn't slow down and stop behaving like the village bull in rut, he'd end up hurting her.

"Come inside with me, Serena," he said, striving to sound welcoming. "It's your home now as well as mine."

She looked past him, at the front of the house. He'd always thought it one of the most handsome on Bloomsbury Square—four elegant stories of brick, picked out with white, and a grand entry—but now he worried that she'd somehow find it wanting. With no claim to the dukedom, his house was not so grand as either his father's house or his older brother's, but thanks to the generous foresight of his mother and aunt, it was his with a hundred-year lease.

"The pictures and furnishings are rather nice," he continued. "You'll see once we're inside."

Some wayward breeze caught the hem of her petticoats, swirling them upward above her ankles.

Of course he looked.

Of course he forgot all about furnishings, and instead recalled what he'd seen of the pretty shape of her ankles and calves. From there he began imagining the rest of her naked, and all bets upon civility were instantly off.

Manfully he cleared his throat, his hand still outstretched toward her.

"All I ask is that you trust me, Serena," he said, his gaze never leaving hers. "Can you do that?"

"Yes," she said, swiftly and without hesitation. "*Yes.*"

Impulsively he plucked her around the waist and swept her from the carriage into his arms. She gasped with surprise, yet clung to his shoulders as he carried her up the two white marble steps and into the house. He'd heard of superstitious country grooms carrying their brides over the threshold like this for good luck and a long life together; he wasn't above hoping it would work for him and Serena as well.

As he set her down in the front hall, her cheeks were pink and her eyes bright with what he hoped was anticipation. He would have kissed her again if they weren't standing before his household's servants, all waiting in a neat line of hierarchy to be presented to the new mistress. It was a ritual that could take a good forty-five minutes or more to review each servant's name, position, and duties—forty-five minutes that Geoffrey was in no mood to stop and squander today.

"Colburn," he began without pausing, addressing his butler as he led Serena through the hall and up the stairs. "Lady Geoffrey has every desire to meet the staff, but she is weary from the day's festivities, and must ask to postpone the greeting until tomorrow."

"We should have stopped," Serena said breathlessly as he hurried her along the upstairs hall to his rooms. "I'm their new mistress. What will they think of me now?"

"They'll think that your husband is more interested in you being his new wife than their new mistress," he said, throwing open the door to his bedchamber for her.

Everything was simply but luxuriously appointed, from the plush Turkish carpet on the floor to the silver candlesticks on the elaborately carved mantelpiece. The mahogany bedstead dominated the room, the tester hung in dark blue damask that matched the counterpane. The servants had pointedly prepared the bed for them, with the counterpane already turned back and the feather pillows plumped. Opposite the bed hung a large Italian painting of Venus and Mars together, their amatory combat eminently suitable for a bachelor bedchamber. Dusk was beginning to fall, and outside in the street the first lamps were being lit for the night. He followed their suit, and lit a handful of candles in the room.

"So this is your bedchamber," Serena said, giving the

room only the most cursory glance. She seemed unable to stand still, unconsciously dancing small steps around the room with the bedraggled bouquet still clutched in one hand, innocently provocative. "Where is mine?"

"Your rooms are at the other end of the hall." He stood before her, intentionally leaving a small distance between them and giving her time to accustom herself to being alone with him. For her sake, he was determined to control his own urgency. After all, she was his wife, and he intended to seduce her, not ravish her. "They overlook the garden."

"So far from yours?" she asked, her disappointment gratifying.

"Farther than I'd like," he said. "Which is why I intend to keep you here as long as I can."

She smiled up at him, a little tremulous. By the candlelight she was achingly beautiful, and innocently vulnerable, too. He'd been, perhaps, a bit impetuous in the carriage.

Slowly he leaned down to kiss her. He didn't draw her into his arms, or touch a hand to her waist or hip. Instead he let his lips alone woo her, kissing her with leisurely assurance, and nipping lightly at her lower lip. Finally he sealed his mouth over hers, letting his tongue thrust and play against hers until she made a smothered moan of frustration, and spun away from him.

"I must call Martha to help me undress," she said. "You know Aunt Morley sent her ahead hours ago, and poor Martha's been waiting for me ever since. It won't take her long—"

"That's not necessary," he said. "I'll assist you, if you need it. I may not be as adept as your Martha, but I'd wager I can make it much more . . . interesting."

To encourage her, he kicked off his shoes and shrugged his arms free of his coat, tossing it over the arm of a nearby chair. Next he untied his linen neck cloth and unfastened the small diamond shirt buckle beneath it, pulling his collar comfortably open.

He'd only revealed a small triangle of his chest and his bare throat above it, but that was sufficient to make her stare, her eyes wide. True, it was a part of a gentleman's anatomy that unmarried ladies would not ordinarily see, but if that caught her attention, then he couldn't imagine how she was going to respond when he removed his breeches.

"Your turn," he suggested. "You could begin with that emerald-studded dagger in your bodice. You know that evil old Lucretia Borgia kept a poisoned stiletto in her stays to ward off unwanted lovers."

"It's not a dagger," she said defensively. "It's a turban ornament that belonged to my father, and it's certainly not poisoned."

She pulled the ornament free and held it briefly above her forehead, showing where it would be worn in an imaginary turban. Now that she'd explained the piece's connection to her father, he understood its significance for her, and regretted teasing her about it.

"One day you can show me how to wrap my head like a rajah," he said, striving to lighten the moment. "That would be a sight, wouldn't it?"

"It would," she murmured, but her expression had grown clouded, looking inward. Carefully she placed the ornament with his coat, and the lace kerchief from around her neck as well. Then she methodically began to unpin her bodice and stomacher, looking down as she plucked each straight pin free, letting them drop to the floor with a little *ping*.

Her determination was oddly seductive, or perhaps it was how her bodice gaped further open as each pin gave way. Without looking, he began unfastening the long row of cut-steel buttons on his waistcoat, shoving it from his shoulders just as she finished with her pins. She worked her arms free of the narrow sleeves, and let the gown fall back to the floor with a *shush* of silk.

"There," she said, almost daring him. Her face was flushed as much from the exertion of removing her clothes as from embarrassment; in fact he didn't think she was embarrassed at all, which both pleased and excited him. She was still wearing her stays over her shift, as well as her hoops and petticoat, standing there defiantly with her hands at her waist. "Are you happy?"

Clearly she believed she was as good as naked already, which she most certainly wasn't.

He smiled. "It's a fair beginning. Now pray remove those abominable hoops."

"They *are* abominable." Deliberately she untied the bow that held her petticoats and shoved them down, followed by the looped cane hoops that had supported her skirts. "They are likely the ugliest things that Englishwomen are compelled to wear. There! Gone!"

She stepped free of the piled petticoats and hoops, giving them an extra kick of contempt with the toe of her shoe.

"You've done well without your maid," he said softly, studying her. She was *worth* studying: her stays were covered in dark red damask that locked his gaze on the narrowness of her waist and the full curve of her hips below, and her white knee-length shift, trimmed with narrow lace, was of such fine linen that it was nearly transparent. The fullness of her breasts raised high by the boned stays, the ivory-gold of her skin, even the shadow of the dark thatch at the top of her thighs was displayed for him.

"I'm not entirely helpless," she said, reaching up to begin pulling the remaining hairpins from her tangled dark hair, the heavy waves already half-undone. "Nor do you appear to require your manservant."

"Not at all," he said absently, distracted by how she

made the simple task of taking down her hair seem so damned seductive. He'd always liked the intimacy of a woman with her hair down, free of all the pins and potions that kept it tortured into place for propriety's sake. Her breasts lifted as she raised her arms, her nipples barely contained by her stays. He could finally see the womanly curves that all that trumpery hid, and he liked what he saw. Her hips and thighs were rounder and more voluptuous than he'd expected, and he was finding it increasingly difficult to be as restrained as he'd ordered himself to be.

Her loose hair fell nearly to her waist, as glossy as a raven's wing. She raked her fingers through the heavy waves, divided it into sections, and began to braid it.

"Leave your hair as it is," he said, and the growl he couldn't keep from his voice made her pause. "I like it that way."

"But I always plait it at night."

"Tonight you won't." He jerked his shirt free from his breeches and whipped it over his head, dropping it to the floor. At once her gaze lowered to his chest, her lips parting in wordless admiration. He recognized that look; he'd seen it before from other women, but their reaction had never mattered the way Serena's did.

Her gaze wandered lower, to the front of his breeches, where his own appreciation of her was flagrantly apparent. Having her look made his cock swell larger still and press uncomfortably against the fall of his already close-fitting breeches. Her blush deepened, spreading over her chest, and he guessed she must be remembering how she'd touched him in the carriage.

"Your stays," he said, but she shook her head.

"I can't," she said. "Martha ties the lace with a knot, and I can't undo it myself."

At once he was behind her, sweeping aside the curtain of her hair. The lace of her stays was in fact tied at the top in that cunning knot that all lady's maids seemed to know, with the thick lace zigzagging between the eyelets along the length of her back. He'd long ago learned the trick of how to tug the loop free, and the rest soon followed.

"How can you do that so quickly?" she marveled as he pulled the freed lace through the eyelets. "No, don't tell me. I don't wish to know, any more than I want to know how many of those other ladies in stays you must have brought to your bedchamber."

"None," he said, the truth. "Not here."

She turned her head to look over her shoulder, her diamond earrings swinging gently against her throat. "None?"

Her voice was hopeful, not prying, and he thought again of how important it was that she trust him.

"None," he said firmly. "I won't deny there have been others, but never in this bed. They'd no place being here. You do."

He held aside her hair and kissed the nape of her neck, brushing his lips from there to the side of her throat. He breathed deeply of her scent, sandalwood and roses, a combination unique to her.

"You have the most beautiful skin," he said. "I've dreamed of losing myself against your skin."

"You're very . . . kind," she whispered, shivering slightly as he kissed her throat. "Considering how sallow I am."

"Truthful, not kind." He tugged the lace through the last eyelet and pushed her stays forward from her shoulders. She gasped as the heavy garment slipped away from her body, and shook her arms with relief to free them and let it drop to the floor with her other clothes. "You're not sallow. You're ivory dusted with gold, and purest perfection. That is the truth."

Now the only thing that lay between them was the

thin linen shift, no barrier at all. He reached forward and filled his hands with her breasts and she gasped again, arching into his chest. Her nipples tightened against his palms, and as he rubbed them with his thumbs, they hardened more. She pressed her head to his shoulder, and moved restlessly against him, her hair falling around them both. Unwittingly she rubbed her plump bottom against his cock, and he bit back an oath, begging for self-restraint. She'd no notion of what she was doing to him, but his cock was all too eager to return the favor.

Still caressing one breast, he moved his other hand lower, pulling up the hem of her shift to slip beneath it. He followed the curve of her hip and thigh to find the soft pillow of her belly and the dark curling hair beneath it. Gently he cupped her, resting his fingers across her plump nether lips.

"Open for me, my Jēsamina," he breathed. "Don't be shy."

"I am not shy," she muttered, and separated her legs a fraction as he'd asked.

"Very well, then, you're not," he said, smiling. Gently he parted her, and eased a single finger between her lips. Damnation, she was tight, but she was already eager for him, too, wet and slick around his finger. She caught her breath, tensing with surprise. Carefully he pushed farther, and she shuddered at the intrusion, her breathing ragged.

"Geoffrey," she said, his name more of an anguished sigh. "Oh, please, Geoffrey."

"Hush, hush," he murmured, lightly stroking the small knot of sensation near the opening of her passage with his thumb to build the fire inside her. She was so snug around his single finger that he wanted her as wet as possible to be able to accept his much larger cock. "Be easy, and let me in."

He loved her breathy little sighs, proof that she was enjoying herself.

"That's it," he whispered, more encouragement as he pushed deeper within her. "My own sweet Jēsamina."

She didn't try to pull away, or cover herself in virginal modesty. Instead she unabashedly writhed against him, her head pressed tight against his shoulder and her back bowed as she moved against his fingers. Swaying toward him for balance, she hooked one foot around his calf, opening herself wider to his caress. Her skin burned over his, the thin shift clinging to her body more erotic than if she'd been entirely naked. There was an innocent wantonness to her motions—or a wanton innocence—that was wildly exciting to him, and made his self-control fray and his cock like iron in his breeches.

He twisted her in his arms to face him, shoving her hair back from her face to kiss her. He had intended the kiss to be a brief respite for them both from the more intimate caresses, but as soon as his lips met hers, he realized how impossible that would be. Unable to help himself, he plunged his tongue deep into her mouth, desperate to possess her however he could. She answered with the same ravenous need, her tongue eagerly dueling with his. She could no more keep still than he, stretching up on her bare toes to be able to reach him and running her hands daringly along his back and shoulders.

And finally it was too much for Geoffrey. For the second time, he scooped her into his arms, and carried her to the bed, his haste making the candle flames dance on the nearby table. Lying crossways on the bed where he'd laid her down, she kept her arms looped around his neck to draw him down beside her.

"I can't part with you, Geoffrey," she whispered feverishly, her dark hair fanned out across the white linen. "Not even for a moment, not one single moment."

He kissed her again, fighting the urge to take her now.

For all her eagerness, she was so small, so delicate. He couldn't risk hurting her, or she'd never forgive him—nor would he forgive himself.

"My Jēsamina," he said, kissing her lips, her chin, her throat. "Nothing is going to take me away."

"Then let me touch you," Serena whispered, sliding her hands down his chest to his belly, and to the fall of his breeches. His body was so strong and lean, and so very different from her own. She was fascinated by the flat, ridged muscles of his abdomen, how the coarse hair that curled on his chest narrowed to a dark trail that disappeared into the top of his breeches. Blindly her fingers began to unbutton the waistband, and he grasped her wrist to stop her.

"Not yet," he said, his voice harsh with restraint. The black silk ribbon on his queue had come undone, the ends trailing over his shoulders, and his dark hair was pulling free, tousled and unruly around his face. "You don't know what you're asking."

"But I *wish* to know," she pleaded. She twisted her hand so she could stroke his cock as it strained through his breeches, curiosity and desire making her bold. "How can I please you otherwise?"

To her it seemed the most obvious thing in the world, and the most important as well. She thought she'd known what to expect from lovemaking, but already she'd realized that all the picture-books and bawdy stories that she'd heard in the *zenana* long ago couldn't begin to explain the mysteries of what she was going to discover with Geoffrey.

But she wanted to discover these mysteries *with* him, not simply be led. The women in the *zenana* had been adamant that pleasure bound lovers together, and that one without the other was only half of life's joy.

She could not fathom why he was holding himself back from her. In the carriage, he'd wanted her to touch his cock, yet now he was pushing her hand aside, and she could tell how much effort it cost him, too. His voice was rough, and his pupils were so dilated from arousal that his blue eyes looked black, the flame from the bedside candlestick reflected in them. It seemed that every muscle in his glorious body was tense and ready for release.

She turned her hand in his grasp, spreading her fingers as far as he would permit over his taut, flat belly, and he jerked back as if he'd been burned.

"Not yet," he said, his breathing ragged as he retreated to the edge of the bed, on his knees and away from her reach. Even in the wavering candlelight, there was no mistaking the intensity of the desire in his eyes as he studied her, a look that made her feel as feverish and light-headed as his caresses had.

"I have to make sure you're ready to take me," he said, "or I fear I'll hurt you."

She pushed herself up on her elbows, intending to coax him back. She wasn't sure how; she was certain she must not look terribly alluring with her hair a tangled mess and her shift pulled down below her breasts and rucked up around her waist, and she tried to wrestle it back into place as she began to sit upright.

"Please, Geoffrey," she began softly. "Please I—*ohh*!"

He'd reached forward suddenly, hooking his arms beneath her knees to drag her forward. She yelped in surprise as he lowered his face between her legs. She wriggled to pull free, suddenly shy to have him so close to her most private parts, but he held her fast. He kissed the inside of her thigh, his beard grazing, giving her a little nip along with the kiss, and then suddenly, shockingly, he was kissing her *there*.

She knew such things were done, but knowing was not the same as experiencing. He held her thighs open, and swept his tongue gently over her lips, her passage, and the small sensitive nub that she'd no English word for. He teased her, lashing his tongue across the tender folds with a magic she'd never imagined. She whimpered and arched upward, unable to keep still as she let herself be carried on the rising waves of pleasure, and he used one forearm across her hips to keep her steady as he increased the wicked torment.

"You're so perfect," he murmured, pausing to open her farther with his thumbs. "Every part of you is beautiful."

His finger glided deep within her and this time she felt herself clutch around him. She was shamefully wet from his tongue and from her own juices. He pushed deeper still, in and out as he began to lick her again, toying with her with just the tip of his tongue. She grabbed at the sheets and pushed against his mouth, at once trying to escape yet wanting more of the delicious tension he was building low in her belly.

She was gasping now, writhing and straining for release, and when he pushed a second thick finger into her passage, all she noticed was the pleasure of it, coming so fast that she could not stop even if she'd wished to. Her climax claimed her, and with a shattering cry she fell back gasping against the pillows, her legs trembling and her body damp with sweat. Her breasts felt heavy and full, her passage impossibly wet and swollen around his fingers.

He held her hips until the last tremors faded, then finally withdrew his fingers from her passage. Instantly she felt empty and chilled in a way she hadn't expected, and she dragged her eyes open, hunting for him.

"I'm here," he said gruffly. He was standing by the bed, yanking off his stockings so that all that remained of his clothing were his breeches—the breeches that were being forced outward by the thick, obvious thrust of his erection. "Nothing would take me from you now, Serena."

"No," she whispered, coherent conversation beyond her. He was so powerfully handsome and almost primitively male in the candlelight, his broad shoulders and narrow waist carved and defined with muscles, and the sight of him made her breath quicken again. "That—that was unexpected, and very fine."

He grimaced. "I promise you it's only a start," he said, tearing at the buttons on the fall of his breeches.

With one quick motion he shoved them down and kicked them aside, standing before her naked at last. His cock was long and thick, crowned by the blunt head, which glistened faintly. This was what she'd wanted, what she'd imagined, what she'd pleaded for all evening, and yet now that she was confronted with the reality of his size, she caught her breath with trepidation.

She knew she was made to accept him—after all, women were fashioned to bear babies, which were far more sizable then any mere cock—but still she flushed, unable to look away as her heart quickened. She remembered once reading a lurid romance where the heroine referred obliquely to the hero's "mighty engine of her maidenly ruin," which had made her laugh at the time. She wasn't laughing now, not with Geoffrey's cock before her.

Her anxiety must have shown on her face.

"Have I frightened you?" he asked, obviously forcing himself to pause. "God knows I never meant to."

She shook her head. "No." She sighed, and tried to smile, as her gaze once again lowered to his cock. He was so shamelessly, aggressively *virile*. "Yes. You are formidable, Geoffrey, and I—I am not."

"Your aunt told you what to expect, yes?" he asked gruffly. "About what husbands and wives do together?"

"Oh, yes," she said, her smile tight at the memory of

the halting, nonspecific wedding-night information Aunt Morley had offered her. "But it wasn't necessary. You forget how much more frank our household was in India. I was raised to think only of the pleasure that lovers give each other, and not of the duty."

He winced. "There will be no duty, Serena. Not with you."

He reached out and brushed her hair back from her forehead, then touched her lips. She smelled the scent of her own arousal on his fingers, reminding her of how those same fingers had felt buried deep within her. Reflexively her inner muscles fluttered and clenched again, as if begging for his return.

"Trust me," he said, his voice a rough whisper. "That's all I ask. I can't pretend that I won't hurt you in the beginning, but what follows will make it worth it. Be brave, and trust me."

All he asked was trust. How could he know it was everything to her?

Her heart racing, she pressed her mouth against his finger, a kiss that was more of a pledge, even an invitation. Then she parted her lips just enough to let his finger slip between them and flicked her tongue against it. His eyes glittered in response, his smile taut.

"Wicked lass," he murmured as he climbed onto the bed beside her. "You do know how to torment me, don't you?"

"What I want is to please you," she whispered, searching his face as he came over her. Her smile was tremulous, not the sort of bravery that he was urging. With determination she pulled the shift—her last scrap of a garment—over her head and tossed it aside.

His eyes lit with unabashed desire as he studied her hungrily. She'd a vague memory of the *zenana* women speaking of how men were helpless before their lust, and that it was entirely in the woman's power to control how hotly that lust grew. If that was so, then clearly she'd just put the final spark to Geoffrey's tinder, and to her surpise, her own as well.

"There," she said, raising her chin as boldly as she could. "I want to give you the same sort of pleasure that you gave me."

"You will." At once he folded his arms around her and kissed her, easing her back against the pillows. The way he stroked her throat, her breasts, the sides of her ribs and waist made her tremble with pleasure and anticipation. She could kiss him all night long and never tire of it, and she tried to focus on that instead of what was to come. His mouth moving over hers was lush and seductive and powerful, more heady and addictive than any wine, and the velvety caress of his tongue against hers made her misgivings begin to fade. She *would* trust him; what choice did she have when he kissed her like this?

While he kissed her, he eased her legs apart, his fingers again stroking and coaxing her to welcome him. She sighed into his mouth and arched restlessly against his hand, and when he nudged his knee between her thighs and eased himself between them, she tensed, but did not stop him.

She tried not to look down, but from the corner of her eyes she still glimpsed his cock, thick and ruddy and veined, and saw him wet the blunt head with spittle in preparation. He was breathing hard, his movements now swift and deliberate, and the faint sheen of sweat on his body gleamed in the candlelight, accentuating every muscle in his shoulders and chest.

She gasped as she felt him press against her, her gasp turning to sighs as he slid his length between her swollen lips and against the opening of her passage. She was so wet and aroused that she glided up against him, instinctively seeking more. She curled her arms over his shoulders to hold him as he kissed her again, and then, suddenly, she felt him inside her.

Startled, she tried to wriggle away, but he was relentless, pushing into her in increasingly deeper increments.

"Shh, Jēsamina, we're nearly there." He kissed her again to try to calm her. "You're so tight, but we're nearly there."

She clung to his shoulders, struggling to accept him, and she could hear his heart pounding, or maybe it was her own. With each stroke, she felt herself stretched further beyond what she'd thought possible. Finally he was buried deep and thick within her, with no space left between their bodies. She felt ravished, taken, possessed, and keenly disappointed, too, with all the giddy pleasure she'd felt earlier vanishing like an insubstantial wisp of smoke.

"The worst is past, I promise," he said. He cradled her face in his hands and kissed her, even as he slowly began to move again. "It will only be better now."

She stiffened at the unfamiliar stretch and tug within her passage. He shifted back, easing his weight upon her, and slipped his hands beneath her hips to raise her up. The angle of his strokes changed, too, pressing against her in an entirely different way. With each slow retreat and return, the sense of invasion lessened as her body accustomed itself to him.

He was watching her closely, responding to her every reaction, adjusting his thrusts, and she'd only to see the tension in his face to know the effort this cost him. But he'd been right: the worst had passed, and with each movement the first discomfort lessened, and the first flutters of the same pleasure she'd felt earlier began to return.

Tentatively she linked her legs around his waist, and began to arch to meet his thrusts as her enjoyment grew. This was better, much better, than when he'd used his fingers and tongue, because with each stroke he was reaching so many unexpected sensitive places within her core.

His cock, which had appeared so daunting, now seemed the ideal size for her, and she moved with greater abandon, twisting and circling her hips as she discovered not only what pleased her, but him as well.

"I told you the pleasure would come," he growled, his breathing harsh. "You're all I want, Serena. All I need, ever."

There was a growing urgency to him now, his back arching and muscular thighs flexing with each driving thrust. She moaned his name, and didn't try to keep back her little mewling cries as the pleasure built, her core tightening around him in intimate embrace. Faster, harder he drove into her as she held tight to his shoulders, her fingers digging deep into his muscles as if her life depended on it. Perhaps it did: the tension was coiling in her body until she feared she could bear no more, yet still he took her further.

Then, abruptly, the tension broke and her release came and she cried out with the force of it, her core convulsing rhythmically around him. He growled her name and followed with a roar, pumping furiously as he emptied himself into her, then shuddered and buried his face in her tangled hair.

Exhausted and overwhelmed, she lay with her legs still tangled with his and his cock still buried inside her. Lightly she smoothed her fingers across the back of his hair, and kissed his forehead, turned toward her. She felt weightless and free, and glowing from the inside out with happy contentment. The stories she'd heard of this moment had been almost right, but not one of them had been able to capture the magic of it, and the closeness she now felt with Geoffrey.

Her lover, her husband: what beautiful words those

were! The tears that trickled down her cheeks weren't from pain, but from emotions that had no other way to escape.

"I love you," she whispered, so softly that she doubted he'd hear her. She couldn't keep the words back, not now, not after he'd just made her his wife in the most primal of ways. "I love you."

He lifted his head, their faces only inches apart. He seemed years younger now, his face relaxed and his smile slow and satisfied.

"My own Serena," he said, kissing her lightly. "I love you, too."

She went very still. "You didn't have to say that just because I did."

"And I didn't, because I wouldn't, unless I did," he said. "I said it because it's true. I love you; I'd be the greatest fool in Christendom if I didn't."

She desperately wanted to believe him, even as a fresh trickle of tears began to slip from her eyes. "I love you, too. It has nothing to do with being foolish."

"No, we'll leave the fools out of it for now," he said. "But I'm endlessly fortunate to have you as my wife, and you've already made me most happy. Why shouldn't I love you as well?"

She tried to smile. He'd said he loved her. That should be enough, shouldn't it?

He frowned, and touched a finger to her cheek. "What is this? Did I hurt you? I tried to take care with you, but if I—"

"I'm happy, too, that's all," she said quickly. "*You've* made me happy."

He reached to the table beside the bed and handed her two of his seemingly inexhaustible supply of handkerchiefs. He shifted just far enough from her that his cock slipped from her body, and with it a gush of wetness. To her mortification she now realized the purpose for the second handkerchief, and she used it to clean herself while he turned away to give her a bit of privacy.

Somehow that tawdry proof of what they'd done—a quantity of his seed streaked with the blood of her maidenhead—made their marriage more sharply real, and put an end to the last of the glowing well-being she'd felt from his lovemaking.

"I am *happy,*" she said again, too late realizing she was also striving to convince herself. "And if you're happy as well, then I pleased you?"

She wished she'd kept the question from her voice. He turned back and looked at her, his expression mystified.

"Of course you pleased me," he said firmly. "Serena, I have never been more pleased in my entire life than I am at this moment with you."

Settling on his side with his head resting on his bent arm, he reached out and pulled her close to fit beside him. He cupped her breast, feathering the nipple with his thumb until it stiffened for him and she sighed restlessly, and then he kissed her lightly, almost sweetly, as he held her.

She liked how different his body was from hers, how his hard-packed muscles seemed so strong even when at ease. Daring, she wriggled a little more closely against him, and to her relief he tightened his arm around her waist, clearly wanting to keep her there. She liked lying with him like this, in the center of the large bed, and the intimacy of it made her feel safe.

"I wanted to please you," she confessed, reassured enough to link her fingers into his. "I know how important that is for a gentleman. My father's first wife was often quarrelsome and unwell, like many of the English ladies who go out to India. She forbade Father from her bed, until in retaliation he brought a *bibi,* a mistress, to share his quarters, and give him pleasure, as any gentleman would do. That *bibi* was only the first of many."

"Your father's wife?" he repeated, curious. "You mean your mother, don't you?"

She froze, staring at their joined hands and realizing too late how badly she'd just betrayed herself. They'd been married only a matter of hours, yet already her secret was forcing her to make a choice.

She could now begin their married life together with honesty and trust, as Aunt Morley had advised. She could tell him the entire truth of who she was and who he'd married. She could stop hiding, stop pretending, stop lying, and trust that he loved her enough to accept her for what she was.

She could . . .

"Of course I meant Mama," she murmured, avoiding his gaze. "How addled I must sound to you!"

"No, you don't," he said indulgently, brushing the back of his fingers over her cheek. "After all that's happened today, it's a wonder we're not both babbling like incoherent Bedlamites."

There it was, her first lie to him and already she felt the dreadful burden of it on her conscience. It wasn't that she hadn't trusted Geoffrey to love her as she was. No, she didn't trust herself to be strong and honorable, and accept the risk of losing him if he didn't. She was a wretched coward, and so she'd lied, and how she hated herself for doing it.

But Geoffrey wasn't done yet. "Do you mean that because your poor mother was unwell, your father used that as justification to keep his mistress in your home, in your company?"

"I have no memory of my mother," she said, taking more care with her words. "She died when I was very young. But I remember Father always having a *bibi,* and sometimes two. Every Englishman there did, and I thought nothing of it."

"They were likely poor, low Indian women, too, who

had no choice in life." The disgust in his voice was clear. "I'm sorry you were forced to witness that, Serena. What an unforgivable thing to do to a daughter! To see your mother put aside like that, and be expected by your father to keep company with his whores—no wonder you've no wish to speak of your past."

"It wasn't like that," she protested. "The *bibis* were always nice to me. It was the best possible childhood, and Father the merriest, most loving of parents."

"I'll wager he was merry," Geoffrey said drily. "Men as cavalier as that always are."

"He *was* a good man, Geoffrey," she insisted. "He was clever and funny, and he loved me. If you'd met, I'm sure you would have liked him."

"Perhaps," he said, unconvinced. "Regardless, know that I'll never treat you as your father did your mother, or subject our daughter to such a circumstance. Never. You have my word of honor, and my word as your husband. You must bear with me through sickness and health and all the rest, for I won't cast you away. I'll be your husband for the rest of our lives."

She was crying again, but this time her tears sprang not from joy, but anguish. It would have been one thing to hear such a promise from him if he'd known the truth about her, but not like this.

"Oh, Geoffrey," she whispered. "You are far too good for me."

"Hardly," he said, with a ruefulness to his voice that touched her even more. "I rather believe I'm not at all good enough to deserve such an angel as you for my wife."

He kissed her again, and with a contented sigh, he tucked her more closely against his body. Soon she heard his breathing slow and his arm relaxed around her, and he slept.

But Serena did not. The peace and security she had felt

earlier was gone, and despite the warmth of Geoffrey's skin against hers and the love she now knew he felt for her, deep inside she was cold and bereft.

Soon after she'd been brought to London, her governess had told her about a common English bird called a cuckoo. The woman had paid little attention to the bird's plumage or calls, instead concentrating on its habit of laying its eggs in the nests of other birds. The cuckoo's egg would hatch first, and the abandoned fledgling would kick the other, rightful eggs from the nest, claiming all its unwitting adopted parents' food and attention as its own. The cuckoo, her governess declared, was a most vile, selfish, and deceitful bird, perhaps the most despicable in the entire avian community.

But Serena had understood the cuckoo's plight. She, too, had done what was needed to survive, flying from one unsuspecting sanctuary to another. Thanks to Geoffrey, she'd landed now in the most lavish of nests, one that was filled with devotion, kindness, and a near-perfect man who she loved beyond all others. Yet she couldn't help but wonder how long she could remain here before she was discovered, and, like the cuckoo, forced to flee again to save herself.

"I love you," she whispered, even though he slept. "I love you."

CHAPTER 12

Geoffrey wasn't sure whether it was Serena's cries that woke him, or the terrified way she was tearing at the bedsheets.

"Serena," he said firmly, taking her by the shoulders to wake her. Her skin was hot, and she was soaked with sweat, her long hair plastered across her shoulders and breasts. "Serena, it's only a dream. Only a dream."

But the dream or nightmare held her tight in its spell. The candles had long since guttered out, and the only light in the room came from the coals in the fireplace, yet still he could make out the abject terror that contorted her features. Her head whipped from side to side, her sweat-soaked hair plastered to her face, and she babbled scraps of Hindi and English that made no sense.

"Serena, please," he said loudly, striving to rouse her. "Serena, it's only a dream."

Yet still she thrashed about, every muscle taut. Perhaps this wasn't a nightmare, but some sort of paroxysm or seizure. He must summon a physician to bring her ease with bleeding or a draft. He released her and ran to the door, shouting for his manservant.

"Allen!" he roared. "Allen, here, at once!"

The man came stumbling down the stairs, groggily stuffing his shirt into his breeches.

"Allen, listen to me," Geoffrey said. "Lady Geoffrey

is unwell. Send a footman at once for Dr. Partridge. Tell him that—"

"Forgive me, my lord, but she won't want a physician," said an unfamiliar young maidservant, curtseying as she joined them with a candlestick in one hand and a small blue bottle in the other. She was fully dressed in the same clothes she'd worn yesterday when she'd greeted them in the hall. Geoffrey realized she must be Serena's lady's maid, Martha, who'd doubtless been waiting in Serena's rooms all night in case her mistress needed her assistance undressing. "Forgive me, but I could hear Lady Geoffrey from down the hall. One of her bad dreams, my lord, isn't it?"

"Yes," Geoffrey said curtly. It was unnecessary to elaborate. Serena's cries could be heard by them all, and by the other servants, who were sleepily appearing in their nightclothes, roused by the noise. Allen stepped forward, holding out Geoffrey's dressing gown, and for the first time Geoffrey realized he was standing before his household staff completely naked. He yanked the dressing gown over his shoulders and around his body, tying it closed as he strode back to the bed. "Come with me, Martha. This has happened before?"

Martha nodded, her round face twisted with concern. "Yes, my lord," she said. "I have the decoction that the physician made up for her."

Geoffrey stared down at Serena, feeling utterly helpless. "Will that help?"

"Sometimes, my lord," Martha said. "Mostly she has to wake, and then the worst will be over."

Serena remained in the grips of the nightmare, fighting the dream as well as the sheets that were tangled around her limbs. Martha lit more candles, and by their light Geoffrey saw not only the fear that twisted Serena's face, but also the tears that streaked it. It was unbearable for him to see her like this, and he hated being unable to do anything to release her, and once again he bent close to try to rouse her.

"Serena, listen to me," he said. "You're safe. No one can hurt you. You're safe."

She muttered something incoherent, her head twisting against the pillow. On impulse he tried the same words in Hindi.

"Serena," he said. "*Tuma surakṣita hō.* You're safe."

At once she gulped and shuddered, and her eyes flew open with a startled cry. Her golden eyes were unfocused and filled with panic as she stared about the unfamiliar room.

"Hush, hush, Serena, you're safe," Geoffrey said, sitting on the edge of the bed. "Nothing is going to hurt you now."

He saw the moment she realized where she was, who she was, and the moment, too, that she understood what had happened.

"Oh, Geoffrey, I'm sorry," she said, her chest heaving, still struggling for breath. "I'm sorry."

"Nonsense," he said gently. "There's nothing for you to apologize for."

Under the circumstances, he wasn't entirely sure what to do, and it was only now, when she seemed to be coming back to herself, that he realized how alarmed he'd been for her sake. He'd gone to sleep blissfully sated and in love, congratulating himself on marrying a beautiful, charming lady who had also turned out to be stunningly sensual, only to be awakened to this.

"Of course I should apologize," she protested with a wistfulness that touched him deeply. "It's our wedding night, and I've spoiled it. What must you think of me?"

"What I think is that I'm glad you're feeling better," he said firmly. He glanced back at Martha, standing respectfully to one side of the bed. "Your maidservant has brought your medicine, too."

"No," she said sharply. She pushed herself upright, modestly pulling the sheet up over her bare breasts. "That is, thank you, Martha, but no laudanum. It only makes things worse. You see I'm better already. Besides, it must be nearly dawn."

"Oh, my lady," Martha said, and the sympathy in her voice told Geoffrey that this had indeed happened before. "It's only half-past three. Surely if you go back to sleep again you won't—"

"No more sleep," she said, and Geoffrey caught a shade of the earlier dread flicker across her face. No matter how exhausted she looked, she wouldn't want to return to whatever demons had plagued her dreams.

"I'm not sleepy, either," he declared heartily, wanting to put her at ease. "But I am quite ravenous, considering how we managed to overlook supper last night. Allen, ask Mrs. Potter to assemble a light supper tray for us. A little cold beef, cheese, buns, that sort of thing. Serena, is there anything in particular you would like?"

"Tea," she said. "Tea would be lovely. And Martha, please bring me a dressing gown, and then you may go to bed. I shan't be needing you further tonight."

The servants left, closing the door and leaving them alone.

Serena sighed, still clutching tightly to the sheets. Her new wedding ring gleamed in the candlelight. "I'm sorry, Geoffrey. Truly."

He reached out and gently pried her hand from the linen, raising her fingers to his lips. "No more apologies, Serena. I told you before. There's no need."

She shook her head, her fingers tightening unconsciously around his. She'd warned him she was complicated. Perhaps this was what she'd meant.

"I cannot help it, you see," she said. "I have bad dreams, and—and they frighten me."

"Everyone does, once in a while," he said, even though

they both knew that what he'd just witnessed was no ordinary bad dream. A childhood in India would have been enough to raise nightmares in any gently bred English girl, but after what she'd told him earlier about her wretch of a father, he could imagine all too well how much worse that childhood must have been. "It's over now."

"Yes," she murmured, clearly struggling to convince herself. "And it's only the one dream."

"Only one?" he asked, surprised. "The same dream every time?"

She bowed her head, pointedly avoiding his gaze, and slipped her hand free of his. "I'd rather not speak of it, Geoffrey."

He rose from the bed, frustrated by her refusal. "Often the best way to conquer a fear, Serena, is to address it head-on."

"No," she said vehemently. "I'm awake, and the dream is done. If I'm fortunate, I won't have another like it for months, even years."

She raised her face, shaking her hair back from her shoulders. She was smiling: not the strongest of smiles, but through sheer will, she'd managed to muster a semblance of one. He'd seen her do this before, composing her features into a beautiful mask to keep the world at bay, and he guessed she did it from habit.

But he didn't want her doing it now, not with him. He couldn't begin to help her, as he longed to do, until she trusted him.

"Serena," he began. "I vowed to be your husband in all things, and that includes this. You don't have to hide anything from me."

"I wasn't hiding from you, Geoffrey," she said softly. Her eyes were so bright that he was sure that tears lurked within them. "I love you far too much for that."

The servants knocked at the door, and with a muttered oath, Geoffrey bid them enter. First through the door was Martha, carrying over her arm a great rustling, ruffled swath of emerald green silk taffeta that must be Serena's dressing gown.

He watched Serena slip from the bed, her breasts trembling and her pale skin luminous in the candlelight. He hadn't had much time in bed to admire her, and now he was struck by the narrowness of her waist, made to appear even smaller by the full swell of her hips, and all of it without the ordinary contrivance of stays or hoops. He was thankful for his own dressing gown, hiding as it did his growing erection inspired by his wife. His *wife*, he thought, marveling. She moved so gracefully, unselfconscious of her nudity, that he couldn't help but watch, and feel a most fortunate man. When Martha stepped forward to wrap the dressing gown swiftly around Serena, he felt chagrined that it was hiding her beauty, and disappointed, too.

Unaware of his thoughts, Serena pulled her hair free of the gown, glancing around the room. "I should like to wash, Geoffrey. I could go to my own rooms—"

"Use my dressing room if you wish," he said, feeling a bit boorish and woefully insensitive. "There, through that door."

She smiled, dazzling him, as she and Martha disappeared. For a long moment, he stood there staring after her, letting the enormity of this night sink in. He was married, yes, and he was also in love. He hadn't expected that to happen so quickly, but it had, or perhaps it had been there for a while and he'd simply been too dense to notice. He noticed now, that was certain. He loved Serena, and he was overwhelmed by the intensity of it. Now he realized he'd never really been in love before, not like this, and he smiled to himself.

He loved his wife, and she loved him. Could there be anything finer, or more right?

Quickly he opened the door for the other servants who'd been waiting with their supper on platters with domed silver covers, plus the necessary linens, plates, goblets, and silverware. He urged them to hurry as they pulled a nearby table before the fireplace and set it for dining. He wanted everything ready when Serena returned—even after the earlier disturbances of nightmare and the fact that it was still a good hour before dawn, an ungodly hour for him to be awake.

He studied the table critically, wishing he'd thought to plan this first meal together, instead of not seeing beyond seducing her. There should have been flowers—lots of flowers—and he should have had Mrs. Potter create some sort of lavish Frenchified specialties instead of humble tea and sandwiches. Perhaps he should have consulted Gus about the niceties of pleasing new wives.

As it was, he was glad he'd hurried the servants, for Serena returned far sooner than he'd expected. He appreciated that, knowing she was as eager to rejoin him as he was to see her again. He was also glad that she hadn't disappeared for hours of primping and preening, the way some ladies would have, and that she'd already dismissed Martha. She'd washed her face and brushed the tangles from her long hair, but that was all: no powder, no paint, no hairpins.

Yet although she smiled, her expression was still guarded, and he couldn't tell how much was due to her nightmare, and how much was the unfamiliarity of being his wife. Clearly if he wanted her trust, he'd have to earn it. He'd been forceful enough earlier in bed—seduction was something he knew how to do—but perhaps a little *politesse* now wouldn't be amiss.

He sent away the footmen, seating her himself, in one of the armchairs. With a flourish, he lifted the cover to find her toast and placed it on her plate, then poured her tea for her. He'd never done that before, not for anyone, and he concentrated hard to make sure the tea didn't come slurping out from the pot.

It was worth it. Her smile warmed at the simple gestures, things most gentlemen—especially the son of a duke—would never do. When he bent to kiss her, tucking his fingers in the back of her hair, she turned her lips up to meet his with an eager little sigh that would undo any man. Immediately he considered forgetting this makeshift meal altogether and taking her back to bed, then just as quickly thought better of it, or at least the thinking part of him did. He had to remember that Serena was his wife, not his doxy. They'd have their entire lives together, and with considerable willpower he sealed the kiss, and took his own chair beside hers.

"Sugar, or cream?" he asked with determined nonchalance as he poured coffee from the other pot into his own cup.

"Only a splash of cream," she said, holding out her cup. When they were alone together, she let more foreignness creep into her voice, or perhaps he simply was more aware of it. Whatever the reason, he found the hint of Indian inflections impossibly seductive and exotic, full of warmth and mystery.

"There you are," he said, adding the requested splash, and trying hard not to think of a more masculine kind of cream he'd like to be offering her. Being so damned domestic was a trial. "Jam?"

"Thank you," she murmured as he set the silver jampot before her. "I see you prefer coffee to tea, the way so many gentleman do."

"At this hour, I do," he said. "And as strong and black as can be."

She smiled shyly, and he realized she was trying to find her way in all this, too.

"I have so many things to learn about your likes and dislikes," she said. "That was what Aunt Morley advised: that I must learn how you take your tea in order to ensure happiness in our marriage."

Immediately he imagined "taking tea" as a euphemism, one that Lady Morley surely had never intended.

"I shall have to consult Her Grace on all your whims," she continued, stirring the silver spoon through the tea and cream. "She'll know them from your boyhood onward."

"I'm afraid she won't," he said. "As charming as Celia may be, she's not party to my deepest peculiarities. She's Father's second wife. My own mother died when I was very young."

"I'm sorry," she said automatically, yet genuine sympathy filled her eyes. "I didn't know."

"Then that's a testament to how contented my father is with her," he said, unable to escape the rush of sadness he still felt whenever he spoke of his mother. "He grieved deeply for Mother, for years and years. We all did. But my brothers and I were pleased when Father married Celia three years ago, for she makes him happy in ways we'd never thought to see again."

"I have no memory of my mother at all," she said wistfully. "Do you of yours?"

"Oh, yes," he said, smiling as he remembered. "Though I was only six when she died, I remember her as if I'd seen her yesterday. I was her favorite, you see. Harry was special to Father, because he was his heir, and Rivers was still in the nursery. Mother always said she and I were two of a kind. She taught me to read, and to ride my pony, and the names of the stars in the sky at night. Toward the end, when she was too ill to rise, I sat on the bed and invented songs and stories to amuse her. She said I was the only one who could make her smile and laugh, no matter how she suffered, and I believe I was."

"I believe it, too," Serena said softly, reaching out to

cover his hand with her own. "Because you do the same for me now."

He nodded, surprised by how grateful he felt for her touch, and turned his hand over to twine their fingers together. He'd intended to stop his reminiscing there. It was all old history now, hardly fit for their wedding night. Yet there was something about the gentle pressure of her fingers around his, the kindness in her eyes, or perhaps the way she didn't pry, but simply waited for him to go on or not, and before he'd quite realized it, he was telling her more, more than he'd ever spoken to anyone beyond his family.

"I was so young that I didn't truly understand what was happening to her," he said. "It was a cancer in her breast that was eating away at her, killing her slowly, and all the surgeons could do was dose her with laudanum against the pain. Everyone told me that we would lose her soon, that Mother's suffering would end when she was called to the angels and other rubbish like that. What I knew was that she was growing weaker and weaker each day—even I could see that—but I believed that as long as I stayed close to her, she wouldn't be lost. It unsettled Father, having me always perched on Mother's bed, but he hadn't the heart to send me back to my own room."

He sighed, recalling how wrongly he'd misinterpreted the genteel expression. "One afternoon Mother seemed better, and an uncle took me to Bartholomew Fair as a lark, to free me from the sickness in our house. But in the middle of a show of dancing dogs, a footman came to summon us at once, for Mother had worsened. I wept and fretted all the way home in the carriage through the fair-crowds, desperate to join my mother, but we were too late, and by the time I reached her bedchamber, they'd already begun to dress her body."

He might think often of his mother, but not the way

she'd been that evening, still and hard and pale as wax, the looking glass on her dressing table already shrouded with black. The joy in their house had vanished, replaced by a crushing darkness that had been very nearly unbearable for his six-year-old self. No: he'd no wish to revisit that day.

"Then that's why you came racing back to England from Calcutta," Serena said. "You needed to save your brother."

He stared at her, almost startled by her voice. How could he have forgotten she was here with him?

"I returned because it was my duty," he said slowly, firmly, the way he'd explained his haste to everyone else who'd asked. "That always came first with Father. It was my duty to be in England in the eventuality that I had become Father's heir. Which, most fortunately, did not happen. I've told you that before. I've never wanted the dukedom, especially at such a cost."

She nodded, her expression solemn as she reached out to place her hand on his chest. "That might have been part of it, yes. But in your heart, here, you believed you could save your brother the way you hadn't been able to save your mother."

He shook his head, resisting what she suggested, yet not wanting to hurt her. He raised her hand from his chest to his lips, lightly kissing her palm to turn her gesture into something more flirtatious.

"Many years separated the two, Serena," he said, striving to lighten the moment. "I don't see how there could be much of a connection."

"I do," she said, her eyes filled with sorrow that went far beyond sympathy. "The past is with us always, Geoffrey, no matter how we might wish it otherwise. It can't be changed. You had to try to join your brother in time, no matter how many months your voyage took. In your heart, your mother was guiding you. You went to him from love, not duty."

"It wasn't that I thought I could change things, Serena," he insisted, for it now seemed oddly important that she understand—or perhaps that he understand himself. "I'm not so great a fool, nor so arrogant, as to believe that. But I suppose what I hoped for most was that last chance to talk, to say things that needed saying. It may sound foolish to you, but—"

"I never said good-bye to Father," she said, her voice scarcely above a whisper. "I was sick, and he was, too, and Asha, and everyone else who could not flee, and then I was the only one left."

"I'm sorry," he said, all he could say. He knew almost nothing of her last days at Sundara Manōra. She'd always made it clear that she'd no wish to speak of it, and he hadn't pushed, not wanting to cause her the pain of remembering. "As you said, the past is always with us, whether we wish it to be or not."

But she was so lost in that past that he doubted she heard him.

"Asha was still alive when I went to her," she said, slipping her hand free of his. She made one hand into a fist, and clasped the other tightly over it, her eyes staring. "I lay beside her and told her that together we would survive, but instead they took me, and left her behind, as if she didn't matter."

"Who was Asha?" he asked carefully. "A servant?"

She shook her head, a quick little jerk. "My sister. She was too weak to fight the fever alone. I loved her, but that wasn't enough."

Geoffrey was stunned. She'd never once mentioned having a sister, nor had he heard it from anyone else. Then he thought of their earlier conversation, of how her father had kept his mistresses in the same house with his true family, and it all made sense. Asha must have been a bastard daughter born to one of these mistresses, and raised side by side with Serena. In England, such an arrangement would have been shockingly scandalous, but in India, Lord Thomas had done what he pleased. And clearly it had pleased Serena, too, for her to feel such devotion to her half sister.

"It could not have been your fault, Serena," he said. "Where were the servants?"

"Gone." She was clenching her hands so tightly together that the knuckles were white, and the fact that she wasn't crying somehow seemed much worse than if she had. "Once Father was dead, they'd no reason to stay. The servants, the guards, the eunuchs, the slaves, all fled if they could, and left the gates open. But many of them died, too, wherever they fell, as is the way with fevers. It was the rainy season, the monsoon, and in the heat and damp the bodies soon bloated and began to rot. There were clouds of flies, and hyenas and other animals came in through the gate to—to feed. I was weak, and I could barely stand, and I was so afraid the hyenas would hunt me down, too."

He rose and went to stand behind her, wrapping his arms around her shoulders to comfort her as best he could. He longed to protect her, even if there was no way he could protect her from the ghosts that haunted her. In all the things that he'd imagined about her unspoken past, he'd never pictured this. His mother's suffering had been very real and grieved him still, but at least she had died in her own bed, with her husband by her side. The horror of what Serena was describing, and what she had witnessed and endured, was unfathomable to him.

"But they didn't," he said. "You escaped. You're here, and you're safe."

She shook her head again, her shoulders bowed with misery. "I didn't *escape*. The English physician that Father had sent for came too late to help. Instead he and the English soldiers carried me away, and burned our house to the ground to destroy the contagion. They left Asha and Father and the others inside, to be burned in the fire with the house. Why was I saved, and they were not?"

Overwhelmed, she slipped forward in the chair. He caught her before she fell and carried her to the bed. She didn't sob or cry aloud, but her face was pale and twisted in sorrow, her eyes empty.

"Listen to me, Serena," he said urgently, bending over her. "None of that affects you now. It's over, done. You're safe here with me."

She reached up and laid her palm against his cheek. Her hand was cold, and she was trembling; he could feel it. "I should never have told you, Geoffrey. Not about the fever, or my sister, or the fire."

"Of course you should have," he said. "I want you to trust me, Serena, in this and in everything else."

"But I've never told anyone, not a word."

He sighed. "It's your nightmare, isn't it? The fever, the wild beasts, the fire. We spoke earlier of your father and India. Likely that was enough to make you remember the rest. It all comes back when you sleep, doesn't it?"

Her eyes widened, answer enough.

"No one knows," she said frantically. "I should never have told you. No one *knows*!"

"Hush now, hush," he said, striving to calm her. "I guessed, that is all."

"But now you know, and—and you shouldn't," she said, the panic rising in her voice.

"It was a long time ago, Serena," he said. "While it may still seem very like yesterday to you, to most other people it will be too long ago for them to care."

"Seven years ago," she said, "and that's no excuse. I still shouldn't have told you any of it."

"And why the devil not?" he demanded. He knew he should be more understanding and show her only kindness, but her instant regret that she'd shared such a momentous confidence made him feel as if he'd already failed her. "You were a young girl in a terrible situation. It has been your secret to keep, and now it's mine as well, until you tell me otherwise."

"But it wasn't my secret to share," she said, faltering. "Not entirely. My sister—no one here knows of her. No one."

"Then we shall change that," he said, determined to prove that he did understand. "She won't be forgotten. We'll have a monument made to her memory for St. Stephen's, beside the one for your father."

"*No!*" she exclaimed vehemently, sitting upright and backing from him against the pillows. "My grandfather and my uncle must never know of Asha, nor your father, either."

"Damnation, Serena, do not mention my father in the same breath as your grandfather!"

"Why shouldn't I?" she said defensively. "Your father may be a duke, but he's just as proud, and as *English*, as my grandfather. If either of them learned of Asha, they would both say nothing but hateful things of her because of who she was."

He hadn't expected that from her. He pushed away from the bed and went to stare down into the dying coals in the fireplace, his arms crossed over his chest as he struggled to control his temper.

"I know they cannot help it," she said, her voice softening a little. "It is how they have always thought the world to be ordered, with themselves at the very top. But I could not bear to hear them speak cruelly of Asha because of things that were never her fault. She does not deserve that, not at all."

She was entirely right, but he couldn't bring himself to

admit it. He'd his measure of pride, too. Instead he simply pretended she hadn't just lumped his father in with her appalling grandfather.

"Very well, then," he said, turning back to face her. "We will have a monument here, in the back garden, where only we will see and understand its significance. A statue, a tree, anything you desire that will help you to keep Asha's memory alive."

She frowned, still troubled. "Why would you do that for her? You never met Asha, or knew her. Because of who she was, in England she would be as nothing to the son of a duke."

He smiled, for the answer to this question was easy, and obvious to him.

"Asha was your sister," he said firmly, "and you loved her dearly. That is sufficient for me to respect her memory as well. I'm not my father, and I'm especially not your grandfather, Serena, or your uncle, nor do I share their misguided bigotry. You might recall that the gentlemen in your family have little use for me, either."

"That is true." She was watching him across the room, her golden eyes guarded.

"It is," he agreed. "There's no help for it, either."

"No," she said softly, looking down. "But it no longer matters, Geoffrey. Now I belong to you, not to Grandfather or anyone else. And you—you are *kind*."

Only one candle remained lit on the table beside her, the rest having guttered out. Against its flickering light, her profile was cast in sharp profile, softened only by the waving wisps of her hair. She was looking down at her hands, lightly touching her finger to the topaz in the center of her ring as if to remind herself of their wedding, and their marriage. Or so he guessed; he wasn't certain, though he'd like to believe it was true.

Yet the longer he studied her, the more he thought of the enormous step they'd taken today. It had been easy to promise to love her in the church, because that was the ceremony, and easier still to say it directly after they'd made love. What gentleman wouldn't tell his bride he loved her when they were in bed together?

But to tell her now, after all he'd learned tonight of her past, of her family, of what she'd endured and what terrified her still, was far, far different. To be sure, he loved her still; there wasn't any doubt of that. No, in fact he loved her more, for by sharing her history with him, she'd given him a sizable part of herself, too.

He'd wanted her to trust him, and he realized now that trust wasn't something that came automatically with their marriage, like the dowry that had been included in their settlement. She had trusted him with the truth about her father, her sister, and her nightmares, and he felt honored and a little awed by such confidence.

And loved. She loved him.

But even better, he realized after this long night how very dear she'd become to him, and how much he did in fact love her. It wasn't just a glib assertion, or a poetical promise, but something true and bright that would only grow with each day and night they were together.

The candle beside her finally burned to the quick, and with a twist of dark smoke, flickered away. The first light of dawn was beginning to show gray behind the curtains, and instead of summoning a servant to bring more candles, Geoffrey went to the window and pulled the curtain open himself. Over the tops of trees in the square and the other houses beyond that, the sun was slowly climbing its way into the sky, the palest of peach against the clouds.

He turned back toward the bed. She was sitting upright, her legs folded beneath her and her back straight, more like a regal Mughal princess than an ordinary English bride.

"Morning," she said softly. "Our first together, my lord Geoffrey."

She did not smile, but she held her hand out to him. He stepped forward and claimed it as his own, then climbed onto the bed beside her. She shifted across the mattress to make way for him, staying close enough that she could rest her head on his shoulder. That was invitation enough, and he slipped his arm around her to draw her closer.

"My own Jēsamina," he said, turning her face up toward his. "Why some of us die while others live is a mystery, and always will be. You survived to marry me, and be my wife. I can't promise I can banish all your nightmares, but I will be here to hold you when you wake, and fight the ghosts and demons for you however I can. I love you, Serena. That is kismet, too: your fate and mine, linking us together."

"Kismet," she repeated, and at last she smiled. She slipped her hand inside his dressing gown to rest it again on his chest, and he wondered if she could tell how that alone could make his heart beat faster. "I love you, Geoffrey. Oh, how I love you!"

It had not been the wedding night he'd expected, but as Geoffrey kissed her, he knew he wouldn't have wanted it any other way.

The next two weeks were the most blissful days—and nights—in Serena's life. Enraptured with their own company, she and Geoffrey did not leave their house, nor see any of the visitors who came to call. There would be time enough for making their formal wedding calls. Now they didn't even bother to dress, and the farthest they ventured was into the walled garden behind the house. Most days they kept to Geoffrey's bedchamber, having their meals brought to them there. No one else in the world existed beyond each other. By tacit agreement, neither of them mentioned what she'd told him that first night, and she slept soundly, deeply, without nightmares. If ever there was a true honeymoon idyll, then this was it: they laughed, and talked, and teased, and made love in a hundred different ways.

Throughout it all, Serena felt cherished and adored and loved beyond measure, and beyond her imagining, too. Even when she and Asha had described their champions long ago, she'd never contrived a gentleman as handsome, generous, and passionate as Geoffrey. Her marriage would in fact be completely, absolutely perfect if not for one thing:

On that first night, she hadn't told Geoffrey the truth.

Now it was the last anguished thought before she finally drifted to sleep in Geoffrey's arms, and the first in her head when she woke. She'd come so close to telling him everything, *everything*, and then at the last moment she'd backed away from the truth. Instead she'd babbled a version that wasn't entirely false, but not pure enough for the truth, either.

Once again, she'd been a coward. As much as she longed to trust him with her greatest secret, she hadn't been able to. She didn't dare. He could say all he wanted about how he'd respect her sister's memory, but a memory wasn't reality. He could be noble and generous because even this half-truth would not affect him, and he could claim his family had been scorned, too, for its baseborn beginnings.

But that long-ago bastard Fitzroy had had a king for a father and a French duchess for a mother. There were no dancing-girls in Geoffrey's pedigree, no murky foreign blood to taint his noble family. He'd no notion of the shame her truth would bring to him, or the disgrace that would envelop his entire family.

She did. Because she loved him, she could not tell him

the whole truth, and risk losing him forever. Yet at the same time, because she loved him, it grieved her to have her monstrous secret always there between them, twisting and gnawing unceasingly at her conscience, and betraying the trust he so freely gave to her.

As long as they were hidden away together here in their house, without any responsibilities or obligations, she could pretend that her past didn't matter. She could tell herself that she would be effortlessly and instantly accepted by his family, with no questions asked. She could believe that with Geoffrey lying beside her at night, she'd never have another nightmare that might give her secret away.

Most of all, she could ignore the too-obvious link between their lovemaking and what could be the most undeniable of evidence as to who she really was: the baby that might already be growing in her belly.

But just like their honeymoon, all that pretending and believing could not last forever, and it came to an end in a way that neither expected.

They were taking their breakfast in the garden, enjoying the summer morning. Geoffrey was reading the latest scandal-sheet out loud to Serena in a silly, affected voice to make her laugh, and he'd succeeded admirably. He'd just added a sly aside about the Countess of Blankblank when Colburn appeared carrying a letter on a small silver salver.

"Forgive me, Lord Geoffrey," the butler said solemnly, bowing as he held the letter out to Geoffrey. "I know you'd left orders not to be disturbed, but this has just arrived from His Grace."

Geoffrey frowned, setting aside the paper to take the envelope.

"What in blazes could induce Father to write to me at this hour of the day?" he said, cracking the wax seal with his thumb. "It's not like him."

"I hope it's not bad news," Serena said. From the somber look on Geoffrey's face, she was already guessing it was. "No accident or misfortune?"

"I suppose to my father it is." He closed the letter, pressing the folds between his fingers. "How soon can you dress? We're expected at Harry's house directly."

That frightened Serena. The duke wouldn't have ordered them so summarily to come to Harry's house without a good reason, nor would Geoffrey instantly obey, either.

"I'll send for Martha," she said, pushing back her chair. "She'll have me dressed before the carriage has arrived. What has happened, Geoffrey?"

"Gus has been been delivered of her child," he said, tossing his father's letter onto the table.

"Is the babe unwell?" Serena asked fearfully, ready to sympathize with the sister-in-law she'd yet to meet. Childbirth was a perilous time, putting both mother and infant at risk. "Or is poor Lady Augusta herself—"

"Both are as fine and healthy as can be," Geoffrey said, and sighed. "There's only one thing wrong, and in Father's eyes, it's most serious, and will influence you and me as well. The child is not the son that everyone wished for, but another daughter."

CHAPTER 13

"I still believe we should be celebrating," Serena said as she sat beside Geoffrey in the carriage. She had in fact been ready in only a half hour's time (far faster than Geoffrey), and while his manner was subdued, she'd chosen to wear a yellow flowered muslin gown and a wide-brimmed hat with silk flowers, determined to be cheerful herself even if everyone else was gloomy. Her single jewel was her yellow topaz and diamond engagement ring, for today when she first visited his family as his wife, she wanted to wear only what Geoffrey had given her, and none of the extravagant reminders of her Indian past. "From your father's letter, it would seem that we've been asked to come mourn rather than rejoice at the birth of a perfectly healthy baby."

"Father probably does see it as a mournful day," Geoffrey said, the sun slanting through the carriage's glass making his eyes very blue. After these last two weeks, it was odd to see him in full dress for day, from his buckled shoes to his beaver-skin hat. "Father was disappointed when Gus produced a daughter the first time, and now for her to do it twice will be unforgivable in his eyes."

"How terribly unfair to Lady Augusta!" Serena exclaimed. "Perhaps I'm mistaken, but I rather believe your brother was somewhere involved in the process."

"Serena, please." Geoffrey sighed. "I don't like this any more than you do, but it's the laws that make it so damned unpleasant, not my father. Not entirely, anyway. There's a title and a great deal of property at stake. None of us wish it to leave the family, but to preserve it requires sons. I agree that it's unfair, especially to little Lady Em, but it can't be helped. Sometimes I believe that one of the main reasons my father so loved my mother was that she bore him three sons in quick succession. No duchess could do better."

Serena looked down, fidgeting with the embroidered edging on her mitt. As much as she loved Geoffrey, she'd no desire to become a ducal broodmare herself. "I don't wish to be a duchess, Geoffrey. Not one bit."

"Nor do I want to be the next duke," Geoffrey said. "I suppose that marks me as woefully lacking in ambition, but I'd rather achieve things on my own than idly sit about and wait for my brother's death."

"I can never see you doing that," she agreed, thinking uneasily of how her father had in part gone to India to avoid being an idle second son. She prayed Geoffrey wouldn't want to do that; as much as she treasured the memories of her childhood, they were far too complicated to make her want to return.

"No," he said, his voice growing more determined as he leaned forward. "I suppose it's as good a time as any to tell you this. I am considering entering Parliament. There is expected to be a by-election for the borough of Apsley later this year, and I have been approached about the seat. I've given it much thought, and I believe I could do some good."

"I'm sure you could," she said faintly.

"I could," he said firmly. "India is becoming increasingly important to England. I've traveled more widely than most members, and I could offer an insight that others would not have. It's all due to you, my love. Having you as my wife made me realize I wished to do something more with my life. I want to make you proud of me, Serena."

"I'm already proud of you," she said wistfully, her head spinning. "What lady wouldn't be?"

He beamed at her. "I mean not just as your husband, but as a gentleman who is known for what he's accomplished, not simply for how much he has wagered at White's or other foolishness."

She nodded, overwhelmed. She knew little of the workings of politics, but she did know that while gentlemen took the seats in Parliament, their wives were expected to hold all manner of entertainments to help support and secure their husbands' positions. They became the same public figures as their husbands, their names and histories known, their faces caricatured, and their habits lampooned. In the heat of an election, these women had no privacy—or secrets.

"Doesn't your father control a borough?" she asked, striving to keep the anxiety from her voice. "One where an election would be uncontested?"

"Oh, he does," Geoffrey said patiently, "just as he sits in the House of Lords himself. But if I take this step, I would prefer to do it on my own, without his assistance. It's all in the future, and much may still change, but I wanted you to know now."

"I thank you for that courtesy," she said. "I agree that it's a very large step to take."

She'd hoped to sound cautious, not negative, but at once Geoffrey's face fell.

"Very well, then," he said, his disappointment clear. "I understand. You have no taste for a husband in politics. Far better to know now than later. I will give the gentlemen my regrets, and—"

"No, Geoffrey, please don't," she said swiftly, turning

to place her hand on his arm. "If taking a seat in Parliament is your dream, then you must do it."

He took a deep breath. "You are sure of this, Serena?"

"I am," she said. She was, too. She wanted him to be happy, and she couldn't let her fears stand in his way. Besides, though she'd never considered being a political hostess or canvasser, she might find she enjoyed it. His love made her brave, and for his sake, she was determined to keep an open mind. "You took me by surprise, that is all. I'd no notion you aspired to such a role."

He pulled his hat down over one eye and winked roguishly, a bit of foolishness that always made her smile.

"There are many things you still have to discover of me, Jēsamina," he said, teasing. "Just as I'm sure you've a few secrets of your own."

Her smile faded as she thought of all he didn't know. She loved him so much, and yet because of her secret their happiness seemed so fragile. Without words, she pushed aside his hat and kissed him passionately, a soul-wrenching kiss that was as much an apology as it was about love.

Unaware of her thoughts, all he tasted was the passion.

"I shall have to make a habit of grand pronouncements, if that's the response they garner," he said softly, his eyes glowing with desire of his own. "If we weren't expected at my brother's, I'd tell the driver to continue, and take you here on the carriage-seat."

Her eyes widened, intrigued by the possibility, and as if by accident, she let her gloved hand slide along the inside of his thigh. "As we drive through the streets, Geoffrey? With the driver and footmen and all?"

"There wouldn't be much point to the experience if we were sitting before our house, would it?" he said, clearly regretting a missed opportunity. "The rocking of the carriage—and the chance of being observed—would make it an adventure. We would have to be inventive in our— Blast, here we are."

The carriage had come to a stop before a large, handsome house on Grosvenor Square. The home of the Earl of Hargreave was four stories of white stone with three bays of windows and an imposing entry with an oversized arched doorway. It was bigger than their own, but not so large nor grand as the one occupied by the duke, while youngest brother Rivers lived in lodgings, all of which, thought Serena, tidily summed up the hierarchy of the family.

It was one thing to be alone with Geoffrey, but very much another to now be a Fitzroy by marriage, and party to this mandatory family gathering, and while Geoffrey climbed down from the carriage and turned to offer her his hand, she hung back, still gazing up at the front of the house before them.

"We won't stay long," Geoffrey promised, sensing her uneasiness. "We'll drink a toast to the baby and be shown her wizened newborn face in the arms of a nursemaid. Harry will dote, Father will be gravely disappointed, and likely we won't see Gus at all. All you must do is be your usual lovely self, and we'll be back on our way in no time."

He was right, of course. What was her reluctance compared to what poor Lady Augusta had endured today: childbirth followed by the duke's disappointment? Serena's role was much the easier, and she smiled as she took Geoffrey's hand and stepped down, shaking her skirts out.

"We must come again later in the week after Lady Augusta has had a few days to recover herself," she said, "and bring a gift for the baby, too."

"Gus," corrected Geoffrey. "You're as good as sisters now. You must call her Gus, the way we all do."

"Not until she gives me leave to do so," Serena said, determined to make the best impression possible on her new sister-in-law. Because she'd always held back a part of herself, she had no real friends in London, but she already liked Lady Augusta, especially after she'd arranged to have their carriage decorated after their wedding. It would be good to have an ally besides Geoffrey. Although he assured her his family welcomed her, she thought otherwise, sensing if not open suspicion, then at least doubt.

"Lady Augusta is of a higher rank than I," she continued. "She's a countess."

"You're both Fitzroys now," Geoffrey said firmly. "That's all that matters."

He gave her hand an extra squeeze for reassurance as they climbed the marble steps to Harry's house. Serena was stunningly beautiful this morning, he thought, as fresh as a spring flower with her light silk skirts fluttering in the breeze, and he could not have been more proud to introduce her as his wife to his family.

Yet her uneasiness was unmistakable, or at least it was to him. As soon as she'd stepped from the carriage, she composed her lovely features into the aloof, reserved distance with which she greeted the world. He'd recognized it immediately; he'd always thought of it as her "great lady" look. Weeks had passed since she'd shown him this face, making him realize how much she'd come to let her guard down with him, and how he'd become accustomed instead to the charming, open Serena.

While he wished she'd show that side of herself to his family as well, he understood why she didn't. The horrors of her childhood had left their mark. He had to remember that Father and Harry and the rest were nearly strangers to her, and she needed time to learn to trust them, just as she'd come to trust him. He would be at her side to help ease the way, and protectively he placed his palm on the small of her back as they stepped through the doorway.

"Good day, Wilton," he said to Harry's longtime butler. "A happy day to welcome a new baby to the family. Are my brother and father still at breakfast?"

"Yes, Lord Geoffrey," the butler said, bowing. "His Grace and his lordship are at present in the breakfast room, and request that you and Lady Geoffrey join—"

"So you're here at last, Geoffrey!" Harry himself burst into the hallway, beaming with happiness. If he were disappointed by his new daughter, he certainly wasn't showing it. "Gus will be delighted. You must meet little Lady Penelope, too. She's another beauty, exactly like Lady Em. She's an obliging little creature as well: she first began to make her impending arrival known shortly after dinner last evening, and by midnight she was here, with no fuss at all."

"Congratulations, brother," Geoffrey said, grinning in return as he clapped his brother on the back. How could he not, when Harry was so obviously overjoyed with his new daughter? "The world is always improved with another beauty. But I wonder if Gus would agree with your description of the child's easy arrival?"

"You may ask her yourself," Harry said. "She specifically requested that you be brought to her when you arrived. You, and your bride."

Harry's smile became more gallant as at last he turned toward Serena, bowing to her.

"Lady Geoffrey, good day," he said. "In my enthusiasm, I've neglected to welcome you to my home. May I congratulate you once again upon your marriage to my brother?"

Serena curtseyed gracefully and nodded in acknowledgment, her smile perfectly measured yet guarded. "I am honored on both counts, Lord Hargreave. And may

I congratulate you and Lady Hargreave on the birth of your daughter?"

Geoffrey saw how Harry's brow flicked upward, taking note of Serena's distance and not approving of it, either. Swiftly he took Serena's hand, making his allegiance to her as clear as possible.

"Would you please give my wife leave to use your given name, Harry?" he said. "She—and you—shouldn't be relying on titles at home, especially not on a day as joyful as this."

Harry's glance flicked down at Geoffrey's and Serena's joined hands, and he smiled. "Of course she may," he said easily. "Serena, my dear, you must call me Harry and my wife Gus."

"Thank you, Harry," she murmured solemnly. "I'm honored."

"No, what you are is part of our family," Harry said expansively. "Now come, let me introduce you to my new daughter."

"Are you certain Gus wants that?" Geoffrey asked warily. He had not seen Gus since that disastrous conversation over breakfast, and while Harry had excused her unfortunate humor on her pregnancy, Geoffrey wasn't convinced that appearing again now, only a matter of hours removed from her giving birth, might not be exactly welcome. The last thing he wished for Serena was that she and Gus begin on the wrong foot—or feet. "Perhaps it would be better if we returned in a few days, after she's had time to recover."

"No, no, not at all," Harry said, already heading toward the stairs. "Gus specifically wanted to see you both, and none of us wish to keep her waiting."

"That we do not," Geoffrey agreed. He glanced at Serena, who was smiling at him anxiously, and in turn he smiled with as much encouragement as he could as they followed Harry up the stairs. Their progress was slow, for Harry's old injury made him take each step one by one, which gave Geoffrey time to ask the question they'd both been studiously avoiding.

"What is Father's humor?"

Harry didn't look back, but it was clear from the change in his voice his earlier smile was now gone. "Disappointed. Sardonic. Not pleasant company."

None of this surprised Geoffrey. "Has he been able to keep his opinions to himself for Gus's sake?"

"He hasn't deigned either to visit Gus or to view the baby."

"Is he still here?" Geoffrey asked.

"Oh, yes," Harry said, his voice hardening. "He and Celia are lingering over breakfast in my back parlor. I believe Celia—who did come see the baby, bless her—is attempting to reason with him, with little success. Otherwise he is eating my eggs and toast and pretending as if everything is exactly as it should be. Which it isn't."

Geoffrey sighed. "Would you like me to go speak to him?"

"To what purpose?" Harry said, resigned. "No, I'd rather you came with me. You know, Penelope truly is a beautiful baby."

"I'm sure she is," Serena said softly, startling Geoffrey. Her eyes glowed with understanding, and her voice held all the warmth that had been missing ever since they'd entered the house. "Your daughter is loved by both her parents, which makes any child a thousand times more beautiful."

Harry paused, and looked over his shoulder. "That is true, Serena," he said thoughtfully, and his smile for her now was genuine. "Those are wise words, and appreciated."

She blushed, and lowered her head. As Harry went ahead to make sure that Gus was awake and still amenable to visitors, Geoffrey bent and quickly kissed Serena, his pride incalculable.

"Thank you," he said. "I've no notion what inspired you to speak so to my brother, but those were the exact right words to say to him in his present humor."

She gave a quick shrug to her shoulders. "I was once loved like that," she said wistfully. "I only spoke the truth."

Harry beckoned to them, and they joined him to walk through the countess's parlor to her bedchamber. Having no experience with either pregnant ladies or childbirth, Geoffrey had been reluctant to venture into Gus's presence, and leery of what unimaginable female mysteries he might be compelled to witness. To his relief, there were none: only Gus herself propped up against a mountain of pillows and crisp fresh linen, sipping chocolate from a tiny porcelain cup. She wore an exuberantly ruffled cap over her red-gold hair, and beneath it her eyes managed to be both utterly exhausted and utterly exhilarated at the same time. In addition to her lady's maid standing guard near the bed, two nursery maids were also in attendance, plus the midwife besides. But the true centerpiece of all this activity was the tiny creature wriggling in an oversized cradle beside Gus's bed, her wrinkled red face surrounded by a ruffled linen cap very much like her mother's.

"You came, Geoffrey!" Gus exclaimed with delight, handing the chocolate cup to her maid. "And you brought your lady, too! Oh, how very glad I am finally to meet you, Serena. You can't know how disappointed I was to not attend your wedding."

She tried to sit up further to reach her hand out to Serena, and grimaced at the effort. The midwife hurried forward, guiding Gus back against the pillows.

"Please, my lady, do not vex yourself," she said sternly. "You must be easy, or risk making yourself ill."

"Oh, please take care, Lady Hargreave," Serena said, joining the midwife at the side of the bed. "I'd never want to be the cause of any distress."

"You won't, I assure you." Gus sighed, studying Serena. "I can see why Geoffrey so wished to marry you. You're quite astonishingly beautiful. And you must call me Gus, since we're now sisters after a fashion."

"Exactly so," Geoffrey said heartily, relieved and pleased that this was going so well.

Serena blushed. "Thank you, Gus," she said shyly. "But I came here not to speak of myself, but to admire your new daughter."

She leaned over the cradle, holding back the ribbons from her hat to keep them from trailing down. Dutifully Geoffrey went to stand beside her. To him Penelope looked much the same as all new babies, impossibly small and fragile and wizened.

"She *is* beautiful," Serena breathed, and as if on cue, the baby made a loud squawking exclamation, her little arms flailing wildly. Everyone laughed but Serena, who stared down at the baby, completely enraptured. She tugged off her right glove, and pressed her pinky into the baby's hand. At once Penelope's fingers closed around it and held tight, and Serena smiled.

"How fortunate you are, Gus," she said without looking up. "Such a sweet little girl!"

"She is," said Gus softly, smiling down at the baby as well. "Would you like to hold her?"

Serena's face lit in a way that Geoffrey would never have predicted. "Truly?"

Gus nodded. "Sit in the armchair, there. She can be wriggly, and it's easiest that way. Mrs. Pratt will hand her to you."

At once Serena sat, eagerly pulling off her left glove. The nursemaid carefully gathered up the baby and her blanket, and placed her in Serena's arms. To Geoffrey's amazement, she knew exactly how to hold Penelope, cradling her securely in the crook of her arm and rocking her gently, and crooning the kind of gentle gibberish that pleased all babies. Only Geoffrey—or so he guessed—realized the nonsense words came from Hindi, not English.

"Not a day old, but she already recognizes her favorite aunt," Harry said proudly, and the others chuckled.

"And pray why not, when she is already my favorite niece?" asked Serena. Her earlier guard was gone entirely, her face wreathed with happiness that bordered on joy as she held the tiny baby. But as secure as Penelope felt in Serena's arms, there was one comfort her aunt could not offer, and fretfully the baby began to whimper and root against the corseted front of Serena's silk gown. With obvious reluctance Serena handed her to Gus, who unfastened the front of her gown and put the baby to her breast.

"Thank you, Gus," Serena said, still unable to look away from the baby. "She is quite a perfect babe."

"Not quite perfect, according to some," Gus said, her sudden sorrow unmistakable as she held her baby a bit more closely. "All because she can never be a duke."

"Now, now, don't upset yourself, sweetheart," Harry said quickly. "We agreed we'd not speak of that."

"So this is where everyone has chosen to gather." Without any fanfare, the duke entered the room, with Celia behind him.

The servants and midwife sank into curtseys to him, as they should. To Geoffrey's dismay, Serena did as well. It wasn't that it was improper, for it was, on the basis of rank. But he wanted his wife to be accepted by his family and not feel she must defer to any of them, especially not Father. Pointedly he went to stand beside her, taking her hand to lead her forward to greet his father.

"Good day, Celia, Father," he said, keeping a steady hand on Serena's arm so she wouldn't curtsey again.

Father nodded, the most acknowledgment he usually made.

"I am glad to see you've finally emerged from your *refuge des amoureux,*" he said drily. "Is the honeymoon over, then?"

Instantly Geoffrey bristled, but before he could spit out words he'd later regret, Serena saved him.

"It's not over, Your Grace," said Serena with one of her most angelic smiles and a languid sweep of her thick dark lashes. She curled her fingers more closely into Geoffrey's hand, leaning slightly against him to make their intimacy unmistakable. "Merely interrupted for this lovely occasion."

"Indeed." Father smiled indulgently. "And please, my dear, call me Brecon. No need for ceremony in the family."

Geoffrey listened, stunned. Serena had just won a small victory for them both, and if it was possible, he loved her even more for it. For all that Father was a duke, he was also a mortal male, and very few could resist Serena when she smiled like that.

"I am honored, Brecon," she said with a charming dip of her chin. "How wonderful to be included in this welcome for Lady Penelope's arrival!"

"Ah, yes, Lady Penelope," he repeated with a sigh at the reminder, and turned from Serena toward Gus's bed. Although he was smiling still, his expression had become blandly, consciously dispassionate, as if making a cursory inspection of livestock rather than meeting a new grandchild. But at least he'd come, thought Geoffrey; when Penelope's older sister, Emily, had been born, Father had taken nearly a week before he'd called.

"That's a fine Homeric name with substance, at any rate," Father continued, several feet from both Gus and the baby, and not coming closer. "Cousin to the beautiful Helen of Troy, faithful wife to the wandering Odysseus."

"She's named for Gus's grandmother," Harry said. "Besides, we thought that Lady Penelope Fitzroy had a pleasing sound to it."

"I suppose it does," Father said grudgingly, frowning as he watched the suckling baby. "Why haven't you engaged a proper wet nurse for poor Augusta, Harry? It hardly seems appropriate for your countess to have to put her child to her teat like some common fishwife or washerwoman."

"It is my choice, Brecon," Gus said defensively. "I see no reason to deprive my child of the nourishment that nature has so generously provided for her, simply because she was born into this family and not another."

But the duke had already spotted something else that concerned him.

"I see you've also chosen to ignore the standard advice regarding swaddling, Augusta," he continued, insisting on using her full name as he always did, loathing the shortened version of it. "A most curious choice. How is the child to grow straight if her limbs are permitted to flop about like that?"

"Gus is following Dr. Cadogan's practices, Father," Harry said earnestly. "His studies have shown that children in the country who grow in simple freedom fare much better than aristocratic children who are constricted by swaddling and tight clothing, and fed an overrich diet."

"What rubbish!" Father declared soundly, appalled. "What does this Cadogan know? All of you boys were swaddled by your mother's choice, and there aren't three taller, stronger, more elegantly made gentlemen in London."

Celia placed a hand on his arm. "Please, Brecon," she

said gently. "Dr. Cadogan is a physician of some renown in the management of children, and his book of advice is very popular with younger mothers. My daughters subscribe to his theories as well, and their children are thriving."

The duke shook his head, unconvinced. "Infants have been swaddled since time immemorial. Even the Christ Child was swaddled. Why should all the wisdom of the past be tossed aside because this charlatan Cadogan presumes to say so?"

"He is no fool, Father," Harry insisted. "He is a Fellow of the Royal Society. It's said that even Her Majesty follows his word."

"I do not believe it," Father said sternly, "and you, sir, are the greater fool for doing so. It's bad enough that you have presented me with another girl in place of the grandson I was expecting, but now you wish to put the child's well-being into jeopardy as well."

Gus made a strangled, gulping sound as if she'd been wounded. She bowed her head protectively over her baby, and Harry immediately went to her.

It was more than Geoffrey could bear. "Father, don't," he said sharply. "Pray consider Gus."

"There is nothing to consider," Father said, his voice equally sharp. "I've only spoken the truth. I'll grant that it's no more Augusta's fault than the child's herself, but the fact remains that a son was required, and a daughter can only be considered a disappointment."

Once again before Geoffrey could answer, Serena spoke.

"If it were my choosing, I'd have only daughters," she said, her cheeks flushed and her words trembling with emotion. "My father had no sons, yet he still showered us with nothing but love."

"And so it shall be for me," Harry said firmly, bending

down to kiss Gus's forehead. "My ladies are my world, and I pray they know it."

Father drew in his breath, his entire posture reflecting the sangfroid that served him so well at Court, if not at home.

"Harry. Geoffrey," he said curtly. "I suggest that we leave the ladies, so that I might have a word or two with you alone."

It was a conversation that none of them wanted, but also one that could no longer be avoided. Grim-faced, Harry led them to a small parlor at the opposite end of the hall from the women in Gus's bedchamber.

"Father, you must listen to me," he began as soon as he'd closed the door. "I cannot stand by and listen to you insult my wife."

Father sat in the armchair facing the mantelpiece and crossed his legs, while both Harry and Geoffrey remained standing, too angry to sit. The arrangement gave Father all the power, reminding Geoffrey all too readily of once again being a schoolboy awaiting his father's reprimand.

Not that Father himself seemed to feel that way.

"I have never insulted Augusta," he said with infuriating calm. "If she believes that I have, then I shall be more than happy to offer her my apology. But can you deny that last night she bore a girl, not a boy?"

Furious, Harry shook his head. "Father, that is not the point. Gus already blames herself. She's nearly made herself ill over it, yet while she's still recovering from childbed, you make barbarously unkind comments that you know will only hurt her."

"There are times when the truth can hurt," Father said calmly, and whether it was the sentiment, or that calmness, it was more than enough for Harry. Without another word, he turned on his heel, and left, slamming the door.

Geoffrey began to go after him, but Father stopped him.

"Stay, Geoffrey," he said. "Please. It's you I wish to address, anyway. Harry will be back when his temper cools, and he can once again see reason."

"I am not so certain," Geoffrey said, but he did turn back. Even now he could not resist the rare moment when Father preferred his company to Harry's. Perhaps Father had already learned somehow of his Parliamentary ambitions; it was possible, given Father's vast network at Court. "He does not like to see Gus suffer. None of us do."

"Oh, Augusta understands," Father said with a cavalier wave of his hand. "She's stronger than the lot of you. But it's your wife who concerns me now, Geoffrey. Tell me of the fair Serena. Does she make you happy?"

"More than I can say," Geoffrey said, unable to keep the foolish grin from his face. So it was Serena, not politics, certainly a far easier topic for him. "I know that the circumstances of our marriage might not have been what either you or her grandfather had planned, but I cannot imagine another woman as my wife, and I dare to say she feels the same."

"I am glad of it," Father said, watching him closely. "She has given you no cause for concern? No questions, no worries?"

Geoffrey frowned, perplexed. "That's a damned strange thing to ask, Father."

"Considering her circumstances before she came to London, I find it perfectly reasonable," Father said. "Even Allwyn himself seemed vague about her early life. Questions are seldom asked when the lady can insulate her past with a sizable fortune, but now that she has wed into our family, there has been considerable talk about town."

Geoffrey's frown deepened. Keeping to themselves as

they had been, he and Serena hadn't heard any of this—which for her sake was just as well.

"No one dares speak this tattle to your face, Father, do they?"

"Oh, no," Father said. "No one would. Still, I hear things."

He added a vague, encompassing wave of one hand, the lace cuffs of his shirt falling back from his wrist. Geoffrey couldn't begin to comprehend the extent of Father's channels through Court and the rest of London; one way or another, there was little that escaped Father's knowledge.

"The usual tattle, of course," he continued. "Entirely unfounded, I am sure, and born more of envy and malice than of fact, yet it cannot be entirely ignored. So I must ask again: has she given you any reason for uncertainties?"

Carefully Geoffrey considered how much he could say to answer his father's doubts, yet honor Serena's request for privacy.

"She has confided in me certain events from her childhood that were not the experiences of an ordinary English lady," he said finally. "Experiences no lady should be compelled to bear, and yet, because of her courage, she survived them. I cannot tell you more, or break my word and confidence to her."

"Your word is safe," Father said, tapping his finger lightly on the arm of the chair. "Suffice it to say that your wife must be an extraordinary woman. Harry and Augusta are considering you both as godparents to Lady Penelope."

Geoffrey smiled, delighted by this show of acceptance by his family. "She would be honored, and so would I."

Father grunted, an ominous sound of nonagreement. "I overheard her with the baby, whispering that Hindi mumbo jumbo," he said bluntly. "Have you determined that she is in fact a Christian?"

"Of course she is," Geoffrey said, his delight instantly dashed. "If that is the sort of rumor you have heard—"

"That's one of them, yes," Father admitted. "But I've only one question that deserves an answer from you, Geoffrey. Do you trust her?"

"Trust Serena?" he repeated, stunned. "Of course I trust her. I love her."

"Love and trust are not necessarily the same," Father said, settling back in the chair. "One would wish it so in an idyllic world, but that is not the one in which we must live. Do you trust her to choose only the truth in what she says and does?"

It seemed a preposterous question to Geoffrey. When he remembered the nightmare on their wedding night, the abject terror on her face when she'd awakened after confronting her past: no, no one could pretend that. What she'd suffered, what she'd told him, was absolutely true. He loved her, and he trusted her.

"I do," he said, aware of how the simple words were an echo of their wedding vows.

"Then permit me to ask another question," Father said. "Were you aware when you pursued her that she had no brothers? Hardly a fortuitous omen for the family."

That one was easy to answer. "Serena's parents died young, before further children were born to them. The Indian climate is not healthy for the British."

Father's expression didn't change. "Her declaration about preferring daughters was worrisome."

"She spoke in the heat of the moment," Geoffrey said. "She'll have no more say than any other woman as to whether she bears boys or girls."

Again Father paused, adding weight to his next question, the one that seemingly mattered most to him.

"Have you gotten her with child yet?"

Geoffrey sighed. After how Father had spoken to Gus earlier, he should have known this was coming. "We've only been wed two weeks, Father."

"Two weeks of marriage, yes," Father said shrewdly. "But as I recall, you'd, ah, tested those waters with the lady before that."

"We didn't," Geoffrey said, defensive for Serena's sake. "We hope for children, of course, but there is plenty of time for that."

Father shook his head. "There isn't," he said sadly. "You are young, and believe that you have all the time in the world, but you don't."

Geoffrey had never seen this kind of sorrow on his father's face before, or heard it in his voice.

"Life is fragile, Geoffrey," he continued. "Your mother and I had hoped for a large family, and she was particularly eager for daughters. She would have adored the little mite that was born last night."

"At least you had us, Father," Geoffrey said, unsure of what else to say under the circumstances. Father never talked to him like this, and never about Mother, either.

"We did have you three," he said. "Your mother couldn't have been more proud of her boys, either, or loved you any more than she did. But Rivers was scarcely a year old when she first took ill, and though she lingered for several more years, there was never a question of more children."

Father sighed heavily, his shoulders uncharacteristically hunched and his still-handsome face sagging. He looked suddenly much older, and with a shock Geoffrey realized for the first time that his father was not ageless, not invincible, the way he'd always seemed. Now Geoffrey understood why he so badly wanted a grandson, not just to preserve the dukedom, but as a continuation of himself.

Silently Geoffrey went to stand beside him, placing his hand on his father's shoulder in empathy.

"Your mother was only twenty-five when she died, the same age that you are now," he said, his voice low yet urgent. "She thought she had time, too, but she didn't. No one knows what Fate has in store for us. Remember that when you kiss your pretty wife, Geoffrey. Remember that, and do not squander a moment."

"*You're not* happy," Serena said softly as they sat together in the carriage on the way back to their house. "What did your father say to you to make you so?"

Geoffrey sighed. He'd taken off his hat so it wouldn't bump against the squabs behind him, and now he tapped the brim lightly against his knee. "It was nothing beyond the usual," he said, "and nothing that bears repeating. What of you and the ladies?"

Serena nodded, accepting his answer. She wouldn't press, but it was clear that heated words had been exchanged among the three men. She guessed that the duke had continued to challenge Harry about an heir, and that Geoffrey had taken his brother's side, the way he had earlier. It couldn't have been enjoyable for any of them. When they'd finally returned to Gus's bedchamber, they were all subdued and gloomy in the way that unresolved but spent anger turns sour, and she and Geoffrey had left soon afterward.

"It was the customary ladies' chatter," she said lightly, and it had been, too. "Celia praised Penelope lavishly, as if to make up for Brecon, and then spoke of her own daughters and grandchildren. Gus knew them all, of course, but I couldn't begin to keep them straight. Then the nursery maid brought in Gus's older daughter, Emily, who is a delightful little creature, though not pleased at becoming a big sister."

"I should fancy not," he said absently, paying more attention to the hat on his knee than to her. "If you do not object, I'm going to leave you at home, and then proceed to White's. Harry has asked me to announce Penelope's birth there for him."

"Of course." She smiled wistfully. "Do you realize that this will be the first time we've been apart since we wed?"

He took her hand, linking his fingers into hers. "It can't be helped, my love," he said. "White's would collapse in an uproar if I tried to bring you inside those sainted doors."

"I know better than to challenge White's," she said, looking down at their joined hands. "I shall simply have to use the time industriously so I don't miss you. Perhaps I'll begin reviewing the household accounts. It's time I became a responsible wife to you."

"I liked seeing you with Penelope in your arms," he said, so completely ignoring what she'd been saying that she looked up, startled.

"I liked holding her," she admitted, remembering the feel, the scent, the trust of little Penelope in the crook of her arm, her tiny fingers clutching at the air and her feet kicking through the layers of embroidered white linen in her own baby-dance. "Babies are so fresh and sweet and new, so full of promise. Most of the servants at Sundara Manōra had children, and Asha and I played with their babies the way English girls play with dolls."

"It would please me greatly to have several of our own," he said. "Soon, too."

She caught her breath. "That's what you were discussing with your father, isn't it? Since poor Gus has failed him, he expects me to produce his precious male heir?"

"I won't lie, Serena," he said. "He did . . . inquire. But I wish for children for us, not for him, nor do I prefer boys to girls, so long as they are happy and healthy. I saw today how fine a mother you will be."

She pulled her hand free of his, and looked away, out the window to the shops they were passing. She should have known this was coming, no matter how much she'd pretended it wouldn't.

"Serena, my love," he said gently. "I don't wish to distress you, but surely you must have considered the possibility of a child after these last weeks. No one could ever say we weren't trying to conceive one, not after all the times we've—"

"I'm not a fool, Geoffrey," she said, more sharply than she'd wished, and far more than he deserved. She instantly regretted it: he'd been so endlessly kind to her, and she loved him so much, that hurting him hurt her more. "Forgive me, but it's so vastly difficult to explain. I—I have certain fears."

"Is it childbirth?" he asked, with a gentle understanding that made her want to weep, because he didn't understand at all. He couldn't. "There is peril to the process, of course, and undeniable suffering, but most women believe the child is the lasting reward."

She turned back, and caught him looking at her waist, as if he could already envision a child growing within her womb.

"Oh, Geoffrey," she said softly. "I'm not very good at explaining this. To bear your child from the love we have would be the most wondrous thing imaginable. How could it not be?"

"It couldn't," he said, almost angrily, as if the very idea was impossible for him to accept. "I love you, Serena, and children, our children, will only make me love you more."

"But what if it didn't?" she asked, finally giving words to her greatest fear. "What if I was—was not the kind of mother you believe I will be to your child, and you stop loving me because of it?"

"I will not let that happen." He thrust his fingers into the back of her hair above her nape, holding her steady as he kissed her roughly, possessively, silencing her doubts in a way that left her breathless with longing.

The carriage stopped before their house, and the footman opened the door. Even though Geoffrey intended to go on to the club, he stepped from the carriage and handed her down rather than let the footman do so. He led her to the steps, and at the door kissed her again, cradling her face in his hands and ignoring the butler, who held the door open and looked steadfastly past them.

"Why don't you trust me, Jēsamina?" he asked in a harsh whisper, holding her face so she could not avoid his gaze. His eyes were very blue in the sunlight, and filled with anger and sorrow. "I love you and defend you, and desire you more than any man could. Why isn't that enough to make you trust me?"

"I love you," she whispered in return, all she could say as slow tears of misery trickled down her cheeks. "I love you, too, oh, so much!"

But it wasn't enough. With a muttered oath, he released her, and climbed back into the carriage. He rapped on the roof for the driver to begin, and he didn't look back.

She dashed away her tears with the heel of her hand, determined not to weep before the servants, and though her heart was breaking, she held her head as high as she could as she entered the hall.

He couldn't know what he asked for when he demanded her trust. He couldn't know that the child he longed for her to bear might not be a twin to little Penelope, rosy pink with a tuft of strawberry-blond hair, but more like the dark-eyed, copper-skinned babies she'd played with in the gardens of Sundara Manōra. He couldn't know, and he wouldn't, unless she gave birth to the undeniable proof of who she truly was. He promised he'd always defend her, always love her, but how could he after that?

"Lady Geoffrey, if you please," said Colburn, the butler. "You have a visitor in the front parlor."

"A visitor?" she asked, surprised. "I wasn't expecting anyone."

Colburn nodded. "Yes, Lady Geoffrey," he said. "His lordship said he had important business with you, and that he would wait until your return. He was most insistent, Lady Geoffrey, and would not be deterred."

"His lordship? Which lord has come calling on me?"

"Forgive me, Lady Geoffrey," Colburn said with a chagrined small bow. "It is your uncle, Lord Radnor."

CHAPTER 14

"My uncle is here? Now?" Serena asked with dismay. A day that had already deteriorated turned even worse. "Pray tell him that I'm indisposed, and that I cannot—"

"Don't bother making any more excuses, Serena," her uncle said, opening the parlor door himself. "I've seen you now, so no more pretending you're not at home or not receiving. That's a low trick to play on one of your family, who only wishes to pay you kind regards."

She blushed furiously at being caught in the social fib, especially by him. She wondered if he had called before; she hadn't bothered to take note of the visitors that had been turned away while she and Geoffrey had been alone together. He had in fact dressed for an important morning call; she'd never seen him in such elegant clothing, from a well-cut frock coat to the maroon-striped waistcoat. As much as she disliked him, she probably did owe him a few minutes of her time, especially after her gaffe.

She sighed, and joined him. "Would you care for tea, or perhaps coffee?"

"No," Radnor said bluntly. "I didn't come here for that."

"Very well." She nodded to the footman to close the

door, and went to sit in the nearest armchair, her hands neatly folded in her lap. The front parlor was a prettily decorated room with bright yellow walls and a pleasing view of the square, intended for receiving and entertaining guests. With any other visitor, Serena would have enjoyed being here, pouring tea from a silver pot and playing the hospitable part of Geoffrey's wife. But with her uncle, she felt on edge and on her guard, and could only pray he wouldn't stay long.

"You're looking well, Serena," he said, openly appraising her. "Fitzroy's bed agrees with you."

She flushed again, from uneasiness, not shame. She sat on the edge of her chair, and she did not remove either her gloves or her hat, determined to keep the conversation as formal—and as brief—as possible.

"If that manner of comment is the extent of your business, Uncle," she said, "then I must—"

"Oh, quit your fussing, niece," he said, dropping heavily into the armchair opposite hers. He pulled the chair closer, scraping the legs across the floor, and leaned forward, elbows on his knees, with a familiarity that she did not like. "Mind you recall that I supported your marriage to Fitzroy, and stood by you against Father. I took the part of you two lovebirds. Surely you remember that."

"I do not recall it," she said, her voice icy. "Not at all."

He smiled, wolfishly showing too many teeth. "I think you do, Serena. You were so grateful for my assistance that you promised you'd speak to the Duke of Breconridge on my behalf."

"No," she said as firmly as she could. "No."

"Oh, yes," he said, chuckling. "I was pleased when your people told me you'd gone to see His Grace. I was sure you were keeping your end of our little bargain."

She raised her chin a fraction higher. "You misremember, Uncle," she said. "You did not support me. You threatened me, telling me you'd have me locked away as a madwoman if I did not do as you wished. You wanted me to marry Lord Geoffrey, and I have, and how thankful I am that I did! Because my *husband* would never believe your lies or your threats."

"Then you see the wisdom of obliging me," he said, completely misinterpreting her point. "Do as I ask regarding the duke, and we both prosper."

"I could tell you I will, Uncle," she said, her voice rising with emotion, "and let you think that of me. But I won't. Nor would I put at risk my relations with my husband's family by endorsing you in any fashion. *That* is the truth, Uncle. I have no intention of obliging or obeying you ever again."

She rose, hoping that Radnor would realize she meant their conversation to be over.

But he rose, too, coming to stand so close to her that she was forced to back away.

"Listen to you, Serena, all high and mighty with your new title!" he jeered. "Better you should listen to me, and then you'll think twice about being so haughty. Because I've heard the talk about you, Lady Geoffrey. I've heard what's being whispered about you since you married into the Fitzroys, about how you're not exactly what you seem."

"I should not think a gentleman such as yourself would heed idle gossip, Uncle," she said as defiantly as she could. "If you care to listen, there are whispers regarding everyone in London."

His smile was an ominous smirk. "Not like what's said of you, Serena," he said. "They're saying you're not my brother's daughter at all, but some conniving Indian lady from the Royal Court of Hyderabad, sent out of India by her true family."

A royal Indian lady! It was so preposterous, and so far from the bitter truth, that she nearly laughed aloud. At least she was able to honestly deny it.

"How could you give credence to such a ridiculous lie?" she said. "I was little more than a child when I arrived in London, and grievously ill at that. How could I possibly have 'connived' my passage in that state? Besides, everyone who knew Father remarks on the likeness between us."

It was a plain and logical defense, or so she thought. But it was only the beginning for her uncle.

"Indeed you do resemble him," he said, surprising her by agreeing. "No one could doubt that. Why, it's an insult to our family, that kind of slander, and to set it right once and for all, I've written to your mama's family in Scotland to prove it."

"They're all dead," she said, relying on years of pretense to keep her voice level and her expression composed. "Grandpapa told me so. He tried to contact my grandparents when I first arrived, only to learn that they were dead."

"Your grandparents, yes," he said, inching closer. "Father went no further than was necessary, not wanting to share you with your mother's family. But it seems your mother had a brother who is an officer in the army, stationed in the north of India."

"She did?" Serena frowned, startled. She recalled the portrait of Asha's mother, hanging in their dining room. But she'd never recalled hearing of this phantom brother, especially not of him being in India. "He never came to our house."

"I doubt Major Dalton had leave to do that," her uncle said. "Soldiers are never their own men. But his regiment has newly returned to Britain, and I've written him for any memories he may have of you or Lady Thomas."

"Why should you think that this gentleman's presence would have any bearing with regards to your request?" she said, striving to sound both firm and unconcerned. "There is nothing he could say that could make me change my mind."

"Because the matter is far more complicated than that," Radnor said easily, his argument well practiced. "If Major Dalton can discover a familial resemblance in you and identify you as his niece, then all that gossip will be put to rest. If he does not, why, then I shall be forced to regard you as an imposter and false claimant to my late brother's estate, and begin proceedings against you."

"I would welcome the truth, Uncle," she said calmly, even as she felt her world cracking and crumbling around her. What had he heard? What made him suspect her now, after so many years? Did this Scottish officer truly exist, or was he only another invention by her uncle to intimidate her? "I thank you for pursuing it."

He drew back and frowned, clearly not expecting that response from her. "Is that all you have to say? That you thank me?"

"It seems sufficient, yes," she said. "What better way to silence this gossip about me and my poor mother than with truth?"

"By God, but you're a cold little chit," he said, anger rippling through his voice. "Truth, eh? I doubt you know the meaning of it. You're as much a lying, deceitful scoundrel as my brother ever was."

That was enough. He could threaten her and call her whatever foul names he pleased, but she refused to listen to him slander her father.

"Good day, Uncle," she said, turning toward the door to summon one of the footman to show him out.

But before she could, her uncle grabbed her by the

arm. She cried out, his fingers hurting her as they tightened. With her free hand, she shoved hard at his chest, struggling to break free, but he held her fast.

"Impudent jade," he said furiously. "I'll leave when I'm ready, after you've heard me out. If you're half the liar I suspect you are, then I'll wager your pretty husband will be done with you. He'll cast you aside for being the wicked little bitch that I always—"

She didn't hear the door open behind her, but from the corner of her eye she saw the flash of Geoffrey's blue coat as he charged forward. He struck swiftly, mercilessly, driving his fist into Radnor's jaw with the full force of his anger. Caught off-balance and by surprise, her uncle staggered backward, and Serena wrenched her arm free of his grasp and pulled away.

But Geoffrey wasn't done. He threw himself at the larger man, knocking him sprawling across the floor. While Serena watched in horror, Geoffrey pinned Radnor down and relentlessly pummeled the other man with his fists, his face fixed and flushed with rage. All her uncle could do was try to defend himself, shielding his face with his arms and attempting to twist away.

"Stop, Geoffrey, I beg you!" she cried, hovering near the grappling men. She'd never seen gentlemen fighting like this and she'd never dreamed her husband would react with such violence: it terrified her. He was so focused on his fury that he didn't seem to hear her at all. "Geoffrey, *stop*!"

Desperate, she glanced back at the doorway, where Colburn and several footmen were crowded together to watch, waiting for orders, the way servants always did. They couldn't lay hands on their master, but she could.

She reached down and grabbed Geoffrey by the shoulder to pull him back, or at least get his attention. She was stunned by the tension in his muscles beneath her hand, the power he'd marshaled to strike her uncle.

"Geoffrey, please," she said breathlessly. "You must stop this. You *must*."

At the touch of her hand he sat back, breathing hard, and stopped his attack. He shoved his hair from his face, his eyes still wild, but at least she'd managed to break the madness that had possessed him.

"Geoffrey," she said. "Please."

He rose in a single agile motion and stepped away from Radnor, who remained groaning on the floor. She placed her hand on Geoffrey's arm, an unspoken restraint. She was shaking after what had just happened, and she prayed he was too preoccupied himself to notice.

Quickly she motioned to the servants, and they hurried forward to help Radnor, groaning and daubing at his battered face with his handkerchief. There was blood splattered on the front of his shirt, and blossoming on the handkerchief from his nose.

"Damn you, Fitzroy," he sputtered as the servants helped him to his feet on shaky legs. "I vow you've broken my nose, and I shall—"

"Leave my house at once," Geoffrey ordered harshly, his voice almost a growl. "Leave now, and never come back. And if I ever learn that you have come near my wife again, so help me, I *will* hunt you down, and I will make you pay."

With a small bow, Colburn handed her uncle his hat, as pointedly as Geoffrey's words. Leaning heavily on the footman's arm, Uncle Radnor snatched the hat and jammed it onto his head, and glared at Serena over the bunched, bloodied handkerchief in his hand.

"You see the manner of rascal you have chosen, niece," he rasped. "Exactly as you deserve."

She felt Geoffrey tense beside her, but before he could react, her uncle had lurched unsteadily through the door. She clung to Geoffrey, watching Radnor's progress as he made his way through the hall and finally out the front door to where his own carriage must be waiting. She didn't know for certain, and she didn't care. All that mattered to her was that he was gone from their house, and that Geoffrey hadn't killed him outright.

She didn't wait for a footman to close the parlor door, but darted away from Geoffrey to shut it herself, not wanting the servants to overhear the conversation that must come next. Yet as soon as the latch clicked, the enormity of everything that she had heard and seen in the last half hour swept over her.

There had always been whispers about her—it was the main reason she'd purposefully kept herself apart from others—but whatever had set her uncle so brazenly on this particular course was new. And if he'd heard it, then likely Geoffrey would as well. Perhaps his father or brother had already shared it with him this morning, which would explain his odd humor in the carriage. No matter how happy she'd been these last weeks, here was fresh proof that she'd never be free of her past. It never ended.

Unsure of what would happen next with Geoffrey, she wearily pulled her hat from her head, and rested her hands and her forehead against the door.

"Serena." Geoffrey came and turned her around to face him, keeping his hands at her waist. She looked down, unable to meet his eye.

"Speak to me," he demanded, his voice low and rough. "Tell me what happened. What did your uncle say? Did he hurt you?"

She knew she couldn't hide, not from him, and forced herself to look up. Despite the furious anger that had driven him to beat her uncle only minutes before, his eyes now were filled with concern for her. Emotion welled up within her and spilled out in a quick sting of tears she could no longer keep back.

"He—he threatened me," she said, her voice breaking. "He wishes me to persuade your father to help him find a place at Court."

"He expected that of you?" he said, stunned, his earlier anger returning. "After all the infamy he has spoken against our family, he desires our help? Did he threaten to hurt you if you didn't obey him?"

She brushed aside her tears and shook her head. So Geoffrey hadn't yet heard the rumors; he wouldn't be shocked now if he had, nor, really, would he likely have come back to defend her.

"Uncle didn't threaten me with force, no," she said, choosing her words with the greatest care. "But he said hateful things of me and of my mother, and threatened to spread them to defame me, and you as well. He said he would instigate a case against me as being unworthy, and try to claim my father's fortune as his own."

"What a greedy, thieving bastard, to think that he could do that to you," Geoffrey fumed, his voice crackling with anger. "Such an ill-founded case would be tossed from any court, of course, but if he dared to do it, he would have to answer to me first."

Oh, this was treacherous ground! As tempting as it was to hear Geoffrey defend her so soundly, she knew she was dancing perilously close to disaster, and before she tripped herself, she retreated to the safety of unquestionable truth.

"Uncle Radnor was very forceful toward me, Geoffrey," she said softly, "and it did frighten me."

"I should have thrashed him in the street for that alone," he said with such vehemence that she pressed her palms on his chest, wanting to calm him. There was a dark mood that remained around him, a lingering hint of the anger and violence with which he'd struck her uncle, and that frightened her nearly as much as had the fight itself.

"Don't say such things," she said anxiously, worried for him. "I don't want you ever again to fight anyone on my behalf."

He curled his fingers around one of her wrists, lightly, possessively, stroking his thumb across her pulse. There was blood on his shirt, her uncle's blood, crimson on the white linen, a reminder she couldn't avoid.

"He was hurting you, Serena," he said. "You can't deny it. I saw it on your face and in your eyes. I will not allow that, not in our house. I would fight anyone, anywhere, who tried to harm you."

"No," she said again. "No! Where would it stop? When one of you is gravely wounded?"

"He would be the one injured, Serena, not me."

"You can't swear to that!" she cried, frustrated by his conviction. "What if he brought a pistol or a sword? What if he challenged you to a duel?"

He leaned into her, his hips crushing into her muslin skirts and hoops, and deftly guided her away from the door until her back bumped into the sturdier pilaster that framed the doorway. He liked this little game of trapping her, almost as much as she liked to be trapped, making their clothes too much of a barrier between them and yet too little as well. Her kerchief had come untucked from the neckline of her bodice, baring the rise and fall of her breasts, and she was acutely aware of the heavy fullness in his breeches as he pressed against her thigh.

"You'd like a duel fought over you," he said, his voice lower, challenging and teasing at the same time. Idly he pulled the kerchief away entirely, his gaze dropping to her breasts. "Admit it. To have two men face death for your sake. Every woman craves that."

"I don't," she said, her words now breathy and making a lie of their meaning.

How could she possibly condone a duel, or the foolish, impulsive danger it signified? And yet at the same time she couldn't deny that having Geoffrey defend her as he had felt like a primal declaration of his love, and an exciting one, too. If there were a dragon in her life, it had always been Uncle Radnor, and now Geoffrey had vanquished him and defended her. He truly *was* her champion.

She reached up to touch his jaw, and he turned his face to nip at her fingers. "I couldn't bear the risk of losing you."

"You can't lose me." His eyes narrowed, and his voice dropped to the rough growl that she adored. "I can't be away from you, even for an hour."

He put his hand to the back of her head, his fingers tangling in the elaborate construction of her hair, and held her steady as he bent to kiss her. He kissed her possessively, reminding her of how he'd saved her and claimed her, how she was his, and she kissed him the same way, hungry for the warm sanctuary of his mouth.

"You came back," she said breathlessly. She threaded her hands inside his coat and under his waistcoat, pulling his long shirttails free to reach up inside his shirt and along his bare back and spine. His skin was heated, the muscles bunching luxuriantly beneath her touch, and she dared to use her nails, raking lightly across his shoulder blades.

"You said you were going to White's," she said, "but when I needed you, you were here. Somehow you knew, and you came. For *me*."

"I was going to White's," he said, "but I had the driver

turn around and bring me back. I couldn't keep away from you."

He knew the intricacies of her dress, and now he pulled out the top pins that closed her bodice and scooped her breasts free of her stays. He bent to draw first one breast, then the other, into his mouth, flicking his tongue across the tender flesh as he sucked until she felt the pull of it deep within her core. She whimpered, clutching his shoulders for support as she arched shamelessly against his mouth.

When he finally lifted his head, her nipples were bright red and ripe and pebbled like berries. Her lips were swollen, almost bruised, from his kisses, and her golden eyes were heavy-lidded and wanton for him.

This was why he'd come back, Geoffrey thought, white-hot desire searing through him as he gazed at her. When he'd left her in the carriage earlier, he'd been frustrated, confused, even angry, thinking of how once again she'd withdrawn from him, and thinking, too, of the rumors that Father had hinted at. As furious as Radnor had made him—and as much as Serena's uncle had deserved the thrashing he'd given him—having a way to vent some of those pent-up emotions had come almost as a relief. She'd been threatened, and he'd defended her, briskly and brutally, paying Radnor back for all the suffering he'd caused Serena both today and in the past. It had felt good in an ungentlemanly way, too good, though it hadn't solved the problem itself.

She'd already confided her difficult childhood, and he'd seen how it had marked her. What else could there be that she still found impossible to share? Each time he'd believed that she had finally come to trust him as a wife should, she retreated, keeping some part of herself away from him. It was as if she were still living in that faraway house where she'd been born, behind an impenetrable wall of stone that he could never breach, no matter how hard he battered against it.

Yet as much as she'd frustrated him earlier, she still had the effortless power to draw him back. No matter how he'd wanted to do otherwise, to find time alone to think and consider, he couldn't keep away. It was as simple, and as complicated, as that. The door of the house had scarcely closed behind her, and he'd already begun thinking of how soon he could return.

No, it had been far more than that: he could think of nothing else besides her, of how she smiled and laughed, of the little kindnesses she showed him and the way she said his name in her lilting hint of an accent, pronouncing it in a way that marked it as her own. He'd thought of the seductive grace that was in every one of her movements, of the golden amber of her eyes, her scent, her taste. He remembered the countless pleasures of making love to her, the shimmering sweetness of her voluptuous body, her little cries and her eager abandon and how she moved so sinuously beneath him and around him.

In their bed, she never held back, never kept apart, and there were no unspoken secrets, doubts, or questions between them. It was the only time she freely gave her entire self, her soul and her heart, to him.

Exactly as she was doing now. How in blazes could he keep away from her? What more could he want?

"You do this to me, Serena," he said roughly, pressing his lips to the side of her throat. "I can't be apart from you. You're a fever in my blood that will never break, nor do I wish it to."

"Then take me, Geoffrey," she whispered, pressing against him. "Here, now. Make me yours, and love me."

He needed no more invitation than that. He swept aside her skirts, bunching them over her hips. He'd a quick glimpse of her legs in scarlet stockings with jeweled garters and her pale skin above—God, he loved the plumpness of her thighs!—and the triangle of dark curls at the top. Shamelessly she parted her legs for him, and when his fingers found her, she let out a long, shuddering sigh of pleasure.

"You're wet already," he said, stroking her swollen flesh with the ridge of his finger and watching how her eyes widened as sensation rippled through her.

"You do that to me, Geoffrey," she said, gasping at his touch, nearly beyond words as her fingers flexed into his shoulders.

Her arousal inflamed him, and he tore at the buttons on his fall, and his cock sprang free, heavy and rampant. There was a small ledge at the base of the pilaster, and he grasped her by the waist and lifted her so her bottom perched upon it.

With her hands on his shoulders for support, she parted her legs farther for him, her breath quickening in anticipation. He opened her with his fingers and lodged the head of his cock within her flushed, blossoming lips. He always marveled at how small and tight her passage was, and yet she was able to accept him, especially when he was as hard and thick as he was now. He bent his knees and thrust, once, twice, until he was buried deep within the lush, wet heaven of her body. Her mouth fell open and her eyes grew heavy as she writhed against him.

"That's it," he said hoarsely, basking in her heat. "That's it."

She made a purring sound that turned into a moan, lifting her leg higher to draw him in more deeply. He hooked his arms beneath her knees and she gasped, curling her ankles around his back as her silk skirts rustled around them. He'd found his pace now, his thrusts steady and strong and relentless, his entire body driving the force of his possession.

He stopped thinking about whether she trusted him or not; he'd stopped thinking of anything that didn't involve his cock. She made him lose all sense of time, and he'd no notion of whether they'd been there in that corner of the parlor for minutes or hours. All that mattered was that he was with her, and together they were glorious.

She rolled her hips to meet him in a sinuous dance of her own, and her breath was now coming in little gulps and pants that matched his thrusts. Her bare breasts shimmied, her nipples red and tight, and her forehead glistened with tiny beads of sweat that made unruly wisps of hair spring out around her face. Her golden eyes were heavy-lidded and wanton, and her lips were parted as she gasped for breath.

He could tell she was riding just on the edge of her release, poised there with her entire body exquisitely taut. She was whimpering as she clung to him, ready for it, and so was he.

He deepened his thrusts, angling so that he stroked her how she liked best, and she shuddered and cried out, arching and coming so convulsively around him that he did as well. His hips bucked as he emptied himself into her sweetness, overwhelmed by how she melted around him in a most intimate embrace.

"Oh, Geoffrey, how I love you!" she whispered raggedly, kissing him as she curled against his chest. "You—you are everything to me."

Everything. He held her tightly, his heart pounding. She'd said it first, but he'd already believed it in his heart, and likely had since the moment he'd met her.

This was why he'd come back. This was why he'd never leave. This was why he loved her more than he'd ever thought possible, and why he'd risk everything to defend her.

She was, quite simply, everything to him. He loved her that much, and he could no longer imagine his life without her in it.

CHAPTER 15

"There's something I wish to show you," Geoffrey said with a great air of mystery as they walked arm in arm through Hyde Park. "Something rare and wondrous, that you will likely appreciate more than most any other lady in London."

Serena smiled from beneath the slanting brim of her hat, intrigued. "Rare and wondrous sounds very fine."

"Oh, it is, it is," he assured her. "I can virtually guarantee that you will not be disappointed."

She laughed, happy to be in his company out-of-doors in the warm sunshine. They had spent this morning much as they had nearly every other morning for the last fortnight, making wedding calls and presenting themselves as a newly married couple to the older, titled ladies of Society: the "lady-grandees," as Geoffrey called them good-naturedly. He'd teased her about all the invitations to tedious teas and good-works now sure to come her way, but Serena had understood the real reason behind the visits.

He had wanted her to be accepted both as his wife and as a member of his family, and by accompanying her in a manner that few other new husbands would, he'd reinforced her new status to an almost unimpeachable degree. Although she had been presented to most of these ladies before, marriage had transformed her so thoroughly that it was as if she were being introduced into Society all over again, with the welcome to Lady Geoffrey Fitzroy considerably warmer than the one that had been accorded to Miss Serena Carew.

Seeing Geoffrey endure so much weak tea and inquisitive conversation for her sake only made Serena love him more. He might have preferred to defend her with his fists, as he had done during that dreadful afternoon with her uncle, but to her these wedding calls were every bit as important, and much less violent.

She tucked her fingers fondly into the crook of his arm. They had left their carriage at the gates so they could walk the paths, but she hadn't dreamed he'd planned a surprise for her.

"Is it something to eat or drink, Geoffrey?" she guessed, trying to coax the answer from him. "Some special sweet?"

He laughed. "Not exactly. But you needn't wait any longer. Here we are."

He grandly ushered her from the path to a clearing beneath a spreading oak. Near the trunk stood a puppet-booth, a wooden box tall enough to hide the puppeteers working inside, with a striped curtain of faded silk across the front like every other raree-show. But what set this one apart was the gaudy Indian scene painted within an oval frame on the front of the box—or rather, thought Serena wryly, an English interpretation of an Indian scene—complete with temples, palaces, monkeys, and exotically dressed men and women.

"You can already see why I brought you here," Geoffrey said solemnly. "The show itself will be even more enlightening."

Serena grinned, knowing he was taking absolutely none of this seriously. She hadn't seen a puppet-play in years, not since she'd been a girl. "A Punch and Judy show?"

"Yes," he said with relish. "But Mr. Punch improved, with an Eastern flair."

"Will there by elephants?" she asked. "And tigers?"

He let his mouth drop open, pretending to be aghast. "However did you guess, madam?"

She laughed, welcoming such foolishness after the stiff-backed formal calls earlier in the day. There was a ring of benches before the box, filled mostly with excited children and a few older apprentices and idlers. The children were not the perfectly dressed little lords and ladies that she usually saw now, but scamps of a sturdier, scruffier variety that reminded her of the servants' children from Sundara Manōra who had been her playmates.

The footman who had accompanied them stepped forward to clear a bench in the front row for Geoffrey and Serena, but Serena stopped him.

"We'll stand, Henry," she said. "These children were already waiting in their places when we arrived. I've no intention of spoiling their fun."

"You are certain?" Geoffrey asked, surprised. "By rights you should have the best place."

"But they came first, and that makes them deserve the front seats," she said, smiling. "I've been sitting all morning, and it will not hurt me to stand now. Besides, we'll see better this way."

This endeared her to the rest of the audience, who offered up a brief round of applause and cheers that made Serena blush self-consciously. She and Geoffrey already stood out because of their dress and the liveried footman, and too late she realized she shouldn't have drawn more attention to herself by such a gesture.

"Well done, love," Geoffrey murmured, smiling fondly at her. "Not one of the lady-grandees could have managed a fraction of your kindness."

Her blush deepened, and she squeezed his hand. But

before she could reply, an out-of-tune horn sounded, followed by a crashing gong, and everyone's attention—including hers—turned expectantly forward.

Mr. Punch was the first to appear, as he always was, but in this show he sported a garish turban with a large glass jewel with his jester's motley and arrived sitting in the howdah on the back of a pasteboard elephant. The children *ooh*ed and *ahh*ed with appreciation, but it wasn't until Judy arrived to quarrel with Mr. Punch that they began to laugh. When she was carried away in the jaws of a giant roaring tiger, they roared along with the tiger, and when Punch had no choice but to rescue his nagging spouse by beating the tiger, the audience cheered as well.

"More amusing than last night's opera, isn't it?" Geoffrey said as they applauded with the others.

"Oh, yes, much more so," Serena agreed as she clapped and cheered. He'd been right to bring her here; as silly as it was, she couldn't remember the last time she'd enjoyed herself more at an entertainment.

As Mr. Punch continued to battle with the tiger (which had roared back to life at the audience's urging), a one-legged man in a worn red coat came from behind the box, leaning heavily on a crude wooden crutch. Clearly he'd been providing the sound effects, for he had a large cow-horn on a cord slung around one shoulder and a tin plate—the makeshift gong—thrust into his pocket. Now his role was to pass benches with a wide-mouthed bottle and collect coins from the audience, bantering with the puppets as he encouraged the audience to be generous.

"Poor beggar," Geoffrey said, reaching into his own pocket. "This is what becomes of our soldiers when they return home from service as broken men. The country should do more for them."

As the man drew closer, Serena now saw that his red coat was all that remained of a uniform. The brass buttons had been cut off and likely sold, as had the regimental insignia. His single boot must have also at one time been military issue, though now it, too, was so patched and worn that his bare shin showed through the holes in the leather. He was younger than she'd first thought, and as he came closer she saw that his face was lined with suffering and poverty, not age.

Pulling off his hat from respect to their obvious rank, he held the bottle out to Geoffrey, who dropped a handful of coins into it.

"Where did you serve, corporal?" Geoffrey asked, reading the faded markings of the rank on the sleeve of his coat.

"Seventy-second of Foot, m'lord," he said. "We was sent to Calcutta to fight alongside the Company men. Queer place for a Lancastershireman, but that's the way of it for the King's men, isn't it?"

Geoffrey nodded. "So that's why Master Punch has a Hindi look to him."

The soldier smiled. "Aye, it's a wee wry joke of mine, tricking him out like that," he said. "Sets us apart from the other boxes in the Park."

"It was most handsomely done," Serena said. Impulsively she reached into her purse and dropped a guinea into the man's bottle.

The soldier smiled again as he recognized the heavier fall of the large coin, and for the first time he looked directly into Serena's face. He caught his breath, then quickly recovered.

"Thank'ee, m'lady," he said, bowing as far as his crutch would permit. "Your servant, *memsahib*."

Serena nodded, suddenly uneasy. She was accustomed to having men be startled, even intimidated, by her unusual beauty; it had been happening to her for years. But she thought she'd glimpsed something more in the corporal's face, a recognition that he'd instantly shuttered. Yet he couldn't have known her from India; she'd been a child when she'd left, and had changed much since then.

He bowed again, and wished them good day, and shuffled back into the crowd. Punch had vanquished the tiger, which now seemed thoroughly dead and finished, and the performance with it.

"Are you unwell, Serena?" Geoffrey asked with concern. "You're pale. I should have insisted you sit, instead of standing for so long."

"I'm fine, Geoffrey," she said, forcing herself to smile as she took his arm. "A bit tired, that is all. It has been a long day."

But Geoffrey didn't accept that. "We'll return to the carriage at once, and home. We needn't go out tonight, either. You can have your supper in bed, and I shall keep you company."

"I'm fine," she said, patting his arm. "I suppose it startled me to hear that man call me *memsahib*. I know it's only the Hindi version of madam, but it's not entirely a compliment. Most Indians only used it for more haughty European ladies."

"I doubt he understood that." Geoffrey sighed, now contrite. "I thought you'd be amused by the puppets. Pray forgive me if they brought up old memories."

"They didn't," she said, reassuring him as best she could. "They were wonderfully foolish, and they made me laugh. What harm could come from that?"

But Geoffrey's misgivings were more well founded than Serena herself realized. For the first time since their wedding night, the old nightmare returned to torment her. No matter how she fought it, the dream held her in its grasp. Relentlessly it forced her to remember and relive again every detail of that last day and night at Sundara Manōra, of being left alone with the dead and sure to perish herself.

Yet when she reached the last part, when she lay beside Asha and burned with the fever, and when her sister's fingers were already still and cold in her own, something changed.

The black-clad doctor bent over her, chafing her hands and forcing her eyelid upward to peer at her eye.

"We must do our best to save her for poor Carew's sake," he said. "She's his daughter, of course. He always boasted of her beauty."

"Brave little lady," one of the soldiers beside the bed said. "She can't stay here, that's for certain. Here, miss, we'll be as gentle as we can."

Strong arms gathered her up, lifting her from the bed and her sister. The necklace with her mother's picture slipped from her fingers and dropped into the tangled sheets. She struggled weakly, wanting to tell them to bring Asha as well, but her mouth was too dry and the words too far away.

"Take her to the wagon, Abbot," said the man in black. "I'll do what I can for her, but it will be a miracle if she survives to see Calcutta."

Her strength spent, she lay limp in the soldier's arms as he carried her from the room. Her eyes stung with the acrid smoke of the burning house, and she whimpered helplessly.

"Be easy, miss, be easy," the soldier said. "You're safe among Christians now."

She dragged her eyes open, struggling to comprehend, and the soldier named Abbot smiled down at her.

"Serena, it's only a dream," Geoffrey was saying. "Please, love, wake, and leave it behind."

She gasped for breath like a swimmer rising from deep water, fighting to orient herself with the waking present.

"You're here, love, you're awake," Geoffrey said softly as he smoothed her tangled hair back from her forehead. "You're awake, and I'm here with you."

She'd frightened him: she saw it in the tension of his

face as he leaned over her. Yet how could she put his fears to rest when she was still terrified herself?

"Hold me," she whispered hoarsely. "Please. Just—just hold me."

He swept her into his arms, holding her tightly against his chest, as if he feared she'd fade away.

"You're safe, Jēsamina," he said fiercely. "You're in London, not India. You're safe here, and I'll never let any harm come to you."

But she wasn't safe, not even here with him.

Because the soldier who'd carried her as a child from her burning home was the same man who had recognized her today in the park.

"Where is Serena?" Harry asked with surprise, glancing past Geoffrey as he entered the back parlor. "Didn't you bring her with you?"

"I'm afraid not," Geoffrey said, dropping into the chair opposite his brother's at the table. Since his marriage to Serena, his routine of taking breakfast several mornings a week with his brother had expanded to include both of their wives and often Harry's older daughter, Lady Emily, as well. "She had a difficult night, and I left her to sleep."

"I'm sorry to hear that," Harry said, motioning for a footman to fill Geoffrey's cup with coffee and refresh his own. "Gus will be disappointed, as will Em. I trust Serena is not seriously unwell? Or perhaps she's in a more interesting condition?"

"No," Geoffrey said quickly. Although Serena had yet to keep away from his bed in the five weeks they'd been married, he knew that women's courses were unpredictable things, and he hadn't let himself read anything further into it. "No. It is more complicated than that."

Harry frowned in sympathy. "Has she been seen by a physician?"

Geoffrey shook his head. He had not shared Serena's nightmares with anyone else, both from respect for her privacy and because he'd no idea himself what to make of them. Perhaps confiding in his brother might help.

"It does not seem to be a case for doctors," he said finally. "It's an, ah, affliction brought on by experiences from her childhood. She has shared with me some of the details of her last days in India, and they were harrowing. I'll beg you not to tell another, not even Gus."

"You have my word," Harry said, setting his coffee down to listen more attentively. "Was it so bad?"

"It was," Geoffrey said, his voice reflecting the grimness of what she'd described to him. "Most of her household was dead or dying with one of those rainy-season fevers. The native servants abandoned them, and Serena was perilously ill herself, surrounded by rotting corpses that had attracted wild beasts from the forests outside. The horror of it haunts her still in her dreams, or rather, nightmares. To watch her in the throes of one is nearly as terrifying. It's as if she's in the grip of some inescapable phantom paroxysm."

"I'd no idea," Harry said. "Poor Serena! She must have been very young, still a girl."

"She was only thirteen," Geoffrey said, "far too young to endure such an experience. Apparently she had a half sister, too, who she regarded with great fondness. One of her father's by-blows with a native woman."

Harry smiled wryly. "So what's said of her libertine father and his private harem is true."

Geoffrey nodded. It was difficult to speak plainly of such appalling subjects in this sunny, genteel room, on the other side of the world from where they'd taken place.

"I suspect there are even more sordid details that Serena has not shared," he admitted. "Her father must have been a rogue, pure and simple. But Serena loved the half sister dearly, and lay beside her as she died. I'm not surprised it affects her still. There seems to be no way to free her from the nightmare except to let her wake on her own. For that reason she refuses to consider laudanum, saying that it only prolongs the dream."

"I recall the same myself, when they tried to dose me for my broken leg," Harry said thoughtfully, rubbing his thigh as he remembered. "Laudanum lessens one pain, yet creates another."

"But what in blazes can I do to help her?" Geoffrey struck his palm flat on the edge of the table in frustration, hard enough to make the china and silverware dance in protest. "She turns to me in our bed to ease her suffering, as a wife should, yet I'm helpless to offer any real aid. How can I fight a demon that only she can see?"

"You can't," Harry said. "All you can do is let her know how much you love her. If she comes to feel that security during the day, then perhaps she won't feel threatened in her dreams."

"That, and to keep her free of any mention of India." Grimly Geoffrey shook his head. "The irony is that her past in India is what first drew me to her, and yet it is the same India that seems most likely to inspire the nightmares. Yesterday I took her to watch a Punch in the park that had an Indian flavor to it, thinking it would amuse her. She was charmed by it, laughing and cheering and as free of care as any of the urchins on the benches. But as soon as she slept, the nightmare returned, and I could do nothing."

Harry sighed, pushing his chair back from the table and looking away, out the window to the garden beyond.

"It may soon become more difficult than you think, Geoffrey," he said. "That vile uncle of hers is telling anyone who'll listen—and as you know, there are plenty of fools about the town who will—that he'll soon have fresh proof that Serena is some sort of an imposter foisted on his family."

Geoffrey swore, his fist tightening. "That's the same sort of rubbish Radnor has always used to threaten Serena. Is it what Father had heard?"

"No one dared say it to his face," Harry said, "but yes, he has heard that rumor, as have I."

"Blast Radnor," Geoffrey said. "What sort of proof could he have after all these years? Serena was a sickly child when she was brought to this country by those who only meant her well. How could she have contrived any sort of malicious intent toward her own family?"

"So you've never wondered if there's a kernel of truth to the rumors?"

Aghast, Geoffrey looked sharply at his brother. "I cannot believe you would doubt my wife like that, Harry, and suggest that she—"

"I'm not suggesting anything about Serena," Harry said mildly. "Nor do I believe any of the tattle, either. I'm only saying that there's often a small, hidden truth behind even the most malicious of rumors. Would it make a difference to you as Serena's husband if some aspect of her past was not exactly as we've believed?"

Geoffrey stared, stunned that Harry would dare ask such a question of him. Yet now that he had, Geoffrey realized it was a question that deserved an answer, at least to himself. Part of the answer he already had, for even before they were wed, he'd come to understand that Serena was not the gently bred English lady in an exotic package that he'd first imagined. She had warned him herself that she was far more complicated than that, and she'd been right. There were parts of her, like the nightmares and the end of her life in India, that were forbiddingly dark and full of shadows.

Yet there were far more facets to her that he would never wish to part with—her warmth; her daring; her laughter; her kindness; her innate, sensual elegance—and with each day of marriage he looked forward to discovering and sharing more. He'd freely accept the dark corners to be able to bask in her warmth as well, and perhaps, in time, to find the key that would finally free her.

"It would not," he said, deliberately and without doubt. "I love her, and she is my wife, and nothing that Radnor or anyone else can say will ever change that. But if Radnor intends to injure her with words or actions, then by the Heavens, I will make him answer for it."

Harry leaned forward, resting a restraining hand on Geoffrey's arm.

"I meant it only as a caution, brother," he said. "You humiliated the man, and denied his ambitions. Now in return he's trying to do the same to you, and to Serena."

"Then he must be compelled to answer for his words." Geoffrey shook off Harry's hand and rose, too agitated to sit any longer. "He must be made to stop his lies about my wife."

"But not by you," Harry said firmly. "You've done enough by force already. Better to take the high road, Geoffrey, for Serena's sake as well as your own. You're a Fitzroy, and now so is she. No more brawling like drunken sailors, or, God forbid, a duel. Hold your temper in check. Let Radnor produce his trumped-up witness, this long-lost uncle, and see how swiftly he'll be dismissed in court."

Geoffrey frowned and rolled his shoulders, unwilling to accept his brother's advice. He knew Harry was right about this, as he too often was, but the afternoon he'd fought Radnor had been the one time that he believed he'd actually defended Serena as she deserved. For her sake, he'd felt strong and invincible, freed of the ineffectual helplessness that her nightmares left him with.

"Radnor is not behaving as a gentleman should," he

insisted. "His actions do not deserve the decency of a court of law."

"Perhaps he doesn't deserve a civilized day in court," Harry said, "but Serena would prefer it. I'd wager she loves you far too well to see you risk your life brawling like ruffians over something as ridiculous as this."

Blast, Harry *was* right. He remembered how Serena had pleaded with him not to do exactly this. Afterward he'd teased her into saying it had excited her, but her conscience—and his—knew that there was nothing to be gained by danger and violence, and everything to lose.

As he stood at the window, he saw Gus and her two daughters in the sun-washed garden. Emily was chasing butterflies among the flowers with more enthusiasm than success, while Gus swayed gently from side to side as she held baby Penelope in her arms: a scene that was peaceful and bright and full of love. That was what he wanted with Serena, and for her as well. That was what she deserved, and he wasn't going to let Radnor or anyone else steal it from her.

"Damnation, Harry, you are right," he grumbled. "As you know you are."

"How seldom I hear you admit it." Harry rose and came to stand beside him, his hand on his shoulder not in restraint, but in support.

"Say nothing of any of this to Serena," Geoffrey said. "Especially not the part regarding Radnor. I don't want her to worry."

"You have my word," Harry said. "All you need do is love her, Geoffrey. That's what she needs from you. Let the truth fight your battles, and trust love to do the rest."

"Hurry, Martha, I beg you," Serena said, scarcely able to stand still as the maid pinned her into her gown. At

Geoffrey's insistence, she'd spent all of the previous day lying idle in bed, and she'd had enough. She'd had a nightmare; she wasn't an invalid.

She'd also had time enough staring at the pink pleated silk inside the canopy of her bed to make sense of recognizing the soldier at the puppet-box. She'd been shocked by seeing him in her dream, but still she could not be sure that this was the same man, the Corporal Abbot who'd carried her. After he had looked at her so closely in the park, it was entirely possible that her imagination had given his face to the soldier in her dream. So much time had passed since that last day at Sundara Manōra, she honestly couldn't be certain.

Besides, it could not be possible. The ladies in the Calcutta hospital had assured her that all her rescuers had sickened and died from the same fever. The odds that one soldier could have survived and returned here to London to haunt her now were very slim indeed. And even if he were the long-ago Corporal Abbot, what could it matter? The doctor had been the first to mistake her for Asha, and there was no reason the soldier should believe otherwise. She was still safe, at least from him, and her secret was as well.

This morning she was determined to join her husband for breakfast to prove that she was perfectly recovered and well—if, that is, Martha could manage to dress her. "His lordship is already dressed and at breakfast, and I do not wish to keep him waiting."

"Yes, my lady," Martha said, her cheeks red from exertion. "As you wish, my lady."

Serena sighed, watching the maid attempt to tug the two halves of her bodice together, to overlap and be pinned into place. She did not understand why Martha was having such trouble this morning. It was usually such a simple process to dress her.

"May I suggest a different gown, my lady?" Martha said finally, uncharacteristically ready to give up. The gap between the two bodice fronts stubbornly remained nearly two inches apart, with Serena's stays and shift on full display in between.

"I'd rather wear this one," Serena said, disappointed. "It's one of Lord Geoffrey's favorites. Perhaps lacing my stays more tightly would help."

"Forgive me, my lady, but I do not believe that will do," Martha said, philosophically standing with her hands on her hips. "Nor will it for many months to come."

"Stop speaking in riddles, Martha," Serena said, attempting to pull her bodice closed herself. "I'm certain it can be closed."

"No, my lady, it cannot," the maid said, then lowered her voice with kindness. "Do you truly not understand the reason, my lady? You haven't asked for rags for your courses since two weeks before you wed, and his lordship has not let you from his bed. It's the way of women and men, my lady. You're breeding."

"*Breeding!*" Serena repeated with horror. "A baby?"

"A baby, my lady," Martha repeated. "It's early days, aye, but there are signs enough."

"But it—it cannot be." Serena fluttered her hands anxiously over her still-slender waist. "I've not been ill in the morning, the way breeding women are. I see no signs."

Martha smiled. "Not all women are poorly, my lady," she said. "Everyone is different. As for signs: why else does that gown no longer close, my lady? The breasts swell long before the waist. No doubt they feel tender, too."

"But so soon!" Serena cried miserably. She should have realized it herself, but she'd been so swept away with being Geoffrey's wife that she'd lost count of the weeks.

Here she'd been worrying about Uncle Radnor's plotting and the soldier with the puppets when she was carrying the most dangerous threat to her secret within herself. "We've scarcely been married a month."

"It doesn't take long, my lady," Martha said, stepping behind Serena to help slip the too-small gown from her shoulders. "Babies are determined to be gotten and born, no matter what their parents may wish."

Serena closed her eyes, the idea of a child slowly becoming real.

"His lordship's manservant swears that every single gentleman in that family has gotten his wife with child in the first month of marriage, my lady," Martha continued. "I'd venture his lordship will be the latest to crow when he learns of it."

"Not yet," Serena said sharply. "I do not wish you speaking of this to anyone in this house or outside it, most especially his lordship. I will tell him when I am certain, and not before."

Martha flushed and dropped her gaze, curtseying. "Yes, my lady," she murmured. "If it pleases you, my lady, I shall find another gown for you."

Alone, Serena sank onto the bench beside her dressing table. Lightly she pressed her hand over her flat belly, trying to picture the child now growing within her. If it weren't for the chance that a baby would betray her blood, then she would be overjoyed. To bear Geoffrey's child, a child born of their love, would be the sweetest thing on earth.

But not like this. Heaven preserve her, not like this.

"*Good morning,* love," Geoffrey said, smiling, his entire mood improving mightily as soon as Serena appeared in the parlor door. He shoved aside his newspaper and rose to greet her. "I thought you'd keep to your bed another day, and now here you are, as lovely as the dawn itself."

She grinned and blushed, and he kissed her warmly, passionately, which made her blush more. He wasn't exaggerating: she did look lovely this morning, and thoroughly delectable in a rustling, ruffled silk dressing gown that displayed her breasts to tempting advantage. He loved all of her dearly, but he'd a special love for her breasts, and having her present them to him like this, framed by lace and silk ruffles, was making it increasingly difficult for him to keep his resolution to let her have another day in her own bed to recover from her nightmare.

He settled her in her armchair at the table himself, not wanting to give up even that small task to a footman, and then sat across the table from her.

"I told you I wasn't ill, Geoffrey," she said as he poured her tea. "As soon as the sun rises, the nightmares are gone. I don't want you to fuss over me on their account."

"I cannot help it, Jēsamina." It was impossible to reconcile her as she was now, blooming and cheerful, with the memory of her pale and wild-eyed and quaking with terror. "It's a difficult thing to witness, without being able to help you."

"But you did," she said softly, reaching across the table to place her hand over his. "You do. You were there when I woke, and you held me, and loved me. I could never want for anything more."

"Because I love you," he said. He turned his hand and linked his fingers into hers. "Words I never tire of saying to you."

"Words I never tire of hearing," she said, so wistfully that he had to kiss her again. Even when everything seemed so perfect between them, there was always that little hint of uncertainty, of insecurity, that he could not make go away. But he was resolved to follow his brother's advice, and love her regardless of everything else. Considering he already did, it was not difficult advice to heed.

"When I thought you'd be resting, I'd planned to meet my brothers to view a stallion at Tattersalls that Harry has his eye on," he said, hoping that such mundane talk would lighten her mood. "But now perhaps I should stay home and keep you company instead."

She smiled, twining her fingers around his. "I'm quite flattered that you'd prefer me to a horse," she teased. "Truly. But you should go with your brothers. If I may have the carriage this afternoon, I should like to visit my mantua-maker, which I doubt would have much interest for you."

"I'd find it most interesting if the visit involved you being undressed," he said, imagining exactly that. But as he did, Colburn brought a silver salver, piled with notes, invitations, and letters, and set it on the table beside Serena.

"Oh, dear," she said, sighing as she gazed down at it. "The obligation of being Lady Geoffrey! I suppose I must set aside time to answer these as well. The lady-grandees will expect replies."

"Shall I stay at home and help you?" he asked gallantly, knowing if he did there would be little actual letter-writing in the process.

She knew it, too, glancing at him over the rim of her teacup. "Not if I truly wish to reply to any of these," she said ruefully. "Better you should go with your brothers, and leave me to this. But tonight . . ."

"Tonight," he said, the single word vibrating with promise as he rose from his chair to kiss her once again.

Nearly two hours later—for it was a leisurely breakfast—he finally left the house to join his brothers. As soon as he was gone, Serena took the salver with the letters and retreated to her own parlor upstairs, leaving word that she was not to be disturbed.

Resolutely she sat at her desk with pen and paper before her, then buried her face in her hands and wept, silently, so the servants wouldn't hear her. The secret that had been with her for so long now felt like an insupportable burden, a weight she could scarcely bear. She could go on pretending as she had this morning, as if nothing had changed and nothing was different, but that could last only so long.

The secret wasn't merely hers now. It belonged both to Geoffrey and their unborn baby, too. She longed to tell Geoffrey she was with child and share the joy she knew he'd feel. She knew, too, that her baby could be born as fair-skinned as she was herself, and no one would ever know the truth.

But what if that poor innocent was a dark-skinned baby thrust into the midst of the noble Fitzroys? She was certain the truth would end her marriage. Geoffrey was such a strong believer in trust between them that he'd be sure to regard this as an unforgivable betrayal. No amount of love could balance that. Her uncle would claim back the inheritance that had never been truly hers. She'd forfeit all the jewels and money that her father had meant for her sister, and she and her child would be penniless.

The best she could hope for would be some sort of allowance from the Fitzroy family if she promised to live far from Society. The worst would be arrest, and prison. The most bitter irony was that she'd be sent back to the same friendless poverty that she'd miraculously escaped in Calcutta.

Except, of course, this time she'd have both a broken heart and a child.

All she dared hope was that over the next months, she'd find some answer. She couldn't begin to know what that might be. Until then, she must live each day, each hour, each minute as it came to her, a precious gift to be savored along with Geoffrey's love.

With a shuddering sigh, she blotted her tears, and set herself to answering the correspondence before her. The first ones in the pile were easily dispatched, acknowledgments of the calls that she and Geoffrey had made together, along with routine invitations to balls, routs, and suppers. She accepted nearly all of them, at Geoffrey's request; he was proud of her as his new wife, and wished them to be seen together often. There were also a smattering of reckonings to be settled from the household accounts as well as her milliner and draper. Those she put aside, to be discussed later with Geoffrey, for he'd still not arranged an account for her to draw upon for such moneys.

Near the bottom of the pile was a letter that made her smile, addressed in Aunt Morley's familiar, tidy hand. She and Fanfan had left London with Grandfather for Allwyn Hall in the country soon after her wedding, and her aunt's letter was filled with good wishes, as well as comfortingly ordinary affairs: the ripening fruit in the orchards, the young vicar's new wife, the roof to be replaced on the summerhouse.

But on the last page, Serena discovered the real reason for her aunt's letter:

I regret to intrude upon these balmy first days of your nuptial bliss, but I do wish to impart certain news to you. Your uncle, Radnor, is determined to bring his old Mischief to you & Lord Geoffrey, & he has been here at the Hall, pestering yr. Grandpapa for his acquiescence. Radnor insists that you are some manner of Imposter, a Thorn in the family's Bosom, & he is determined to prove it. He has discovered a Relation of your poor late Mama, & is having the man brought to London to deter-

mine your parentage. I myself do not believe a blessed Word of Radnor's Blather, nor see the Use in it, knowing you to be a true Daughter to our family. But I would caution you & Lord Geoffrey to take care, & prepare your defenses against Radnor's machinations & unpleasantness.

Serena read the letter twice, then carefully refolded it and tucked it away in her desk. She doubted her aunt knew of how her uncle had already threatened her, or how Geoffrey had beaten him after he had. Geoffrey was confident that her uncle would not bother her again, but she wasn't nearly as certain, and her aunt's letter proved her right. But the last thing she wished was to have Geoffrey lose his temper and challenge her uncle again, so for now she would keep Aunt Morley's letter to herself.

Another sin of omission, she thought grimly, one more that she could not share with Geoffrey.

Only a single letter remained in the salver, one written on coarse paper in a smudged, clumsy hand, and sealed with a blob of plain candle wax. Likely it was a false appeal for money, the kind of unscrupulous begging-letter claiming to be from a nonexistent foundling hospital or almshouse. She considered simply tossing it into the fire unread, but opened it, anyway.

And gasped.

My Lady,

You know me. I saw it yesterday when you looked at me close. I know you too though you are much changed into a great lady.

But I know more. I know your mother was not what you pretend but your father's vēśyā, *his Hindoo whore. I know because I kept the picture of her that was with you, a small picture once with diamonds all around. In it the whore wears green stone ear-bobs and a gold necklace and a red rag around her head. Her face is like yours. Anyone can see it. You are her twin except her skin is brown like mud and you pretend to be English.*

I will sell you this picture if you come alone to me at the puppet-box Thurs. If you do not come I will go to His Lordship.

Yr. s'v't.
Stephen Abbot

She pressed her hand over her mouth to keep back the whimper of surprise, shock, and fear. So it *had* been the same man, the soldier who had carried her from the burning house. Corporal Abbot. The man had always been part of her nightmare, and here he was again, unforgettable and undeniable.

She couldn't remember a time in Sundara Manōra when she hadn't worn the gold locket with her mother's portrait. Father had given it to her as a way both to honor the mother she'd never known, and to be protected by her, too. The miniature portrait had been exquisitely painted on ivory and surrounded by a ring of diamonds. As a girl, Serena would tip the necklace this way and that to make the diamonds catch the sunlight and reflect a thousand tiny fractured rainbows, and pretend that they were sent from her mother in Heaven.

She was sure her mother was in Heaven, because Father had said she was so beautiful that she'd put the very angels to shame. Staring at the little painted face, Serena had only agreed. Her mother had been named *Ramya*—Hindi for *enchanting*—and in the portrait, she was beautiful indeed, with coppery dark skin, glossy black hair, wide pale-gold eyes, and a tiny mouth. The emeralds in her ears and the scarlet silk *ohrni* wrapped around her head had served to set off the perfection of her features.

Each night Serena would hold the portrait cupped in

her hand when she went to sleep, knowing her mother would keep her safe. That last day, when she'd been so ill and had gone to find Asha, she'd taken the locket from around her neck and held it up for her sister to see, hoping her mother's smiling face would protect them both.

It hadn't.

When the soldier had picked her up from the bed, she'd been too weak to hold the chain in her fingers, and the locket had slipped away and fallen back into the bed with Asha. She'd mourned its loss, certain it had been destroyed with everything else in the purging fires.

Now the locket with her mother's face had found her again, from the other side of the world and seven years in the past. But this time the locket wouldn't protect her; it could ruin her in a way that neither her father nor her poor mother ever could have anticipated. It was the proof that Uncle Radnor had so desperately sought, the hard, unimpeachable proof of who and what she was.

Blackmail was an ugly word, but the consequences could be uglier still, and Serena would not let that happen. She tucked Abbot's note in her pocket, gathered up all the hard money she had in her rooms, and called for the carriage to take her to her mantua-maker, and then, when that was done, to confront her past.

CHAPTER 16

"*Wait here with* the carriage, Henry," Serena said as she stepped down. "I wish to continue by myself."

"Is that wise, my lady?" the footman said uneasily. "Begging pardon, but his lordship wouldn't—"

"His lordship is not here," Serena said firmly. "I will never leave your sight. I will walk to the same puppet-box as before, there beneath the tree, and I will address the same fellow in the red coat that his lordship spoke to. Then I shall return directly to the carriage."

Henry scowled. "Forgive me, my lady, but that fellow's a rum sort of rogue, for all he's got but one leg."

"You have my word that I'll take the greatest of care, Henry, rum rogue or not," Serena said, turning away before he could object further.

The day was overcast and cooler than it had been when she and Geoffrey had watched the puppets together, and the benches that had been filled now held only a handful of children. Serena went to stand to one side, waiting for the performance to come to its usual break. She was plainly dressed, in the kind of clothing a lady wore for a day of errands or traveling—a dark blue worsted habit and a black silk bonnet with a single black plume, the brim pulled low to shield her face—yet because she was alone, she felt self-conscious. While

Mr. Punch battled Judy and the tiger, there was still no sign of Abbot. She rubbed her gloved hands together, praying that his letter hadn't been some monstrous prank.

But at last he appeared, rattling his bottle of coins as he made his way between the benches. With such a small audience, it didn't take him long, though it seemed to Serena that he pointedly took his time to make her wait. Finally he tucked the half-filled bottle inside his coat, and came to her.

"You came, m'lady," he said, his smile more of a leer, uneven with gaps from missing teeth. "The third time we meet, eh?"

"How much do you wish for the locket?" She was trying hard not to be intimidated by him, and desperately wanted their transaction over as soon as was possible. It had been different when she'd had Geoffrey beside her. Now the man stood closer to her than was proper, near enough that she could smell both his clothes and his person, with a whiff of stale drink besides.

Abbot drew his brows together and pursed his lips. "That's harsh, m'lady, powerfully harsh, considering how I once saved your life."

"You also plundered my home," she said bluntly, anger at what he'd done giving her words strength. She'd lost all the sympathy she'd felt for him previously. "You stole from my sister's corpse."

"Spoils of war, m'lady, spoils of war," he said easily. "You lived fine as royalty, with jewels and baubles scattered about like some pasha's treasure-house. Would've been a shame to burn all of that, 'specially for a poor soldier like me with only the king's shilling to his name."

"Show me the locket," she said.

"I'm not a fool, m'lady," he said in a way that told her that he thought her one. "It's in safekeeping elsewhere.

If I had it here, you could order your footmen over there to come knock me on the head and steal it away, and then where'd I be?"

She glanced back at the carriage, relieved to see that Henry and the other footmen were watching. "How am I to know you truly have it?"

"Because I do," he said succinctly. "Because no one else *could* have it, could they? It's a gold locket with your mama's face painted on it, and a twist of black hair inside. There used to be diamonds around the outside, but I pried them out and sold them long ago."

She thought of all the tiny rainbows she'd made with those diamonds. "Why didn't you sell the locket, too?"

"Because no one wanted it," he said. "Who'd buy a locket painted with a black chit's face like that?"

"I would," she said, her voice trembling with emotion. "I'll give you twenty-five pounds for it."

"Twenty-five pounds!" he exclaimed. "Fah, you *do* take me for a fool!"

"That's more than a fair price, especially with the diamonds gone," she said. "More than you made in a year of soldiering."

His face hardened. "If you're talking fair, m'lady, I'd still have the leg I gave up for the Crown," he said. "Fair would be me earning my bread like a man, not beggaring to brats with those damned puppets. But life's not fair, m'lady, not to me, nor to you, neither. Think of what His Grace the Duke o' Breconridge would make if he were to see this, and learn his precious son's wife has native blood in her veins."

She jerked her head as if he'd struck her. "You would dare show it to His Grace?"

"I would, m'lady," he said. "You're the very picture of your mother. His Grace couldn't miss it. Though maybe I should take it to the papers first. What a story that would make for them, eh?"

When she'd been a girl, she'd studied her mother's face and prayed that one day she'd share the same beauty. "Fifty, then. That's all I have with me."

"But it's not all you have, m'lady, is it?" He turned and spat contemptuously against the roots of the tree. "I've asked about, you see, and it's said that you're worth ten thousand a year on your own, without what your lord's worth. Compared to that, fifty pounds is pitiful poor. I'd say five hundred would be closer to fair."

She gasped. "Five hundred pounds!"

"Five hundred pounds," he repeated. "Has a nice round sound to it, don't it?"

"But I do not have five hundred pounds, not in my possession!" she cried, aghast. No married lady would have that at her disposal, no matter how much she was considered worth. Her money had been overseen by her grandfather before her marriage, and her husband after it. A sum like that would require a draft from the bank, drawn at Geoffrey's request. "How am I to come by five hundred pounds?"

"That is not my affair, m'lady," he said. "If you cannot come by it, then I'm sure your lord would."

Frantically she shook her head, as if denial would change his mind. "You cannot tell my husband of this! He knows nothing of any of this!"

"Then I'd say you best find that money, m'lady," he said. "I'll be generous, and give you until tomorrow afternoon. Then you'd best be back here, else I'll be calling on his lordship. Good day, m'lady."

He doffed his hat briefly, settled his shoulder onto his crutch, and turned toward the puppet-box without looking back. He'd as much as dismissed her, and as she stiffly returned to the carriage she felt humiliation and fear in every step of her retreat.

She stared blindly from the carriage windows as they

drove through the streets, seeing nothing beyond the glass. She did not know which would be worse for Geoffrey: to learn that she was an imposter, the illegitimate daughter of a *nautch* dancer from Lucknow, or that she hadn't trusted him enough to share such a monumental secret. Either one would be enough to end their marriage, but together they would entirely destroy his love for her, and that—that would devastate her. Once she considered their child as well, she felt as if she were standing on the edge of a very deep, very dark hole, with no way to pull back.

When she reached the house, she went directly upstairs to her rooms and locked her door, telling Martha she wished to be undisturbed to rest. With feverish haste, she searched through all her drawers and trunks, hunting for every last coin of her pin money. Altogether it was less than a hundred pounds, not nearly enough. She would have to sell one of the jewels that Father had left—not that she'd any notion at all of what any of them would fetch. Why should she, when she'd never once had to step into a jeweler's shop to purchase anything for herself?

With growing desperation, she unlocked the jewel box in the back of her wardrobe and began to pull out the leather-covered cases. Their distinctive shapes would be a giveaway, and sure to be missed by Martha as well. Instead she took bracelets, a necklace, earrings, and rings, all rich with diamonds and other precious stones, wrapped them in handkerchiefs, and tucked them into a single small velvet bag before she replaced the empty cases in the locked box. Surely together they would be worth the five hundred pounds she needed. Tomorrow she would take them to a jeweler that did not serve the Fitzroys, use a false name to be sure, and pray she'd be given a fair amount.

She heard a carriage stopping in the street outside the house, and men's voices. That must be Geoffrey and his brothers, back earlier than expected, and eagerly she ran to the window, hoping to see them.

But instead of the three Fitzroys, there were five men she most definitely did not want to see. First from the carriage was a man dressed somberly in plain dark clothes that marked him as a lawyer or other legal personage and his clerk, followed closely by a strong, stout constable, the thick brass-crowned tipstaff of his profession grasped firmly in his hand, and doubtless an arrest warrant waiting within it. Next from the carriage was a middle-aged army officer, his scarlet uniform coat a brilliant spot on this gray afternoon. Last to step from the pavement was the one she least wanted to see: her Uncle Radnor, a grim smile of satisfaction on his face as he sent a footman ahead to knock on her front door.

"No," she whispered, panicking. She'd been so concerned with stopping Abbot's blackmail that she'd completely forgotten her aunt's warning regarding her uncle. Here he'd brought the Scottish officer to identify her, and clearly confident that her other uncle wouldn't, he'd also brought a lawyer and his clerk to act as witnesses, and finally a constable to arrest her. "No, no, *no*!"

She had to flee. She could not stay and risk being put into irons before Geoffrey and his brothers. Colburn would show the men into the front parlor to wait. She'd already left word that she did not wish to be disturbed, which would buy her more time. Colburn could be very firm, even when confronted by Uncle Radnor.

She pulled a small leather traveling satchel from her wardrobe and as fast as she could, she threw into it a few necessities for a journey. She grabbed the velvet sack with her jewels and stuffed it down the front of her gown, sandwiched for safekeeping between the whalebone of her stays and her linen shift.

She paused, trying to calm herself. Radnor and the others were in the house now; she could hear his voice echoing against the marble floor of the front hall. As much as she longed to, she didn't have time to leave a lengthy letter for Geoffrey to explain. Instead she swiftly dipped her pen in the ink and wrote a few hasty lines that she prayed would say everything she'd never be able to tell him in person.

Please forgive me, my own dearest G., though I cannot deserve it. I love you and always will. Forever yours, S.

She flipped back the bed's counterpane to uncover the pillow, and placed the note in the center, where he'd be sure to see it. Then with infinite sorrow, she pulled her betrothal ring from her hand and placed it beside the note.

With tears in her eyes, she hooked a dark cloak around her shoulders and gathered up the traveling bag. She pressed her ear to the door to make sure that there were no servants in the hall, then carefully opened the door. Her heart pounding, she slipped through the opening, and ran as lightly as she could down the hall to the back stairs. At this time of day, the servants should have finished all their tasks about the house, and would be gathered in the hall in the kitchen to dine before they began the preparations for the evening meal for the abovestairs table. She heard their voices and their laughter as she crept down the stairs, yet saw no one, and in the next minutes she was out the garden door, down the side alley, and out the back gate.

For now she was free. The clouds that had threatened all day were finally beginning to give way, splattering wet drops on her cloak. She did not look back at the house, nor let herself think that she might never see

Geoffrey again. Instead she pulled the hood of her cloak up to shield her face, and with her head bowed against the rain, she hurried away from Bloomsbury Square to look for a hansom cab to take her to an inn near the docks. Tomorrow she would find passage for France, and make her way across the Channel to Calais.

The idea came to her so suddenly that she realized she must have already unconsciously made such a plan for escape. She'd visited often with her aunt, and she was comfortable speaking French. She could live frugally on the sale of her jewels until after her child was born. Then together they would return to Calcutta, where no one ever asked questions of an Englishwoman. If she took another name, she could disappear completely, and never be found.

That is, if Geoffrey bothered to look for her.

Kismet, she thought miserably. Kismet.

"*It's the* absolute truth, Harry," Rivers said, deftly blowing the smoke from his cheroot over the glass of the open carriage window. "Bay horses are slow as mud, and always have been. In all racing history, you'll never find a bay horse standing to take the cup."

"What's the absolute truth, Rivers, is that you are as wise in such matters as that bay horse's ass," Harry said crossly, waving his hand through the haze of tobacco smoke. "For God's sake, must you smoke that infernal sot-weed in my carriage? Even if you have the windows open, the stink clings to the silk panels. You know Gus will sniff it out, and blame me for letting you light the damned thing in the first place."

Geoffrey leaned forward, frowning as the carriage slowed. "Whose coach is that before my door, taking the space before my curb on a rainy evening?"

"Most likely it belongs to some friend of Serena," Rivers said blithely. "What a territorial old Turk you've become since you wed, Geoffrey! You can't lay claim to every paving stone as if you're the everlasting satrap of Bloomsbury Square."

But Geoffrey wasn't listening. "Damnation, it's Radnor. Driver, stop at once! How the devil does he have the audacity to come to my house again?"

Harry grabbed his arm. "Wait until the carriage stops. We'll be with you to make sure you do nothing rash."

"But if he's hurt Serena—"

"Then he'll answer to all three of us," Harry said firmly.

Despite the warning, Geoffrey charged into his front hall moments later, prepared for another fight even with his brothers following close at his heels. Yet the scene he found was hardly what he expected. True, Radnor was there, standing to one side, with three strangers and a constable clustered around him.

But there was no sign of Serena. Instead, Colburn was attempting to calm Serena's lady's maid, Martha, who was sobbing inconsolably against the shoulder of the housekeeper, Mrs. Harris. Other servants were hovering about in the hall to watch, in the way that servants did.

None of it made any sense, and instinctively Geoffrey began with Radnor.

"Where the devil is my wife?" he demanded. "You were forbidden to enter this house again, Radnor, yet you've returned to distress her."

"I might ask you the same question, Fitzroy," Radnor said, daring to interrupt Geoffrey. "Where is Serena? Where have you hidden her? You'll be named as an accomplice, you know."

"Damn your accomplice!" Geoffrey said furiously, lunging for Radnor, only to be pulled back by his brothers.

"Lady Geoffrey is not here, my lord," Colburn said, a solemn voice of reason. "We were attempting to determine what has become of her."

"What in blazes do you mean she's not here?" Geoffrey demanded, shaking his brothers away. "She can't simply vanish as if it were some conjurer's trick."

"She's gone, my lord," Martha said, curtseying even as she wept, her words running together in a teary babble. "She came home in the carriage, and said she wished to rest, and then when she didn't send for me, I went to make sure she was well, and she was gone. Gone!"

"Gone," Geoffrey repeated, unable to comprehend. He thought of how he'd seen her last, blushing and laughing as he'd kissed her good-bye. How could she be gone? "How? Where?"

"The driver said she asked to be taken into the park this afternoon, my lord," Colburn said. "She stopped and spoke with the puppet-master you saw the other day, my lord. The driver says that afterward she appeared most distraught, my lord."

Geoffrey shook his head in disbelief. It made no sense, none of it. "What possible reason could she have for addressing a one-legged beggar like that?"

That made a fresh torrent of tears flood Martha's face. "She—she left this for you, my lord," she said, holding out a single sheet of paper. "This, and her betrothal ring, both on her pillow-bier."

He took the ring and the paper, and read the hurried words. It was Serena's handwriting, and Serena's words as well. But what could she possibly have done to beg his forgiveness? What could have driven her to such an action? If she loved him as she claimed—no, as he *knew*—then what could have made her flee like this?

He looked down at the ring in his palm, the bright golden stone that was so much like her eyes. She'd left it behind, which hurt. But she must still be wearing her wedding band, which gave him hope.

"We came to ask her certain questions of her past, that is all," Radnor was saying. "Questions I've a right to have answered. But I never intended any harm to her, not like this, and I—"

"Go at once, Radnor," Geoffrey ordered curtly. "Now."

Whatever nonsense Radnor was sputtering could wait. All that mattered now was finding Serena.

Serena sat alone in the tiny room, lit by a single candlestick. She'd paid extra for a room that she wouldn't have to share with other women, for she could not have borne their company, not tonight. As it was, the inn was bustling with other travelers coming and going, the noise unfamiliar to her ears. Tomorrow she would be joining them, sailing on the noon tide; the innkeeper had helped secure her a place on a packet for Calais. He'd told her she was fortunate, very fortunate, for most ships bound for Calais left from Dover, not London. Silently she'd listened to him ramble on, and nodded, and paid him what he'd asked for the service and the passage, but she'd volunteered nothing in return. The less anyone else knew of her, the better.

Now she sat beside the room's single, narrow window, numb to the world as she watched the rain fall and the twinkle of lights in other windows. She was not tired, and had no desire to sleep on the damp and musty sheets. By luck her room faced the river, and she forced herself to think to the future, and try to forget the past that lay behind her on Bloomsbury Square. From the window she could make out the ships at their moorings in the river, their masts with furled sails like a black forest of leafless trees. The tallest belonged to great ships of the East India Company, the same fleet that had once brought her to London seven years before. She had arrived with few possessions, and she'd leave tomorrow with the same.

The only difference was that this time, she'd be leaving her heart behind with Geoffrey.

It had taken Geoffrey less than an hour to find the one-legged soldier from the puppet-box, here in this grimy, smoke-filled tavern not far from the river. At his father's insistence, he was accompanied by two large and menacing hired men, while a small legion of their fellows helped comb the city in search of Serena. Geoffrey wasn't surprised that Father had such men at his disposal—to say the Duke of Breconridge was well connected would be an understatement—but Geoffrey was endlessly grateful that he had.

Now he stood in the small storeroom that the barkeep had provided for privacy in exchange for a few coins while the soldier from the puppet-show sat on a bench before him, nervously rubbing his remaining leg as his gaze shifted from Geoffrey to the two guards and back again.

"I told you, m'lord, I don't know where her ladyship's gone," he whined. "How could I, a poor wretch like me?"

"My driver said she went specifically to speak to you, Abbot," Geoffrey said curtly, his patience long gone. "Whatever you told her distressed her."

"Forgive me, m'lord, forgive me," Abbot said, ducking his head to avoid Geoffrey's scrutiny. "But how am I to know what a fine lady like that was thinking?"

The guard beside Geoffrey reached out and snatched the man's hat from his head. "Show more respect to your betters," he barked. "What do you know of Lady Geoffrey?"

"The barkeep told us you were boasting of becoming a rich man," Geoffrey said with disgust. "He said you promised you'd buy everyone a dram on tomorrow night. I'd wager that had something to do with my wife."

Still Abbot didn't answer, muttering to himself and looking away.

"Tell his lordship what you know," the guard growled, "or I'll shake the truth from your worthless body, see if I don't."

Abbot looked up at the guard, obviously weighing the consequences, then heaved a great sigh, and swore to himself.

"I'd something her ladyship wished to buy," he said grudgingly. "Something of great value to her, but to no one else."

Geoffrey frowned. "What could you possibly possess that would be of any value to my wife?"

"This, m'lord," Abbot said, fumbling inside his coat and finally pulling out a filthy cloth knotted into a tight, small bundle. He held it up to Geoffrey, who hesitated.

"Go ahead, m'lord, take it," Abbot said bitterly. "It will be worth my loss to see the look on your face when you unwrap it."

Unsure what he'd discover, Geoffrey took the bundle and began to pull away the cloth. Something small, hard, and round was wrapped inside. A coin, he guessed, or a medallion. At last the object fell into his palm, a small gold pendant or locket, decorated with bright enamelwork of swirling vines and flowers that had to be Indian.

"Look inside, m'lord," Abbot urged. "It's that what made your lady weep."

Geoffrey flipped open the locket in his hand, and caught

his breath. Surrounded by a ring of bent, empty prongs was a portrait of a strikingly beautiful dark-skinned Indian woman, dressed in rich clothing and covered with jewels. It was a face to captivate, and except for her coloring, she could have been Serena.

"Oh, aye, m'lord, you can't believe what your eyes are telling you, can you?" Abbot jeered. "That's your precious lady's mother, m'lord. She was a *nautch* girl, a dancing whore. You can tell by how she's dressed. You married a native bastard, born of that chit and the great Lord Thomas Carew."

Geoffrey stared at the locket, his thoughts spinning. "How did you come by this?"

Abbot cackled. "You should be thanking me, m'lord," he said, "because I was the one that saved your dear wife. When Lord Thomas's household was struck with a terrible fever, he sent to Hyderabad for a doctor, and I was one of the party sent to escort him. Like a plague, it was, with bodies everywhere, including Lord Thomas himself, and we'd orders to burn the place to the ground to stop the sickness."

Abbot paused, reaching for the tankard on the bench beside him.

"Go on," Geoffrey ordered, striking the tankard from the man's hand. "Damnation, go on. Tell me all."

"Not much more to tell, m'lord," Abbot said. "We found his lordship's two daughters, one English, and the other a bastard, the pair of them kept like princesses. The English one was dead, but the bastard still lived. On account of not wishing to leave her behind, the doctor pretended the bastard was the true daughter, and had us save her. I took the locket and more besides—we all did—before we burned the lot. That's God's own truth, m'lord, and you have the proof in your hand."

Still Geoffrey stared at the locket. Abbot's story

matched Serena's nightmare perfectly. It had to be the truth, for there was no other way the man could have known what had happened.

Everything about Serena made sense to him now, and at last he understood all the mysteries that had always hovered between them. He understood the little things, like why she danced with sensual grace, as well as the big ones, like why her nightmares held such power over her. He even understood why, when her past seemed at last to be catching her, she'd run away. She'd had every reason to be reserved, to hold back, to keep the secret of who and what she was that would be her undoing. He didn't fault her for any of it, either. He could imagine all too well what her fate would have been in India as a penniless, fair-skinned girl without a family to protect her.

The only thing he didn't understand was why she believed he'd care about any of it.

"Her ladyship was going to buy the locket from me," Abbot said, wheedling. "A hundred pounds, she promised me."

"It wasn't a sale," Geoffrey said sharply. "It was blackmail, wasn't it?"

Abbot cringed. "I'm a poor man, m'lord, what needs to earn my bread however I can."

"Here." Geoffrey dropped five guineas into the man's lap. "That's for saving my wife's life, not for trying to blackmail her. Be grateful I won't have you charged for that, or for the theft of the locket from her, either."

Swiftly Abbot tucked the coins away, and then looked up at Geoffrey with surprise as he realized what Geoffrey had said.

"'Your wife', m'lord?" he asked, unable to keep back his curiosity. "She's still that to you, now that you know what she is?"

"She is my *wife*," Geoffrey said, for to him there'd never been any doubt or question. "And now I must find her."

Despite her intentions, Serena must have fallen asleep; she knew the moment she awoke in the dark room, the candlestick guttered out on the table beside her. Her face was pillowed awkwardly against her arms on the windowsill, her thoughts groggy and disoriented as she heard the innkeeper's voice outside her door.

"She seems respectable enough, sir," he said. "A grieving widow, if I'm not mistaken. I wouldn't have taken her in otherwise. I run an honest house, sir, and I don't take strumpets."

He knocked, his fingers rapping sharply on the thin wooden door.

Serena didn't answer, her heart racing. Who would come asking after her at this hour? Who would care if she were respectable or not?

"I expect she's asleep, sir," the innkeeper said apologetically. "She seemed all worn out, and she's a long journey ahead of her tomorrow."

"Open the door."

She pressed her hand over her mouth. Was her mind playing tricks upon her, or could that truly be Geoffrey?

"I can't, sir," the innkeeper said, balking. "I told you, this is a respectable house, and I can't go opening the doors of my lady-guests for gentlemen who—"

"The lady is my wife," Geoffrey said. "Open the door now."

Serena rose, her heart racing with anticipation, or perhaps dread, and she clutched the chair beside her for support.

The innkeeper's passkey scraped in the lock, and the

door swung open. There by the light of the candlestick in the innkeeper's hand stood Geoffrey, his face expressionless.

"Leave us," he said curtly. "I wish to speak to my wife alone."

The innkeeper nodded, leaving the candlestick on the table before he closed the door.

For a long moment she and Geoffrey simply stood there, the silence growing deeper and deeper between them until she could bear it no longer.

"You—you came," she stammered, her trembling voice echoing hollowly in her ears. "Why?"

Without a word, he held out his open hand to her. In his palm was the locket with her mother's portrait. With a little cry, she sank into the chair.

"So you know," she said. "You know."

"Not everything," he said, his voice surprisingly quiet. "Tell me more of your mother."

She twisted uneasily in the chair, unsure of what he wanted. "Likely you've heard all there is to know."

He came closer to take her hand, and pressed the locket into it. "Not from you," he said. "Tell me."

She looked down at her mother's painted face, and seven years disappeared.

"I did not know her," she said softly, tracing her fingertip around the damaged frame where the diamonds once had been. "She died while I was a baby. Father was devastated, and ever after spoke of his grief. He had other *bibis*, but he swore he never loved again after she died."

"Tell me more," he said, drawing a second chair close beside hers. "Please."

She took a deep breath, her mother's little smile giving her courage. "Her name was Ramya Das, and she was—she was not a lady. She was a *nautch* dancer, and Father met her in a brothel near the fort at Golconda, where she danced for the foreign soldiers, and likely—likely did other things for them as well. Father did not care. He said he loved her at once, and took her from that place to Sundara Manōra, where they lived in great happiness together until she died. She was his favorite, but they never wed. I am their only child, their illegitimate daughter."

She steeled herself to look up at Geoffrey's face, to see the repulsion that surely must be there.

"You pretended to be your sister," he said, his voice so full of gentleness that she felt tears welling up behind her eyes. "She was the real Serena, wasn't she?"

She bowed her head over the locket. "My true name is Savitri Das," she said. "'Daughter of the sun.' But I have been called Serena for so long it seems more true than any other."

"Why didn't you tell me?" he asked roughly, unable to keep back his emotions. "Why couldn't you trust me?"

She shook her head. She was crying now, and she didn't try to stop. "I was afraid you'd despise me if you knew the truth."

"I don't," he said. "I couldn't, not you."

She closed her eyes, not believing, not yet. She had come this far, and she had to finish. He had to know everything. She owed it to her mother's memory, and to Geoffrey as well. Slowly she looked up again, letting the hot tears slide down her face.

"I never contrived to take my sister's place," she said. "The English who saved me mistook me for her when I was ill, and by the time I was well enough to understand what they'd done, I was too frightened to correct them. If they'd known, they would have sent me into the streets, and I would not have found a man as kind as my father to rescue me."

"Not in Calcutta, no," he said. "But here you have me."

"But consider who I am, Geoffrey, what I am!" she cried miserably. "I'm half Hindi. I'm the daughter of a dancer from a brothel. I'm a bastard. For seven years, I've taken my dead sister's place in her true family. I've taken the love that was meant for her, the fortune, the blessings and good wishes. From that last day at Sundara Manōra, I have been nothing but a falsehood, a deceiver, a liar, and a thief."

He took her hand and raised it to his lips, his gaze never leaving hers.

"You are the woman I love more than any other," he said, his blue eyes intent on hers so there would be no doubt of his meaning. "You are my love, my life, and my wife, and that is all that matters to me. All."

"But what of my uncle? What of his threats to tell all the world who and what I am?"

She saw his jaw tighten, and at once she regretted mentioning her uncle.

"I'm not afraid of Radnor," he said firmly. "I believe I've proven that well enough. Together we'll find a way to end his interference in your life once and for all."

She swallowed, wanting desperately to believe him.

"You are the son of the Duke of Breconridge, a peer of the realm," she said, the long years of guilt and shame too strong a memory to let go easily. "What will he say? What will your friends, your family, your—"

"I told you, Jēsamina," he said, every word deep and rich and filled with magic to her. "You are my love, my life, and my wife, and that is all that matters to me."

"I love you, too, Geoffrey, oh, so much." She gulped through her tears. "But there is one more thing you must know. I think—I believe—that I'm with child. Your child. *Our* child."

"A child?" he asked, stunned. "You are sure?"

She'd never seen him smile so warmly. "It's early," she said. "But Geoffrey, you must realize that this child may more resemble my mother. He or she may be—be dark."

"*Our* child," he said fiercely. "That is all that matters to me. He or she will be *our* child."

Joy and relief left her speechless. And love: so much love for this man who loved her as she was, as she always had been.

He pulled her from her chair onto his lap, into his arms, and threaded his fingers into her hair to draw her face closer to his. "Now come home with me, Serena. Come home, and be mine forever."

"Forever," she echoed as he kissed her. "Forever."

CHAPTER 17

"They're here."

Geoffrey stood at the window of the upstairs parlor with his hands clasped behind him. Below him in the street, his father's carriage had drawn before their house, with all the usual pomp and fuss that a duke's carriage made, and which his father thoroughly enjoyed. Already passersby were stopping on the pavement to gawk, but then, a gilded ducal crest on a carriage door, four matched gray horses, and footmen in plum livery trimmed in silver braid would stop most anyone, and that was before Father and Celia themselves had even stepped from the carriage.

"Shall we go downstairs to greet them?" Serena asked behind him, still rearranging the tea table to suit herself after the servants had left them. "It's the first time they've been to our home."

"It's the first time they've been here at all," Geoffrey said. He hadn't really given the fact much thought until she mentioned it, but it was surprising that in all the time since he'd taken the lease on this house, his father had never once entered the door. "Father always prefers that my brothers and I come to him, but today it seemed right that he come here. And now he has."

"Because of me," Serena said, her nervousness clear in her voice.

"Because of us," Geoffrey said firmly, watching the footmen open the carriage door. After the events of yesterday and last night, he would rather have taken the day to let her rest, but given those same circumstances, he wanted his father to learn what had happened—and what Serena had told him—from them, not from anyone else. There was simply too much at stake.

"We'll let Colburn show them upstairs," he continued. "We'll receive them here."

He turned away from the window and back toward her. He smiled; he couldn't help it. She was wearing a pale sky-blue silk gown, trimmed with white lawn ruffles at the wrist to match the filmy white embroidered kerchief modestly covering her neckline. Her dark hair was simply dressed, and her only jewels were a single strand of pearls around her throat, and his betrothal ring back on her finger, where it belonged.

He knew she had cautioned that it was early days in her pregnancy, but to his eye there was a glow and a ripeness to her that he could only attribute to the child. As she stood there with her hands lightly clasped at her waist, he sensed a new serenity as well, completely in keeping with her name. Whether that came from being with child, or from finally sharing the truth about her past with him, he couldn't say. All he knew for certain was that she had never looked more enchantingly beautiful, and that he'd never loved her more.

"My own Jēsamina," he said softly. "It's not too late to spare yourself, and let me do the telling. You are certain you wish to do this?"

She nodded, her smile radiant.

"I am," she said. "I won't deny that I am anxious, Geoffrey, but this is something I must do for myself, and for you, and for my mother's memory, too."

"You're very brave as well as very beautiful." He heard his father's voice on the stairs, and he kissed Serena, a quick burst of passion. "No wonder I love you so much."

"And I you," she said, swiftly linking her hands with his.

Lightly he squeezed her fingers, and she smiled up at him. This was how he wished his father to find them, joined together as one. He couldn't guess what Father would make of Serena's revelations, but his reaction would not change Geoffrey's own feelings one bit. Serena was his wife, and nothing else mattered.

"The Duke and Duchess of Breconridge," Colburn announced solemnly (if unnecessarily), and Father and Celia joined them.

For the first minutes, it was all smiles and small talk of last night's rain and the loveliness of the parlor's decoration. Chairs were taken and tea was dispensed, and finally Father opened the true conversation.

"We are glad to see you safely returned to your proper place, Serena," he said, smiling warmly. "I trust you are none the worse for your, ah, adventure?"

"Thank you, Brecon," Serena said with a graceful nod of her head. "As you see, I am quite recovered, and even improved by it."

"It was but a misunderstanding between us, Father," Geoffrey said, watching Serena with careful concern. What she planned to say would not be easy for her, and he worried that it might prove to be too much.

"Ah, the misunderstandings of newlyweds," Father said indulgently. "Common enough, to be sure, though perhaps yours had more of the high drama to it than most."

Celia leaned closer, gently placing her hand in its silk mitt on Serena's arm. "But everything is quite resolved between you and Geoffrey now, my dear? Everything is settled to your satisfaction? We cannot have you running away like that again. It's so very dangerous."

Serena smiled. "I won't, Celia, I promise, and I am sorry for the distress I must have caused. There were many things I needed to say to Geoffrey that were finally said. Things that I now must say to you as well."

She put down her teacup, and took a deep breath. Geoffrey rose from his chair, and came to stand behind her, placing his hands protectively on her shoulders.

"My history is not as you believe it to be," she began. "I am indeed the daughter of Lord Thomas Carew, but my mother was not his wife. I am instead his second daughter, his illegitimate child with his *bibi*, his Hindi mistress, whom he loved above all others. My mother was named Ramya Das, and was a *nautch* dancer from a brothel."

She drew the locket with her mother's portrait from her pocket, and set it on the tablecloth before Father and Celia. Father took the locket from the table to study the portrait, frowning with concentration, not disapproval, and Geoffrey realized he was holding his breath.

"You are quite like her, and as beautiful as she," Father said finally. "Does your grandfather know of this?"

She lifted her chin a fraction with determination.

"No," she said. "He does not. He knows nothing of who I am, or what carried me to London. Geoffrey is the first person in England to whom I have told my story, and now you shall be the second and third."

And tell it she did, from the blissful days of her childhood through the horrors of the fever and the first misunderstanding that changed her life forever, all the way to the soldier who'd tried to blackmail her yesterday. As Geoffrey listened, he was struck again by her strength and courage. He could not fathom how she alone had survived in the face of so much, nor how she had borne the guilt of such a secret for so long.

Yet she never faltered, her voice even and sure with every difficult word, and he realized why this telling was so important to her. As much as he wanted to protect her, this was something she had to do for herself. It was a confession, seeking absolution in the truth from the deception that had become part of her life. He had longed for her trust, but the magnitude of what she'd given him was stunning, and humbling as well.

"Oh, my dear," Celia murmured, reaching out to pat Serena's arm. "I had no idea. What an astonishing history!"

Father didn't say anything, his silence stretching out uncomfortably as he waited to make sure Serena was done. He was sitting with his fingertips tented together, his expression noncommittal. He'd always been good at that, hiding his true thoughts and feelings; it was why he'd been so successful at Court.

Finally he glanced down at the locket on the table, and back at Serena.

"So, Serena," he said. "It would seem that you are by birth half English and half Hindi."

Of all the things he might have said after Serena had told her story, this struck Geoffrey as the most appallingly insensitive, and at once he rose up to defend her.

"She is, Father," he said furiously. "She has made that abundantly clear. Does this knowledge disturb you?"

Father looked at him, his expression still unreadable. "Does it disturb *you*, Geoffrey?"

"She is my *wife,*" Geoffrey answered sharply. "I love Serena for herself, with no regard for the bigoted perceptions of others."

"I am glad of it," Father said, smiling at last, "because that is what this estimable lady deserves after the trials she has faced. My only regret is that she has suffered from fear of disappointing us, when such ill favor could not be further from the truth."

"But you are an English duke with royal blood," Serena protested, and for the first time this day Geoffrey heard that little tremor of uncertainty. "My grandfather does not believe it, of course, but most others say the Fitzroys are second in the realm only to His Majesty's family."

Father sighed. "People like your grandfather believe that noblemen should be like overbred horses, limited to a certain breeding stock and no more," he said. "It's an impractical course that leads to spavined horses and weak-brained lordlings, rather like your uncle, Radnor. But consider our own family. We can count a king among our ancestors, true. But his royal blood included that from Italy, France, Austria, and Germany, and we're all improved by it."

Relief washed over Geoffrey with such force that he realized how much he'd dreaded this moment with his father, fearing a much different resolution. He would have chosen Serena even if it meant breaking with the rest of his family, but how much better for them both—and for their child, and other children sure to follow—that it hadn't been necessary.

But Serena remained unconvinced. "To be from India is much different than to be born in Italy or Spain," she said wistfully. "You see from that portrait how dark my mother was."

"And I counter with Her Majesty Queen Charlotte," Father said easily. "You have been presented to her. Her skin may be fair, but her features bear the mark of her royal Portuguese and Moorish ancestors, who were African, and a good deal darker than your mother. Yet Her Majesty is the first lady of our realm."

Geoffrey nodded. He'd heard this story of the queen before, of course, and he did not doubt its veracity. But he was impressed that Father had thought to tell it now to Serena. What better way to ease her worries about her mixed blood than to say that Her Majesty herself was much the same? He'd always known his father was a clever man, but until this moment he hadn't credited him with being so wise as well.

"I had not known that of the queen," Serena said slowly. "Her Majesty is a most refined lady."

"And her heritage has no effect on that refinement, except to improve it," Father said firmly. "All that matters to me, Serena, is that you love my son, and he loves you."

"Thank you," Geoffrey said, stepping forward to offer his father his hand. "You cannot know what that means to me."

He couldn't recall his father ever smiling at him like this before, with warmth but with pride as well, and he held his clasped hand another moment longer, savoring the connection. It was ironic how neither of them had wanted this match in the beginning, yet through the unpredictable nature of love, Serena had brought them to a kind of rapprochement that he never would have anticipated.

"It is a marvel that Serena found her way here to become your wife," Father said. "We couldn't possibly let something as petty as this stand in the way of your happiness now, could we?"

"Not at all," Geoffrey agreed heartily. "Once we've confounded Radnor, then everything shall be as it should."

"I thank you, too," Serena said with a graciousness that Geoffrey knew masked her uncertainty. "But how exactly do you mean to confound my uncle? Once he learns of my secret, he will not stop his persecution."

"But why must he learn of it?" Father said with a dismissive twist of his hand, the way he often addressed other people's problems. "A secret implies some shame, some mortification. But if we regard your past as a matter of privacy, to be shared within our family and no further, then it simply becomes a question of discretion.

I see no reason for either him or your grandfather to be told."

Abruptly Serena rose, and went to stand before the fireplace and placed her hands on the edge of the mantel. Her head was bowed, her shoulders stiff, and her hands in tight, clenched knots.

"It's my father's fortune," she said to the window, though he was certain she was seeing nothing of what lay beyond it. "My uncle has always believed it should belong to him, not to me, and has resented my very existence because of it. He has done so many hateful things to me over the years that I would gladly give him every last farthing if he pledged to leave me alone."

Geoffrey rose and went to her at once. Heedless of his father and Celia, he circled his arms around her waist.

"If I believed that would bring you peace, then I would carry the bank draft to him myself," he said softly, against her cheek. "I didn't marry you for your fortune, and if you'd come to me in your shift alone, I would love you the same. But giving Radnor the money would be the last thing your father would have wished. If what you say of how much the two brothers disliked each other is true, then your father would likely prefer that you toss it all in the Thames rather than give it to Radnor."

Behind them, Father sighed. "You needn't do anything so wastefully dramatic," he said, ever the pragmatist. "Don't touch the money yourself if you don't wish to, but put it into trust for your children."

"Our children," Geoffrey echoed, wanting to remind her of that first child in particular. She had not wanted to announce her pregnancy to his family yet, but he couldn't help sliding his hands a little lower from her waist, protectively over her unborn child. "I'd much rather they received your father's largesse than Radnor."

But she shook her head. "Everyone advises me on

what I should do, how I should behave, and what I should say and think," she said with a mixture of sorrow and frustration. "Yet how can I decide anything for my future? I've pretended to be my sister for so long that now I've no notion at all of who I truly am, or who I'm supposed to *be*."

"Oh, my love." Gently he turned her around to face him, and cradled her cheek in his palm. "You may have borrowed your sister's name, but everything else is entirely your own. What you've experienced, good and bad, has made you who you are. Let people judge you for that, not for how you were born. You're brave and strong and determined, kind and intelligent and endlessly fascinating, and there is no other woman like you anywhere. As long as you know that, nothing anyone else says can harm you, because it will not matter."

"Geoffrey, Geoffrey," she said, trying to smile. "When you say it like that, I can almost believe you."

"You should believe me, because it's the truth," he said. "You're an entire original, and no one can take that from you."

"I am," she said, marveling at the sound and the power of the two small words. "I *am*."

"That you are," he said, smiling. "You are Serena Fitzroy, and I'm honored to have you as my wife."

He'd intended to kiss her then, but she kissed him first, arching up to capture his mouth for herself. It was sweet and sensual, the way kissing her always was, but this time it was more than that. It was a pledge, a trust, a promise for their future together, and he loved her more in that moment than he'd ever thought possible.

"What is it, Colburn?" Father said behind them.

Lost in the moment, Geoffrey had forgotten that his father and Celia were in the room with them, and reluctantly he turned back toward them, his arm still around Serena's waist. His butler was standing there at the door, and as practiced as Colburn was at revealing little, his entire posture couldn't help but betray anxiety.

"Forgive me for interrupting, Your Grace, my lord," he said. "But Lord Radnor and his party are here. His lordship says he knows you are at home, and he will remain until he is seen."

"Blast Radnor," Geoffrey said. It was exactly like Radnor to reappear now, at this inopportune moment, trailing his trumped-up Scottish officer as a witness and his jackanapes of a lawyer. "He has no decent business being in this house, and he can wait until Hell turns to ice for all I care."

"I will see him," Serena said. "Show my uncle here, Colburn."

"That is not necessary, my dear," Father said quickly. "Let him challenge you in a court of law if he chooses, but not in your own drawing room."

"Forgive me, Brecon," she said, "but if I end this now, I will never need face him again."

There was a steely resolve in her voice that Geoffrey hadn't heard before, nor expected. Her earlier forlorn uncertainty had vanished, and she now had the expression of a female warrior ready for battle, her golden eyes flashing.

"You are certain of this?" he asked, although he already knew the answer.

"Entirely," she said. "My uncle has brought a man that he believes will discredit me as a lowborn, foreign imposter. You have reminded me of whom I have become, Geoffrey, and how no one else can make me into something I'm not unless I let them. When they enter this room, they will see only what I am: an unimpeachable English lady, surrounded by my family."

Geoffrey smiled, and bent to quickly kiss her again. He motioned to the butler to have Radnor and the others join them as Serena took her seat beside the tea table.

She sat with even more grace than usual, her silk skirts arranged elegantly over her legs and her body turned the exact degree to display both her posture and her figure. She sipped her tea, the translucent porcelain cup in one hand and the dish in the other, with the perfect precision of both art and nourishment.

Most of all, she managed to compose her face to be welcoming yet reserved, pleasant but distant, exactly what was expected of an English lady of rank. It was the same face with which Serena had greeted him on the night they'd met, and Geoffrey realized how very far they'd come together since then.

He returned to stand behind her chair, one hand resting lightly on her shoulder, and she smiled up at him. He'd follow her wishes and not interfere, but at the first sign of difficulty from her uncle he would be ready to step in and defend her.

Yet as soon as the door opened and her uncle entered the room, he felt her shoulder tense beneath his hand, and he wondered if this idea of hers truly was such a good one.

Serena wondered as well. She hadn't thought her uncle could still have an effect on her, especially not with Geoffrey beside her. She'd believed she was brave enough to confront Uncle Radnor like this, and put an end to his plots against her once and for all. She *needed* to be that brave, or else she'd let him haunt her for the rest of her life—and that she was determined not to do.

But the moment her uncle entered the room, her resolve faltered, and her courage with it. How had she forgotten the contempt and dislike that was always in his eyes when he regarded her, as if she were some offensive scrap of nothingness that must be crushed and swept from sight?

"Be brave, love," Geoffrey whispered beside her, under

his breath, for only her to hear. "Remember who you are."

She nodded imperceptibly. That was the key, to remember who she was. She wasn't the sickly, terrified orphan-girl that he'd bullied so easily when she'd first come from India, though that girl had helped mold her into the woman she was now. For the sake of that lost girl, she would be strong now, and she would triumph.

His face flushed as soon as he saw she was not alone, with both the duke and duchess as well as Geoffrey to support her. Displeasure flickered through his eyes, but he recovered quickly, smiling as he bowed to each of them in turn and ending before Serena.

"Good day, niece," he said. "I am pleased to see you looking so well. The married state must agree with you."

"Good day, Uncle," she said. His smile reminded her of a jackal's, false and cunning. Without looking, she reached her hand back and rested it over Geoffrey's on her shoulder. "Thank you, yes. I have never been happier, nor more content."

She glanced past him to the footmen who stood near the door, motioning for them to bring chairs from along the walls of the room for her uncle and the other four men. The very presence of these four—the same four that had so frightened her when she'd spied them from the window—was awkward and unwelcome and humiliating, which was likely what her uncle had intended. The officer in his scarlet coat was at least a gentleman, but the lawyer, legal clerk and constable were not. They'd no place in a lady's drawing room and especially not in the company of her ducal in-laws.

But she was able to pay him back in a similar fashion. The chairs occupied by the duke and duchess were mahogany armchairs with silk-worked cushions, while the ones for her uncle and the others were plain and straight-backed: a subtle difference, and a proper one under the circumstances. If Radnor had in fact been a favorite relative, he would have received an armchair as well, and he knew it, too, his face clouding with displeasure.

The lawyer's clerk made a great show of opening his letter case and producing paper and stylus, poised to take down everything that was said, and the constable, too, sat on the edge of his chair with his tipstaff leaning against his knee, much like a hunting dog that's scented prey and is waiting to be released. The officer stood behind her uncle, his face still hidden from her.

"You have called with a purpose, Uncle?" she said once they all were settled. "You have a reason for bringing this—this *party* into my home?"

"I have," he said, smiling that jackal smile again. "As I have told you before, I thought it a great pity that you should marry without any members of your poor, late mother's family in attendance, or even aware of your marriage. Thus I discovered your mother's only brother, and he is as eager to meet you as you must be him."

"Indeed," she murmured, her heart racing even as she told herself the man was likely an imposter. "Shall you make the introductions, Uncle?"

"I am remiss," he said, pointedly taking his time as he turned back toward the duke. "Your Grace, may I present Major Andrew Dalton of the 2nd Battalion of the 73rd Foot?"

His introductions continued, but as Major Dalton stepped forward to bow to her, his black cocked hat tucked tidily beneath his arm, she stopped hearing her uncle, and perhaps she stopped breathing as well.

The face of the thickset man before her was weathered and lined from a lifetime of harsh conditions, his yellow-blond hair streaked with gray and his eyes a pale and faded blue. Yet the resemblance between this man and her sister, Asha, was so striking that she couldn't keep back a little cry, her hand flying to her mouth with shock.

Quickly Geoffrey bent beside her. "Are you all right? If this is too much for you to bear, then—"

"No," she said as firmly as she could. She'd convinced herself that the man couldn't possibly be Asha's real uncle, that he was sure to be a false contrivance, and yet one look at his face, and she'd no doubt that he was in fact Major Dalton. He was exactly the man her uncle claimed him to be, exactly the man who could drag her and Geoffrey and the rest of the Fitzroys into a bitter court battle over her inheritance. The major must already see that there was no resemblance between her and the rest of his family. How, really, could he not? "I am . . . surprised, that is all."

"Pray forgive me, Lady Geoffrey," the major said with gruff contrition. "I've no wish to distress you."

"You heard my niece, Dalton," Radnor said with a misplaced heartiness. He nodded at the lawyer, indicating that he should pay extra attention to what followed. "She's fine enough. You startled her, and little wonder, if you're long-separated family."

The major shook his head even as he continued to study Serena, running his fingers lightly around the brim of his hat.

"It has been a considerable time since I saw my poor sister, my lord," he said, hedging. "At least twenty years, and likely more. She was newly wed to Lord Thomas, and residing with him in Calcutta."

"That was before I was born, Major Dalton," Serena said, striving to regain her composure. She must remember who she had become, not who she had been born, exactly as Geoffrey had told her, and as if he could read her thoughts, he gave her shoulder a small pat of encouragement. If she wished Major Dalton to believe who she was, then she must first believe it herself.

"At that time, my father still maintained his commission with the East India Company," she continued. "It was not until after my mother died that he resigned, and moved to the neighborhood of Hyderabad."

"He knows that already, niece," Radnor said impatiently. "We all know that."

She turned her face toward her uncle, keeping her head straight and her features composed. She wouldn't let him intimidate her.

"Forgive me, Uncle." No matter how she tried, she was unable to keep the tension from her voice. There was simply too much at stake. "But I believed this to be a conversation, not an interrogation."

She heard the duke make a small cough of amusement behind her, a response her uncle did not share.

"You know perfectly well why this gentleman is here, Serena," he said, his irritation clear. "Yes, he has come to see you as a member of his family, but he is also here to answer the question of who exactly you are."

"She is my *wife*," Geoffrey said sharply, and at once Serena pressed her hand over his, silently begging him not to challenge her uncle.

"Lord Geoffrey is right." After so many lies, she was determined now to speak only the truth, and she chose her words slowly and with great care. "I am his wife, Lady Geoffrey, Uncle. To you and others in our family, I am Serena Carew Fitzroy."

"But if Major Dalton tells us otherwise, then it will most certainly matter," Radnor declared. "Then you are guilty of fraud, and malicious deception, and thievery, too, as these two men will attest before a court of law."

"Mind what you say to my wife, Radnor," Geoffrey began again, and again Serena pressed her hand over his.

"While I welcome Major Dalton as a member of our family, Uncle," she said, "I do not see how the opinion of anyone else should be held against me, or used to defame me in this manner."

"Damnation, Serena, all of London speaks of it!" her uncle said, swinging his fist through the air as his resentment finally spilled over. "Everyone believes you are an imposter, foisted upon my family by my scoundrel of a brother to deprive the Carews of the fortune that by all rights belongs to us, not to you—you damnable Fitzroys!"

Serena gasped, and beside her Geoffrey swore, and she twisted in her chair, desperate to keep him from lunging at Radnor. The duke had risen to his feet, as ready as Geoffrey for a brawl, and around them the footmen were waiting only for an order to charge into whatever happened next.

And none of this was what she wanted, not at all.

She clambered to her feet, forgetting all her resolutions to be genteel and demure, and pushed herself between her uncle and her husband.

"No more of this, Uncle," she ordered breathlessly, her hands outstretched. "No more of any of this!"

"Step aside, Serena," Radnor said brusquely. "I won't have your interference in this."

He put his hand out to shove her aside, but before he could, the major deftly seized her uncle's arm and twisted it behind his back.

"Forgive me, my lord," he said. "But I cannot stand here and let you attack this lady with no reason beyond your own greed and malice."

Furious, Radnor struggled to break free. "How dare you handle me in this fashion!" he sputtered. "I will see you broken, sir, and stripped of your commission for daring to treat me like this! You there, Constable. Act as my witness. Mark how I am being abused!"

The constable stood with his tipstaff ready in his hand as if longing to strike Radnor with it. "What I see, my lord, is how this officer has defended her ladyship against your unwarranted attack."

"No!" Radnor raged. "Dalton, you promised that you'd swear she was a lying little chit. You promised you'd swear against her, as is only right."

"What I promised, my lord, is that I would swear to the truth," the major said curtly, "and what you desire me to say has not a speck of truth to it."

He gave Radnor a final shake, then let him go. Radnor scuttled out of reach, breathing hard.

"You cannot believe that she is one of us," he demanded hoarsely. "You cannot swear that she is anything but a false pretender!"

"I can, my lord," the major said curtly, "and I will. In her ladyship I recognize every grace and virtue that my dear sister possessed. I am honored to be her ladyship's uncle, my lord, and it will give me the greatest pleasure to testify to that effect in any court of this land."

Serena caught her breath, stunned. This man that she'd only just met was *choosing* to be her uncle, with kindness and regard that her real uncle had never once shown her.

"Damn you, Dalton," Radnor growled. "This isn't over."

"But it is," Geoffrey said, his voice so taut with anger that Serena pressed back against him. "Your attacks end here, in this room."

She'd never seen the kind of fury that flooded her uncle's face. "Then damn you, too, Fitzroy! Damn you and your bitch of a wife!"

"Go," Serena said, her voice slicing through the hostility that filled the room. "Go. Your lies and hatred have no place in my home, or in my life. Go, and never, ever return."

He stared at her, his eyes red-rimmed and his mouth working with impotent rage. Somehow, she did not flinch or look away, but met his gaze. She would be brave; she wouldn't back down.

And at last, she won. Radnor snatched up his hat from his chair, and stormed from the room, and as soon as he was gone, she felt all the tension in her body rush away in a wave. Her knees buckled beneath her and she swayed forward, only to have Geoffrey gather her in his arms and hold her tight, his strength all that she needed.

"It's done," he whispered. "It's done."

LONDON
July 1772

The celebrations at the Royal Hall for Foundling Girls could not have gone any better. The new lodgings had been dedicated and pronounced a great improvement, stirring anthems had been played by a brass consort, and many toasts drunk by the ladies and gentlemen and sundry dignitaries who had joined the directors in marking the auspicious day. As the late afternoon sunshine began to slip over the Hall's tall brick walls, the children who had been on such good behavior throughout the ceremonies had at last been freed to play, and they darted across the lawn in their bright blue petticoats with white aprons and caps, laughing and shouting in playful abandon.

For Serena, it was the best sight of the day, far better than all the weighty speeches and toasts and self-satisfied dignitaries. She couldn't help but smile as she stood watching from the Hall's front steps, her hand firmly tucked into the crook of Geoffrey's arm.

"This is why I did it," she said proudly. "So that these girls may be as lighthearted as children should be, and not need to worry about which alley doorway will be their bed tonight, or who will prey upon them, or what they must do to earn their bread. They're safe here, Geoffrey, where none of the evil of the streets can touch them. It's only a start, to be sure, but a start nonetheless."

"It's a very large start," he said, smiling at her instead of the children. "Your gift is the greatest the Hall has ever received. Not even Her Majesty has been as generous."

"I have a special interest in these girls," she said, knowing he'd understand in a way that no one else would.

As soon as it was clear last year that her uncle, Radnor, had finally abandoned his intention to press a case in court against her, she had decided to give the majority of her father's fortune to the Foundling Hall for the boarding and education of young girls and infants rescued from the city streets. The girls would have a home at the Hall until they were old enough to be entered as apprentices to a useful trade, with the aim, in time, of supporting themselves honestly. Today had been the first step, opening the refurbished older rooms to accommodate more girls, while construction had also begun on a new addition that would double the size of the existing Hall.

It was a very lofty goal, and one to which Serena had determinedly devoted much time as well as money. Yet what had pleased her most today was the simple sight of the girls playing on the lawn, behaving exactly as children should.

But at this moment, there was one child in particular that she wished most to see.

"Where is Mrs. Betty?" she asked Geoffrey, looking in both directions. "She should be back here by now."

"I believe they went to inspect the chickens," Geoffrey said. "Ahh, here they are now."

The nursemaid bustled up the steps toward them, with a footman close behind. In the nursemaid's arms was an impatient bundle of infant energy with wispy dark curls and bright blue eyes, snug in drifting layers of embroidered linen and lambs' wool: Miss Caroline Fitzroy, exactly twelve weeks old. Few aristocratic babies would be brought from their nurseries to such an event at such an age, but Serena wanted her daughter to be aware of how fortunate she was and how she must look to the welfare of those who weren't. At least that was what Serena had told anyone who'd shown surprise at the baby's presence. What was closer to the truth was that Serena could not bear to be apart from Caroline, not even for an afternoon.

"Thank you, Mrs. Betty," she said, carefully scooping the baby from the nurse's arms. "I'll hold her now. Isn't that so, little lamb?"

Caroline blinked and squawked and shoved her baby-fists at the lace edging her bonnet, then smiled rapturously, a feat she had just newly learned, and one sure to reduce her parents to babbling idiocy.

"Who's Papa's favorite girl?" Geoffrey asked in his best crooning baby-voice. "Who's Papa's only— Oh, blast, Serena, she's just spit up on your sleeve."

Unperturbed, Serena turned toward Mrs. Betty, ready with a cloth to blot away at the now-stained silk sleeve. "How fortunate that it is the end of the day, and not the beginning. I doubt anyone would've wished to sit beside me otherwise."

"I should always wish to sit beside you, Lady Geoffrey," said the Earl of Westover with a gallantry that didn't quite fit with sour-smelling baby spit-up. He and the countess, beaming beside him, were two other benefactors to the Hall, and had also been lauded today for their contributions. "What a little beauty your daughter is! She'll break her share of hearts one day, won't she?"

"Not until she learns better dining manners, I'm afraid," Geoffrey said. "But she is a beauty, just like her mother."

"She's more Fitzroy than Carew," Serena said, a fact that still stunned her. No matter how much Geoffrey and her family had assured her that her child would be loved and accepted, she had worried throughout her pregnancy, only to bear Caroline, who was as fair-skinned as any baby in Britain. True, she had not been the longed-for heir; that title must wait for another baby. But to Serena, Caroline could not be more perfect. "And she's happier and more merry than both Lord Geoffrey and me together."

"Of course she is happy, Lady Geoffrey," said Lady Westover. "Your daughter is truly blessed in every way. Consider her place in the world, especially in comparison to the poor fatherless creatures here."

Serena hugged Caroline a little more closely. "It was never their choice to be orphans, Lady Westover," she said. "Pray recall that I, too, was left without parents at a tender age."

"Yes, yes," the countess said, unperturbed. "But the difference, Lady Geoffrey, is that you were loved."

Before Serena could answer, their carriage drew before the steps, and with many farewells and good wishes, she, Geoffrey, and Caroline climbed inside, Mrs. Betty riding with the driver. It was not the most graceful of departures, everything being infinitely more complicated when Caroline was included, but at last they were on their way, and the three of them were alone together. Serena rested her head on Geoffrey's shoulder, and he curled his arm protectively around both her and the baby nestled against her breast.

"Happy?" he asked, kissing her lightly on the forehead.

"Oh, yes," she said. "How could I not be? Yet I cannot put Lady Westover's words from my head about the difference between me and the girls at the Hall."

"Your circumstances were different," he said. "They

all were born within ten miles of this place, while your journey from Sundara Manōra to Bloomsbury Square is the stuff of novels."

"That's not what I meant," she said, shifting so she could see his face. "It's the part about how I was different because I was loved. My father, my mother, my sister, Aunt Morley, and Grandpapa. And now you."

He smiled warmly. "You met me, and I loved you at once. I believe you did the same, as I recall."

"I did," she said. "I didn't wish to, but I could not help it."

"At least we agreed," he said, pulling her more closely into his arms. "And a most excellent thing it was, too, considering that I've no intention of ever not loving you."

She smiled at him, her heart filled with joy. "Kismet," she whispered as she reached up to kiss him. "Kismet."

Read on for an exciting preview
of Isabella Bradford's
next Breconridge Brothers novel

A Reckless Desire

LONDON
May, 1775

"I'm telling you the truth, Everett," said Lord Rivers Fitzroy. "The famous Madame Adelaide Mornay is the sorriest, most wretched excuse for a queen that I have ever witnessed."

"Speak it louder, Fitzroy," said his friend Sir Edward Everett as they squeezed through the narrow, noisy passage of King's Theatre. The leading actors and actresses had scarcely taken their final bows, yet already the cramped spaces backstage were crowded with friends and other well-wishers. "There may have been one or two people in Drury Lane who didn't hear you."

"Let them hear me," Rivers said as he maneuvered around a plaster statue of Charlemagne that had figured in the second act. "She was abominable, and you know it, too."

"What I know is that she's currently warming Mansfield's bed," Everett said, following close, "and I've no wish to make an enemy of a man like that. *He* doesn't seem to find fault with her, at least not when he's buried between her legs."

"He wouldn't, considering how sorry his own performance likely is on that same field of battle," Rivers said, dodging a porter carrying a basket filled with masks and wooden swords. As the third son of the Duke of Breconridge, Rivers wasn't particularly intimidated by the Marquess of Mansfield or anyone else, unlike poor Everett, who as a lowly baronet, lived in constant dread of offending one peer or another. "Damnation, but it's crowded here tonight. Who *are* all these rogues?"

"We're like blasted salmon in Scotland, fighting our way upstream," Everett grumbled, struggling to stay close behind Rivers. "We've all the same goal as those fish, too."

"What, you mean to spawn?" Rivers asked over his shoulder.

"Call it what you will," Everett said darkly. "Although spawning's a peculiar term for it."

"Not if you're a male salmon, it's not," Rivers said seriously. "If you were, then you'd think there was nothing finer than to chase upstream after a handsome hen-salmon until she reaches her redd, that's a spawning site, and then he—"

"Spare me, Rivers, if you please," Everett said, wincing. "Backstage at King's is hardly the time or the place for one of your infernal tutor's lectures."

Rivers laughed ruefully, too accustomed to such a rebuff to be offended by it. It had been the same his entire life. He read voraciously and always had, which meant he had such a wealth of disjointed information packed into his head that occasionally it spilled out in a way that his friends and family found . . . tedious.

But Everett had been right about the salmon. The gentlemen around them did have the overwrought, pop-eyed eagerness that marked men in the pursuit of beautiful women who'd welcome their advances.

The door of the dancers' dressing room stood open, and already Rivers could glimpse the intoxicating delights inside. Lovely, laughing young women, all in the process of shedding their gauzy, spangled costumes without a shred of modesty: what man with breath in his body could wish to be anywhere else? He loved how they darted confidently about in the crowded room, graceful and sleek, slipping teasingly among servants and well-wishers. He loved even their scent, a heady, sensual mixture of face powder and pomatum, rosin and perfume, and female exertion.

"*Buoni sera, innamorati!*" he called from the doorway, cheerfully greeting them in the Italian that was the native language of so many of the dancers. "Good evening to you all!"

"*Buoni sera,* Lord Rivers!" they chimed back, like schoolgirls with a recitation, and like schoolgirls, they collapsed into laughter afterward, while the other male visitors glowered unhappily.

Rivers was a favorite with the dancers, and not just because he was a duke's son with deep pockets, either. He was tall and he was handsome, with glinting gold hair and bright blue eyes, but most of all, he genuinely liked this company of dancers. He sent them punch and chocolate biscuits. He knew all their names, which none of the other gentlemen who prowled about the dressing room had bothered to do. He not only spoke Italian, but he spoke Italian with a Neapolitan accent on account of having spent much time in Naples with a cousin who had a villa there.

He was also the only gentleman in London who'd managed last year to have a brief love affair—a *poco amore,* or little love—with Magdalena di Rossi, the lead dancer of their troop, and survive unscathed. Even more amazingly, he'd managed to emerge after those two months in her bed as her friend. He'd the rare gift of knowing the exact moment to end affairs to make such a transition possible (although a handsome diamond brooch had helped immeasurably.) All of which was why now, as soon as he sat in the chair that was offered to him, Magdalena immediately came to sit on his knee with territorial affection.

"*Mio caro amico.*" She swept off his hat so she could kiss him loudly on each cheek without being poked in the eye. "Our evening is complete now that you are here, my lord."

"Hah, you say that to every gentleman who comes through the door," he said, and kissed her in return as he slipped his arm around her waist. Dancing had made her body firm and compact, and he'd always appreciated how her waist was narrow without stays. "Truth has never been your strongest suit."

She pouted coyly. She still wore her stage paint; with blackened brows and dark rings around her eyes and her lips painted scarlet, it was a formidable pout indeed.

"I am not truthful like you, my lord, no," she admitted, trailing an idle finger along the collar of his silk coat. "But then I am not English, with your English love of truth and, um, *franchezza.*"

"*Franchezza?*" repeated Everett, who was sitting nearby with another of the dancers on his knee. "I can only guess what manner of wickedness that may be."

"It's frankness," Rivers said. "Magdalena has always believed I am too frank for my own good."

"True enough," Everett said. "You *are* frank to a dangerous fault. Do you dare repeat what you told me about Madame Adelaide's performance?"

That instantly captured Magdalena's interest. There was neither love nor respect between the acting side of the playhouse's company and the dancers, with both groups claiming they were the real favorites with audiences.

"Oh, that lead-footed cow Adelaide," she scoffed. "*Vacca!* I wonder that you could keep sufficiently awake to judge her, my lord. What did you say to Sir Edward, eh? What did you say of the vile Adelaide?"

For half a second, Rivers hesitated, considering not repeating the opinion he'd given to Everett earlier. It would only serve to inflate Magdalena's considerable pride further—an inflation that it did not need—to hear him criticize her rival. He'd had a quantity of excellent smuggled wine with his dinner, enough to give him bravado, yet not quite enough to make him completely unaware of the peril of making foolhardy statements. His father had always cautioned him against that, reminding him of the fine line between confidence and being a braggart.

But in that half second of reflection, he decided that this was confidence, not boasting. More important, it was the truth, and so with a smile he answered her.

"I said that Madame Adelaide is the sorriest, most wretched excuse for a queen that ever I have witnessed," he declared, heedless of who overheard him. "There is not one iota of royalty to her or to her performance, and if it were not for the lord who's keeping her and paying for the production, she wouldn't have a place on this stage."

"Bah, that's nothing new," Magdalena said, disappointed. "Everyone knows that of her."

"But why doesn't she make a study of Her Majesty, so that she might better play queens?" he asked. He was serious, too, for willful ignorance was incomprehensible to him; with study and application, anything seemed possible. "If she'd rather not model herself on the queen, then there are plenty of regal duchesses about London. Why doesn't she observe them to perfect her art?"

"Because she has no art, that is why," Magdalena said with a dismissive sweep of her hand. "My dancers and I practice every day of our lives, hour after hour until we fall from weariness, but actresses like Adelaide are idle and useless—useless! They do not believe they need to do more than mumble through their lines, and they expect their suffering audience to be grateful for that."

"Madame Adelaide should take lessons from you, Rivers," Everett said. "Give her training in how to behave like a queen."

Rivers smiled, entertained by the idea of giving lessons in regal deportment. God knows he'd seen his share of haughty, queenly ladies, and those were just in his own family.

"I could do it," he said, "and do it well, too. Given the time to develop a proper course of study and a woman who is reasonably clever and willing to apply herself, anything would be possible."

Everett groaned. "Only if the poor thing didn't perish from boredom first. 'A proper course of study'! My God, Rivers, could you make it sound any more tedious?"

"It would be an education, Everett, not a seduction," Rivers said. "Not that you would know the difference. But it's only the most idle of speculation, since I doubt that Madame would agree to become my student."

"No, she would not," Magdalena agreed, and heaved a bosom-raising sigh directly beneath Rivers's nose. "More's the pity, *mio caro*. It would be something to see, yes?"

A small tiring-girl—one of the servants who helped the dancers dress—scurried up to her, bobbing a quick curtsey. In her arms was an enormous bouquet of flowers, so large that it dwarfed the girl holding it, a vibrant splash of floral color against her white apron and kerchief. Magdalena plucked the sender's note free, read it, and scowled, shoving it disdainfully back among the flowers.

"Such beautiful flowers from such a ridiculous man," she said derisively. "But it's not the fault of the poor blossoms to have been sent by a churlish oaf. *Allocco!*"

Rivers sympathized with the poor oaf. Any romantic attachment with Magdalena was fraught with such scenes. At first the drama was exciting, yes, but over time it became too exhausting to be pleasurable. He had to keep reminding himself of that as she sat on his leg, her bottom pressing against his thigh in a very enticing manner.

Magdalena's thoughts, however, had already gone elsewhere.

"Tell me, my lord," she said in the coaxing voice she employed to get what she wanted. "What if you attempted to train a lesser actress? One who was not as proud? One who, with your, ah, education, could knock the vile Adelaide from her post?"

"Do better than that, Rivers," Everett said with a bit of bravado of his own. "Take some ordinary hussy and turn her into your regal actress, the toast of London. Take this chit here. She'd do."

He seized the arm of the tiring-girl who had just presented the bouquet to Magdalena and pulled her back. The young woman caught her heel on the hem of her petticoats and stumbled, nearly dropping the flowers, and Magdalena rolled her eyes with disgust.

"So clumsy, Lucia," she scolded, bored, as if she couldn't really be bothered to say more. "Mind you don't drop my flowers."

"No, *signora,*" the young woman murmured, her dark eyes enormous in her small face. Although she was obviously from Naples like Magdalena and the rest of the dancers, she lacked their lush figures as well as their voluptuous beauty. She was more delicate, her skin paler, and the dark linen clothes she wore were in stark contrast to the gaudy bright silks and ribbons around her. Like too many young servants, Rivers saw a waifish quality to her that spoke of long hours and low wages.

Yet there was also an unmistakable spark in her eyes, a defiant fire that not even the somber clothes could completely douse, and Rivers guessed that she would like nothing better than to hurl the flowers into Magdalena's face. He sympathized. He'd often felt that way himself.

"Make it a true challenge, Rivers," Everett said, still grasping the young woman's arm to keep her from escaping. "I'll wager fifty guineas you can't turn this little drab into your stage queen."

"Fifty guineas, my lord!" she exclaimed. "*Madre di Dio*, fifty blessed guineas!"

"A whole fifty *blessed* guineas!" Everett repeated, imitating her accent, lower-class London with a foreign fillip. "Fancy!"

He laughed, and the dancer on his lap tittered with him. The tiring-girl flushed, but with more of the same defiance—or was it simply confidence?—Rivers had seen in her before. She did not look down, or apologize, either.

Nor did Rivers laugh along with Everett. He never enjoyed scenes like this one, when those with privilege and wealth made jests of those who didn't. The young woman had every right to find fifty guineas a staggering proposition; he doubted she earned even a fifth of that amount in an entire year.

"Enough, Everett," he said, a single word of warning.

Surprised, Everett nodded. Indulgently he winked at the tiring-girl.

"Very well, lass," he said, attempting an empty show of kindness. "If you feel you're worth more, than I'll raise my stake to a round one hundred guineas."

She gasped, her eyes even wider as she looked to Rivers. "I'd make you proud, my lord," she said eagerly. "I swear I would."

Rivers smiled, liking the young woman more by the moment. It took courage for her to speak up like this, especially after Everett had been such an ass. Her spirit intrigued him. She was a bold little thing, and he'd always had a weakness for women who weren't afraid to speak their minds.

"What do you say, Rivers?" Everett asked. "Will you take this little scrap on as your pupil?"

"Of course he will not, my lord," Magdalena said indignantly, sliding quickly from Rivers's knee to pull the girl's arm free of the baronet's grasp. "Lucia is a cousin and an orphan, entrusted to our care and keeping, and I won't have you ruining her usefulness for the sake of some foolish gentlemen's wager. Back to my room with those flowers, Lucia, *pronto, pronto*!"

She gave Lucia a light smack between the shoulder blades with the flat of her palm to urge her on, and the girl curtseyed and hurried away, the flowers held high in her arms for safekeeping. But as she curtseyed, Rivers glimpsed regret in those large dark eyes, a genuine wish that things had gone otherwise. Could she truly have wanted to be part of this, of what Magdalena had accurately described as a foolish gentlemen's wager? Would she really have wanted to cast away her lot on the whim of a man she didn't know, gambling that he could do what he'd grandly claimed?

As Rivers watched her slender figure weave among the others, he speculated as to whether he could have made so great a transformation. He wondered, trying to imagine her commanding both a stage and an audience as she played a queen.

Could he have done it? Could she?

Yet as soon as she disappeared from the room, she faded from his thoughts as well, and within minutes he'd forgotten both the tiring-girl and the wager entirely.